ZANE PRESENTS

# IN MY
# Rearview
# MIRROR

D0733230

# Dear Reader:

*In My Rearview Mirror* by Suzetta Perkins is, as always with this author, a page-turner. Perkins has the gift of painting vivid pictures of characters, right down to their surroundings and style. In yet another story of both redemption and love conquering all, a married couple struggles to get over both of their numerous past mistakes before their imminent divorce is finalized.

What happens when both the wife and husband have babies outside of their marriage? What happens when one of them has children with the spouse of one of their older children that they conceived together? What happens when scandal runs amok in a community that threatens their very livelihood? How does love prevail when every day is filled with yet another heart-wrenching discovery about someone close to them and people are even turning up dead? All of those questions and more are answered within the pages of *In My Rearview Mirror*.

As always, thanks for supporting Suzetta Perkins and the authors that I publish under Strebor Books. We appreciate the love and we strive to bring you the best, most prolific authors who write outside of the traditional publishing box. You can contact me directly at zane@ eroticanoir.com and find me on Twitter @planetzane and on Facebook at www.facebook.com/AuthorZane.

Blessings,

*Zane*

Publisher
Strebor Books International
www.simonandschuster.com/streborbooks

ZANE PRESENTS

# IN MY
# Rearview
# MIRROR

# Suzetta Perkins

STREBOR BOOKS
NEW YORK LONDON TORONTO SYDNEY

**SBI**

Strebor Books
P.O. Box 6505
Largo, MD 20792
http://www.streborbooks.com

ISBN 978-1-59309-476-8
ISBN 978-1-4516-9634-9 (e-book)
LCCN 2012951575

First Strebor Books trade paperback edition May 2013

Cover design: www.mariondesigns.com
Cover photograph: © Keith Saunders/Keith Saunders Photos
Rearview mirror art: © i3alda/Shutterstock.com

10 9 8 7 6 5 4 3 2 1

Manufactured in the United States of America

For information regarding special discounts for bulk purchases, please contact Simon & Schuster Special Sales at 1-866-506-1949 or business@simonandschuster.com

The Simon & Schuster Speakers Bureau can bring authors to your live event. For more information or to book an event, contact the Simon & Schuster Speakers Bureau at 1-866-248-3049 or visit our website at www.simonspeakers.com.

To my children, *Teliza and Gerald Jr.*
To my grandchildren, *Samayya and Maliah*
To my son-in-law, *Will*
To my dad, *Calvin Sr.*
To my brothers and sisters: *Calvin Jr., Michael,
Jennifer, Gloria, Wayne, Mark, and DeShone*
To my nieces and nephews who are
too numerous to name
Family is what we are; family is all we have...
I love you.

## One

S weat covered her face like molasses on a hot-buttered biscuit. The contractions were coming every two minutes and the pain in her pelvic region was almost too much to bear. Margo's swollen brown body lay on its back, her legs spread apart, obliging the commands of the doctor as she readied herself to bring forth her babies into the world.

She had to be out of her mind to decline the epidural that would have made this delivery less painful. Maybe she forgot that she was in her forties and that child bearing should've been left to the younger women who had a lot of elasticity in their bodies, who weren't facing menopause, and who had loving husbands to hold their hands and help them through their labor with the information they learned in Lamaze classes.

It had been two hours since her water broke and left a trail of liquid streaking down each leg as if in a race to the finish line. She had to take another shower and then call an ambulance because there was no man in her life to whisk her away to the hospital, although the large pouch on her body that was carrying twins said somebody had stopped by and paid a visit. Yes, that was true, but she hadn't a clue as to who her babies' daddy was—Jefferson or Malik.

"Push," Dr. Dixon ordered, her long sinewy-gloved fingers examining the cervix. "You're almost there."

Margo pushed and took several deep breaths.

Dr. Dixon twisted her head to the left, pushing a braid that had fallen from her meticulously wrapped bun away from her face. "Push again. The head is crowning."

On command, Margo gave it all she had and pushed again.

"One more time," Dr. Dixon said and added a little chuckle at the end. "You're doing well."

Margo held on to the bed rails, the sweat continuing to pour down her face and other parts of her body. "One for the Father, two for the Son, three for the *oooly* ghost," Margo said as the pain hit hard, then gave her release in a matter of seconds.

"Congratulations, it's a boy," Dr. Dixon said, as the nurse cut the umbilical cord.

"Waa, waa," came the healthy sound of the newcomer who was quickly whisked away to be cleaned.

"Margo, we've got one more. Let's rock and roll, baby," the doctor said.

Margo pushed down again and stopped, her chest rising and falling as she inhaled and exhaled. She opened her mouth to say something, then squirmed as another pain made her blow air. Then she let go. "All right now, you need to come on out of there so Momma can get some rest. Momma's tired."

"Come on, Margo," Dr. Dixon admonished. "Give it all you've got, girl. It's about to be over. Your baby's twin wants access to the new world."

"All right, I'm ready."

"Here it comes. Yes, another baby boy!"

Margo's body relaxed as she heard the squeal of another tiny voice. Minutes later, two nurses rushed in, each carrying what seemed to Margo to be gifts wrapped in thin, white blankets, bundled up as if they were about to travel to the arctic North. In turn, each nurse held the bundles of joy in front of Margo for her to view. They were beautiful with heads full of black, straight hair, wrapped in swaddling clothes like Jesus, and sucking on their fingers.

Margo beamed. She couldn't tell who her boys looked like. They were angelic in every way, both getting ready to cry for mother's milk. Margo closed her eyes, and it was Jefferson she saw—her beloved husband, her soon to be ex-husband, her former lover and friend. She batted her eyes, and there was Malik—her confidant, her shoulder to lean on when Jefferson was away in prison, the man she gave her body to when she thought her husband was being unfaithful…again.

The movie screen in her subconscious faded to black, and when she opened her eyes, there stood the nurses still holding her babies. "I can't do this right now," Margo said. "Give me some time."

Two

**M**argo sat up in her four-poster queen bed in her exquisite City Cottage residence at North Hills, reviewing the last years of her life and contemplating what her outlook for the future would be. She had raised four children whose personalities were as different as night and day, suffered through her husband's infidelity and incarceration, and when it seemed clear that her life, which had taken some critical turns, was headed for recovery, her life had somehow completely bottomed out.

At forty-five years old, Margo felt trapped. Her life should've been uncomplicated because all of her hard work had paid off and provided dividends that would allow her to cruise on Easy Street and even quit the job that made her rich and independent. Real Estate had been Margo's forte for the last twenty-five years and because of it, she had received numerous awards and been dubbed the Real Estate *Queen*. And this was how she was able to afford her new lavish lifestyle on her own, without the husband who'd been a part of her life for just as many and then some years. But she was independent and alone to raise two babies…two baby boys whose father's identity was unknown.

"Waaa, waaa, waaa."

Margo listened as her boys crooned out the Waaa, Waaa song in chorus. It was hard for her to fathom that at this stage in her life she'd be changing diapers and preparing formula for her own children, although she had already tagged one breast Ian and the other Evan. It was easier in the wee hours of the morning to give the twins her breasts when they tried to act as if they'd never been fed.

Neither of her four elder children had given her a grandchild or spoken of walking down the aisle, although walking down the aisle should come before having children. Her current life with the twins might have to suffice.

"I'm coming," Margo said out loud, although the babies continued to holler. She pulled her body to the edge of the bed and sat a moment, not in any hurry, and sought her bedroom slippers when it was apparent the boys were not taking a no-show for an answer.

Although her master suite was on the first floor, she chose to stay in one of the three bedrooms on the second floor so she'd be close to the nursery where her babies slept. Two baby cribs, a dresser, and a dressing table occupied the room that was not yet decorated in fashionable baby attire. The walls were stark white with no cutesy baby appliqués to make the babies feel at home. A vintage rocking chair made out of walnut hugged a corner of the room.

"Hi, sweeties," Margo said in a soothing voice, as she reached down and scooped both of the little fellas up in her arms. "Mommy is here." She kissed them both and smiled.

The boys stopped crying; however, as soon as she laid Evan down to check his diaper, Ian began to cry. "Okay, Ian, Mommy is going to take care of you in a minute."

Margo changed both diapers, washed the babies' faces, and stuck pacifiers in their mouths. She kissed them both again. "Mommy is going to run downstairs and get her doughnut so I can sit on my bottom. I'll be back as quick as I can." Margo retreated but turned around and returned to the cribs. "I love you both, although Mommy hadn't made plans for you to be present in her life, especially not at this time." She tickled their tummies; Evan cooed. "But God doesn't make mistakes. For whatever reason you're here in my life, at this place and time, and know that Mommy will always love you."

All of a sudden the alarm began to beep. Margo jerked her head around and then walked from the nursery into the hallway.

"Mom, you should've been up a long time ago," Winter shouted from the first floor, disarming the alarm. "Shame on you; it's twelve-thirty."

"And you're supposed to be at work and not trespassing in my house. I'm going to take that key away from you. What gives you the right to walk up in my house anytime you get good and ready, girl? The least you can do is ring the doorbell first."

"I took the rest of the day off. I'm here to help you with the babies."

"Well, good. I'm getting ready to feed them now."

"Mom, I have a visitor with me."

"Winter, please. You can't waltz in here with a visitor without calling me first. I may not be presentable."

Margo stood in her bare feet on the hardwood floor in the foyer with her hair tousled and wearing her lavender silk lounger. "Why is the door open? Is that your brother with you?"

A head appeared from behind the door, and Margo went into shock. It had been at least six months since she'd seen him last, but he looked good; in fact, damn good. His rugged good looks made her back up and run her hand over her hair in an effort to brush it down, and then she realized her headlights might be beaming too bright at the sight of him as his eyes seemed transfixed on the upper part of her body, specifically, the swell of her breasts. Margo let her eyes wander to the place that she willed herself to avoid, but she was weak, and when she looked, he was still packing the right size toolbox.

"Hey, Margo," Jefferson said in a deep, seductive voice, offering her a peace smile.

"Uhh, Jefferson, hello," she said in return, still caught in her trance. "You were the last person I expected to see."

After pushing her braids away from her face, Winter grabbed Jefferson's hand and closed the front door. "Mom, I'm going to take Dad on a tour of the house. You don't mind, do you?"

"And what if I say I do? Would it matter?"

Winter laughed. "Mom, it's only Dad. He knows what you look like. He knows how you keep house—immaculate. How many years were the two of you married?"

"You aren't too old for me to whip that butt. And I want my key before you leave."

Jefferson smiled at the banter between mother and daughter.

"Come on, Daddy; let me take you around. Go ahead and take care of the babies, Mom. We'll be up in a minute."

Margo watched as Winter whisked her father away to check out her private abode. It made her smile to see that Winter and Jefferson got along so well, especially after what the family had been through. But Margo was going to give that girl a good talking to. She didn't care how grown Winter thought she was, she wasn't going to come up in her house and disrespect her—father or no father. But Margo understood that Winter was showing off so that Jefferson could see how well she'd done without him. Jefferson looked good, but her life with him was over. In three months, their divorce would be final.

## Three

Jefferson's eyes darted in and out, not missing a nook or cranny, as Winter gave him the grand tour of Margo's new townhouse. He realized it cost a pretty penny. He had himself inquired about the purchase of one of the luxury condos in the same vicinity. It didn't surprise Jefferson one bit that his soon-to-be ex-wife had opted for a place like this; after all, she'd worked hard and made the greenbacks to afford it. He wished Margo would let him advise her about the best financial portfolio that would suit her needs, but it was evident she didn't need him.

"Daddy, isn't this kitchen to die for?" Winter said, waving her arm around as if she were in a showroom.

"Uhm, hmm."

"Look at these top-of-the-line stainless steel appliances," Winter went on, her hand gently brushing over the surface of the refrigerator, microwave and stove that appeared embedded into the wall. "And look, Daddy, a small, flat-screen TV on the door of the refrigerator."

"Isn't that overkill? Doesn't seem like Margo at all."

"Well, I did pick it out for her. You know your woman;

she didn't want that mess. I figured if I was going to hang out at her house all the time, I wanted to have a few amenities of my own."

Jefferson looked at his daughter. "You are unreal, Winter, but I love you. And stop calling your mother, my woman. You know good and well that she discarded me like yesterday's trash."

"That's not fair, Daddy. If it weren't for your drama, you and Mom would be a happily married couple."

"You need to tame that tongue of yours and remember I'm still your daddy. My advice? You need to save your money and get out of that dump you're living in and purchase your own place."

"Okay, okay. I know my place. There's something about this home I like, though. And I'll probably be spending a lot of time here. Hear those babies crying up there?"

Jefferson leaned against the granite countertop and sighed. "Why was it so urgent that I come with you today? Yes, you managed to surprise your mother, but it's obvious she doesn't want me here."

"Daddy, I didn't think I had to lead you by the hand. Mom needs help. She has twins. Your children."

"How do you know they're my babies?"

"What are you talking about, Daddy?"

"Just ponder the question. Now finish showing me the house. I need to be somewhere in an hour."

As if the question hadn't been asked, Jefferson followed behind Winter as she continued her tour. "And this is the dining room."

"I'm happy that Margo has carved out her life the way she wants it to be."

"I don't think it's quite the way she wants it to be," Winter said, pointing toward the ceiling to indicate Margo's new additions to her family she was attending to upstairs.

"As I've already said, she doesn't want my help. And maybe that's because I'm not those babies' daddy."

Winter put her hand on her hip and stared at Jefferson. She loved him. Hated what he'd done to her mother in the past, but still she loved him. "Daddy, please. Don't try and deny that my baby brothers aren't yours. You're only mad because Mom wanted a divorce when you thought that you all were going to be all right."

"Enough, Winter," Jefferson said, staring back as hard as Winter was staring at him. "There may be some wisdom in what you're saying, but I didn't ask for your assessment of your mother's and my situation. It is what it is." Jefferson sighed. "Why don't we go see your brothers now? I have to leave in a moment."

Winter grabbed Jefferson around the waist and steered him toward the stairs.

Jefferson stopped, then looked down at his daughter. He kissed Winter on the top of her head that was full of braids and squeezed her. "I love you, baby."

"I love you too, Daddy."

The duo walked up the stairs in silence, each holding the other around the waist. They stopped at the entrance to the nursery and listened as Margo sang a lullaby to

Ian and Evan and then ensured her boys they would be all right in this world. When Jefferson and Winter looked in, Margo was rocking the boys in her rocking chair. She looked up when they stepped through the doorway. Margo waved them in with her head and started her lullaby again.

Jefferson came and stood over Margo and stared at the baby boys. They were too young for him to ascertain any real resemblance to himself, but he smiled at Margo lovingly. "Cute. Reminds me of when Ivy was a baby," Jefferson said. "You rocked her the same way and sang the very same lullaby. Your boys are beautiful."

Margo lifted her head and smiled. "I remember. In fact, all of our children were blessed to have their mother sing them this lullaby. Have you spoken to Ivy?"

"Nope, not a word. I thought since she and J.R. were so close, she'd be in contact with him."

"Did Mom look like this when she had Winston and me?" Winter asked Jefferson, interrupting her parents' banter about Ivy.

"A carbon copy, except you were a girl."

Jefferson and Winter watched a few moments longer until Margo stopped rocking and moved to get up. Winter rushed over and took one baby out of Margo's arm.

"Who is this?" Winter asked.

"That's Evan. He has a birthmark on his leg like…" Margo paused as if reconsidering what she was about to say.

"Like what?" Winter asked, giving Evan a kiss on the nose.

"Like I do?" Jefferson asked, trying to make direct eye contact with Margo.

Margo wouldn't look at him. In fact, she held Ian tight in her arms and didn't respond.

"I hear Malik is running for public office in Fayetteville," Jefferson said, diverting the conversation. Margo's head jerked upon hearing Malik's name. "My frats said they heard he was getting engaged to some young chick, but she must be a big secret. Malik hasn't introduced her publically, let alone been seen with a woman."

Margo was silent for more than a minute before she finally spoke. "It's probably best for his career that he has a woman who will stand behind him to give him the support he'll need during a campaign. I guess congratulations are in order."

"Well, hopefully he's scrubbed the skeletons from his closet," Jefferson said, looking at Margo. "The Edwards scandal is more than North Carolina can handle as far as scandals go."

"Daddy, what are you talking about? You aren't making any sense. What does that have to do with Malik?"

"I'd like to know, too," Margo said, her eyes piercing through Jefferson's.

"It's time for me to go."

Margo stood up. "No need to rush off, Jefferson," Margo said, advancing toward him with Ian cupped in her arms. "Stay a minute. After all, it's been awhile since I've seen you. How's J.R. doing?"

Jefferson looked between Margo and Winter before looking at the bundle of joy Margo caressed tight to her bosom. "I only have a minute…and J.R. is doing well."

"Tell him he needs to come by and see his mother," Margo said, taking her eyes away from Jefferson's after lingering a little too long.

"I will. I guess you know that Winston is going to join J.R. and me in the business."

"Yes, I've heard. You'll have to rename your business Father and Son's Media Connection, although I like The Web Connection. It has a nice ring to it."

Jefferson smiled. Before anyone could react, he took Ian out of Margo's arms. Bulging eyes protruded from both Margo and Winter. And they smiled.

"Daddy, you look natural holding that baby," Winter teased.

Jefferson handed Ian back to Margo. They made eye contact, and Jefferson turned toward the door. "I've got to go. I have an appointment with a client in twenty minutes." He took a liberty and swallowed Margo up with his eyes. "You look good, Margo; you really do. I like you in this element. It's sassy. Reminds me of a tossed salad…the lettuce, the tomatoes, the croutons…"

Margo stood there and stared.

"Okay, Daddy, too much for my ears," Winter said, covering her ears with her hands. "You and Mom need to get over yourselves and do the right thing."

"Shut up, Winter," both Jefferson and Margo said simultaneously.

"But if you need any help...want my help," Jefferson said, not willing to take his eyes off of Margo just yet, "I'm here. You know how to get in touch with me. And you know I take care of my children."

It was Margo's turn to smile. "Thank you, babe...ah, ah, Jefferson. I may be calling you sooner than later."

Jefferson stood there transfixed and continued to stare at Margo. No words were necessary. He smiled, but his expression was mixed with sadness. "Okay." And he turned and walked away.

"Bye, Daddy," Winter said as Jefferson walked out of the room.


Jefferson jumped in his Mercedes coupe and drove away in a hurry. He held the steering wheel tight with one hand and held his head up with the other, his elbow lodged in the window frame of the car door.

Mixed emotions clouded his thinking. He wanted more than anything to be the father of the twins. Seeing Margo this afternoon for the first time in six months made his insides rattle and his heart skip a beat, causing it to palpitate out of rhythm. Although she had delivered twins only days before, Margo's body was still in great form—a brick house no matter the interpretation. Her hips were sturdy and round and her breasts were full from carrying mother's milk. He'd love to be one of the twins at feeding time.

Jefferson hit the steering wheel with the palm of his hand. He missed her; he still loved her...almost as much as he did when they were young, foolish and had first fallen in love.

He drove blindly through the streets of Raleigh, his mind distorted and unfocused. Were the babies his? Was he the father of the twins? Winston and Winter were twins. Then Jefferson remembered how Margo stopped short of saying that one of the twins had a birthmark. *Like his?*

Jefferson wanted her. It took all the courage within him to not touch her. He wanted her bad...and her sitting only a few feet away, holding what was more than likely his son, confused him. It might have been lust at the moment, but Margo was still his wife. If Winter hadn't been in the room, he might have missed his important appointment. Then again, Margo might have called the police and requested a restraining order to keep him away. He wouldn't have been there in the first place if his daughter hadn't begged him to come.

He wanted her. Jefferson wanted Margo.

# Four

I vy put her hands on her hips and made a last inventory of the boxes she'd packed that now crowded the small living room in her condo. The movers were due in a couple of hours, and she wiped the sweat from her brow. She counted…"one, two, three, and four…" until she reached twenty-six. She stood up straight, then sighed, pushing through the faraway look on her face while brushing back the long strands of hair that fell into her eyes.

Ivy was taking a huge risk, a huge step backward in her way of thinking. Returning to Fayetteville, North Carolina had never been an item on her short or long-range plans, especially having experienced life in Atlanta that was exciting, rewarding, and so full of opportunities. Although her brother, J.R., had moved back to Raleigh several months ago to work on a business venture with their father, Ivy had not once felt alone. She was happy.

Another sigh escaped Ivy's lips, glad to have the last bit of packing done. She glided through the vacant hall with the empty walls of her condo and headed toward the bathroom to shower but stopped abruptly when she heard her cell phone ring.

Ivy nearly tripped over a box trying to get to her cell that sat on a coffee table that was surrounded by boxes before it stopped ringing. She reached it in time and smiled.

"Hey, baby," Ivy said into the phone. "You miss me?" Pause.

"I can't wait to see you." Pause.

"All I've been doing is thinking about you...me...us... together. You consume my thoughts day and night. As much as I hate moving back to Fayetteville, I'd do anything to be with you, baby." Pause.

"A surprise? What is it?" Pause.

"Give me a hint. Please, pretty, please." Pause.

"You're so fresh." Ivy blushed. Pause.

"You're making me wet," Ivy said seductively. Pause.

"I love you, too." Pause.

"I'm going to make it worth your while, Senator." Pause.

"I know you're going to win the election. I've got faith. I've got faith in you, and I've got faith in us." Pause.

"I can't wait for your surprise." *I've got a surprise for you, too,* Ivy thought to herself.

"Okay, baby. I'll see you day after tomorrow." Pause.

"I love you. Smooches."

Ivy held the phone in her hand and closed her eyes. Another smile erupted on her face as she reminisced about how only a few nights ago her lover had made her feel like the woman she knew she was, how he tenderly and gingerly caressed her whole body with the soft and supple strokes of his hands, how he snatched her to him and worked her lips and delighted her with his tongue, and how she felt when her body trembled…like a climactic earth-quake that swallowed up everything in its path.

Eyes still closed, Ivy held her body and squeezed. She squeezed her breasts through the thin cotton T-shirt, rubbed her stomach with her hand and finally touched herself in her private garden, then moved her hand away quickly as if the memory was too much to bear. Ivy began to laugh, then covered her mouth with both hands…the memory taking hold of her, not letting go. She walked over to the couch and found a small place to sit and sat down, pushing her thighs together as if trying to fight the earthquake that wanted to erupt within her, not wanting to be consumed by the orgasm of her thoughts. She laced her fingers together and rocked back and forth, unable to hide the smile that forced itself out in the open, exposing her hidden thoughts of pleasure. And then Ivy shuddered…her whole body trembled while she tried to catch her breath. And then she opened her eyes and looked around and saw the cardboard boxes that sat like lifeless creatures waiting to be awakened and devour her.

And just like that, Ivy came to her senses. She jumped up from the couch and shook her hand in the air. "Hell, let me get my funky body up out of here and take a shower so I can be presentable by the time the movers arrive."

## Five

"J.R., my man," Jefferson said as he strolled through the front entrance of The Web Connection with extra pep in his step and an enormous smile on his face to go with it.

"Whuzup, Pops?" J.R. asked Jefferson, flicking one of his braids out of his eye as he looked up. "Must've hit pay dirt, with all those pearly whites you've got showing in your mouth."

"J.R., we are designing the website and all other media material for Dr. Shelton Wright."

"You mean the dude who's running for senator?"

Jefferson walked over and stood beside J.R.'s desk. "Our name is already out there, but we're getting ready to blow the joint up." Jefferson and J.R. slapped each other's hand. "This is a big deal. From all accounts of our interview, we will also be handling his TV ad campaigns. I'm on the way into my office now to draw up the contract. Get ready. I've also been looking for another location to set up shop—you, Winston, and I will each have our own office."

"You the man, Pops. I hope Winston plans on starting

sometime this week; we're going to need all the help we can get."

"Your brother promised me he would be here by Thursday to help out. Trying to finish up some project he's working on. I may be able to bring him in full-time with what's getting ready to happen to us, not that we're doing bad now."

"Yeah, I wouldn't mind a raise."

"Son, you'll get your raise. You're doing a damn good job. We've got a large number of contracts under our belt but nothing as lucrative as this. This will put us on the map."

J.R. pulled on the lapels of his Old Navy plaid poplin shirt that sat over a white wife beater and smiled. "Pop, I'm glad you and me," J.R. pointed to himself, then back at Jefferson, "have made amends and are friends. We didn't always see eye-to-eye while I was growing up, but you giving me this chance to make something of myself has allowed me to see who you really are, besides being my Pop, and what you're made of. And I like it a lot."

Jefferson looked at J.R. thoughtfully and patted his chest with his fist. He pulled J.R. up by the arm, and they hugged in a gentleman's embrace. "I'm glad you're here, son." Jefferson began to choke up. "I…I love you." He and J.R. embraced again.

Jefferson moved away before their father and son love fest got sloppy. And the last thing Jefferson wanted was for J.R. to see him cry. "Oh, by the way, your mother wants you to stop by. She hasn't seen you in awhile."

J.R. was silent but continued working, putting the finishing touches on a website he was building for a local church. "So you saw Mom?" J.R. finally said.

"Your sister nearly dragged me over there...I guess to rub those twin babies in my face. Winter thinks I need to own up to them and do the right thing by your mother. But I can't make someone love me if they don't."

"So why did you and Mom break up? Why did she want a divorce?"

"Life and love is a hard thing, J.R. I've hurt your mom something awful in the past, but I was praying that when I got out of jail, things were going to turn around—be better, especially since she waited for me those five long years. It was for a moment."

"So, did it have to do with you and Angelica?"

"What do you mean by Angelica and me?"

"Who doesn't know about you and Angelica?"

"J.R., there was never anything between Angelica and me. I was her husband's accountant. I don't think Hamilton knew how Angelica was, although, they did end up in divorce court. True, Angelica tried to put the moves on me a time or two, but she'd changed after she got out of prison. She wanted to create a new life for herself until Santiago showed back up on the scene, trying to exact revenge on all of us who'd been a part of his organization, Operation Stingray. I don't know why I let Hamilton talk me into it. Now he's dead, I lost my company, but I thank God I've been given another chance to make my life right."

"So, did it have to do with Linda, our ex-next-door neighbor? I thought Mom forgave you of that mess."

"Uhmm, she did. However, we learned something right before your mother left me that was the proverbial straw that broke the camel's back."

Jefferson looked at J.R. and blew air from his mouth. He was in a good place, having the prodigal son return home, but he was afraid that if he shared this bit of news, he might lose J.R. again. But he wanted to be honest and upfront. Maybe it was time to share this news with his kids.

"What is it, Pops? You can tell me…trust me with anything. I've got your back."

Jefferson looked into his son's eyes, those inquiring eyes that said they understood.

"You have another brother; he's about six now. Linda gave birth to a son that I had no knowledge of until your mother and I bumped into them at an ice cream parlor."

At first, J.R. took the news in and ingested it, rolled it around in his head a moment, then looked up at Jefferson. "How do you know he's yours?"

"I don't, but the one thing Margo and I agreed on, he looked a lot like you. There was no mistaking that co-incidence."

J.R. laughed and slapped his dad on the arm. "Is he old enough to join the family business?"

Jefferson smiled. "Whew, I was afraid…"

"Afraid I was going to run away again? Naw, I said I

had your back. You've paid for your sins. It is what it is. So, did you see the new twins?"

"Yeah."

"So, is she going to raise them by herself?"

"Looks that way. I had to hurry up and get out of there, though. Your mother looked so good."

J.R. smiled. "You still love her, don't you?"

"I've got mad love for that woman."

J.R. took a last look at the website he created. Satisfied, he began the process of publishing it. The fee netted them a few thousand dollars, but the money was in the mega churches.

He landed a huge account for the firm when he joined a mega church and soon after, submitted his proposal. Although he had an ulterior motive for joining, he found that he rather liked the services, except the keeping track of his tithe paying. The extras were the truckloads of women who came every Sunday, distracting him from his time with Jesus. The church, though, helped him get his head together, to heal, to be in the place he was now in with his dad. He hadn't quite gotten there with his mother.

Hungry as a bear, J.R. got up from his chair hoping their part-time receptionist, Cheryl Richards, was on her way in. He needed some air—a moment to think. His mind drifted to what his Pops had said about visiting his mother. It wasn't that he hated her; he was mad that she didn't want to keep the family together. Although, now, he understood some of her frustrations.

Sitting back down, J.R. reached for the telephone. Before he was able to pick it up, the phone rang. He recognized the number right away.

"Hey, sis, what are you doing calling me on the work number?"

"You must have turned your cell off or didn't charge the battery," Ivy said. "Can't talk to a brother on his cell if he doesn't pick it up."

J.R. and Ivy laughed.

"So whuzup? What are you doing calling me in the middle of the day, Ms. Girl About Town—the next Ms. Hot Atlanta."

"J.R., you're so crazy. I miss you."

"Didn't seem that way when I was moving back home. You couldn't wait for me to leave."

"What if I tell you that I'm moving back to Fayetteville…like in two days?"

J.R. sat up in his seat. "For real? Something happened? I thought you said you were never coming back?"

"Yeah, I did, but I kind of miss the place."

"Girl, this is J.R. No need to lie to me; I know you… remember? I expect Winter to say something stupid like that. So what's the real deal?"

"Nothing, J.R. I like Atlanta, but I need to come home."

"For what? No one lives in Fayetteville anymore. Where

are you going to live? If you want to, you can move to Raleigh and hang out with me awhile."

"Love to, brother dear, but I'd rather be on my own."

"Should I tell Dad?"

"J.R., no. I don't want Momma or Dad to know that I'm moving back to the area. I haven't spoken to Momma in three or four months. She probably hates me. So you and Dad have gotten close?"

"Yeah, I love the old man. He's cool, even if he is my Pops."

"Even after all the crap he put Momma through?"

"Got to forgive. Plus he's given me a new lease on life."

"Have you seen Momma?"

"You won't believe this, but I was getting ready to call her. Get this, Dad saw her for the first time in I don't know how many months. Winter dragged him over to Mom's house to see the new twins. I bet you didn't know Mom had given birth. Dad said Mom asked me to call her."

"Well, good for you. Do as your daddy instructed. I was on Winter's Facebook page and she dropped pictures of the babies on her page and was talking about them as if she had given birth to them. Momma is a drama queen and, at her age, who in their right mind would go and get pregnant, especially when her older children are all over twenty? Now she has babies to raise—not one but two."

"Don't be so dramatic, Ivy. It's her life; you don't have to raise those babies."

"I know, but how is it going to look telling everyone that 'these are my baby brothers' when I'm the one who should be saying, these are my children?"

J.R. thought about Jefferson's confession about the other little boy, Linda's six-year-old son, who was also their brother. He decided not to tell Ivy—let that be his and Pop's secret. J.R. liked that Jefferson trusted him enough to share such an intimate secret.

"Are you still there, J.R.?"

"Yeah, yeah. Just thinking about our family and all of the drama we've been through. And to your last question, why don't you have some children so you can say that they're yours?"

"I don't know why I bother to talk to you sometimes. You don't get it…never seem to get the point. Have you talked to Winter? She's probably peppering up Momma; you know Winter is her favorite."

"Don't you mean the twins, Winter and Winston, are her favorites?"

"Whatever. I'd talk to Winter, but she talks too damn much. She tells Momma everything."

"Well, I've got to get something to eat. Let me know when you get in the Ville."

"Okay, but don't forget. You can't tell Momma or Dad I'm coming. They'll find out in time."

"Dog, everybody has secrets except for me."

"You need to get some nice, young honey to cuddle up with…take the edge off, brother. Then you might gain a secret or two."

"Whatever, Ivy. Dad's coming out of his office. Gotta run."

"Bye."

"You okay?" Jefferson asked, seeing the perplexed look on J.R.'s face.

"Yeah, I'm okay. It's women and their complicated issues." J.R. smiled.

"Oh, a girlfriend thing. You've been holding out on me." Jefferson slapped J.R. on the back. "Man, you've got a lifetime of complicated issues and drama ahead of you." Jefferson laughed. "I'm out. On my way to ink this deal."

"Go get 'em, Pops."

## Six

Holding Ian in her arms, Winter watched Margo feed baby Evan as she swayed in the rocking chair. Her mother seemed so natural breast-feeding the baby, as if it wasn't that long ago she or one of her other brothers and sisters were drinking from their mother's breast. Then she thought about the slave mothers who bore babies until their dying day, producing milk not only for their babies but for half of the plantation population. One day, she was going to have one of those small wonders for herself so she could hold and love, Winter thought.

"Pass Ian to me and burp Evan," Margo said, making the switch with ease. "I was thinking about weaning them off my breasts and giving them a bottle. But there's something holistic about giving them mother's milk."

"I'd help you out, Mom, but I don't have any milk to give my brothers."

"You keep those little titties inside that itty bitty bra of yours until you have your own babies."

Margo and Winter shared a laugh.

"I want to have a baby," Winter said out of the blue.

"When you get a man who's committed to spending

the rest of his life with you and is willing, as Beyoncé says, to *put a ring on it*, then you can think about having babies."

"And if I don't find that man?"

"Listen up, my wayward child. A lot of responsibility comes with raising a child and even more if you're a single parent. There's no way I should be pulling baby-sitting duties at my age with the exception of my grand-children, and even then I wouldn't be at everyone's beck and call. I made a mistake, and now I've got to pay the consequences for my actions."

"Mistake?" Winter asked with a frown on her face. "You were doing the freaky sneaky with your husband. I know…you forgot to get back on the pill."

Margo looked away, pulled her breast out of a sleeping Ian's mouth, and then looked back at Winter. "What if they're not your daddy's babies?"

Winter's eyes jutted out of their sockets. She jumped up from her seat, almost forgetting that Evan was in her arms. "Mom, what do you mean that they may not be my daddy's babies?"

Margo stared at Winter but didn't say a word.

"Oh my God! Oh my God. Mom please tell me that you and Malik didn't do the…do the…that you didn't get busy. Oh my God. I don't want to envision it. Oh, Mom, how could you? What would Pastor Dixon say if he knew you'd sinned—broke one of the commandments?"

"Don't be so dramatic, Winter. You're going on and

on for nothing. No one said that I slept with Malik. Anyway, it's not Pastor Dixon's business what I do. It's between me and Jesus. That's why I left that congregation; those sisters were too busy getting in my business instead of doing the Lord's work."

"Back to the subject. You didn't deny you slept with Malik. Now I understand why Daddy kept making those snide remarks. He knows, doesn't he? He knows that you let Malik do the nasty. No wonder he's not owning up to his responsibilities; Ian and Evan may not be his. Mom, why?"

"Shut up and sit down with my baby, Winter. If you drop him, I'm going to beat your little ass down to the white meat."

"Don't try to change the subject. Mom, you're a loose woman." Winter laughed.

"Watch your mouth, Winter; I'm still your mother. Be glad I've got this baby in my arms because you'd have a print across your face. Then I'd tie together those funky little braids that you've got twisted all over your head until your brain hurt."

Winter started laughing and couldn't stop. "Mom, you are too funny. Can't get out of this one."

"You want to be let in on a secret?"

"Can't be better than you slept with Malik. Damn, damn, and double damn."

"It may not be, but it's going to make you sit back down in that chair, and make you say, Jesus."

"What is it, Mom, since you're trying to take the spotlight off of yourself?"

"How about you have another brother you don't know about?"

Winter looked at Margo before sitting back down. "Another brother where?"

"Do you remember our next-door neighbor, Linda? She has a little boy who should be six about now. Looks exactly like your father and J.R. Things that make you go hmmm."

It was Winter's turn to be quiet. Ian burped and she rubbed his back. "Jesus," she finally said.

"Let's put the babies down and go into my room," Margo said.

Winter put Ian down next to Evan. She followed Margo into her room without a word. "Does Daddy know?"

"He and I were together when we ran into them at Cold Stone Creamery almost a year ago. Linda wouldn't acknowledge it, but in our heart of hearts, your dad and I knew. That's when I decided to get a divorce."

"So when did you and Malik get together?"

"That's a long story, but your father found out about it, and I'd say our marriage was truly in jeopardy. Too much had gone on. I love your dad, but I was having mixed feelings about Malik also. But I shouldn't have done it."

"So, have you and Malik…how can I say this?"

"Spit it out. You never seem to have trouble saying anything else you want to say."

"Yeah, Mom, but to learn that your momma's been screwing around..."

"Watch it; you've crossed the line. You aren't that grown. Just because we're having a mother/daughter discussion doesn't mean you can say whatever comes out of your mouth."

"Just a minute ago, you said speak your mind."

Margo raised her finger to her lips.

"Okay, Mom. No disrespect. The question is...have you and Malik been intimate recently? I saw how you perked up when Dad announced that Malik was running for office. I'm sure he saw it, too."

"So, you and your daddy have gotten close, I see."

"He's a lot of things, but he's still my daddy and I love him. I don't know if I told you this, but we hang out every now and then. One Sunday, we all went to church with J.R. Can you believe we were following J.R. to church? But J.R. loves it, and I think he's caught some of those young women's eyes."

"I wish he'd call or stop by. I don't know why J.R. is so angry at me."

"J.R. has been angry at the world. He felt like an outcast in the family, but now that Daddy has taken him under his wings, he's another person."

Margo smiled. "That's good to hear, but the next time you see your brother, tell him his mother wants to see him. Have you talked to Ivy? She and J.R. seemed to have slipped in some black hole. Ivy and I used to talk all the time. It's like she's being secretive and her family is off limits."

"She and J.R. talk all the time, from what Winston has told me. After all, they lived together when J.R. was in Atlanta. Ivy is closer to J.R. than I am."

"Did you know that Malik was running for Senator?"

"No, ma'am. First time I heard it was when you heard it."

The phone began to ring, interrupting their conversation. "Answer it."

Winter picked up the phone on the third ring. "Hello, this is Margo Myles' residence."

"Hey, Winter, this is your big brother, J.R. Where's Ma?"

Winter arched her eyebrows and made a wide circle with her mouth. "She's right here." Winter put her hand over the receiver and pointed at the phone. "Mom, it's your son, Jefferson Jr."

## Seven

The drive from Atlanta was rather dull although Ivy was grateful that the weather had held up, considering the weatherman had announced that a big storm was getting ready to engulf the southern states. She hated the five-hour drive and the long stretch of road on Interstate 20, but she celebrated each time she closed in on a milestone that would get her closer to her destination.

"Augusta, Columbia, and Florence," Ivy shouted out loud. "Four more miles to Interstate 95 and then home."

Excitement mounted as Ivy crossed over from South Carolina into North Carolina. Forty-five minutes to go, and then she'd be in Fayetteville. She rode as if the forty-five minutes of travel would be her last forty-five minutes on earth. She could smell Malik's cologne and could feel his sloppy kisses all over her, which made her mash the pedal to the metal in her quest to get to her man.

Before she knew it, she was in Fayetteville. She exited Interstate 95 and headed into the city, where she was to meet Malik at his campaign headquarters. She pulled out her cell and punched in his number, her stomach doing flip-flops as she waited anxiously to hear his voice.

"Baby, this is Ivy." She grinned into the phone when Malik answered. "Guess where I am?"

"You're in Timbuktu?" Malik teased.

"No," Ivy said, laughing at his attempt to be funny. "I'll be at your door in fifteen minutes."

"Girl, I can't wait to see you. Why don't I meet you at Luigi's instead, since you like Italian food? I don't want these people to see me make a fool out of myself when you walk in the door. I want that to be a private moment between us. Anyway, I want to make some kind of official announcement when you do come to campaign head-quarters."

"What kind of announcement?"

"That my woman just arrived in the Ville and has come to take her rightful place and shake this campaign up."

"I like that, baby. Okay, I'll meet you at Luigi's. Hurry, I don't want to wait too long in the lobby. Smooches."

"Back at ya."

Ivy drove into Fayetteville. Nothing seemed to have changed since the last time she was there. She drove down Owen Drive and onto the All American Freeway, finally exiting at Morganton Road.

Ivy smiled at some memory as she continued to ride down the street. She sat up straight in her seat when she saw a good-looking brother dressed in a slate gray business suit rush into one of the restaurants to probably meet a client or his woman. Yes, she was back in the Ville—her old stomping grounds.

Turning left onto McPherson Church Street, Ivy eased down the street until she pulled into the parking lot of Luigi's. Her mouth began to water, thinking about her favorite, She-Crab Soup.

She wondered what her mother would say if she knew that she was having dinner with an older man, her daddy's ex-friend, a man she believed her mother secretly had a crush on but was too afraid to explore the possibilities of a romantic relationship with him because she made a vow to her husband to love and to cherish until death they did part. Ivy didn't understand a woman, her mother, who'd wait for a man who had put her and the family through hell, who sat in a federal prison for five years for stealing from his own company, only to divorce him in the end. Well, it was too late now. As much as she believed her mother had a crush on Malik, the man was all hers and she was carrying his baby, although he didn't know it yet.

Ivy got out of the car and closed the door. She'd have to get a new car if she was going to be paraded around as the girlfriend of the newest senator for the State of North Carolina. Maybe she could talk Malik into loaning her a sizable down payment so she could ride in that nice BMW650i coupe she'd been eyeing for awhile. She temporarily threw a lid on her thoughts upon seeing Malik drive up.

## Eight

He was handsome in his Versace suit, black and white shirt with the white tuxedo collar, and a custom-made black, gray and white tie with the words *I'm Your Next Senator* running the length of it. His chiseled features wrapped up in his arrogance was what attracted her to him, although he had been a challenge most of her teen and adult life.

Ivy smiled as she watched Malik get out of his car and saunter toward her. He was her man—a man who knew what he wanted and how to get it, a man who had the grace and style to back it up. When Malik finally stood in front of her, Ivy welcomed him with open arms, enveloping him in her embrace. She laid her lips on his and assaulted him with kisses.

Malik gently pulled back, and looked around to see if anyone was watching. Ivy smiled again, wiping lipstick from Malik's lips. She hoped their public display didn't cause too much attention, although she knew Malik enjoyed every minute of it. Holding hands, Malik ushered Ivy into the restaurant where they were seated almost immediately.

"You're beautiful," Malik said, rubbing the top of Ivy's hand that sat on the table.

"You're handsome, Senator Malik Mason. That does have a nice ring to it."

"Thank you. And it will happen." Malik looked thoughtfully at Ivy. "How was the ride up?"

"Not bad. No, it was horrible. I counted every second, minute and hour before I would see you again. I can say this for sure, it was well worth the wait."

Malik's eyes roamed over her, which made Ivy blush. She wished she could get into Malik's head for only a moment to see what was bouncing around in there. Probably only politics resided inside, but that couldn't be totally true because she wouldn't have been sitting in the restaurant with him, if that were the case. So maybe she was a welcomed distraction.

They both jumped when the waitress approached. "Are you ready to order?"

"Yes, I'm famished," was Ivy's reply. "A bowl of your She-Crab Soup and your Country Salad with Salmon for me."

"I'll have what the lady's having," Malik said with a smile.

"Got it," the waitress said. "Hey, aren't you Malik Mason who's running for State Senator?"

Malik was grinning now. "Yes, I'm one in the same."

The waitress shook Malik's hand. "You have my vote. I've been following you closely, especially after you helped that daycare center get back on its feet after someone stole all of their equipment. My child goes to that center, and everyone sings your praises. You'll be good for North Carolina."

"Well, thank you, ma'am."

"Call me Sharon."

"Thank you, Sharon. I appreciate your vote of confidence." Malik stood and shook the waitress' hand.

"Great! I'm happy to serve you today." She looked at Ivy and smiled. "And you, too, ma'am."

"She's pushing for a hefty tip," Malik said when the waitress was gone.

"Well, Mr. Mason, you made her day. I think you can count on fifty extra votes on account of it."

"I think you're right, Ivy. But I figured seventy-five extra votes." Malik and Ivy laughed.

It was obvious the waitress had run back and told all the help that Malik was dining with them. Every few minutes, a waiter or waitress happened to pass by, hovering around long enough to get a glimpse of Ivy and Malik.

"You are a bona fide celebrity," Ivy said, unable to converse with Malik as she planned. "I can't wait to get you away from here so we can have some privacy. I need some 'me time' with the senator-to-be without his fan club."

"You're not jealous, I hope. There will be plenty more days and nights to come when there will be demand for my attention. I hope you'll be by my side."

"There's no question about it. I'll always be there for you, baby."

Malik smiled. "How does Senator and Mrs. Malik Mason sound?" Malik sat back in his seat, ready to assess Ivy's response to his question.

Ivy gasped. Her eyes bulged from their sockets. She stared at Malik as if he were a mirage, then held her chest. "Malik…are you asking me…are you saying what I think you're… Are you asking me to be your wife?" Ivy felt embarrassed when Malik didn't reply. She waited for a response.

"You're so funny to watch, but you're not imagining a thing. Unless your brain waves were turned off, you interpreted everything correctly."

"That wasn't fair, having me sit on pins and needles looking as if I'd lost my mind."

"Shhhh," Malik said, as he drew her fingers to his lips and kissed them. Ivy watched as Malik went into his coat pocket and pulled out a black velvet box. He opened the box and there sat a five-carat, Princess-cut diamond engagement ring. "I haven't had an opportunity to ask your dad for his blessing, which I'm sure he wouldn't give."

Ivy ignored what Malik said about asking her father for her hand in marriage. Her eyes were glued on the ring. "Oh, oh, oh," was all that came from Ivy's mouth.

"May I have your hand?"

Ivy gently laid her hand in Malik's.

"Will you, Ivy Nicole Myles, marry me?"

Tears gushed from Ivy's eyes. "Will I...will I marry you? Yes, yes, yes!" Ivy almost shouted out loud. "Oh my God, yes." Tears continued to flow.

Malik took the ring and placed it on Ivy's finger. She gawked at the size of the ring and held out her hand to admire it. "It's so beautiful, Malik."

"Not half as beautiful as you are."

"I love you, Malik. You've made me so happy." Ivy cried some more, stopping a moment to gaze at the sparkling diamond that sat on her finger. "I love you," she mouthed again.

"I love you, too, Ivy. Let's not make this a long engagement."

The waitress returned with their food and saw Ivy admiring her ring. "Your She-Crab Soup."

"Thank you," Ivy and Malik said simultaneously.

"I'm sorry to be so nosey, but...is that what I think it is?"

"Yes," Ivy blurted out without shame. "I'm engaged."

The sound of hands clapping erupted throughout the restaurant. Ivy stood up, held out her hand, and put her ring on display. Malik watched her with a grin on his face. "I'm going to be Mrs. Malik Mason," Ivy said out loud. The crowd continued to clap. Ivy sat and the applause subsided.

"Oh my God," the waitress exclaimed. "I can't believe this is happening at my table. You need to order something to celebrate the occasion," Sharon said to Malik.

"I think you're right. I'll order a bottle of your best wine. Surprise me."

"Okay. I'll never forget this day."

"I'll never forget it either," Ivy muttered, her eyes drawn once again to the brilliance of the ring. She wanted to tell Malik her surprise…about the embryo that was growing inside of her, but there was no way she'd upstage this moment with her little announcement. It was a good day…a romantic day, one she had envisioned for a long time. No, today was not the day to tell Malik he was going to be a father. Then a thought came to her. She looked up and saw Malik staring at her.

"Baby, why don't we get married today…tonight? I want to be your wife, now."

Malik looked at Ivy with surprise in his eyes. "Okay, baby, I know that you're overcome, but there's no need to rush. I'm sure you want to have a huge wedding with the beautiful white gown and all the bells and whistles, and, of course, with all of your family around."

"Let's not wait. I don't mean to sound selfish, but I don't need a church wedding, family or friends."

Malik watched Ivy as she continued to speak.

"My family is so dysfunctional now. They'd only add stress to a day that was meant to be perfect and the happiest day of my life. I hope you understand."

"If that will make you happy," Malik said with some reservation. "Your dad may not agree with us getting married but surely your mom will want to be a part of your wonderful day."

Ivy pulled her hand back and sat it in her lap. Malik was once in love with her mother, and as far as she was concerned, there wasn't going to be any other opportunity for Malik to start having feelings for her mother again. She would see to that.

Ivy sat almost expressionless in her seat. "Is it important that I tell her? I haven't seen or spoken to my mom in four or five months. She and I aren't connecting, and this announcement would blow her away." Ivy watched Malik and wondered what he was thinking.

"Margo had her chance," Malik began. "She blew it. Let's go to South Carolina tonight and get married."

Ivy couldn't hide her delight. Things were going to fall into place. She'd make passionate love to Malik, and as soon as they said "I do," the baby she carried inside of her would have a father without the illegitimate sign hanging around his or her neck. "I love you, Malik."

"I love you, too, Ivy. You're going to make a wonderful wife and companion."

Ivy's dream was coming to pass. Older men always appealed to her. Twenty-five years young, Ivy felt on top of the world. The man she secretly admired and wanted for years was now hers and she was going to be Mrs. Malik Mason, Senator Mason's beautiful wife.

## Nine

I vy was awakened by the sudden shift in the bed. Her eyes now adjusted to the semi-darkness, she was able to make out the silhouette of her husband with his taunt pajamaless back with its well-defined muscles. Turning on her side, Ivy reached out to him, her ring sparkling in the early morning from the few strands of light that peeked through the blinds.

"Hey, baby," she said in a sweet, soft voice.

Malik turned around and took Ivy's hand and kissed it and inched his way up the length of her arm, planting kisses along the way until he found her lips. He held her head in a lover's embrace and kissed her passionately, opening her mouth with his tongue, inhaling and tasting until Ivy moaned.

Malik travelled to her neck and painted kisses all around until he was ready for a new adventure. He pushed his body up and was now on his hands and knees looking to see what else he could devour. Malik straddled Ivy and gently took her arms and pinned them behind her. With her head pushed back, the soft mounds of her breasts were now exposed, her nipples erect just above the skimpy lace-trimmed teddy she wore. Malik continued his gentle probe, taking each nipple in his mouth and sucking them as if they were an irresistible fruit of passion.

Ivy squirmed and moaned underneath him, the sensation too much to bear. Then Malik took each breast and fondled them, squeezing the nipples gently before tasting them again. Ivy's body writhed from the excitement of it all and begged Malik to make love to her.

"Good morning, Mrs. Mason. I love you," Malik said as he came up for air.

"I love you, too, baby, but we can talk later. I have needs only you can fulfill since you've taken me to the mountaintop."

Ivy was naive in many ways when it came to matters of the heart, but Malik was going to relish being a good teacher. He covered her mouth again with his and then began his long, tedious journey to find the pot of gold. He humbled her as he caressed her body with his tongue, discovering Ivy's erogenous zones that she never knew existed. And for the first time Malik truly discovered the gateway to pure satisfaction for himself and his wife. Ivy was now in total surrender—the young lady finally becoming a full-grown woman.

They lay spent from their lovemaking. Malik hadn't felt this satisfied in a long time. Lying on his back, he pushed up on his elbows and rolled toward Ivy but she was fast asleep. Malik wasn't sure how long he had dozed off, but it was past time to get up and go to his place of business before stopping by campaign headquarters.

Malik looked again at the sleeping beauty. She had the look of innocence. While he and Ivy had been intimate before their marriage, she hadn't let go of her soul. She held back the best part of her—the thunder and the roar—maybe because she was afraid or inexperienced in the ways of true seduction and romance. And then he remembered her mother.

He watched Ivy with loving eyes, her chest rising slightly and then retreating. Ivy shifted, and at that moment she looked so much like Margo. Malik shook his face as the image of Margo replaced that of Ivy—so vivid the memory of their one night together. He sat up straight and caught his breath, eager to leave the image behind. Malik wondered what Margo would say when she found out that he had married her daughter and that he was giving Ivy what he'd always wanted to give her.

He got up and turned on his Walter Murphy CD—the music soothing to his ears. Then he headed straight for the shower to rinse the lust for another woman from his body. Malik hadn't thought about Margo in a long time, but now her image had come to haunt him. When he'd run into Ivy that day in the coffee shop in Atlanta, he was sure that seducing her was to exact revenge on Margo for rejecting him. He had fallen madly in love with Margo, and Malik knew that Margo had felt something for him, too. And then, just like that, Jefferson was released from prison, and he'd become a thorn in her side, although they were together almost always after his wife, Toni, died.

And then Margo had come running, no begging him to make love to her. She thought Jefferson was with Angelica. Wow, Angelica. He'd forgotten her, but how could anyone forget Angelica with the angelic body that any man would die for? She was once Margo's best friend, but that came with a price. Angelica tried to seduce him, and he would have let her if he wasn't so sure that Margo was going to be his.

Malik turned the water on high. Those old feelings of lust had to go away. He had a beautiful new wife that was going to keep him happy for years. He'd win the state senate seat, and then he'd run for governor. And if the political road seemed promising for him, he'd run for President of the United States.

He scrubbed harder as images of Margo tried to seize his mind and his groin. The pounding water didn't seem to help, only exacerbate the feelings and the memories. He jumped at the pounding on the glass to the shower door and felt condemned when he opened the door to a beautiful and naked Ivy who begged to join him.

"You want me to scrub your back?" Ivy asked, planting kisses all over Malik's chest.

"Yeah, baby."

"And I see you're still thinking about that good lovin' I threw on you last night." Ivy laughed.

"Yeah, baby," Malik said, trying to hide his erection.

"Why don't you let Momma take care of that for you?"

"Gotta go to the shop. Baby, you know I want to, bad. What are my customers going to say?"

"They'll understand when you don't show up. You need to call your assistant and tell him you're married now."

Malik laughed. "Come here, baby." With the water raining on them, he kissed Ivy and pinned her against the shower wall, admiring her beauty, kissing and feeling her all over until he entered her. Their bodies melded together, they made love to Walter Murphy's recording *"A Fifth of Beethoven,"* each moan and groan delivered at a fever pitch. Malik gave Ivy what she wanted. And then they were spent, each collapsing in the arms of the other. After a brief moment, he held her arms and moved her back so that he could admire her body. "Hurry up and get dressed. I'm ready to announce to the world that Malik Mason is no longer single."

"I'll be ready in five, Mr. Mason."

## Ten

After leaving SuperComp Technical Solutions, Malik and Ivy headed for his campaign head-quarters. Ivy felt on top of the world, driving around Fayetteville with her brand new husband in his black BMW 750i without a care in the world. She'd given up her job in Atlanta as a financial analyst assistant making decent money to be with Malik. She wasn't sure where her next dime would come from, but now she was Mrs. Malik Mason whose husband was now running for Senator in the State of North Carolina. Yes, she was on top of the world.

She felt giddy as they neared Malik's campaign head-quarters and relished in the thought of what it was going to be like when Malik announced that he had gotten married. Would they love and embrace her like they did Malik? Of course they would.

"Okay, baby, this is it," Malik said as he turned into the parking lot. "It's time for the great reveal."

"I'm ready."

Malik came around and opened the door for his wife, who slid out of the seat like she was a princess. Ivy flexed her hand and ring finger as if practicing for a part in a movie or a play. She wore an orange and yellow two-piece cotton suit with matching pumps and a yellow sleeveless shell. Malik wore a tan gabardine suit set off by an off-white, lightweight knit shirt. On his feet, he wore a shiny pair of tan Stacy Adams that would have sufficed as a crystal ball.

Arm in arm they walked through the doors of Malik's campaign headquarters. There were four or five staffers who volunteered their time and were busy on the phones. There were two males in their early-twenties and three ladies who were in their mid-twenties to late-thirties. Ivy recognized a couple of the girls as long lost acquaintances that she had ceased to keep in contact with. She smiled and waved but they ignored her, continuing their telephone conversations with their backs to her.

Ivy sniffed. She was going to get some respect up in here. There was no way they were going to ignore Mrs. Ivy Mason.

Malik held up his hand and got everyone's attention. "I need to talk to everyone as soon as you conclude your telephone conversations."

One by one, each of his staffers put their phones down as soon as their calls were completed. Many of them had been at the office since early morning calling folks to ask for their donations, time, and most importantly their votes. The phones were silent for the next five minutes.

Ivy stood back as Malik took center stage with the

staffers standing around him in a semi-circle. "Hey, every-one, I appreciate your hard work."

"You could've brought us some lunch," one of the young men replied. Everyone laughed.

"Sure you're right, my young friend. I just might do that, but before I do, I have a very important announce-ment to make." He waved for Ivy to come and stand next to him. "This beautiful lady standing next to me is Mrs. Ivy Mason, my wife."

The demeanor on the faces of the women changed several times as they looked from one to the other. The news had caught them off-guard because at no time had the man they were volunteering their services in hopes of him gaining a win for a seat in the North Carolina Senate given any indication that he was off the market and, least of all, was headed for the altar. In fact, LaShea, one of the workers, had made it known to Malik and everyone else in the camp that she was single and unat-tached and that Malik Mason would make a nice catch.

"Don't just stand there," Malik said, not sure it was the right thing to say.

Milo, the young brother began to clap, and the others followed, softly.

"You'll see a lot of my wife here at headquarters," Malik began.

"Um-hmm," LaShea said under her breath although everyone in the room heard it.

Ivy fidgeted and rocked back and forth in her shoes,

not feeling the love. It was all right because she didn't care about any of those heifers who acted as if they had an attitude about her new status. It was what it was. She was Malik's wife. She cocked her head and listened to Malik's final announcement.

"I wanted you to know first. I want to have a press conference in a couple of days to share the news with my constituency. We have a lot of hurdles to cross and I understand that I'm running against a very tough opponent. But we can win, and we will win."

"Yes, we will win," Milo began the chat.

Everyone chimed in except LaShea. She walked up to Malik and stood in front of him and rolled her eyes at Ivy. "I quit." And she walked out of the door.

"Is there anyone else who feels like LaShea? Speak now."

"Naw, Mr. Mason," Mychele, the older woman, said. "We're with you. And welcome, Mrs. Mason."

Ivy smiled for the first time since walking into campaign headquarters. "Thank you," she mouthed.

"Baby, how about I take you out for a nice lunch, drop you home, before I head back here?"

"That'll be fine, baby."

"I've got a lot to do. I'll bring back pizzas for the rest of you."

"Yeah," Milo shouted. "I don't know what the rest of these folks want, but make mine a double pepperoni with lots of cheese."

Malik laughed. "You're going to have to share that pizza young blood."

Milo bowed. "That's okay by me."

"See you all later," Malik said as he and Ivy proceeded out of the building.

Ivy smiled and waved goodbye to Mychele and Donna. They did the same. Ivy was glad that the preliminaries were over. It was very uncomfortable, but these were the kinds of things she would have to endure as a political candidate's wife. She was ready.

Lunch was brief but Ivy enjoyed the time with Malik. Their courtship, if you could call it that, was brief, and their engagement even briefer, but the last two days had been wonderful. She didn't fully understand what made Malik tick, but she studied him, getting to know his mannerisms and his idiosyncrasies. She walked around his townhouse and familiarized herself with the man she married, although she realized that it wouldn't be long before she began to add her feminine touches to the place.

For a fleeting moment she thought of her mother, wishing they weren't so estranged and that she could share her good news with her. It was her mother's fault for the distance between them, Ivy decided. It was her mother who pulled away from everyone after the split up from her father, acting as if she and her siblings were to blame for the ruination of the marriage. Hell, her mother had gone overseas without telling anyone for three whole months, knowing that she had babies growing inside of her. Why should she run to her now? Let her understanding daughter, Winter, be there for her. Ivy loved her mother, but she had pushed her away when she needed her most.

Ivy learned from J.R. that her mother didn't want her dad's assistance when the babies came, and now she had a set of twins she had to raise on her own. She understood why her mother left her dad, but damn, they were his babies, too. Maybe that's where Ivy got some of her stubbornness from.

She picked up her purse off the couch and pulled out her cell. Sighing, she finally dialed a number and waited. Ivy paced back and forth until she heard his voice. She sighed again and answered.

"Hey, J.R., your sister reporting in."

"Hey, Ivy. Where are you? Have you made it to Fayette-ville yet?"

"Yep. I'm in Fayetteville."

"Where are you staying? Do you want me to come down?"

"Not so fast, brother dear. I'm staying with a friend of mine at the moment until I get a permanent residence. I just wanted to say hey to my big brother."

"Girl, I'm glad you're here. Did you get your stuff moved and all?"

"It will get here in a couple of days. I'll put it in storage for awhile."

"Like I told you, you're welcome to stay at my place. It's small but comfortable."

"I'm good. I see that Fayetteville hasn't changed much. The only thing that's changed is me."

"Yeah, how so?"

"I'm in love, J.R. I'm in love with a wonderful man. I never thought I'd feel this way about anyone, but I've found the man of my dreams."

"The man of your dreams? Where is this coming from? It wasn't but four months ago that you were with that Andre dude? Don't tell me it's him. Last I remember, you dumped him out like two-hour-old oatmeal."

"J.R., you are funny, man. I wasn't that bad, was I?"

"You know I know you, sis. You'd kiss them like you were a black widow spider and leave 'em the next day. You are a cold-blooded sister, but unlike the black widow, you let your prey live. Why do you think I never introduced you to any of my friends? I wouldn't have any once you got through." Ivy and J.R. laughed.

"You're telling the truth, brother, but I've changed. I'm a one-man woman now. I'm with a serious man who's going places and is going to take the world by storm."

"So when do I get to meet this knight-in-shining-armor?"

"Sometime soon. We're getting to know each other better right now. I'm not ready to share him with the rest of the world yet."

"Sounds like some crazy reality show. So how many bachelors did you start off with before you gave this one the final rose?"

"Too much TV. You need to get your butt up off the couch and get involved with what's happening in the world...dibble and dabble in a little politics?"

"What's up with you? You don't sound like the Ivy Myles I know. And for your information, how do you know that I'm not dibble and dabbling in politics? I'm more invested than you know."

"Okay, J.R. This is not about tit for tat. You don't have to pretend with me. I'm sure Dad's got you stuck up in some hole in the wall, making promises to you he can't keep."

"Hold it, Ivy. You don't know a damn thing, okay. Dad is cool, and he's going to be on top again; you wait and see. And I'm going to be right there with him."

"Hmmm," Ivy retorted. "Such strong words, my brother. Sorry if I offended you; didn't mean to."

"Well, it's been good talking to you, sis. If you want to get together, give me a call. Got to run."

"Okay," Ivy said as she heard the phone go dead at the other end. "So that's how it is. Uhmm."

## Eleven

"Pops, Winston, check out this website." Jefferson and Winston rushed to J.R.'s computer. "Look at this home page; check how it opens up."

"That's tight," Winston said, thoroughly delighted at his brother's work.

"Good job, J.R.," Jefferson complimented.

"Thanks. See…it opens up to the image of Dr. Shelton Wright, the businessman, and then rotates to the image of him as a family man, and finally as a man of the people. I've also placed his campaign ad on the site."

"Yeah, I understand that it will be airing tomorrow," Jefferson said. "Have you finished with all of the other media paraphernalia, Winston?"

"Yeah, Dad. I'm on my way to the sign shop now to pick up the yard posters and the large signs that we'll post at different locations around town. I'm going to head over to headquarters when I'm done and then back to the office."

"Don't forget about dinner. We will be dining with Dr. Wright around six tonight."

"Got it; I'm out," Winston said. "If I don't catch up

with you guys, I'll meet you at the restaurant. The website is off the chain, J.R. Great job." Winston patted his chest with his closed hand, and J.R. did likewise.

"It would be nice if Ivy was going to be with us tonight," Jefferson said, pouring a cup of coffee for himself. "It's going to be a family affair having all of my children together, as we toast the candidacy of Dr. Wright."

"Yeah, it would be," J.R. said without any emotion.

Jefferson turned around and looked at J.R. thoughtfully. "You heard from Ivy?"

J.R. turned away from his computer screen and looked in Jefferson's direction. "Why do you ask?"

"Maybe it's because of your body language and your nonchalant response."

"Pops, I was engrossed in this website and barely heard what you were saying."

"Okay, if that's what you want me to believe. However, I've known you all of my life, and I can tell when something is not right."

J.R. leaned back and swiveled around in his seat. He looked past Jefferson, then back at his dad who watched him like he was his favorite ESPN commentator for the Sunday afternoon NFL Game of the Week. Jefferson put his cup down on a file cabinet and waited for J.R. to speak.

J.R. sighed. "I spoke to Ivy a couple of days ago. She was acting weird. You can't say I told you, but she's back in Fayetteville."

"Fayetteville? How long has she been there? Does your mother know?"

"Pops, something's up with Ivy. She was talking crazy… like she was in a cloud talking about some man she was so in love with…and that the man was the reason she came back to the Ville. If you ask me, she sounded like she was high on drugs. But I know my sister; she doesn't do drugs. Plus, she's had a number of boyfriends, or whatever you want to call them, since she's been in Atlanta that she's discarded like the plastic wrap on a Twinkie. None of them lasted a week, if that. I don't see her being serious with just one person because no one is good enough for her."

"Do you have her number?" ⸱

"Pops, she doesn't want you or Mom to know that she's here. In fact, she doesn't want anyone to know and that includes Winter and Winston."

"You think someone has her strung out on drugs?" Jefferson popped his fist in his hand. "I don't want to have to hurt anyone."

"I don't think it's as serious as that. I can't put my finger on it, but something is different about her."

"Maybe she'll feel differently about contacting us soon. Why don't we get up out of here and get ready for dinner tonight?"

"Sounds like a plan, Pops. What would you say if I brought a date?"

A smile flew over Jefferson's face. "A date? We have

room enough for another person. Didn't know you were interested in someone special."

"Come on now. Don't make a big deal about it…but she's special. Goes to the church."

Jefferson slapped J.R. on the back. "You go, son. At least one of my children is interested in the dating game. Can't wait to meet her."

J.R. smiled back. For the first time in a long time, he was glad to be part of the family.

*Twelve*

Campaign headquarters was overflowing with activity. There were several wooden tables with file cabinets in the medium-sized room, lined up on either side of two walls, and one desk that sat up against the back wall. Dr. Wright sat at a desk with his phone to his ear, no doubt contacting constituents to drum up votes. Dr. Wright watched as Winston approached his desk carrying a bundle of signs and other campaign material after an aide pointed Winston in his direction.

Dr. Wright held up a finger, and Winston stood a few feet away until Dr. Wright was finished with his phone call. Dr. Wright was a distinguished-looking gentleman who appeared to be in his late-forties. Winston noted that streaks of gray highlighted his rather black sideburns that complemented his medium-brown complexion. Dr. Wright wore a navy-blue suit, plain white dress shirt, and a conservative blue, white, and gray-patterned neck-tie. A thin, black moustache was draped nicely over his thin lips. Winston stepped forward when Dr. Wright motioned for him to come forward.

"How are you doing, young man?" Dr. Wright asked,

standing up to assist Winston with the signs. "You must be one of Myles' sons."

"Yes, sir; I'm Winston Myles at your service."

After Winston set all of the campaign material down with the help of Dr. Wright, Dr. Wright gave him a hearty handshake. "Nice to meet you, son. You all did a fine job on the website and the ad campaigns."

"My brother, Jefferson Jr., is the mastermind behind the web-site. I'm a techie, too, but I can't take credit for it. I did work on the ad campaign with him. Just know that my dad and our company are committed to your run for the North Carolina Senate."

"Thank you, thank you. That's good to hear. Let's look at what you've got."

Dr. Wright looked at the postcards, buttons, flyers, signs and placards that Winston brought in. "These are great. Can't wait to get them into the voters' hands and posted on lawns. I think we have a fair chance of winning."

"Yes, sir. Well, I won't take up any more of your time. We look forward to seeing you at dinner tonight."

"That's right. I want you to meet my beautiful wife of twenty-five years. Fine woman; she's stood beside me every step of the way. I'll also bring my son; he's going to be a doctor like myself. He's finishing up at Duke University School of Medicine."

Winston grinned. "My sister will like that."

"Jefferson didn't mention he had a daughter."

"Actually, two daughters. My twin sister is the one

who'll join us this evening. My sister, Ivy, lives in Atlanta."

Dr. Wright patted Winston on the shoulder. "I can't wait to meet all the members of your family. See you at six o'clock."

Winston shook Dr. Wright's hand. "See you at six."

Margo pulled the baked chicken from the oven and sat it on the stove. She had done more cooking in the past week than she'd done in the last six or seven months. Since Winter always seemed to be hanging around and expecting to have a home-cooked meal, she acquiesced. It was great having her daughter around to help with the babies, though. It helped to ease the loneliness she sometimes felt while also giving her a break.

She tasted the mashed potatoes and added a little salt. The spinach was done; dinner was done. All that was left was for Winter to come downstairs and eat.

With spoon in hand, Margo rested her body against the granite countertop and looked around at her kitchen. She was in love with it…in fact, she loved her townhouse. It had all the nuances and more than a regular house boasted. Margo twisted her lips. But her house didn't have the warmth of a man, something she missed.

Her mind wandered and there was Jefferson, her beloved husband who was soon to be her ex-husband. He looked so good the last time she saw him; he was aging gracefully. Margo still loved him, but too much drama, hurt and pain had interrupted their lives. There was no way their marriage could survive another stroke; so she'd made up her mind it was the end. But she loved him.

"Hey, Mom," Winter said as she entered the kitchen. "How do you like my dress?" Winter twirled around.

Margo seemed confused. "Why are you all dressed up? I've got dinner on the stove…"

"I'm sorry, Mom. I've got a date tonight."

"A date? And you didn't tell me? I've fixed dinner for us and now you tell me you've got a date."

"I'm sorry, Mom. Forgot to tell you. Smooches."

"So who is the lucky guy?"

"Promise you won't get mad?"

"Am I going to be upset?"

"You might."

"Well."

"I'm going to dinner with Dad, J.R., and Winston. We're meeting the candidate who's running for North Carolina state senator."

"I thought your dad said that Malik was running for senator?"

"He is but in a different district. It's complicated."

"So you're going to ditch me for a date with your dad?"

"It's not like that, Mom. You know I love you." Margo smiled. "It's nice that the guys asked me to join them. So, how do I look?"

"Other than showing more cleavage than usual and

your dress being a little too short to be meeting a sena-torial candidate, I say you look absolutely fabulous. Black is wicked on you, Ms. Winter."

Winter kissed Margo. "Thank you, Mom. I do want to make a good impression. You made my day, though. Kiss, kiss. I may go to my apartment tonight. Get a change of clothes, check my mail. I'll stop by tomorrow."

"What if I'm not home? Don't you think my babies and I have a life?"

"I'll see you tomorrow, Mom. Sorry about dinner. I'll give you the lowdown when I see you."

"Okay, sweetheart. Have a good time with your daddy."

Ivy put her hands on her hip and gave Margo an inquiring look.

"What's on your mind?" Margo asked. "You better get out of here before you're late. I've got a date with the TV and my boys. Whatever's on your mind take it with you."

"Either you've been thinking a lot about Dad or you're jealous. I like to think the former."

"Girl, I don't know what you're talking about. Your dad and I are history."

"I saw the way you were scoping him out when he was here the other day."

"Winter, I don't know what you're talking about."

"Yeah, right."

"Well, I will admit your daddy still has it going on. He did look good. Now get out of here and have a good time."

Winter laughed. "All right, I will. And I'm going to tell Daddy what you said."

"You do, Winter, and I'll bust your butt wide open."

"Mommy, stop the violence. Love you."

"Love you, too, baby girl. Night, night. Drive safe."

Margo went to the front door and watched as Winter climbed down the few steps to the sidewalk. Her big babies were all grown up, and she was proud of all of them—even the ones who had distanced themselves from her. Children went through phases, and whatever was going on with Ivy would hopefully be short-lived. She and Ivy were very close at one time and Margo missed her.

Locking the front door, Margo went upstairs to check on the boys. They were so peaceful as they slept. Margo was going to use this time to eat something since she cooked and watch a little TV. She missed Winter already.

*Thirteen*

Jefferson pulled his Mercedes in front of the Mint restaurant and paid for valet parking. He was a few minutes early, but he'd rather be on time than late. It had been a good while since he'd been to the Mint, but he looked forward to a good meal with his family and the man he believed would be one of their next state senators.

The Mint had a flare of its own and people called it a culinary jewel considering its location in the heart of downtown Raleigh. The cuisine featured contemporary Southern food with a global influence. The ambiance made one feel special, romantic if you felt the mood. It was said to be the best in fine dining.

Not seeing anyone, Jefferson entered the restaurant and looked around. He couldn't believe that not one member of his family besides himself had arrived, noting it was five-fifty by his watch. Seeing no one, he alerted the maître d that he has reservations for eight that included Dr. Shelton Wright. The maître d' acknowledged Jefferson's reservation and offered to show him to his table just as Winston stepped through the door.

"Hey, Dad," Winston greeted Jefferson, hitting him

with a fist bump. "New suit?" he whispered, running his fingers along the lapel of Jefferson's jacket. "Looking sharp."

"Hey, son. You're looking and smelling pretty good yourself, if a father can say so." Winston laughed.

"Are we ready?" the maître d' asked. Jefferson and Winston nodded. "Follow me."

Light dinner music played throughout the restaurant. There weren't many diners seated, although the night was still young. Jefferson and Winston were seated and accepted menus from the maître d.

"You've been here before, Dad? Looks expensive."

"Yeah, I've taken your mother here on several occasions. Those were special times."

"You still love her, don't you?"

Jefferson looked thoughtfully at his son. "Winston, how can you stop loving someone who has been your whole life? Sometimes life throws us a curve ball or we make a mess of it, and I've paid for my sins. But to answer your question, no, I've never stopped loving Margo. When I saw her the other day..."

"You saw Mom?"

"Leave it to your sister to drag me over there. It was hard. I wanted to go to your mother, pick her up, kiss her, and hold her forever. I don't think she's as happy as she pretends to be."

"Well, why don't you tell her, Dad? Man up, swallow your pride and tell her what you just told me."

"Hold that thought. Here comes Dr. Wright and his family."

Jefferson and Winston stood up as Dr. Wright, Mrs. Wright, and their son, Phillip, joined them at the table. Dr. Wright shook Jefferson and Winston's hands and sat down.

"Good evening, Jefferson...Winston," Shelton Wright said, unbuttoning the jacket to his suit.

"Dr. Wright," both Jefferson and Winston said.

"This is my wife, Betty, and my son, Phillip," Dr. Wright said by way of introduction. "Baby, this is Jefferson Myles and his son, Winston. I met Winston today. He's a fine young man, Jefferson."

"Thank you," Jefferson replied.

"My son, Phillip, is a student of medicine at Duke. He's going to be a fine doctor one day."

"That's great," Jefferson said. "We need more fine doctors, especially African-American doctors."

"Thank you, Mr. Myles...," Phillip began but stopped mid-sentence. Everyone followed his gaze.

"Oh, here's my daughter, Winter...Winston's twin sister," Jefferson offered, standing up to wait for Winter to be seated.

"She's very attractive," Phillip said as he watched Winter approach the table.

"Good evening, everyone," Winter said with a bright smile. She stopped at Jefferson and gave him a peck on the cheek and tapped Winston on the shoulder.

"Sexy dress you've got on, sis," Winston whispered in Winter's ear. "You've got an admirer."

"Mom said black looked wicked on me; so it's doing its job."

"Winter," Jefferson began, "this is Dr. Shelton Wright, our choice for North Carolina state senator, his wife, Betty, and their son, Phillip, who by the way is studying to be a medical doctor at Duke.

"Nice to meet you all," Winter said, holding her gaze much longer than the rest as she acknowledged Phillip. Winter smiled, and Phillip's eyes met hers.

The waiter approached the table. "Would you like a Cabernet or another wine of your choice?"

"What do you recommend?" Dr. Wright asked.

"I recommend a Pinot Grigio."

"Sounds good. How about you, Jefferson?"

"That sounds good to me as well."

"I'd like a glass of water with lemon, please," Winter said. The waiter nodded his head.

Jefferson looked at his watch. It was fifteen after six. Just as he was about to make an excuse for J.R., he strolled in with a very attractive lady on his arms.

"Here's J.R.," Winston said. He and Winter glanced at each other with amazement in their eyes.

"Sorry I'm late," J.R. said. "We were held up by a train. I'm Jefferson Jr., better known as J.R., and this is my friend, Elaine." J.R. and Elaine sat down.

"Glad to meet you," Dr. Wright said. He introduced

his wife and son. "I've got to tell you the website is awe-some. I was telling your brother this afternoon that you did a top-notch job on it. The ads are outstanding. The Web Connection is going to be getting a lot of referrals."

J.R. smiled, as well as Jefferson and Winston. "Thank you, sir," J.R. said. "I pride myself on my work, and most of all, I believe in your campaign as do the rest of my family."

"That's right," Jefferson said. "We will be campaigning right along with you, and whatever you need, we'll be there for you."

For the first time Betty Wright broke her silence. "I appreciate your vision for my husband." Dr. Wright's smile was long and endearing. "My husband is a wonderful man, and I believe he is the best man for the senate seat. He's devoted his whole life to serving people, whether in the doctor's office, hospital, the community, or church. He has the heart for people, and I want him to win."

"That was so sweet," Winter said. "You have such a warm and loving mother, Phillip."

Winston hit Winter. She was going overboard.

"It's all right." Betty Wright laughed. "I see my son making goo-goo eyes at Winter."

"Okay, Mom," Phillip said. "I'm not making goo-goo eyes at the gorgeous woman sitting across from me."

Everyone broke out in laughter.

"Okay, let's loosen this party up," Dr. Wright said. "Oh great, the wine is here. Let's celebrate."

"Dear, we can celebrate as soon as we give our dinner order to the waiter," Betty Wright interjected.

"I agree with you, Mrs. Wright," Winston said, fumbling with his menu. "This place is filling up fast, and I'm famished."

Everyone laughed again. After the orders were given, everyone picked up their glasses of wine or water upon the request of Dr. Wright.

"I'd like to make a toast," Dr. Wright began. "To a bright and successful campaign."

"Here, here," the group said in unison before taking sips of their drinks.

"I'd like to make a toast, also," Jefferson said. Everyone held their glasses up once more. "To one of the next senators of the State of North Carolina."

"Here, here," the group said again.

"I'm grateful to all of you," Dr. Wright said. "Thank you for being a part of my journey."

The night was progressing well. The Wrights and the Myles were getting along fine. The food was divine, and the wine was still going around.

"J.R., you're looking good in that navy blue suit and white silk turtleneck you're wearing," Winter said, pushing J.R.'s elbows with hers. "I like your dreads pulled back like that on the back of your head. You've got the look of a well-accomplished man...a man who's going places."

"What are you talking about, sis? You need to talk to the man sitting across from you whose eyes have been hanging out in your cleavage the whole night."

Winter hit J.R., who laughed. "Mom said I look good."

"I can't believe she let you leave the house like that. I'll admit that if I weren't your brother, I'd try to hit on you, too, but as you can see, I've got a fine sister with me already."

"Elaine," Winter said, reaching over J.R., "how did you get my brother to suit up? I don't remember the last time I've seen him look this good."

"Well, you've got to come to our church more often. Most Sundays, but not all, J.R. does wear a suit."

"Shut up. A regular church member; I've got to get my life right with God."

"Elaine, don't pay my sister any mind," J.R. said. "She is the number one drama queen, although I'll say she's a smart drama queen. Girlfriend has a good job and makes good money. She needs a significant other to spice up her life."

"I don't need a man to complete me," Winter said, taking a peek at Phillip. "Watch this, J.R." Winter turned to Phillip. "Phillip, would you like to get some air..."

"Damn, Winter," J.R. whispered. "You sound like you're trying to pick up somebody."

Winter frowned. "I'm only being sociable."

Phillip tried to keep from laughing. "Hey, J.R., since I couldn't help but hear what you said, I love a girl who's forward."

J.R. wrinkled his face. "Okay, my man. My sister is a handful."

Jefferson, Winston, Dr. and Mrs. Wright, J.R. and Elaine watched as Winter and Phillip both stood up and preceded to leave the table. Jefferson smiled, as did the Wrights. No one said a word. Before Winter could move into the aisle, she stopped cold.

"What's the matter?" Phillip asked.

"Isn't that Malik Mason?" Dr. Wright asked Jefferson.

Jefferson turned in the direction Dr. Wright was looking. Winter was blocking his view and he couldn't get a good look.

"It is him," Dr. Wright said before Jefferson could reply. "He has a woman with him."

"I didn't know he had a girlfriend," Mrs. Wright said, studying the couple.

Stunned, Winter turned to look at her brothers with her mouth hanging open just as Phillip came up behind her. She looked at J.R., Winston, and Jefferson. "That's Ivy with Malik. I didn't even know she was in North Carolina."

"Who's Ivy?" Phillip asked as he looked from Winter to her brothers.

J.R.'s mood changed. He looked at Jefferson, whose mood had also changed. No one moved until Winter opened her mouth.

"What is Ivy doing with Malik?"

"Who's Ivy?" Phillip asked again.

Phillip was getting on Winter's nerve. This was a Myles family situation and he needed to go and sit down somewhere and mind his own business, regardless of how fine of a specimen he was. But she heard herself say, "She's my sister."

Fourteen

Ivy hung on Malik's arm as if it was stuck there with crazy glue. She wore a slate blue taffeta sleeveless dress with ruffles circling the dress at the knees. Malik complemented Ivy by wearing a dark gray suit and sky blue dress shirt with a blue, white and silver patterned tie that brought it all together. They walked to their seats like they were royalty, with ease and without a care in the world, preparing themselves for a romantic dinner as Ivy hung on to Malik's every word.

They hadn't noticed Winter standing a few tables away gawking at them. The Masons were in their own world, unable to keep their eyes from each other, and every now and then reaching for spot kisses on the lips.

"I love this place," Ivy began. "It's so romantic, Malik."

"A fitting place for my new bride." Malik took Ivy's ring finger and looked at it and then whispered in her ear. "Girl, your lovemaking was on point last night. I didn't know you were that hot."

"I'm a believer if you give all the goodies away up front, there's nothing left to come back to. My mother used to tell my sister and me that all the time."

"Well, Margo was very wise because, honey, I wasn't

in the least bit disappointed. You've set the bar high; so you've got to deliver."

"Listen up, Mr. Malik Mason, the well isn't dry and I've got more tricks than any magician. I love you."

"I love you, too."

"Cabernet or another wine of your choosing?" the waiter asked.

"Yes, we would like one of your good French wines," Malik said, winking at Ivy. "Something special for the madam."

The waiter smiled. "I've got just the one for you...a Sauvignon..."

Malik puckered his lips and answered before the waiter could finish. "Mighty fine choice. Please bring us a bottle."

The waiter nodded and left the table.

"This place is popular," Ivy observed, glancing around for the first time. Then she stopped and stared. "That can't be..."

"That can't be what," Malik asked, turning around in his seat.

"Oh my God. It is...my family. Damn, Winter is coming over here."

"Be calm. We don't want to make a scene in the restaurant. This is a very nice establishment..."

"Well, hello, Ivy," Winter said, glaring at her and Malik. "So when did you get into town? When were you going to call someone and tell us you were here? You have a mother who just gave birth to twins who keeps asking about you."

Malik looked at Ivy with a puzzled look on her face. "Your mother was pregnant and had twins?"

"Oh, so Ivy here hasn't given you the four-one-one about our family, especially since you were so closely connected? Shame on her. Well, just so you know, Dad, Winston, J.R. and his girlfriend, Elaine, and soon to be North Carolina Senator Wright are sitting over there." Winter pointed. She smiled at Ivy's irritation.

"It's good to see you, too, Winter," Ivy said with a frown. "My husband and I are trying to have dinner, and you're interrupting our good mood." Ivy flashed her wedding ring so Winter could see it. It was Ivy's turn to smile as Winter's eyes protruded from their sockets.

"Let's keep this civil," Malik interjected.

"I'm trying to do just that, honey," Ivy said, her voice controlled but angry.

"Well," Winter said, crossing her chest with her hand. "Sounds like we're the ones that didn't get the four-one-one or the wedding invitation. Your mother is going to be deeply disappointed."

"Winter, go back to your seat. We can chat another time."

"To think we were once very close. All right, sister dear, I'll leave you two lovebirds. Wait until Daddy hears this. He's going to go off." With that, Winter strutted back to her seat in double time.

"You can be sure Miss CNN has just broadcasted our business across the globe," Ivy said.

"After our press conference this afternoon, anyone

she tells will have already heard the news. It broadcasted on the evening news. I DVR'd it so we can see it when we get home."

"Good," was all Ivy could say as she stared at the table where her family sat. No one turned around and looked in her direction, although she knew that little Miss-can't-keep-anything-to-herself had already told everyone at the table. Ivy looked down at her ring and then up at her husband and smiled.

"Why didn't you tell me your mother was pregnant and had twins?"

"I didn't think it was important, Malik. As I said, my mother and I haven't been getting along. I only learned a few days ago that she had the babies. Look, I didn't intentionally forget to tell you. It's just that I'm estranged from my family. As much as my dad hates you, he hasn't gotten up from his table to come over here and say something to me."

"And if he knows what's good for him, it would be best that he stay put where he is. I know that you are his daughter, but you are old enough to make your own decisions about who you want to spend the rest of your life with...not him."

"Thanks, baby." Ivy grinned. "I appreciate the support. Let's try to get through our dinner without any more drama."

"Good idea."

Every now and then, Ivy looked toward the table where her family sat while she continued to eat her meal with her husband. Malik's mood seemed a bit off-kilter as they ate in silence. Ivy peeked again and saw her family glance her way as they prepared to leave. The nerves in her stomach churned as she picked at her salad and prayed that this night would soon be over.

Ivy saw Malik look up and put his fork down with a severe frown on his face. Then a shadow loomed over their table as Jefferson came into view.

"Good evening, Ivy," Jefferson said.

"Hi, Daddy," was her response.

Jefferson's eyes tore into Malik like a torpedo. "You couldn't have Margo, so you settled for my daughter." Ivy looked at Jefferson with disgust. "You hurt Ivy and I'll find you and break every bone in your body." And then Jefferson walked away without waiting for a response from Malik, followed by the rest of the family who hadn't bothered to speak.

Ivy put her fork down and excused herself.

Malik was seething but he reached out and grabbed Ivy's hand. "Baby, are you okay? Where are you going?"

"To the restroom; I won't be long." Malik let go of Ivy's hand and watched her walk away.

Ivy flew into the restroom and stood over the commode and threw up her dinner. She flushed the toilet, pulled the toilet seat down, and sat on it. She dropped her head into her hands and cried until the tears refused to come.

Sighing, Ivy got up from the commode, washed her hands and returned to her dinner table.

"Are you all right?" Malik asked, truly concerned as she returned to the table.

"Yes. And I'm ready to go."

Ivy looked toward the entrance of the building. Her heart didn't pass the test. Her father had no right to accost Malik the way he did. She was a grown woman who made her own decisions. J.R.'s rejection surprised her the most; in the last two or three years, they had gotten along well and enjoyed each other's company. She missed her family, but if they thought she was going to run behind them, they had another thing to think about. They could all kiss her black ass.

# Fifteen

**M**argo pranced around the kitchen and fixed her plate. Her chicken was baked to perfection, and she ate until she couldn't eat any more. When she finished, she took her plate to the sink and placed it in. She'd get the dishes later.

She listened to the baby monitors as her babies begged for her to come and get them. "I'm coming, Ian and Evan." Margo took two steps at a time. "Whew," she said when she reached the top. "I've got to exercise more."

The babies were crying loudly when Margo entered their room. Their diapers were wet upon examination, and she changed each baby in turn, then tried to decide which of her two sons she'd nurse first.

Margo put Ian in the swing and Evan on her breast. Trying to nurse two babies at the same time proved difficult, so taking care of one at a time seemed to be the best option.

Evan fretted throughout his whole feeding. Maybe he didn't like her milk, but he'd done well up to this point. She checked Evan's head and he seemed to have a slight fever. She laid him down and rubbed his stomach. She touched his forehead and it seemed warm.

Baby Ian began to cry. Margo sat in her rocker and fed him, all the while watching out for Evan. Baby fed, Margo looked for some Tylenol for children and gave a smidgen to Evan. She went to her bedroom and sat on the bed, holding both babies in her arms. They were quiet for the moment, looking around at the strange place that was their mother's room. They were fascinated by the television when Margo turned it on.

News Fourteen provided local and state news every half-hour. It was about ten o'clock, Margo noticed—time to get the top of the news. The babies went to sleep and Margo lay up against the backboard of her bed.

"And in Fayetteville, Mr. Malik Mason, candidate for state senator, gave a press conference this afternoon. We will go to Sharon Wells, who has the story."

Margo sat up straight with the babies tight in her arms.

"Today, senatorial candidate, Mr. Malik Mason of Fayetteville, gave a surprising announcement. In a private ceremony performed in the state of South Carolina, candidate Mason married Ms. Ivy Myles, who as recently as a few days ago, lived in Atlanta, Georgia, but grew up in Fayetteville. From talking with several people who attended the press conference and knew Mr. Mason well, none of them had any knowledge that Mason was seriously dating anyone. This was a well-kept secret. Again, senatorial candidate, Malik Mason, was recently married to Ivy Myles in a secret ceremony in South Carolina. This is Sharon Wells, News Fourteen."

Margo sat frozen on top of her bed, her bundles of joy still snuggled up against her. She now ignored the voices coming from the TV set as she tried to digest what she had heard. *Did the newscaster say that her daughter, Ivy, got married to a man she had feelings for once?*

Scooting from the bed, Margo deposited the twins in their cribs and covered them lightly with blankets. Her brain was working overtime, unable to fathom what she had heard. Margo tried to suppress the anger that began to well up inside of her. She walked briskly to her room and grabbed her cell phone. She had to talk to Winter.

Before she was able to dial Winter's number, the doorbell rang. She looked at the clock. It was ten-fifteen. Who would be coming to her house this time of night without calling first? Maybe it was Winter, but she had a key. The doorbell rang again.

Illuminating the house, Margo walked stealthily to the front door. She peeked through the peephole and pulled back and looked again. "Winston?" she asked.

"Yeah, Mom, it's me. Open up."

"Boy, you need to call and let me know you're coming when you come this late," Margo said as she opened up the door. Winston came in and Margo clamped her hands over her mouth when she saw J.R. and a young woman.

"Hey, Ma," J.R. said, falling into her open arms. When J.R. pulled away, he introduced his friend. "And this is Elaine, my friend."

"Hello," Margo said, in a low, sweet voice with tears

streaming down her face. "I'm sorry, Elaine. I haven't seen my son in awhile, and I'm so happy after the news I just learned. Give me a hug, J.R."

"What happened, Mom?" Winston asked.

"Look, this is not the time. I'm...I'm so glad you're here. J.R. dressed up in a suit. My God, son, you're looking good. Sorry, Elaine, but I've got to make a fuss over him."

"You ain't got to do that, Ma. It's cool. I love you. Miss you, too."

"So how did the dinner with your dad and the senatorial candidate go?"

"Everything was great," Winston replied. "It's what happened afterward that has us stunned."

"What happened?" Margo asked.

"You tell us what you learned, and we'll save the juicy gossip for last. It's going to blow your mind," J.R. said.

"I don't know about that," Margo said. "I'm still in the state of shock with my bit of news."

"So spill it, Mom," Winston encouraged.

"Where do I start? I had just finished feeding the boys and was sitting in my room watching television. It was tuned to News Fourteen. At first, I wasn't sure if I had dozed off and had some kind of horrific dream, but hearing it from the newscaster's lips made it a nightmare. Do you know where your sister, Ivy, has been?"

Winston and J.R. looked between each other.

"There was a press conference in Fayetteville today

where Malik announced that he had married Ivy. Imagine my shock when I see my daughter that I haven't heard from in four of five months smiling that fake smile and waving like she was the Queen of Sheba. Married? How long has she been in Fayetteville? I was so hurt. Mad to be exact." Margo caught her breath. "Mad as hell."

"You're right," Winston began, "our news has lost its punch."

"So what happened at dinner? I still want to know. Your mother has been in prison and needs to hear some exciting news."

J.R. went to Margo. "Ma, why don't we all sit down? What you got cooking in the kitchen?"

"Boy, this is the first time I've seen you in God knows when and you're talking about food. I thought you just ate."

"Yeah, but I know my momma, and I know you've got some food stashed in here somewhere."

"Nothing but baked chicken, mashed potatoes, and spinach."

Winston and J.R. took off.

"I don't know about my boys, Elaine. There's nothing fancy in those pots. Let's follow them."

Elaine followed Margo into the kitchen. "This is a nice house, Mrs. Myles. Oooh, I like."

"Thank you, Elaine. Look at my boys eating up my chicken and licking their fingers. I hope you washed your hands."

"Ma, I don't care if it is baked, this chicken is so good," J.R. exclaimed.

Margo laughed. "Y'all eat it all up if you want to. This makes me happy. Now somebody tell me what happened at dinner. It looks like you didn't eat anything."

"Mom," Winston began, after wiping his face with a napkin. "We know about Ivy. She and Malik showed up at the Mint."

"The Mint? Your father and I used to go there on special occasions."

"He told me," Winston said. "Anyway, Ivy didn't see us at first, but your drama queen daughter, my twin sister, had to go over to make it known that we were in the house. You could tell that Ivy was shocked, and to have Winter tell it, Ivy flashed her great big rock and told her that she and Malik were married."

"What did your daddy do?"

"He didn't want to make a scene, especially since we were in a nice restaurant and Dr. Wright and his family were there," Winston continued. "Dr. Wright is our client and loves our work with guarantees for more contracts. That saved Malik's ass tonight."

"Pops threatened him," J.R. put in, eating the last of the mashed potatoes. "Pops wanted to pound Malik into the ground."

"Well, I'm glad he didn't. So did Ivy say when she was going to get up with us?" Margo inquired.

"You mean with you, Ma?"

"Yes, J.R. With me."

"Ivy didn't say anything to us and we didn't say anything to her. She had her 'don't mess with her tonight' mask on. And we left her alone."

"This is so sad. I can't believe that my own daughter didn't have the decency to call me after I've left her a ton of messages, and then to go off and marry Malik. J.R., were they seeing each other while you were in Atlanta?"

"Ma, I can't divulge information like that, but to answer your question, not to my knowledge. I haven't seen Malik since God knows when."

"Too much drama for one night," Elaine finally said. "I'm going to pray for all of you."

"Please do that, Elaine," Margo said. "We do need Him."

"Can I see my little brothers?" J.R. asked, looking at Margo.

"Yeah, baby, go on up. Winston will take you to the room. I'll be up in a second."

J.R. held Elaine's hand and followed Winston out of the room. Margo smiled. "My baby has come home."

## Sixteen

W hat was meant to be a night of celebration quickly turned into an evening that Ivy wished she could erase from her memory. The silence that ensued during the long ride home from Raleigh to Fayetteville only complicated matters because she could read the distrust all over her husband's face.

Yes, she knew her mother was pregnant, but why should Malik care? It wasn't a secret that her mother led Malik on, laid in his bed, gave up her goodies and was in denial when her daddy found out and then threw Malik away like yesterday's trash, talking about she had made a mistake and that she only loved her husband, Jefferson. Her mother made her sick, but Ivy wasn't going to let it get her down because she was now Malik's wife and she was carrying his baby.

Ivy flipped these thoughts in her mind like a tossed salad as she leaned on the passenger side window and prayed that the ride would soon be over. She wished Malik would say something, anything to open the door that would allow her to explain her reasons for not saying anything about her mother. As much as she tried to remain civil tonight, Ivy was hard pressed to do so with her sister, Winter, looking down at her as if she was the family outcast, hurling her accusations and insults like she was the family spokesperson. If the situation had been different, she would have knocked Winter to the ground.

Sighing, she could feel Malik's eyes on her, probably trying to process her mood, maybe contemplating what he would say when he finally decided to break the silence. They drove on.

Ivy nearly jumped when she heard his voice. She shook her head, not certain where she was.

"Ivy, we're home," Malik said softly, still sitting in his seat.

She buttoned her coat and grabbed her clutch and waited for Malik to come around and open the door. He did so, but without a word, and Ivy vowed to not speak first. She followed him into the house and went straight to their master bedroom while he took a detour for the kitchen.

The silence was killing her. Ivy dropped her clutch onto the bed, took off her coat and dress, and hung them up. She stood for a moment in her black lacy bra and panties, thinking about how she was going to break the ice. Malik Mason was going to talk to her tonight. They were going to get it all out in the open so they could begin to live their lives on the good foot.

Thirty minutes passed and Malik had not yet come into the bedroom. Maybe a hot shower would soothe the tension that now coursed through Ivy's body. Yes, that would do it, and if Malik had not come into the room by the time she finished, she was going to march out to the kitchen or wherever he was and confront him. She was ready to put her cards on the table—all of them.

Fifteen minutes later Ivy felt great, the tension from her body melted away—nothing that a good, hot shower couldn't take care of. She looked at her image in the mirror and smiled, and as if on cue she brought her left hand out in front of her and looked at her magnificent rock that bound her to Malik. She brushed her hand with the other and delighted in how she felt. Tonight's little event was just that, a small and minor event that some good lovin' would cure. She was counting on it; she was counting on Malik being in their bedroom when she exited the bathroom, waiting to take her in his embrace and say that all was forgiven.

Ivy took the shower cap off of her head and swished her hair. She never thought she'd get rid of her dreads, but she liked her new look. It made her look like a senatorial candidate's wife, one who could wield influence for her man and possibly earn him a bid for the governorship or stretching it a bit, President of the United States of America. Ivy repressed her night dream, picked up her gown from the vanity chair, pulled it over her head and proceeded from the bathroom.

Entering their master bedroom, there was no sign of Malik. In fact, the house was deadly quiet. Ivy put on her robe and went in search of her husband. She found him in front of the fireplace with his arm resting on the mantel with a glass of wine in the other. Malik looked up as she came close.

"Malik, are you okay?"

"You tell me," he said, as he looked Ivy up and down with sultry eyes, not oblivious of her beauty.

"Come on, baby. Let's not end this night like this. It started out so well. I'll admit it was awkward seeing my family in the same restaurant where we chose to dine, and maybe I could've handled the situation with my sister a little better, although she was being a complete asshole. But one thing is for sure, Malik, and that's how I feel about you. I love you with all my heart and soul."

Malik moved his elbow from the mantel and turned to face Ivy. He took a sip of his drink, then put it down on the coffee table.

"Yes, it was a very awkward situation for the both of us. Seeing your father unnerved me somewhat, considering how we left each other the last time we saw each other. He brutally attacked me with his words, but I should have seen it coming." Malik seemed far away. "A vivid memory of one of the last times I saw him came to mind. We were at Texas Roadhouse for a farewell luncheon or dinner—I can't remember—for Angelica Barnes. It was after Hamilton's funeral. Ivy, I acted like a complete ass." Malik stopped and looked at Ivy; then he turned and looked anywhere but straight at her.

"I was obsessed with being with your mother, although she had blatantly stated that she was staying with your father. Damn, I had slept with your mother." Ivy cringed. "She told me she wanted me to make love to her and that she would tell Jefferson that he was history. But I don't know what happened between the time of our last kiss, when she left my house, and when she got home. She snapped. And she turned on me and made me look like a pure fool at the repast after Hamilton's funeral.

"I was angry, and I told Jefferson that Margo slept with me and wanted to be with me. Your dad was my boy. We loved each other once. But in that restaurant, we were two different people—we hated each other, and hate is a strong word. There was no mistaking the venom, and right there in front of hundreds of patrons in that restaurant we fought like archenemies, looking like the fools that we were before we were thrown out and banned from the restaurant for good. I'm glad the manager didn't ask me for my name."

For the first time in minutes, Ivy spoke. "Do you still have feelings for my mother? Is that the reason you reacted when you heard about her pregnancy?"

"That's a stupid thing to say, Ivy. Aren't I with you?"

Tears formed in Ivy's eyes. "Yes, you are, but even talking about her now, it almost sounds like you wish it was her instead of me you're with. And…the way you reacted when you learned my mother gave birth to twins is haunting me."

"Ivy, you are worrying for no reason. Margo told me she wanted nothing to do with me. I haven't seen her in almost a year. Why would I care what she's doing with her life?"

Ivy blinked several times and gave out a sigh. She had ideas of her own, but this was not the time to verbalize them. She hid them in her bosom and smiled instead. "I guess it's my insecurity," she finally said, although not wanting to admit it, she was probably right.

Malik went to her and grabbed her by the shoulders. He pulled her to him and kissed her on the lips like a starved animal. After releasing some of the pent-up emotions, he kissed her gingerly. He came up for air and held her head between his hands. "I love you, Ivy. I'm happy that you're my wife. We are going to make a great team."

Ivy kissed him back when he drew her into him, his yearning to please now sure and more intense. The one thing Ivy missed when Malik declared his love for her was his desire to have a family. While not spoken, it was the left unspoken part that left her vulnerable, especially since a new member of their family was already growing in her womb. She'd take it a day at a time, but tonight she'd take whatever Malik presented as a peace offering.

Seventeen

**M**argo sat up in bed as the crackle on the baby monitor announced that the twins were awake. She yawned and then looked back at the clock on her nightstand that read six-thirty. Margo wasn't ready to get up after tossing and turning all night, unable to get a good night's sleep and unable to get the visual out of her head of Malik and her daughter, Ivy, together.

"Married," Margo said out loud. "Ivy has gone and married a man almost twice her age. Has she lost her damn mind?" Then a voice deep inside said *admit it, you want Malik for yourself.* Margo shook her head, then turned toward the monitor where her crying babies were calling out for their mother. "I'm coming."

She pushed herself off the bed and ran into the twin's nursery. They were both screaming, their little arms moving and feet kicking. Evan settled down upon feeling his mother's touch, but Ian continued to holler regardless of what Margo did to try and quiet him.

Quickly, Margo changed each twin's diaper and rubbed their backs. She picked up Ian to feed him, and although he had a dry bottom, his screams seemed to intensify.

Margo touched his forehead to see if he had a temperature. It was slight but not enough to make him holler as he did. He was too young to be teething, so it must be something else. Margo sat in her rocker and began to breast feed, but that didn't satisfy Ian. In fact, he refused to eat. Now Margo was concerned.

She laid Ian down and picked Evan out of the crib and fed him. He seemed to be pacified after Margo burped him and put him back in his crib. Ian was still whining, and when Margo touched him, his whole body seemed to be on fire. As if knowing he would now receive attention, Ian began to wail again.

"It's going to be all right, Ian," Margo whispered, leaning over into the crib to plant a kiss on his chubby cheek. She picked him up. "Mommy is going to take you to the hospital to see why you're so hot. I've got to find the doctor's number so he can meet me at the emergency room. Don't cry, little baby, don't cry. Mommy's got you in her arms."

Instead of calling the doctor, Margo dialed Winter's cell. Margo prayed that she wasn't in a meeting or away from her phone. She didn't have to wait long.

"Mom, what's up?"

"I need your help, Winter. Something is wrong with Ian. He's been screaming at the top of his lungs and his body is hot. I've got to take him to the doctor and I need you to watch Evan."

"I hear Ian. He's either mad at you or something is

truly wrong with him. Did you take his temperature?" Winter asked, concerned.

"I don't know where the thermometer is but if you know, please tell me. Can you come?"

Winter sighed. "Give me an hour. I'm getting ready to go into a meeting, but as soon as I give my presentation I'll be there. I wish I could drop everything right now, but my boss is giving me the *I need to get into the conference room* look now."

"Okay, Winter. I'll see you as soon as you get here."

"Okay, the thermometer is in the layette tray. See you in an hour."

"Thanks, babe."

Margo found the thermometer and before she could check Ian's temperature, Evan began to cry. Margo sighed and shook her head. "I'm going to have to hire a nanny."

She checked on Evan and reached over into the crib and gave him a kiss. He quieted down, although Ian's screaming had crawled to a nagging whine. Margo sat down in the rocker and proceeded to take Ian's temperature, and just as she was getting ready to put it into his rectum, her cell phone rang. Thinking it might be Winter, Margo scooped Ian up and reached for her cell phone that she had set in the layette. Before the caller hung up, Margo pushed the TALK button.

"Margo?"

A frown formed on her face. "Who is this?" Margo asked, not recognizing the voice. She pulled her Black-

Berry away from her face and looked at the number. The person's ID wasn't recorded, which meant the caller wasn't a friend or acquaintance. So how did this person get her number?

"Has it been that long?"

"Been long for what?"

"Okay, I get it," the voice at the other end of the line said. "I'm a complete stranger."

"If you don't identify yourself in the next three seconds, this call is history. I've got more important matters to attend to."

"Margo, this is Malik."

Margo froze with Ian still on her lap and his diaper open to expose his buttocks. "Malik...I didn't recognize your voice. I guess I should be calling you son-in-law. It's funny how life evolves and changes at the drop of a hat. Are you in love with her?"

"If you're talking about Ivy, the answer is yes. Surely you're not objecting. As I recall, you rejected my affection on more than one occasion; a man can only take so much rejection."

"It's not even about that, Malik. How could you and Ivy sneak behind my back and get married without even a phone call to say you wanted her hand in marriage like any other decent suitor? She's my daughter, and she's half your age. I've been calling Ivy for weeks and have yet to receive a return phone call. And then I had to see it on TV in living color from your campaign headquarters in Fayetteville—your big announcement—candidate for

Senator, Malik Mason, is now married to Ivy Myles. How long has Ivy been in Fayetteville?"

"Not long, but I'll talk to Ivy about getting in touch with you."

"You're so cavalier. You don't feel the pain that this family feels." Ian began to wail.

"Are the babies mine? Is that my baby crying?"

"You've got some nerve, Malik. You aren't anybody's daddy. These are Jefferson's babies. Evan has a birthmark in the same place that Jefferson does."

"I'm happy for you, Margo, although you won't admit the obvious that I could well be the father of those babies. You're in denial."

"Well, it's my business, Malik. And there's nothing going on over here that you need to worry about. You need to watch your back because that child of mine that you're married to is the sneaky one."

"Bitterness doesn't become you, Margo. It's a shame to see a woman who I adored, who was talented, beautiful and amazing, with such a stank attitude. You've changed. You seem so...hostile...so angry."

"For your information, I am angry. I'm angry at you for taking advantage of Ivy and angry at Ivy for being inconsiderate and stupid."

"That was unkind. Do you still go to church? And by the way, when you see Jefferson, tell him his threats don't scare me."

"Don't worry about what I'm doing. And as far as Jefferson is concerned, you tell him yourself. He doesn't live here. Whatever has gone on between you and Jefferson is your business."

"I love my wife, Margo. I'm going to take good care of Ivy."

"That sounds promising. But why, Malik? Ivy is much too young for you. You have no right to use my daughter to get back at me."

"You are crazy, Margo. I put you out of my mind a long time ago. You don't even exist in my life. If it wasn't for Ivy, I wouldn't give you a second thought, Mother-in-Law."

"Let me tell you something and hear me well. If you are using my child as a pawn in your desire to exact revenge on me, you will pay."

"Ivy loves me, and she will be a senator's wife come Election Day. Can't say the same for you. You wasted five long years pining for Jefferson while he was locked up in prison where he belonged. I was there for you, at your beck and call, and in the end you kicked me to the curb like I was piece of chewing gum that you chewed the flavor out of until there was nothing left but to discard it."

"You said it, I didn't. But let's not forget, I was still a married woman."

"But you did spread your legs for me. It was good, Margo. Your nectar was so sweet."

Margo hit the END button and threw the phone down on the floor. She picked up Ian and held him tight in her arms and cried some bitter tears.

## Eighteen

M alik sat in his office at SuperComp Technical Solutions and pondered his conversation with Margo. Margo acted strange and Malik couldn't put his finger on it. What if the babies were his? He'd want to do the right thing, but acknowledging such at this time might ruin his chances to become Senator. Maybe it was best to leave it alone, but he couldn't. He always wanted a son...his son.

At that moment, Malik thought of his first wife, Toni, who died in a car accident with their unborn child in her womb. And then he thought of, Ivy, so young...so beautiful who reminded him so much of her mother... her mother, Margo. He reached deep into his heart and searched for the answer as to why he was with Ivy.

Sitting in the quiet of his office made Malik think about Margo's words, *if you are using my child as a pawn in your desire to exact revenge on me.* Malik loved Ivy. He was sure about that. Their chance meeting in Atlanta was not orchestrated or planned. He'd be lying, though, if Ivy's resemblance to Margo didn't make him stop and take a second look, but it was Ivy herself who had captured his heart and tapped him with a love Jones. Malik was sure about his love for Ivy but something deep within was telling him he still loved Margo. "But I'm married now," Malik said out loud.

Malik pulled out of his daydream when the phone began to ring. "Hello," he said on the second ring.

"Hey, babe, how's your day going?"

Malik sat up straight in his seat. "Good, couldn't be better. How's my beautiful wife today?"

"I feel great, especially after the way we made love to each other last night. Wow, Malik, you were so gentle and thorough."

"The only way to treat a lady. I love you, Ivy."

"I love you, too. I'm going to go out and look for some things for the house to give it a little feminine touch. You've lived here a long time, but I want to feel like I'm a part of it as well."

"I just had a thought; well, maybe I've been thinking about it for a short time. Why don't we go house-hunting for a place we can call our own?"

"Do you mean it?"

"Yes, baby, and once we find our dream home, we can go together and look for new furniture and other furnishings for the house. I was ready to get some new stuff anyway."

"Malik, I'm so happy. Thank you, baby, for wanting to do this now."

"Well, we need a realtor. Your mother would be perfect."

There was silence on the line and then a heavy sigh.

"Sweetheart," Ivy took her time getting the words out of her mouth, "sweetheart, I don't want my mother in our business. I'm sure Winter has told her by now that she saw us at the restaurant. I haven't spoken to my mother in a long time, and this shouldn't be the basis for us getting together."

There was a pause on the other end of the line, and then Malik spoke. "Ivy, you need to contact your mother and make peace with her. I'm a believer that when you communicate it makes a world of difference."

"Okay, okay, I'll call my mother, but I'm not sure when. With that said, I'm still adamant about not having her in our business. It would be different if you and my mother weren't close friends. My mother had feelings for you, and she may still have them for all I know. She's divorcing my dad after all they've been through. But why? My dad still loves her."

"How do you know?"

"Because my brother, J.R., told me so. My dad is hurt by this divorce. I'm not saying he didn't have it coming, but my mother wanted her husband despite all he'd done. So her doing this now doesn't make sense."

"Are you afraid that if Margo still loves me that I might go to her?"

"Why would you say that, Malik? We're married. I can't allow those thoughts to go through my head."

"But you did think them, didn't you?"

"This conversation is over. You have a senatorial race

to win and you need to keep your mind focused on getting those votes. I'm going to pamper myself, and I'll see you later."

"I love you and only you, Ivy. I mean that from the bottom of my heart. Don't spend too much money. We're buying a house."

"Okay, sweetheart, I'll talk to you later." And the line was dead.

Malik sat a moment longer. Yes, he loved Ivy, but the hunger for Margo hadn't gone away.


Margo paced the floor with a whimpering Ian on her shoulder, trying to soothe his little body. On her tenth walk around the house, she heard the key in the door and was glad to see Winter come inside.

"Hey, Mom, how's Ian doing?"

"He's still the same. He has a fever and I've got to see about my little fellow."

"Where's Evan?"

"He's upstairs, asleep. I pumped some milk and left it in the refrigerator. He should sleep for awhile."

"I've got him. You run on to the hospital."

"Thanks," Margo said as she finished putting Ian's knit cap on his head. She grabbed the diaper bag and headed for the door to the garage. Almost as if she forgot something, Margo turned on her heels. "You wouldn't guess who called me today."

"Daddy," Winter said playfully. "Mom, you can stop

the divorce proceedings at anytime. Daddy doesn't want this and he's still madly in love with you."

"Your father is okay with the divorce. We've decided to go our separate ways, and that's what we're doing."

"After seeing you the other day, Daddy ain't sure about going separate ways."

"Well, it's over and that's that. You still haven't guessed the name of my caller."

"Instead of playing twenty questions, why don't you just tell me? And aren't you in a hurry?"

"Malik called me. Now watch your baby brother so that I can get to the hospital to see about the other one. Love you."

"Mother, I see the gleam in your eye, but please tell me you don't still have feelings for Malik. I'm sure you haven't forgotten that he's married to your daughter— the daughter who's forgotten we exist."

"I'll see you later. Take care of Evan."

"I will. And, mother, I have a date this evening."

"A date? I didn't know you were even talking to anyone."

"I just met him. His name is Phillip and he's Dr. Wright's son."

"The Dr. Wright who's running for senator?"

"Yes, one and the same. I met him at dinner. He's gorgeous."

"I don't know why I'm the last to know anything. Well, take care of my baby." And with that Margo let herself out the door.

Margo strapped Ian in the baby seat and stepped up

into her SUV. Before putting the key in the ignition, she thought about what Winter had said about Jefferson. She missed him...still loved him, but too much garbage had built up between them.

For a fleeting moment, she wondered if the babies could be Malik's. She did allow herself that one indiscretion and she didn't have any protection. How long had she waited for Jefferson while he was in jail without giving herself to another man? Five long years, but her faith had brought her through.

Margo closed her eyes, and then sighed. *The messes people make out of their lives,* she thought. How could she have been so stupid? However, part of her desired Malik. Was it because he had forgotten about her and was now making her daughter feel the way he used to make her feel, even when she hadn't admitted it? Disgusting thought. "Lord, forgive me. My thoughts are not my own. I need some direction," Margo cried out. Then she heard Ian crying. "We're on our way, baby. Mommy's sorry for being so selfish."

Margo put the key in the ignition and drove out of the garage and headed to the hospital. There was no doubt about what she needed to do. She wasn't sure when, but at the appropriate time, whenever that was, she'd have both babies tested for their DNA. That would give a value to the unknown. Maybe it was best to leave the unknown the way it was, but Margo had to know.

## Nineteen

The whole idea of Margo with twins scrambled Malik's mind. He calculated and recalculated from the moment he'd made love to her until the approximate time she'd given birth to the twins. Malik shook his head because each time he'd gone over his calculation, the equation added up to the same theory—that those boys she'd just delivered could possibly be his. No, they were more than likely his. As far as he knew, Margo hadn't consummated…hadn't resumed her marriage with Jefferson in the bedroom once he was out of prison. And the fact that Margo and Jefferson had filed for a divorce, made it all the more evident that the whole of their marriage was in ruins.

Malik looked at his watch and got up from his desk. The time was a little past one o'clock. He had an errand to run and he needed to be away from the office for awhile.

"Reggie," Malik called to his retail clerk, "I need to leave the office for awhile—campaign business. If anyone should call, tell them I'm on campaign business although I'm not going to campaign headquarters. You don't have to tell them the latter. I've got to go on a fact finding mission."

"All right, boss," Reggie said. "I've got this. Corky should be back from lunch in fifteen minutes."

"Good. If you or Corky should need me, you can reach me on my cell."

With that, Malik left his place of business that was virtually empty except for a browser who came in periodically to see if there was something new on the market. Malik jumped in his Beamer and headed out of town. He took the scenic route to Raleigh by way of Highway 210, eventually connecting to Highway 401, coasting and in no real hurry. Taking the scenic route always quieted his nerves; he wasn't sure why.

He cruised through the towns of Lillington and Fuquay Varina, inching his way to Raleigh. Once Malik got there, he wasn't quite sure what his approach would be. The only thing on his mind was seeing Margo. He remembered how Ivy, in one of her rants, had talked about her mother living high on the hog in a brand-new townhouse in a new development called City Cottage in North Hills. He'd have no problem finding North Hills. Getting her address was the real hurdle, and if he hadn't been in such a big hurry, he would've searched for it on the Internet before he left. "Damn, damn, and double damn. This can't be a wasted trip," Malik said out loud.

Malik's iPad was in the trunk of his car. He'd find a place that had Wi-Fi and look up Margo's address. Malik drove on, his desire to see Margo intensifying with each mile he drove. Every now and then, he'd glance in his rearview mirror to see if the city's law enforcement or paparazzi were following him.

Traffic was heavy when Malik pulled onto Interstate 40. He drove a mile or two until he reached the Beltline, Interstate 440, the route that would take him to North Raleigh and North Hills. He drove a bit and took the off-ramp at Six Forks Road. He passed North Hills that had been completely redeveloped and went in search of a place to stop in hopes of acquiring Margo's address.

Stopping in the road, he asked a plump gentleman who took his time walking across the street if there were any book retailers close by. Malik was in luck as he had two choices, but he took the closest, which was on Sandy Forks Road. He thanked the gentleman and in less than two minutes Malik was exiting his car and entering the store.

The store was quiet considering the time of day. Noonday was a prime time for customers to breeze in and out of a bookstore or some other retail place while on their lunch hour. Malik bought a small cup of cappuccino and sat down with his iPad. He quickly went into action and found the white pages. He brought up the White Pages and entered Margo's name to include city and state. As he predicted, Margo didn't have an unlisted number.

Without giving it another thought, Malik shut down his iPad and quickly exited the store. He jumped into his car and headed for North Hills. His adrenaline flowed at the thought of laying eyes on Margo. What would she say? Would she invite him in? Their phone call hadn't gone as he had hoped, but given his very presence, hopefully Margo would have a forgiving heart.

Malik pushed down Six Forks Road, following the explicit instructions of the navigation guide in his car. A thin film of sweat seemed to sweep over his face as he neared the street he was to turn on, putting him closer to his goal. After a series of right and left turns, Malik was there…at Margo's house…his wife's mother…and possibly his babies' mother.

Getting up the nerve for a face-to-face with Margo, Malik exhaled and then took a look at his surroundings. Margo Myles had done well for herself. He heard that North Hills was serving up prime real estate, and Margo's townhome, from the outside at least, appeared to fit the bill and the pocket of only those who could afford it, especially in these economic times. Malik was happy for Margo. After all, she lived and breathed real estate—you could go to the bank at the precise moment she'd close a deal because her pulse jumped out of her skin.

Nerves under wraps, Malik exited his BMW. It was unbecoming of him to sweat as he did. After all, he was a top contender for a senatorial seat in his district and was in line to win it. Malik walked briskly up the steps to Margo's place, and before he could change his mind, rang the buzzer.

At first he thought no one was there or that Margo had spotted him and refused to answer the door. After a third ring, the door finally opened and he faced a defiant Winter.

"What do you want? In fact, what are you doing here?" Winter asked, her hand on one hip while holding the door with the other.

A smile painted Malik's face. "I'd like to see your mother, if you don't mind."

"Well, I do mind, unless you have that ungrateful sister of mine with you."

The smile slid from Malik's face. "Winter, I've come in peace. I would like to talk with your mother about Ivy as well as some other things; however, I'd prefer that Margo tell me herself that she doesn't want to speak with me."

"Well, Mr. Mason, today isn't your lucky day. My mother isn't here and I have no earthly idea as to when she'll return."

Malik looked past Winter into the house, but didn't see any signs of life. His range of sight was very limited, but the stillness within was very evident. Then all of a sudden he heard a baby's cry. Winter turned slightly at the sound of the baby's voice.

"So, are you sure your mother isn't in?"

"There's no need for me to lie," Winter said abrasively, turning back to face Malik. She looked him up and down, and for a moment Malik felt uncomfortable. "Look, I've got to go and see about my little brother."

"Maybe...I can wait."

Winter stopped, put her foot out, and gave Malik a cold stare. "Not here, you won't. I don't know what you're doing at my mother's house without my sister in tow, but I hope you have a very good reason. It would be terrible if Ivy should happen to find out that her husband had come to see her mother without her knowledge."

Malik thrust his finger in Winter's face. "I don't know what you're trying to insinuate, but you're dead wrong. I'd appreciate it very much if you'd tell your mother that I came by to see her, and let me worry about my wife."

"Struck a nerve, didn't I? You see, it wouldn't be so obvious if you hadn't called my mother earlier today." Surprise registered on Malik's face. "Oh yeah, she told me. In fact, it was the last thing she told me before she left home this afternoon. I wonder why?"

"I'm glad that I chose the right sister to be my wife. I'd have to give you a tongue-lashing and put you in line."

"Oh really? This tells me you really don't know my sister, Ivy, at all. She's worse than I am. Subservient, she's not, and she'd give domestic violence a new face. Good day, and I'll be sure and tell my mother you stopped by."

Malik turned away and high-tailed it to his car. He turned in time to see the smile on Winter's face. She might have been an obstruction today, but he was going to see Margo and get some answers.

The North Carolina senatorial race was in full swing. Television campaign ads endorsing or deflecting a candidate heated up the airways. Jefferson was proud and satisfied at the quality of the television advertisements J.R. had developed for Dr. Shelton Wright. It personified Dr. Wright as the candidate for the people as well as acknowledged his accomplishments that gave credence to his being in the senatorial race. It was Jefferson's hope that Dr. Shelton wouldn't have to do a lot of mudslinging since he was a well-respected individual in the community. However, if they had to go there, the Web Connection was ready to accommodate.

Business at the Web Connection had increased by thirty percent since they'd taken Dr. Wright on as a client. As promised, Dr. Wright directed several of his clients their way, for which Jefferson was grateful. With the talent of Winston added to the team on a part-time basis, there was no doubt their company would be able to handle the growth.

Jefferson sat in his office working on a proposal for a web design for a fairly new company that was looking to expand its brand in the baby business. He lacked concentration because all he could think of was Margo. Seeing those babies in the crib was déjà vu—Winter and Winston reincarnated. It was crazy, given his immediate situation with Margo, but Jefferson needed to know if those babies were his own.

The sudden buzz on the intercom caused Jefferson to look away from the proposal and provided a brief interruption from his thoughts. "Yes, Cheryl, what's up?"

"I have a Ms. Toni Gillette in the office who'd like to see you about having a website constructed."

"See if you can make an appointment. I'm right in the middle of a project that I need to complete for another customer."

"All right, I'll let her know."

Thirty seconds hadn't gone by before Jefferson's intercom buzzed again. "Mr. Myles, Ms. Gillette is really adamant about seeing you now. She said she'd make it worth your while."

Jefferson sighed. "Send her in, Cheryl."

Shuffling papers aside, Jefferson stood up to greet his visitor. His eyes became transfixed as the frame of the tall, statuesque golden goddess enveloped his doorway. She wasn't drop-dead gorgeous, however, Ms. Gillette's semi-slanted grayish-green eyes with the long, jet-black eyelashes extending from them, set in a honey-colored oval face, shadowed by her black, shoulder-length hair and slightly plump red lips made her look like a pastry that made your mouth water. Draped in a form-fitted avocado knit dress that hit just above the knees and topped off by a short-sleeve bolero jacket, showcased what one would call Ms. Gillette's major assets—her muscular legs and arms.

Jefferson couldn't resist riding the elevator from the top to the bottom of her shapely frame. Her stocking-less, well-oiled legs looked as if they had run thousands of marathons and her arms had pumped weights well over one hundred pounds. Regaining his composure, Jefferson offered Ms. Gillette a seat, forgetting momentarily why she'd come in the first place.

Before she sat down, Toni extended her hand. "Thank you for seeing me on such short notice, Mr. Myles."

Jefferson shook her hand. "Call me, Jefferson, Ms. Gillette."

"Toni," she said seductively.

"Well, Toni," Jefferson stuttered, "how may I help you today?"

"Let me cut to the chase." Jefferson lifted an eyebrow but listened intently. "You come highly recommended as a web designer and I believe you won't have any problems navigating through the complexities of my project."

"Go on," Jefferson said, his curiosity aroused but wishing Toni would get on with it.

"I'm a journalist, and I've started a news magazine."

"So far, so good. I'm still interested."

"It's a news magazine with a twist."

"A twist?" Jefferson sat forward in his chair and gave Ms. Toni Gillette another personal examination and his undivided attention.

"Yes, a twist. Think *Access Hollywood*...ah, ah...*Entertainment Tonight*. I will be following the careers of our local government officials and celebrities that make a rumble in our state."

For a moment, Jefferson didn't say anything, processing and reprocessing what Toni Gillette was proposing. She stared at him, as if by assessing his body language she'd be able to tell that he was on board. Then Jefferson looked up into Toni's face. "A rag magazine?" he politely asked.

"Not quite that, Jefferson. The way you say it sounds vulgar. This magazine will allow the reader to stay abreast of the candidates who are running for political office. We can't be too careful with this anti-Obama climate swirling around us."

"I still don't understand your take on this except that it's sensational journalism in which you hope to make a name for yourself."

"Now that didn't take long. You hit the nail on the head, Jefferson. Capturing and reporting the news is my niche. And I say, the climate is ripe for it. What I need from you is a simple website that will allow us to post the latest news in a newsletter format, set up a blog within the site so that we give daily opinion pieces, contact information, and a place to purchase a subscription for a small fee using PayPal. Once the frame is set up, my assistant can maintain it."

"Doesn't sound complex at all. Why not have the assistant set up the website and save yourself some money? My fee might be too exorbitant for what you are proposing."

"I'm sure you'd be fair in your pricing. I have every faith in you."

"But you don't even know me."

"I know what I've read and heard."

Jefferson held up his hand and sighed. He wasn't sure where this was going and why Toni Gillette had chosen The Web Connection to do the job. "I'm not sure..."

Toni rushed to cut him off. "Before you rush to judgment and entertain a 'no' verdict on my request, please let me finish. As I stated, it will be worth your while."

"Ms. Gillette, I don't feel that this is a venture I'd like to affiliate myself with as I see it as a potential conflict of interest. One of my biggest clients happens to be running for a political office and to take you on as a client would certainly put a question mark next to my integrity and my reputation."

Toni seemed mildly disappointed. She pursed her lips and pointed her finger casually at Jefferson. "What if I promised to leave your client alone...maybe give him the edge?"

"Sounds like a bribe to me. Ms. Gillette, I'm not one for playing dirty politics, and there's no guarantee that you'll do what you say."

"True, there aren't any guarantees other than my word, and I give you that. Your expertise is what I need, unless you're afraid that working on this website might influence you to peek inside my world and become a willing participant."

This woman was more than Jefferson had bargained for—straight, no chaser. She was going to bulldoze her way into Jefferson's good graces whether he wanted her to or not. Maybe he wasn't convincing enough, but he was trying to grow a business. It had been tough coming out of prison with all that he had worked for only a distant memory—stuck in the annals of the *Fayetteville Observer* and other local publications, serving only to remind him of where he had been.

As Jefferson started to respond, Toni stood up and sat on the edge of Jefferson's desk, the hem of her form-fitting dress riding up to her thighs. "How does a ten-thousand-dollar design fee with an additional two-thousand-dollar a year maintenance fee for five years sound?"

It took all of Jefferson's willpower to not stare at the sculptured legs and thighs that extended beyond Toni's hemline. He coughed to regain his composure and put an abrupt end to the interview. "I'll have to think about it. I'll give you my decision in a day or two."

"I can't believe that you'd turn down ten-thousand dollars."

"It wasn't as if you offered me a million dollars."

"Would that make a difference?" Toni paused as if waiting for a response from Jefferson, who only stared at her. "I was made to believe that you'd jump at the chance to take this offer, given that your recent stint in prison caused you to lose your lucrative business in Fayetteville."

Dropping his hands to his sides, Jefferson gave Toni Gillette a hard stare. "Ms. Gillette, I don't care what you believe or who may have planted you with seeds about my past; the bottom line is that The Web Connection is a legitimate business, and I won't be coerced into doing something I have reservations about. Now, Ms. Gillette, our business has concluded and as promised, I'll call you today or tomorrow after I give your proposal some thought."

Toni slid off of Jefferson's desk and offered a slight smile. "Thank you, Jefferson. I appreciate you taking the time out of your busy schedule to listen to my proposal. I like how you operate. And so that you know I don't have any hard feelings, I look forward to hearing your favorable reply to my offer." Toni stood tall and gave Jefferson a once over. "Take care, and tell Margo I said hello."

"Margo? How do you know my wife?"

There was a big smile on Toni's face as she sashayed out of the office with Jefferson left to stare at her backside. Jefferson searched his internal database for a name that matched Toni Gillette, but he couldn't come up with one as he randomly went down the list of Margo's friends—the ones he could remember. He walked back to his desk and hit the intercom.

"Yes, Mr. Myles?"

"Cheryl, do a Google search for me and see what you can find on a Toni Gillette."

"Gotcha. Is there anything in particular you're looking for?"

"I'm not sure, Cheryl. I'm hoping your search will answer that question for me."

"I will say this, Mr. Myles. When Ms. Gillette opened up her purse to give me her business card, a postcard with Malik Mason for Senator was sitting on top. I don't know Mr. Mason, but I do know we're endorsing Dr. Wright."

Jefferson cocked his head. "Hmph, now I know for sure Ms. Gillette is worth checking out." A smile crossed Jefferson's face. "Okay, Cheryl. Get that information I asked for. We'll curtail our discussion of Ms. Gillette for now."

"Uhm-hmmm," Cheryl retorted.

## Twenty-One

The more Jefferson tried to forget, the more he couldn't leave it alone. Who was Toni Gillette and what was her real motive for coming to his office? Jefferson pondered it some more. Surely, this wasn't an attempt to get close to him so that she could obtain information to hurt Dr. Wright's campaign. Dr. Wright had always been on the up and up. Maybe Malik was behind this because of the threat Jefferson made about Malik marrying his daughter.

Still disturbed, Jefferson reached for his telephone and dialed Margo's number. Maybe she could shed some light on the mystery.

"Hey, Dad," Winter said, upon answering the phone.

"Why are you at your mother's house instead of at work, Winter?" Jefferson asked.

"Ian was ill, and Mom took him to the hospital. She asked me to watch Evan."

"It isn't anything serious, is it?"

"Mom seems to think it is, which is why I flew over here. I haven't heard anything since she's been gone."

"How long has that been?"

"You're talking like a concerned father and husband."

"I am concerned," Jefferson said, in a matter-of-fact way.

"Speaking of husbands, you won't guess who came by to see Mom today."

"Put me out of my misery. I don't feel like guessing."

"Daddy, please take at least one guess. I'm still in a state of shock."

"Was it Ivy? I know your mother would be elated."

"That trifling child of yours has yet to call her mother to say she's back in town and married. No, it wasn't Ivy, but how about her husband, Malik?"

"What in the hell was he doing there?"

"Calm down, Daddy. I was as shocked as you. Imagine him standing on Mom's front porch when I answered the door. Anyway, he asked if Mom was here, and I told him no. Then I asked if his wife was with him. You should've seen his face, Dad. Malik isn't slick. He wanted to wait, but I sent his tail packing."

"I wonder what that was all about."

"Dad, I think it has something to do with the babies."

"What about the babies? Those babies have my DNA running through them. Malik can go to hell."

"So...are you saying that Mom had a...a...a sexual relationship...uh...with Malik?"

"This isn't a conversation that you and I should be having. Have your mother call me as soon as she comes home, Winter. I had a visitor in the office today asking about a website. There was something strange about her, and she knew your mother."

"What's so strange about that?"

"I know most of your mother's friends, but I have never met this one. My hunch is that Malik may have something to do with her sudden appearance."

"Why would you say that? Why couldn't the woman be one of Mom's old friends?"

"As long as your mother and I were together, don't you think I'd remember her friends? I didn't know this woman at all, and it was the way she said Margo—like they had history. And then Cheryl told me later she saw one of Malik's postcards in the woman's purse."

"Yeah, I'd check out her credentials. What is her name?"

"I think I'll keep it to myself. Have your mother call me. And don't go trying to solve something you don't have any information on."

"Did that make sense, Dad?"

"You know how you are."

"You do know me. Okay, Dad, I'll tell Mom as soon as she comes through the door."

Jefferson sighed. "All right, sweetheart, go take care of Evan. I've got work to do."

Toni Gillette sat in the back of the Bonefish Grill restaurant and ordered a Pomegranate Martini. She smirked while having her own private hooray as she recounted in her mind the encounter with Jefferson Myles. It was hard not to notice that he tried with all his might to resist the temptation to admire her body, and when he thought she wasn't looking, took a peek anyway. Jefferson was a nice-looking man, and from what Margo had told her, it was about time their divorce was final since Margo had said she was giving him his walking papers the evening they spoke last.

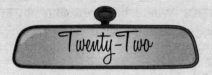

## Twenty-Two

W inter jumped when she heard the door open that led from the garage into the kitchen. She forced her eyes open, having drifted off to sleep. Curled up in her lap was Evan, who was fast asleep. Winter didn't want to wake him, but she was anxious to get downstairs to see her mother and baby Ian.

Gently, Winter lifted Evan up and placed him in his crib. Before she was out of the room, she heard Margo call out her name.

"Hey, Mom, I'm up here. How's Ian? I'm on my way down."

When Winter entered the kitchen, Margo was emptying one arm of her purse, while holding Ian with the other. "He has a very bad ear infection," Margo said, handing Ian to Winter. "Thank God that's all it was. The nurse gave him some amoxicillin, and within minutes, Ian had calmed down. I've already gone to the drugstore to pick up his prescription. How's Evan?"

"He's fast asleep." Winter kissed Ian on the cheek. "Guess who stopped by the house looking for you?"

Margo stopped what she was doing and turned around

and looked at Winter, her face void of any expression and a hand on her hip. "Who?"

Winter smiled and made Margo wait for the answer. "Guess."

"I don't have time to play games with you, Winter. Tell me."

"Malik was here…and, without his wife. Can you believe that?"

There was no emotion on Margo's face. She stood and stared at Winter as if she was an aberration. And as quickly she thawed. "What did he want?" Margo snapped.

"I will tell you this, Mother Dearest, he didn't come to talk about his new wife. No, it was all about you and these twins. If it makes you feel any better, I sent his tail packing. But he did leave a message; please call him."

"Winter, you're so dramatic and you don't know what you're talking about. Give me Ian. You can go on back to work now."

Winter smiled. "So, you're trying to get rid of me so you can talk to Malik in private?"

"Winter, I can still whip your butt. You need to get a life of your own—find you a nice young man to be with so you can stay out of my business."

"You forgot already that I have a date this evening with Dr. Wright's son. I'm praying that it will blossom into a hot romance. We need some excitement in our lives—well, besides the excitement you and Ivy have got going."

"Out of this house now, girl."

"Okay, Mommy. Smooches."

"Winter, I love you. Have a good time this evening."

"Love you, too, Mom. Oh, I almost forgot." Winter wagged her finger up and down at Margo. "Your husband wants you to call him. He has a mystery he needs you to solve. I would love to stay and see who you're going to call first." Winter laughed.

"Out!"

## Twenty-Three

I vy paced the floors of the condo she shared with her husband, Malik. She'd been calling him for the past two hours with no luck. He had the audacity to shut off his phone so that all incoming calls went straight to voicemail. Why? *He could be in an important meeting*, Ivy thought, although there didn't seem to be any hint of one as they discussed their calendars with each other that very morning.

Picking up her purse, Ivy clutched it under her arm and set out to find Malik. She didn't want to appear to be the nagging wife or even one that had to be in control of everything, although that was a thought. Ivy was genuinely concerned about Malik's where-abouts since she'd been unable to reach him for most of the afternoon. Dressed in a purple, pink, and black floral chemise and four-inch leather pumps, Ivy headed out the door.

Pulling in front of Malik's place of business, Ivy stepped out of her car and went inside. A few men were browsing, but there wasn't any sign of Malik.

"Hello, Mrs. Mason," Reggie said as he rounded the bend. "You really brighten up this place."

Ivy smiled. "Thank you." She patted Reggie on the shoulder, making sure that she got the most out of the rock on her ring finger. As if looking at her wedding ring reminded of her of why she was there, she pushed flattery aside and stated her case. "I'm looking for Malik. Have you seen him?"

"He went out early this afternoon…on business. Told me that I could reach him by cell phone if I needed him."

"That's only good if your cell phone is turned on." Ivy let out a heavy sigh. "I've tried to reach him all afternoon, but his calls have all gone straight to voicemail."

"Have you tried calling campaign headquarters?" Reggie asked, knowing that Malik wasn't there either.

"No," Ivy said. "Thanks. I'll drive over there." All of a sudden, Ivy grabbed her stomach. "Where's your bathroom? My stomach feels queasy; it must be something I ate this morning."

"Right this way, Mrs. Mason. Are you going to be all right?"

Ivy couldn't talk. She nodded her head in the affirmative.


With her hands on her hips, Margo paced around the room trying to fix her mind on why Malik was so anxious to talk with her. She hadn't spoken to him in almost a year and now, out of the blue, he wanted to have a conversation with her. Certainly, he didn't think that the twins belonged to him. Just as Jefferson had said, Evan had a birthmark on his leg that resembled the one on his leg.

Her mind continued to race. Maybe Malik was trying to make amends because he married her daughter without asking for her hand in marriage—that he had done it out of spite to get back at her for how they ended their relationship that wasn't.

Margo sighed. With both of the boys asleep, she moved to her purse and retrieved her BlackBerry. She held it in her hand and looked down at it as if it had the power to read her mind. She touched the TALK button but couldn't·bring herself to select his number from her call log...the number that would connect her to Malik and possibly open a can of worms that she wasn't ready for. Instead, she pulled up Jefferson's number on her touch screen, selected it, and waited while it dialed.

Upon hearing Jefferson's voice, her stomach rumbled, betraying her once calm demeanor for the nervous wreck she really was. There was something about that man's voice that made her insides flutter like a teenage girl on a first date. And now, after she was nearing the end of her legal separation and on the road to her final divorce decree, here she was confused about what she was doing to her life.

"Margo?" Jefferson called.

"Hey, Jefferson, I'm returning your call. Winter said you needed to talk to me about some mystery...something or other. I didn't really understand it. What's up?"

"First, how are you doing and how is Ian?"

"I'm fine now. Ian had an ear infection. The doctor said they are common, but told me what to watch out for to keep him from getting them, if at all possible."

"Well, that's good. They are too young to be enduring unnecessary pain."

"You called?" Margo interrupted, steering him from talking about the twins.

"Yeah, yeah. Met this friend of yours...at least that's what she said. I thought I knew all of your friends, but I don't recall having met this one before."

"What's her name?"

"Toni Gillette."

"Ohhhhhhhhh, Ms. Toni, huh? What did she want?"

"She said she wanted me to design a website for her and some other promotional stuff. She's starting one of those political rag magazines."

"Toni is a piece of work. I met her when I was selling the house. She had just started at the real estate office I was working out of when I decided to leave. Asked a lot of questions about why I was moving...you know."

"No, I don't know. Something about her tells me she's up to something that I might not want to be a part of."

"The only problem you'll have with Ms. Toni is keeping her at bay. I'd watch your back because I've heard she's a man-eater. She's probably already poised to hook her claws into you."

"Would you have a problem with that?"

"What do you want me to say, Jefferson? That I mind so your ego will be stroked?"

"Of course not." Jefferson cleared his throat and tried to hide a small laugh that threatened to expose him. "Anyway, I'm not looking to get with anybody. If the love of my life doesn't want me, I'm no good for anyone else."

There was a long pause before Margo spoke again. Why was Jefferson doing this to her? In truth, she would always love him. It was the heartache that came along with being his wife—the infidelity that had her emotionally spent.

"Are you still there?"

"Yeah, I'm still here. I don't know what else to tell you, Jefferson, but be careful. You are in the business to make money, but some money ain't worth the headache that comes with it. But it's ultimately your decision."

"True. I needed to get some background…history on Ms. Gillette since she seemed to be armed with information about my family when I knew nothing about her. I get that it's her business to be in the know, but if I can set up her website and she can be the invisible client, I can work with that. I don't need any drama, especially now that I'm working with Dr. Wright."

"Winter told me that she's going out on a date with Dr. Wright's son tonight."

"Oh, really? She didn't mention it to me when we talked. However, she was eager to tell me that Malik stopped by the house."

"That child of ours is a busy body. It wasn't her business to be sharing that kind of information with you."

"So, are you and Malik sneaking behind Ivy's back?"

"Damn, Jefferson. What kind of question is that? Malik is our daughter's husband, and I would never stoop that low. I haven't seen him in almost a year—probably the last time we both saw him in that restaurant where the fight broke out. Malik doesn't mean a cotton-pickin' thing to me."

"Hmph," Jefferson retorted. "Well, as you said, it's your business. But I don't want to catch him sniffing around my sons."

"Hold it. Ian and Evan are my sons," Margo hammered back.

"Your sons have a biological father, and Evan's birthmark is exactly like mine. Don't deny me my sons, Margo. Please don't do that. If you want to divorce me, I can't do anything about that, but don't deny me my sons. I've got to go."

"Okay." And the line was dead.

## Twenty-Four

Toni Gillette took a last sip of her drink and prepared to leave. Before she was able to hoist herself from her seat, her BlackBerry began to vibrate. She reached into her purse to retrieve the phone, and after looking at the name of the caller, her countenance changed from moody to very pleased.

With a smile on her face, Toni answered on the third ring. "Well, hello. I hadn't expected to hear from you so soon."

"Well, after you left, I gave your proposal some thought, and I've decided that my firm will develop your site. If you're not busy later on, I was hoping we could get together to discuss the terms of our pending business relationship."

"I like how you say…our pending business relationship, Mr. Myles, or Jefferson, if you don't mind me calling you by your given name."

"Jefferson is fine, as I've already told you."

"I'm sitting at the Bonefish Grill off Capitol Boulevard. If you'd like to join me, now would be a great time."

"All right, I'm on the way over. I'll see you in twenty minutes."

"I'll be waiting."

Toni ended her call and smiled so hard that the smile almost became a permanent fixture on her face. The first phase of her plan was underway. That was the easy part because Toni already knew that she was a great journalist and with state elections in full swing, there probably wouldn't be a shortage of stories to elevate her status. With the feds hot on former senator and once presidential hopeful, John Edwards' case, she could chew off the fat from that story for some time.

The second phase of her plan wasn't as cut and dry. It included Jefferson Myles as her new eye candy—the new man in her life. He was attractive and a go-getter, and with Dr. Wright in his corner, Jefferson's status could only go up in spite of the fact that he had done a short stint in prison. If Toni wanted him right away, she could rope him with her feminine lasso, but she didn't want to scare him off. It had to be a gradual, subtle meeting of the minds and spirit that would eventually lead to intimacy.

By no means was Toni innocent in the clever trap she was laying for Jefferson because when she played, she played hard and it was for keeps. She wanted this man. And thanks to the Internet and the Office of Vital Statistics, it appeared that Jefferson and Margo were close to receiving word that their divorce was final.

Ivy drove to Malik's campaign headquarters, but the volunteers hadn't seen him all day. Exhausted, she gave up and drove home, her mind wandering and allowing ill-conceived thoughts to seep in. "Where in the hell could he be?" Ivy said aloud as she plopped down onto the brown leather couch, which was going to be the first piece of furniture to be tossed out when they purchased their new home.

Ivy continued to sit and tried to shake the terrible thoughts from her head. She pulled her cell from her purse and tried dialing Malik's number once again. Her eyebrows arched, surprised that her call didn't go straight to voicemail. She waited and on the fourth ring, she heard Malik's voice.

"Where have you been?" Ivy asked, her tone cool but with a hint of anger in her voice.

"I've been out doing some campaigning," Malik said non-committally.

"Well, I've called you all afternoon and all of your calls have gone to voicemail. I might have had an emergency."

"Did you?"

"Don't get smart, Malik. I looked like a fool today when I went by the store to look for you, and Reggie said that you were out but could be reached by cell, except that was next to impossible since you had your cell turned off. Not having any idea where you were certainly didn't make my image as your wife, especially a future senator's wife, look good."

"Trying to track me down like a bloodhound? Baby, we've got to set some parameters about you being possessive of my time. You have to understand I've been a single man a long time, and I'm not used to charting my every move for someone. I do hope you aren't one of those wives."

"For your information, you're a married man now. I will have you to know that I'm a very independent woman, and I don't need a man to survive. However, I thought I had a husband who I could share anything with—my joys and pains or whatever. I was only worried when I couldn't reach you. Nothing more, nothing less. I'm sorry that I called and interrupted your flow."

"Look, I'm sorry, Ivy. I've been out trying to raise some money for my campaign. I can't win this senatorial race on my looks alone." Malik laughed but stopped short when Ivy didn't chime in. "I'm on the way home now, and you will have all of my attention. In fact, let me take you out to dinner. Was it something important that you needed to tell me?"

Ivy sighed. She wasn't happy about Malik's dismissive attitude. This wasn't what she bargained for. "We need to talk, but it can wait. I'll be here when you get here."

"O-kay," Malik said hesitantly. "I love you."

"I love you, too," Ivy responded without any real enthusiasm.

Ivy ended the call and thought about the conversation with her husband. Something wasn't right; she could feel it in her bones, like a sudden chill that had come out of nowhere. There wasn't anything tangible or intangible that she could tie her feelings to, but her gut reflexes didn't lie. Maybe it was because of the embryo nestled in her stomach that she had yet to share with her husband that made her jittery...made her question his sincerity. And maybe it was guilt because of how she came to marry Malik knowing full well her family's sordid relationship with him the last year and a half—a time bomb waiting to explode. It was a time like this that Ivy needed her mother. And she picked up her cell phone.

Maybe, in some way or another, Ivy wanted what she thought her mother craved but couldn't have because she was a married woman, although Ivy was fully aware that Malik's desire for his mother was much stronger than any Margo had for him. And for the first time since Ivy had said *I do*, she had reservations.

Now that she had the man, she didn't feel the same wonderful tension that he elicited and had coursed through her body whenever Malik touched or looked at her with those dreamy eyes of his. It could be her pregnancy, like her menstrual cycle, that caused her to be irritable and out of kilter, although she wasn't sure that was a good comparison.

Ivy recalled how Malik once made her feel. Her body would tremble like a thousand crashing cymbals—the vibrations touching every nerve and pulse, sending out signals that made her want to lose her soul and satisfy all the erotic urges that were awakened. Making love to Malik was like a drug—so addictive that her body craved a fix on the regular. Nothing else seemed to matter except wrapping her body around his, while Malik took every liberty to satisfy the deep and superficial emotions Ivy's body desired, taking her to the ends of the earth and back. There should've been a law against feeling that good, so much so that Ivy had to take care of her own needs if she couldn't get a fix from Malik.

Still holding the cell phone in her hand, Ivy hit her mother's number on the touch screen. A thin veil of perspiration formed at her hairline as she anticipated her mother's voice. On the third ring, just before Ivy decided to end the call, she heard her mother say hello.

Ivy held the phone to her ear and savored her mother's voice. It was at that moment she realized that she wasn't ready to speak to Margo—to share her intimate thoughts and now her possible reservations. She wasn't the same girl who used to sit on her mother's bed and talk openly about life with all of its possibilities as well as its short-comings. She, Ivy Myles Mason, had changed, and she abruptly ended the call.

For a moment, Ivy felt terrible because she'd lost the moment to settle things with her mother…to get back in her good graces. But then she thought about Malik, her husband, who was on his way home to her arms, who she truly loved and wasn't going to let no one—her family, mother, or anyone else stand in the way of her loving her man. At first, the sound of the key in the door startled her, but she put all reservations aside, smiled, and waited for her man to walk through the door.

## Twenty-Five

Toni Gillette looked up from nursing her second Pomegranate Martini when Jefferson Myles strode into the restaurant dressed in a pair of washed jeans belted at the waist and a red Polo shirt that highlighted his gorgeous chocolate complexion. *Gosh, that man is fine*, Toni thought to herself, as she watched the movement of his body parts as he approached her table. His stride was smooth and lithe like a cheetah stalking his prey—his taunt muscles flexing and contracting as he advanced. A broad smile lit her face, and to her surprise, Jefferson bestowed one back at her.

"Hello again, pretty lady," Jefferson said, surprising the hell out of Toni. "How are you?"

"Doing much better now that you've arrived." Toni coughed and patted her chest gently with her hand. "Please have a seat."

Jefferson squeezed into the booth and sat opposite Toni, glancing at her repeatedly as if he'd noticed something different and unique about her that he hadn't captured the first time they met. Anyone else might have felt uncomfortable at his repeated assault on her body, but Toni wanted Jefferson to get a good look because she knew that it was only a precursor to what was yet in store for him—if she was lucky.

Toni sipped her drink. "What are you drinking?" Jefferson asked.

"A Pomegranate Martini," Toni responded. "It's very good." She took the tip of her tongue and licked the top of the straw for emphasis. "You ought to try it."

"I don't usually drink while I'm transacting business. I like to keep a level head."

"One drink won't hurt."

"Maybe not, but I don't want any hindrances to our business meeting."

"I know that you aren't going to just sit there and let a sister drink alone. Let's have a congratulatory drink on sealing the deal."

"Well, we haven't quite done that yet, but I guess one won't hurt." Jefferson waved for the waitress. "I'd like to have a Corona and give the lady another of what she's drinking." Toni gave Jefferson an appreciative smile.

After they received their drink order, Toni and Jefferson put their heads together, nodding continuously in animated motion as they worked out the details of Ms. Gillette's venture, agreeing and disagreeing on certain aspects of the proposal, but finally ending up in unanimous agreement on the how, when, what, why and how much. Jefferson was easy to talk to, and Toni wondered if pillow talk would be as easy.

"Now that all the preliminaries are over, what would you say to stopping by my house for a nice steak dinner? I bet you haven't had a real meal today."

"I don't like to mix business with pleasure," Jefferson said. "In fact, I was hoping to get back to the office, draw up this contract, and get you to sign it so that my team could get started on it tomorrow."

"You are a hard sell, but how about a compromise? You can still go back to your office and do what you were going to do, and when you're finished, bring the contract by for me to sign. And, I'll still have that steak dinner waiting for you." Toni smiled.

There was hesitation in Jefferson's voice, but in the end he acquiesced. "Okay. Is eight too late for me to stop by with the contract?"

"Eight or nine, I'll be waiting."

Jefferson stood up. "I'll see you then. And if you're ready to leave, I'll walk you to your car."

Toni gathered her things, stood up, locked arms with Jefferson and proceeded to her car. She wanted to reach over and give him a quick peck on the cheek, but she thought better of it. Didn't want to scare him off. There would be plenty of time tonight to make a move on her subject. Shoot, she might have to write her own story and put it in her magazine if indeed what she had in mind panned out, sizzled, and sparkled like she hoped it would.

Toni grinned and smiled as Jefferson held her door

open for her. He was a keeper and she was going to play for keeps.

Flowers seemed to always have a way of appeasing the spirit when one is down and depressed. And Malik knew that. The two dozen red and yellow roses Malik held in his hands as he came through the front door made Ivy forget all about the afternoon she had and the momentary reservations she'd entertained about their status as man and wife. The flowers caused a temporary amnesia, and for now, Malik was back in her good graces.

"For my lady," Malik said softly, offering the beautiful blooms to his wife.

Ivy's smile was infectious, unable to hide the joy she felt inside when Malik gently set the roses in her arms. "Thank you, baby." And she kissed him.

"You're welcome. Only the best for you."

Ivy looked up at Malik and knew he was sincere…that this was his way of apologizing without going through all the babble.

"I'm ready for dinner if you are," Ivy said, as she placed the roses in a vase.

Malik went to Ivy and put his arms around her, cutting through the temporary silence. "You look beautiful tonight. If I haven't told you lately—like in the last hour—that I love you, know that I do. You mean the world to me." He kissed Ivy on the lips while staring into space.

"I love you, too, Malik. If ever I had a doubt about our being together, this moment put all ill-conceived thoughts to rest." He managed a smile.

"How does Carrabba's sound?" Malik offered. "I happen to know that it's one of your favorites."

"A good choice and I do believe I'm hungry."

The ride to Carrabba's was met with silence. The man who sat next to Ivy had somehow changed from the time she came back to Fayetteville, got married, until today. Maybe Malik was truly concerned about winning the senate seat because a new political figure had come on the scene and announced his candidacy for the same seat. And if the air wasn't already thick, it became unbearable when Sterling Garrison walked into the same restaurant they had come to sup.

Sterling was tall, slender, and in his late-thirties. He looked as if he'd been carved from a block of creamy, whipped chocolate. Ivy couldn't help but notice his long, slender hands and manicured fingers as he passed by with his attorney wife attached to him like Saran Wrap on a chicken salad sandwich. They complemented each other, Sterling wearing a sandstone-colored linen suit; a brown shirt; and a brown, white, and black designer tie; while his wife wore a two-piece suit of almost the same color with a pair of brown and egg-shell knock-'em-dead Jimmy Choos on her feet. Sterling played basketball at the University of North Carolina at Chapel Hill, better known as Carolina, back in the day and he also played several years in the pros for the Lakers before a horrific Achilles' heel injury sidelined him for good. His doctors had said that his Achilles' heel injury was problematic long before basketball—when he was a sprinter in high school and had been put through an excessive amount of training in hopes of a spot on the USA Olympic team.

"You look much better than that woman," Malik said to Ivy after the couple passed. "She has too much makeup on, and something about them doesn't seem natural."

"You're just hating, Malik. Anyway, just because he was somebody's somebody when he was at Carolina doesn't mean he's going to beat my husband come Election Day."

Malik really smiled for the first time that evening. "You're right. Let's enjoy our dinner and forget about them. They aren't competition anyway. Ah, the waitress is here to take our order."

Malik and Ivy ordered their food and enjoyed the moment, although Ivy would catch Malik staring at her and in deep thought. She hated that Sterling and his wife had chosen Carrabba's to dine because it was affecting Malik more than she first thought. Then out of the blue he started on his rant.

"Why haven't you called your mother?"

"Huh? What brought that on?"

"I'm sure your brothers and sister have already told your mother about their encounter with us last night."

"Malik, I don't want to entertain this right now. We're supposed to be out for a nice dinner—enjoying us. Let's not go round and round about my mother tonight."

"I called her today."

"You did what? Why in the hell would you go behind my back and call my mother? What's up with that, Malik?"

"I only wanted to explain to Margo that I didn't mean any disrespect about not telling her about our marriage. It has been months since I last saw her, and the way we left each other…I would rather forget and erase permanently from my mind, I somehow wanted to make amends."

Ivy sat paralyzed while Malik talked about Margo, her mother, like he was recalling some past moment that he had cherished. "How could you? You couldn't wait until I was ready to talk to her?"

"I told her that I would talk to you and encourage you to make that step. She misses you, Ivy."

There was no smile on her face, only contempt. "My relationship with my mother is my business, not yours."

"She's my mother-in-law now."

"I don't know why you're doing this…." Before Ivy was able to finish her sentence, she grabbed her head and stomach. She jumped up from her seat and headed for the bathroom with Malik right on her heels. As Ivy opened the door to go into the women's restroom, she turned around and pushed him in the chest. "Get out of my face." Before the door closed, she lost it and vomited all over the floor.

"Ivy!" And the door shut behind her.

## Twenty-Six

Sitting at his desk, Jefferson sifted through the last few hours of his life. There he was sitting in a restaurant with a woman that he wasn't attracted to, although physically she may have sparked an emotion. She had all the right curves and who could forget those fine legs of hers. She was attractive in a different sort of way—her intelligence and intellect on top of being a great conversationalist. He found himself wanting to know more about her although somewhat reluctant to tread that way for fear of what his body wanted instead of his heart.

His mind immediately went to Margo. She had suffered something awful at his hands. Margo was still the love of his life and he wanted nothing more than to be with her, to continue being her husband. But he had to face the facts; she didn't want to be married and she had terminated once and for all the lifelines that kept them together with no hopes of mending the broken cord.

Jefferson went over the contract one last time. He still wasn't convinced that he was making the right decision by taking on this project, but when all was said and done, he resigned himself to the obvious. He was only the designer, and business was business.

He put the document in a manila envelope and prepared to leave. Before he got up from his desk, he picked up the phone and called Margo. She picked up on the first ring.

"Waiting for someone?"

"What do you want, Jefferson?"

"Only checking to see if Ian is okay."

"I'm sorry; just a little tired. I'm not as young as I used to be."

"I could come by and help you, if you like. If you need a babysitter..."

"Jefferson, don't do this. Our divorce will be final soon, and both of us will be able to go on with our lives. There's been too much heartache for us to continue on as before. You have Jaylin, and I have the twins."

"Margo, I don't have a relationship with Linda's son. I haven't been given the opportunity to claim paternity. If this is how you really feel, I'll leave you alone." It was quiet for a moment, and Jefferson wiped tears from his grown-man eyes. "I'll always love you, and I'm here if you ever need me. Goodnight."

Jefferson hung up the phone without waiting for a response from Margo. He picked up the envelope with the contract in it and headed to Toni's.

Jefferson put Toni's address in his navigation system and headed in the direction the guide instructed. Unable to bear the quiet, Jefferson turned on his CD player and Sade seductively cooed about her sweetest taboo. The music made him relax and before too long, Jefferson found himself in North Raleigh at the Wakefield Plantation condos. He found Toni's building, pulled into a parking space, turned off the ignition, and headed to the unknown with the manila folder tucked under his arm. That's what this meeting was all about—getting paid, although Sade's words lingered in his ears like milk residue around the lips after a cool dip into its milky pond.

He brushed down the collar of his red polo shirt—the one he'd worn to the restaurant—and rang the doorbell. Jefferson's eyes were wide with curiosity when Toni opened the door in a bright magenta and orange-colored silk sheath that covered her main attraction, which Jefferson had anticipated seeing again. And now he was even more intrigued as his imagination was left to run wild. This was the beginning of a night that was full of mystery, and Jefferson was set to play the game to see what it would reveal. A vision of Margo came to his forethought, but he tossed it back to the recesses of his mind.

Toni flung her arm across her body, ushering Jefferson in. "Come in to my humble abode. I see you brought the contract with you."

Jefferson stammered, mesmerized with Toni's place

and the mystique she brought with it. "Yes, yes, I've got it right here. Nice place you've got. I love the oriental flare."

"Yes, I spent some time in Japan...Tokyo to be exact. My father was in the Marines, and we were stationed there when I was younger. I remember being intrigued by the country and went back there after graduating college. I thought I wanted to do something in international trade."

Jefferson looked at Toni in awe. "A well-rounded individual..."

"Who was trying to find herself."

"It looks as if you've done a good job of it. At least you've convinced me that you know what you want for yourself."

"That hasn't always been a true statement, but I think I do now. Anyway, I loved Japan, and I brought a lot of its culture back with me. I almost wore a kimono tonight, but I thought it would be overkill."

"Well, I like what you have on, although it's much different from what you wore earlier today."

"So you noticed?"

Jefferson felt awkward having revealed his hand to Toni. *A man should never let a woman know what he's thinking*, he thought. But he 'fessed up. "Yes, I did notice. It also smells good in here."

"Well, I hope you like filet mignon."

"A good cut of meat."

Toni smiled. "You almost got me to say something that would've been out of order."

"What were you going to say?"

Toni waved her finger, no. "Maybe...maybe if you eat all of your food I might share with you, but not right now. So why don't we get business out of the way so we can enjoy dinner?"

"Ms. Gillette..."

"Toni..."

"Toni, let's take care of business because I'm famished and I'm dying to hear what you were going to say about a good cut of meat."

Toni laughed and pounded her arms into Jefferson's shoulders. He grabbed them and pulled her to him. The envelope fell to the floor, and their lips fell upon each other's for a moment of silence.

Dinner was getting cold and the contract had yet to be signed. Ten, eleven, fifteen minutes had gone by and Toni enjoyed the feel of this man against her body. Jefferson was hungry all right. He sucked her tongue greedily and probed her mouth like a doctor with a stethoscope, exploring her larynx for possible polyps. She felt his wonderful hands caress her shoulders and move along the curvature of her back, examining and reexamining it like a fine piece of sculpture. Then she exhaled and let her body totally relax as those wonderful hands of his inched down slowly and cradled her buttocks in his hands, squeezing them repeatedly with his long, thick fingers until she released a long, overdue sigh.

Briefly, Jefferson parted his lips and held Toni's face in his hands. He looked deep into her eyes, and Toni melted. "I trust you don't hold it against me that I didn't take heed to my own advice about not mixing business with pleasure."

With intoxicated eyes, Toni shook her head no. "Not at all," she finally said. "The pleasure is all mine. And now, if you continue where you left off, that would please me even more."

Jefferson moved his hands from Toni's face, but instead of grabbing her buttocks, he took a liberty and drew the sheath Toni was wearing up her sides, an inch at a time. When he felt the hem of her garment, he put his hand underneath until he felt her buttocks. Toni could tell that he was surprised because his hands stopped momentarily upon realizing that all she had on was a thong, and when he grabbed her flesh and squeezed this time, there was no doubt in her mind that what she felt was his hardness up against her...his unbridled elation at what her body had done to him. And she was wet, wet, wet and ready for all that Jefferson was willing to give now that she was on fire.

Loud groans and moans of passion were all that could be heard as Jefferson took the liberty to explore further. Toni leaned into him with Jefferson's every touch, so gentle, so thoughtful, and so erotically arousing. Eyes closed, she felt him lifting her body, trying to assess where he was and where he needed to go. Toni let her right arm fall backward as she pointed toward her bedroom.

While still holding Toni, Jefferson lifted the silk comforter on the king-size bed and lowered her onto the antique-gold satin sheet. It was cool to the touch and helped to cool Toni's body only a smidgen. In truth, she didn't want to cool down because the fire was all over her, especially between her thighs, and just as Jefferson cleared Toni's sheath from the rest of her body, he melted into her flesh, fire and desire consuming them both.

He clutched her breasts and squeezed them like Charmin, before rolling his tongue over her ripe nipples, which he found inviting. Then he explored the rest of Toni's body, letting his hands roam over the calves of her legs, and then moving to her thighs, languishing in some places longer than others until he was unable to contain himself much longer. Quickly, he removed his clothes and waved Toni off when she tried to help. He wanted to make love to Toni while she was in total surrender as if he knew that there would be another time—more than likely that evening when it would be her opportunity to take care of him.

When Jefferson entered her, Toni could tell that he let go of his pent-up passion because he gave her the ride of her life and the satisfaction beyond all other satisfactions. He was insatiable—a winged stallion that

I vy woke up from a restless night. She couldn't even remember the dream that had her tossing and turning. She rubbed her eyes and forced herself to look at the clock on the nightstand. It was ten-thirty, and she was still in bed.

Turning over, there was no Malik. Given the time, she knew that he was already gone to work. She pushed herself up to a sitting position and shook her head with her eyes closed. She thought she'd see stars; instead, her mother and father stared back at her.

While she didn't want to admit it openly, Ivy missed her parents, especially her mother. She and her mother had been the best mother and daughter team, and Ivy could always share anything with Margo. Breathing in, she tried to erase the memory from her mind. But it wouldn't go away. And then part of the dream came to her.

There was sweat pouring from her head. She was having morning sickness, and she couldn't stop throwing up. She had yet to go the hospital to be checked and get some vitamins for fear that Malik would accidently find out before she told him, but she had to look out for herself.

Ivy was pretty sure that Malik had no idea because he hadn't even questioned her little incident at the restaurant on the prior evening, let alone acknowledged it. This was a time that she needed her mother, and she reached for her phone.

She touched a number and waited for it to dial. Within minutes she heard a familiar, warm voice.

"Hey, sis," J.R. said. "What's up? Everything down there okay with you and Malik? I wished you had talked with me about hooking up with him before you did the 'I do.'"

"Why does everybody feel that I don't have the good sense God gave me? I knew what I was doing and getting into. I love Malik."

"This is your brother, J.R. Do you really love him, Ivy?"

There was a short pause. "Yes, I love him, J.R. Maybe I should've waited before I actually got hitched, but it was the size of that rock that blinded me."

"I knew it. When I get married, I'm going to do so because I'm in love."

"Please, J.R., you wouldn't know what love looked like if it bit you in the face."

"Oh, really? You see, I am in love, Ivy, with a wonderful woman. She completes me and we have so much in common. Most of all, she's a Christian and has the same values I do."

"When did you get a girlfriend? I've never seen you with anybody. Wait a minute. She's the girl that was hanging on your arm when Malik and I ran into you all at the restaurant."

J.R. ignored Ivy's comment. "Why don't you come up one day so I can introduce you to Elaine? You'll like her. She's down to earth and not pretentious."

"Maybe I will. J.R., I need another favor."

"What do you need, sis?"

"I want to see Mom. When I come up there, I want you to go with me. It has to be a time when Winter isn't around. I don't want her gloating with her judgmental eyes."

"Sure. How about tomorrow?"

"I'll let you know. We've got a lot to talk about. Love you, J."

"Love you, too. Don't forget to get back with me."

"I won't."

Campaign headquarters was in a frenzy when Malik arrived. Polls had Sterling Garrison gaining on Malik, even if it was by a small margin. Malik needed to bring his A-game, which meant that he was going to have to put his curiosity about Margo and her twins aside for the moment. He wasn't going to let a two-bit hustler like Sterling steal the territory that he'd already chartered for himself. He needed to organize a few big-time fund-raisers, and instead of Ivy romping around like a lost soul, she had to become active in his game and help organize his future.

He huddled for most of the morning with his campaign manager, Perry Rush, strategizing about how to proceed with the next phase of the campaign. Perry agreed that Ivy needed to become more involved, which would help bolster Malik's image.

"You seem to be preoccupied," Perry said out of the blue. "I'm glad you've come down to earth because we're winning this seat. We're not just stopping here at senator central; you're going to be the first black Governor of the State of North Carolina one day, and who knows, possibly the second black President of the United States."

Malik laughed. "I like the sound of that, Perry. You've got my undivided attention."

"I know that new wife of yours is wearing you out. It's nothing like having a fresh pair of panties."

"Okay, Perry, you've overstepped your bounds. My personal life is off limits. I do remember, though, how I used to hound the women back in the day, but it's been many moons since I was a true player. In fact, I was in love with only one woman for a good while before my wife and I got together."

"Could have fooled me. I consider myself to be one of your good friends, next to Jefferson Myles, and I didn't even know you were even seeing anybody, let alone entertaining a woman who keeps you warm at night."

Malik leaned forward in his chair and whispered to Perry. "It was Jefferson's wife, soon to be ex-wife."

Perry gasped for affect. "Well, you know the rumor was running around the frat house. I also heard that Jefferson whipped your ass at a local restaurant."

It was Malik's time to be surprised. "You heard all of that? When?"

"You know how the streets work, man. Ain't nothing sacred. Frats be talking all the time. You won't believe some of the crap that our line brothers have been involved in. Ain't nobody squeaky clean."

"Including you?"

"You know, dawg, I'm like you. I've got a checkered past, but like the apostle Paul, I found my Damascus Road and have been trying to live the straight and narrow life."

Malik laughed. "Yeah, right. See, I heard that while your wife, Shirley, was getting her groove on in Jamaica, that you were skinning dipping with..."

"Hold up, Malik. That's a boldface lie. Some of the brothers set it up to make it look like I was with old girl. I was minding my own business when she came out of nowhere and got in the pool."

"So why was your ass naked?"

"I was in a private pool, and..."

"Don't try to lie your way out of it, Perry. That fine-ass, Toni Braxton look-alike had you drooling."

"Look, I wasn't naked when I got into the pool. The woman pulled down my swim gear after she got into the pool. My body reacted, and she reacted. After the night was over, I haven't seen hide nor hair of her again. I love my wife. How about you?"

"What in the hell are you talking about, Perry? I love my wife, too."

"We heard that you might still be in love with Jefferson's soon-to-be ex, but in the meantime, you married her daughter because she reminded you of her mother and you couldn't let it go."

"That's why I don't go around you thugs because you keep crap stirred up without a cause. Damn frats need to mind their business and let me handle mine. Now, we've got a campaign to run. There is no way Sterling is going to win this race."

"I hear that he's coming out with a negative campaign ad about you. Better brace yourself."

"I need you to squash the rumors and set up rumor control. That's what I'm paying you for."

"Don't be upset at me, dawg. I'm already your eyes and ears. I just want you to get serious about what you want to do, so we can send Sterling packing early. I hear his wife likes to run around and spread her offerings wide, if you know what I mean."

"Although I don't want to partake in any negative campaign fest, do what you have to do."

"In case we have to go there, I'll get the ammunition ready. I heard from a friend of mine that a Ms. Toni Gillette is going to start a political news magazine to air candidates' dirty laundry. A little tidbit to put in your back pocket. My advice to you is keep it clean, love up on your wife, and make her a part of your up-and-coming career. Don't let the skeletons fall before you close the closet door."

Perry got up and went back to his office, leaving Malik to ponder what he said. *Time out for discovery in the paternity of Margo's twins*, Malik thought. *They're probably Jefferson's and I'm making a big fool out of myself.* Malik picked up the phone and called his wife. "I'm going to take my lovely wife out to lunch. I'm going to win."

## Twenty-Eight

Jefferson woke with a big smile on his face. He couldn't get enough of Toni Gillette. An hour of sexual bliss turned into four divine hours of drive-you-off-the cliff lovemaking. He never got to taste the filet mignon...well, not the one Toni had taken tender care to cook for him. He did take a doggie bag but made sure he got the contract signed. He wasn't sure if Toni even read it, but she was eager to get the work started having given Jefferson the retainer she promised.

He breathed in the air and swore he could smell Toni on him. Being with a woman for the first time in a long time was exhilarating, especially since Toni knew how to make it worth his while. Without her major assets, Jefferson was sure he wouldn't have given her the time of day. He smiled because not once had he thought of Margo, and if she didn't want him, he knew someone who liked, no enjoyed his company.

Rising to take a shower, Jefferson looked at his psyche as he passed the wardrobe mirror that took in his whole, naked body. He ran his hand over his chest and stomach. *I need to do some situps—start going to the gym*, he thought to himself. Jefferson flexed his muscles and was pleased that he still looked halfway decent, although Toni didn't seem to mind. His limp, which was caused by the accident when his car was riddled with bullets by the mob six, almost seven, years before, was almost unnoticeable.

Jefferson sang to himself in the shower, allowing the water to soothe him and his good mood. As soon as he got to the office, he would have J.R. begin right away on Toni's project, and if he wasn't available, he'd do it himself. He also needed to check on the progress of Dr. Wright's upcoming ads. He was proud of what he and his two sons had accomplished.

Before Jefferson could finish dressing, his BlackBerry went off. A smile parted his lips as Toni's number lit up the screen.

"How are you doing, beautiful?" Jefferson asked.

"I'm doing wonderful. I need another helping of what you served last night. Thank you, Jefferson. I haven't felt that whole in a long time."

"I'll let you in on a secret. Neither have I. I enjoyed being with you last night, and I look forward to spending more time with you."

"If you aren't too tired at the end of your day, maybe we can have an encore of our previous production, only I promise to feed you a home-cooked meal this time."

"Strawberries and whipped cream sounds good."

"Oh, Jefferson, I'm so embarrassed."

"Why?"

"You made me *come*. I've done nothing else but think

about you. I hated that you had to leave my bed, but I'll relish your warmth tonight. I haven't been blessed with such mind-blowing sexing in a long time."

Jefferson smiled on his end of the phone. "Come on, tell the truth. I'm sure there were many others before me."

"Well, not to say that isn't true, but I have had a three-month drought. I'm here to tell you that the drought is over. And you don't have to worry about mixing business with pleasure because the pleasure is all mine. Tonight, I'm going to have something extra special for you. I can guarantee that after tonight's session, you'll want to be with me day and night."

"Whoa, let's take it slow. I'll agree that you've turned me into a cookie monster, but let's enjoy each other's company for now."

"Jefferson, you've got my nose wide open. You should've behaved yourself last night because now I'm strung out."

"I'm flattered, Toni. I had a great time, too. My thinking is we should take baby steps—tiptoe if you will. I'm not ready for a full-blown relationship at this moment."

"Okay. That's fair. I'll back off, if you promise to come and see me tonight and wet my whistle."

"I can do that. Now, I've got to run, but I'll see you tonight. I'm anxious to get started on your project so you can work your thing—not that you didn't work it last night."

"You're so naughty."

"Just the way you like it."

"See you tonight."

Jefferson smiled when he hung up the phone. Then he stopped abruptly. He hoped he hadn't bitten off more than he could chew. He had been sexually deprived for too long to let some hot, molten lava mess up his mind. But he had to admit that he had suddenly been fulfilled. There was no doubt that Toni was a good lover, in fact she would be grade-A competition if it were indeed that.

She felt so good...so right, and he had to agree with Toni that the sex was so good that it had the capacity to drive him to the insane asylum. Maybe it was because she used her gift of seduction well and was everything Jefferson envisioned a real woman to be. Jefferson only hoped that while his immediate needs were met that he wouldn't disappoint Toni by tiring of her too soon. And then thoughts of Margo rose to his forefront. He put his jacket on, picked up the envelope with the signed contract and retainer from the coffee table and headed to work.

All heads looked up when Jefferson strolled through the office. It was too quiet for Jefferson's liking, although he didn't want to be the one to disturb the atmosphere because he had "things" on his mind. He stopped at Cheryl's desk and handed over the envelope.

"For you," Jefferson said with a big smile on his face.

"What's got you grinning like that, Mr. Myles?" Cheryl asked, looking from Jefferson to the package she was fumbling to open.

Jefferson waited while Cheryl opened the envelope and emptied the contents. Then he put on another smile when Cheryl looked up.

"Log it in," Jefferson said.

"So, you and Ms. Toni Gillette sealed the deal," Cheryl said sarcastically.

"She's paying your salary," Jefferson reminded her before putting on another broad smile before walking to his office. "Is J.R. here?"

"Yes, he's in with Winston working on some project."

"Thanks, Cheryl."

Jefferson sauntered to the space that was created for Winston and smiled broadly when he saw his two sons hard at work.

"Hey, Pops," J.R. said as Jefferson came through the door.

"What's up, Dad?" Winston asked.

"I've got a hot new project for you guys when you finish up with what you're working on. I bagged a new account yesterday, and it may prove to be very lucrative over time."

"What is it?" J.R. wanted to know.

"A news magazine."

"Doesn't sound like much of a challenge," Winston countered.

"A political online magazine that will keep voters informed about the candidates."

"Umph, there may be something to that," J.R. said matter-of-factly.

"Sounds like a news rag to me," Winston said.

"We're getting paid well," Jefferson interjected. "However, the one thing I won't do is compromise this company. I've worked too hard to get back on my feet, and I like working with my sons. This is a happy day."

Both J.R. and Winston stopped what they were doing to give Jefferson a high five.

"I'm with you on that, Pops," J.R. said. "I must say that it feels good to be working with you and my brother—family."

Silence ensued and all eyes were on Jefferson. J.R.'s words touched him and he couldn't express in words the impact of what J.R. had said. His face puffed up, Jefferson held his lips together, trying to push back the emotion of joy that suddenly enveloped him. Then he made a fist and tapped his chest twice. "Thank you, J.R. That really meant a lot."

J.R. got up from his seat, went to Jefferson, and hugged him. Jefferson couldn't stop the tears this time. When he pulled back, he wiped away the tears. "I love you, son." He stopped and looked over at Winston. "Come on over here. I love you, too." Winston joined his brother and father and formed a perfect circle. And they held each other in their embrace for the next five minutes.

Twenty-Nine

Tension was flying high in the Mason household. Ivy threw her purse down on the nearest chair and proceeded to the bathroom. She bent over the porcelain toilet bowl and regurgitated until there seemed to be nothing left in her body. Sweat began to pour from her face, leaving her faint and exhausted.

Flushing the toilet, Ivy pulled down the lid, sat on top of the stool, and held her head in her hand. This was not what she'd bargained for and happiness seemed to be elusive. She wouldn't be able to keep her secret long from Malik, and what did it matter now? They were married.

She gathered herself together and proceeded out of the bathroom. Malik was waiting for her in the den as she passed through en route to the kitchen to get a drink of water.

"Is there something you want to share with me?" Malik asked, as he peered into Ivy's flushed face.

"Why do you ask?"

"Ivy, I'm not blind. Something is going on with you. Twice tonight you've puked in the toilet and on the floor. So I feel that it's time you come clean because there is an explanation for your erratic behavior. Are you pregnant?"

Ivy stared at Malik as if he'd lost his mind and then cast her eyes away from him. She blew air from her lips and contemplated on what she'd say. There was no recourse but to tell the truth because the tell-tale signs were there. So what if she was pregnant before they'd said I do? They were married now, which legitimized the seed that was growing inside.

"I'll assume your silence means you are. Were you pregnant prior to us getting married?"

"Look, Malik," Ivy finally said, stretching out her hand. "I've held off telling you because I didn't want you to think that I was trying to trick you into this relationship. I hadn't expected that you'd ask me to marry you…at least not right away. But when you did, I was beside myself with joy, and I didn't want the news that I was pregnant to destroy our moment and possibly face rejection if you weren't on board."

"Ivy, look at me." Malik managed a smile. "I'm happy for us…happy that I'm going to be a father, although I would've rather you told me without all the melodrama." Ivy looked at Malik and pushed back the tears that threatened to moisten her eyes. "Come here."

Malik held out his arms and wrapped them around Ivy when she came to him. He squeezed her and closed his eyes and then pushed her back. "I've always wanted a son. My first wife, Toni, was pregnant with our son, but as you know, they were killed in a car accident."

Surprising Ivy, Malik held her again and kissed her full on the lips, finally parting them with his tongue. He kissed her passionately, consumed with a fire that tore through the cavern within her mouth, sucking and tasting her like a luscious fruit. Still holding her close, Malik left her mouth and tasted her neck, stopping every now and then to mark his territory with purple passion marks.

As abruptly as Malik held Ivy's lips, he withdrew, picked her up, and carried her to their bedroom, gently placing her across the bed. He swooped down on her like a swan diving for its prey, enveloping her head in his arms. Malik continued to kiss Ivy passionately, stopping momentarily to look into her eyes. There was love for him in those doe-like eyes, and he lost himself in her embrace.

Their bodies melded together like butter on a stack of hot pancakes. Each touch, each caress demanded more. Malik and Ivy were like starved children in Somalia, feeding on each other in an effort to survive. And they removed their clothes in between the sucking and grinding, sweat forming on the surface of their bodies like a thin coat of paint. And when they were naked, Malik turned into a ravenous beast, eating all he could devour.

Ivy was so accommodating for her man. She took her time and loved him up, leaving no doubt about her prowess and ability to serve her man in bed. Malik shuddered as Ivy stalked him with her tongue and body, straddling him like a goddess who ruled the world. As

## Thirty

Today was a brand-new day. Margo was determined that she was going to rid herself of the funk that had engulfed her in the belly of a thick, cumulus cloud since her baby boys were born. Some would call it postpartum blues but, in reality, it was being strapped to not one, but two newborns to raise alone—two babies she loved dearly. But that was her reality, and she needed to get on with life, embrace it, suck it up to what it was. No matter how she tried to color the thing, it was what it was. She was a middle-aged woman with brand new babies.

The weather forecast called for sunny skies and it would do her good if she and the babies got out of the house for a while. A stroll through the park seemed to be the perfect antidote for her blues.

Margo got up and rushed through the shower, taking an extra minute or two to pamper herself with a splash of sensual oils and lotions. She blow-dried her hair and curled it, after which she twirled in front of the mirror, arched her back, did a couple of body stretches and proceeded to get dressed, opting for a simple pair of salmon-colored shorts that cuffed at the edges topped off by a white-ribbed tee. She looked good.

She hurried and got the babies up, fed and bathed them, then dressed them in matching plaid shorts and white tees with neck-lines made of the same plaid material. Gathering up Pampers and light blankets in the event she'd need them, Margo neatly placed them in the black and gray Eddie Bauer diaper bag that matched the twin's double stroller. Picking up the bag, Margo kissed her little men and marched downstairs where she grabbed their essentials like milk and juice and added them to the diaper bag. And then they were off—Margo and her boys.

After tucking the boys in their respective car seats, Margo drove to downtown Raleigh, the capital of North Carolina, ending up in its heart and finally at Moore Square Park. Moore Square Park, with its manicured landscaping, housed a giant copper acorn that symbolized Raleigh as the "City of Oaks." Its old-style lampposts and cobblestone streets in the City Market gave it an old European feel that excited Margo, conjuring memories of long ago when Jefferson served in the military overseas.

It was one in the afternoon, and mothers with their young children milled about. This was the last week of summer vacation before the children had to give up their days of leisure for the classrooms and their continuing education. Margo strolled around, letting the slight breeze waft around her face, checking the twins every few moments to make sure they were all right.

They seemed to enjoy the activity that surrounded

them. Both Ian and Evan waved their little hands and cooed as Margo pushed their stroller into the thick of the park. They seemed to sense that other children were just as delighted to be at the park as they were—every now and then beating the little white food tray on the stroller.

About an hour into their tour, the boys began to wine, and Margo found a bench and sat down, taking each twin in her arms independent of the other and feeding them. Other mothers with their children stopped in front of Margo to gawk, coo, and offer congratulations about her beautiful bundles of joy. Margo smiled. This was the best idea she had in a long time. Nothing else mattered; it was she and her boys.

Two more hours passed and Margo couldn't believe that the time had flown by. The twins were getting restless, a true indication that it was time to go home. Margo pushed the babies down Blount Street and headed for the parking garage on South Wilmington Street along with several other mothers. Traffic was beginning to get heavy, and there was no way Margo wanted to be in the middle of downtown when all the government employees bailed out of their offices in an half-hour.

One more block to go. Babies content again, Margo marched along. She could see South Wilmington Street and she breathed a sigh of relief...ready to begin her trek home. Easing the stroller off the sidewalk and into the street, she proceeded to cross the street.

Then she heard it before she saw it. The long squeal

of an automobile as it made an attempt to brake to a stop as it rounded the corner without stopping at the stop sign—*SCREECH...BAM.*

A deafening, stillness filled the street...the kind of feeling that folks who've claimed to have encountered a UFO must feel when they say a bright light from a spaceship engulfs them. And then in an instant, the real-time switch was turned back on. People watched transfixed while others raced to Margo's rescue as she fell to the ground but not before she tried to shield her babies from harm. Even in her intense pain, she became the protective mother hen.

Holding her side, Margo pushed up on her knees but the pain was too severe. Wherever her strength came from, she released her babies from the stroller, held them to her bosom as droplets of blood from their tiny hands drenched her tee. Margo screamed to the heavens and both Ian and Evan screamed louder. "Please help me and my babies," Margo cried, rocking back and forth but falling back to the ground, holding onto the twins for dear life.

"Let me help you," a young, black sister with a short, close-cropped snazzy hairdo said, admonishing her two girls that looked to be seven and eight, their heads full of micro-braids, to stay on the sidewalk. "Let me hold one of them for you."

"My babies. My babies," Margo cried. "Somebody call 911. Please help me; don't let me die."

"Don't worry, sister, I'm right here with you."

"I can't lift my leg," Margo said, her voice rasping and the tears still flowing.

"I'm a nurse," a white woman said, pushing through the crowd of onlookers. She knelt down and tried to take Evan from Margo.

"Please don't take my babies," Margo cried, as blood flowed from her leg.

"What's your name?" the nurse asked.

"Margo."

"Margo, lay still and let me look at your babies. We don't want to move them too much in the event they've sustained any injuries, critical or otherwise. Moving them will compromise their recovery."

"Okay," Margo whispered.

Looking at each twin, it was easy to assess on the surface that they had both sustained lacerations and Ian had a small gash on his tiny forehead. His constant crying indicated that the extent of his injuries might be bigger than she could see.

"We're going to let this kind lady hold your other baby and keep them both warm until the ambulance arrives," the nurse said. "Now let me look at you." After a moment, the nurse looked at Margo, who looked pale. "Your leg is broken...hopefully your hip isn't. Don't move. I'm going to take this blanket from the back of the stroller and tie it around your leg to stop the bleeding. An ambulance should be here soon."

"Thank you," Margo said to the nurse, and then looked around for the sister who held both Ian and Evan. "Thank you, too," Margo said faintly.

"Stay with us...keep talking," the nurse said.

"Get him," someone shouted, as the driver of the automobile attempted to get away. There was so much commotion that it was hard to ascertain what was going on. But it was clear in an instant as the brave men in the group of spectators jumped on the car of the driver that hit Margo and her babies and pulled him out of the car. The driver, a young white man in his late-teens or early-twenties, tried to fend off the mob that had formed and shouted obscenities at him.

Margo lay in the street, a sweater that someone had offered underneath her head. "How are my babies?" Margo whined. "I want my babies. Please don't let anything happen to my babies."

Sirens could be heard in the distance—first the police and then the ambulance. The crowd moved to allow the emergency vehicles access so they could take care of the victims. The para-medics rushed to Margo's side, while witnesses gave the police their accounts of the accident. The driver was handcuffed and put in the back of a patrol car, while the paramedics whisked Margo and the babies off to the hospital.

"Please save my babies," Margo begged, as the para-medics administered first aid to the twins first, Ian seeming to have suffered the brunt of the accident, along with Margo.

"Ma'am," one of the paramedics began, "we are going to do our best. All I can say is that you had someone in high authority watching over you and your kids...your angel, if you believe in them...because this could've been a totally different outcome. I'm a believer, and I'm telling you that God fixed it so that the car sideswiped you instead of hitting you full force."

Margo finally looked up into the face of the man who talked about faith, angels, and God. Tears spilled from her eyes, and she was rendered speechless. When Margo regained her composure, she looked at the man again. "Thank you. Thank you. God, please save my babies."

The ambulance flew to Wake Med in lightning speed. Hospital interns from the emergency room met the ambulance and whisked Margo and the babies away to a triage room to access the trauma to the babies while they waited for the pediatric doctor to arrive. Margo clutched her heart and prayed. Then she pulled her Black-Berry from her purse and dialed Jefferson's number.

## Thirty-One

It was mid-afternoon, and the Myles' brothers had something to show their father.

"Hey, Pops, you busy?" J.R. asked, followed by Winston.

Jefferson looked up when his sons entered his office. "Got all the time for the two of you. What you got?"

"Not much," Winston said, stealing the conversation away from J.R. who looked at his brother in disbelief. "We've got a design without text or photos. We aren't sure what anything is supposed to look like. Did you get any idea from this woman while you were taking her money and getting her to sign the contract?"

Jefferson was quiet for a moment.

"Ohhhhhh," J.R. said playfully. "I get it. You had to give up something to get the goods."

"And you must be on crack," Jefferson retorted. "What kind of businessman do you think I am?"

"Winston, I think I touched a nerve. Am I right, Pops?" J.R. egged. "Look at you. You're in that place where you want to lie, but you already know we've got your number. Spill it, Pops. We're all grown men here."

Jefferson laughed. "J.R., you are out of your mind.

We've got plenty of work here, and I'm not going to chase any tail to get any."

"Well, is he right, Dad?" Winston pressed, then laughed. J.R. joined him.

"Of course not. I didn't even want to take Toni on as a client."

"Did you hear that, J.R.? Dad called the client by her first name—not Ms. Gillette, or Ms. Toni Gillette, just Toni. I hope you didn't screw her, Dad."

"Gentlemen, you need to slow your roll, and recognize that this is your father you're talking to. Secondly, I'm a businessman who doesn't need to lay with any woman to get business. As I've said time and time again, I'm running a reputable business here, and..."

"Saved by the phone," J.R. said, allowing the laughter that was caught in between his diaphragm and ribcage to escape. "Pops, you got to get up early to put a lie like that over on us."

"Quiet while I take this phone call."

J.R. and Winston held their waists to keep from laughing outright. Jefferson picked up the phone and was surprised that Cheryl had called his private number instead of using the intercom.

"Cheryl?"

"Yes, Mr. Myles, Ms. Toni Gillette is here and she says she needs to see you right away. Do you have a minute you can spare to meet with her?"

"Sure, Cheryl. I hope you're treating our new client

well. In fact, the guys and I were talking about her project, and I must say she's right on time."

"Well, I'll send her to your office. Thank you."

Jefferson hung up the phone.

"What was that all about?" Winston asked.

"Ms. Gillette is here and wants to see me about her project."

"I guess that means we've got to exit, Winston," J.R. said, rapping his brother on the chest while trying to keep his composure.

"No, I want the two of you to stay," Jefferson said. "You are an integral part of this project, so you need to hear what she has to say."

Before the guys were able to move away from Jefferson's desk, the door to his office flung open. A statuesque woman, her skin the color of Beyoncé's, slid into the room. She wore a yellow, satin-cotton, shirtwaist dress that was belted around the waist. The hem of the dress rested two inches above her knees, while the top two buttons of the dress were unbuttoned, showing just enough cleavage to excite everyone in the room. "Jeffer...son," Toni said, but stopped short of saying anything else, surprised to see the two young men huddled at Jefferson's desk.

"Ms. Gillette, come in. Let me introduce you to my sons."

A look of surprise and delight crossed her face. "Your sons? They're as handsome as you are." Toni gave J.R. an extra special once over.

Jefferson cleared his throat. "My sons and I were just talking about you."

"I'm flattered."

"Would you like a seat, Ms. Gillette?" Winston offered, pulling back a chair that he was leaning on that sat in front of his father's desk.

"Would love to sit," Toni said, now giving Winston a second helping of her flirting.

Toni sat down and crossed her bare legs, causing both J.R. and Winston to drop their eyes momentarily to view one her fine assets. And then she dangled her yellow mule on the tip of her foot that crossed her leg, distracting the brothers totally. Jefferson watched his sons and he smiled internally.

"The guys are ready to place text and photos into the website and get a good understanding of how you would like for it to look. They've designed some templates for you to review."

"Intelligence and efficiency," Toni said. "I like that in my men."

The three males in the room remained quiet, sharing a private observation between them. "That's why we're a team. J.R. and Winston will get you started, and..."

"Before I go off with your handsome sons to do some real work, I'd like to know if you're available for a late lunch when I'm finished."

Jefferson wasn't ready to answer Toni's question, especially in light of their conversation prior to Toni walking into their office. He could see Winston and J.R. rolling their eyes and trying their best to keep from laughing out loud. While he was up for a leisurely meal, he didn't want to sound desperate...respond too quickly. He was about to say yes, when his cell phone rang. Jefferson hit the TALK button and before he could say anything, Margo started talking.

"Jefferson, baby, I need you."

"What is it, Margo?" Jefferson looked up at Winston and J.R., who stared back at him.

"The babies..."

"What about the babies?"

"The babies...we were hit by a car."

"Are you all right? Are the babies all right? Where are you?"

"Come quick, Jefferson. We're at Wake Med. I need you."

"Hold on, Margo. I'm on the way." Jefferson hit the END button, grabbed his keys off the desk and proceeded to leave the room.

"Dad, what's up with Mom?" Winston asked.

"Your mother and the babies were in an accident. They're at Wake Med."

"We're going with you," J.R. said, as he rushed to his office to get his jacket and keys. "I'll drive."

"And I'll call Winter," Winston chimed in.

"Another time, Toni," Jefferson said, looking back at her. "I've got an emergency."

"I understand."

Father and sons rushed from the building on their way to Wake Med to see about their mother and Jefferson's soon-to-be ex-wife.

Toni sat back in the office, not sure what had just happened. One moment she was enjoying the view—Jefferson, J.R. and Winston, and in the next, she wasn't sure. Daddy had blessed each son with his genes, and each one looked as good as the next. But the one she had her eyes set on was the eldest of the bunch—the mature sapling that had turned her world inside out only the night before. Now, she wanted all of him and there was no way Margo was going to take him from her, even in an emergency.

Toni looked up when she heard footsteps along the tiled floor leading to Jefferson's office. Cheryl walked through the door, giving Toni the once-over like she didn't belong. Toni knew that Cheryl didn't like her, but Cheryl was like crumbs at the bottom of a cookie bag—ready to be tossed out.

Cheryl continued to look Toni up and down. "So, you got left high and dry. You weren't as important as you thought you were."

Toni uncrossed her leg and stood up and stared straight into Cheryl's eyes. "You need to mind your manners, little girl, before Mr. Myles loses this contract. I don't know what your issue is, but I don't take kindly to being disrespected, especially as a well-paying client. And I'm sure Mr. Myles won't like it either when I tell him."

"You don't scare me."

"We'll see. Let me leave you with a little something because I'm going to be around. You better put that little attitude of yours in check because if you don't, it may have harmful effects."

"Is that a threat, Ms. Gillette?"

"Call it what you'd like, but don't ever say I didn't warn you." It was Toni's turn to give Cheryl the once-over. "Umph. Honey, I don't know why you've got your nose turned up at me because you're not even in my league. Now, I've wasted too much time in idle chitchat with the likes of you. Good day." And as Toni came, she left… alone—this time.

## Thirty-Two

The emergency room was chaotic by the time Jefferson, J.R., and Winston arrived. Victims of yet another accident that involved a school bus carrying thirty children and a large SUV had just arrived at the emergency room and everyone was scrambling to assist. Jefferson rushed to the receptionist desk to see if they could locate Margo and the babies.

"I'll take you to her," one of the triage nurses, a Ms. Cassandra Little by her nametag, said. "All of you won't be able to go in, but..."

"I'm her husband," Jefferson said, cutting off Ms. Little. Winston and J.R. gave each other the eye.

"Hey, everybody," Winter said, out of breath, "I got here as fast as I could. How are Mom and the twins?"

"We just arrived, too. I'm on my way back to see them now," Jefferson said. He turned and followed Cassandra.

"Why can't we go back and see them?" Winter asked, crossing her arms over her chest. "I can't believe this has happened."

"Policy," Winston said. "Hopefully, they'll let us know something soon."

The trio sat down in the waiting room without a word. People came and went, and although only ten minutes had gone by, it seemed like an eternity.

"Has anyone called Ivy?" Winter asked finally. "She ought to be here. I think she'd want to know."

"No, we didn't think to call her," Winston said. "But we should wait until we know something. No need for all of us to be in panic mode."

"You would be the one to sympathize with her feelings, while the rest of us are worried stiff."

"Lighten up, Winter," J.R. cautioned, getting up from his seat. "Ivy is your sister and she hasn't done anything to you. You ought to be the bigger person and give her a call. I'm going out for some air, but come and get me as soon as you hear from Pops."

J.R. went outside and out of sight. "He's right, Winter," Winston said. "Ivy hasn't done a cotton pickin' thing to you. You're angry because of the way she's treated Mom, but woman up and call your sister." Silence. "Cat got your tongue?"

Jefferson stepped back when he saw Margo's blood-soaked clothes. She looked like a budding teenager—so young and innocent. The doctors were cleaning her off and preparing her for surgery. She was drifting in and out of consciousness.

"Where are my babies?" Margo said in a soft voice,

opening her eyes. When no one spoke, she turned to the right, and Jefferson knew she had seen him. "Jefferson?"

"Baby, I'm here," he said, going over to where she lay. Jefferson took her hand in his and squeezed.

"Where are Ian and Evan? Where are my babies?"

"Shhh," Jefferson whispered. "Relax, I'll find them."

A tall, older gentleman with sandy-red hair looked over at Jefferson. "Hello, I'm Dr. Calvin Betts, Chief Orthopedic Surgeon. Ms. Myles has a broken pelvis and fibula fracture from the x-rays we've taken. We are going to move her to the operating room as soon as we get clearance."

"Thank you, Dr. Betts. I'm glad it isn't any worse than it is."

"She's lucky, and so are those twins boys. If she hadn't sacrificed herself by falling over on them, their outcome certainly would've been much different."

"Dr. Betts, where are the twins?"

At that moment, as if on cue, a middle-aged, African-American female doctor approached them from another room. She looked from Margo to Jefferson. "Mr. Myles, I presume?"

Jefferson extended his hand. "Yes, Jefferson Myles. I'm Margo's husband. I got here as fast as I could when I received the phone call."

"I'm Dr. LaTika Anderson, and I'm the boys' doctor. I'm glad you're here. I was coming to tell Mrs. Myles that while Evan suffered minor lacerations, Ian suffered a minor concussion, lacerations, and is experiencing what seems to be some internal bleeding for which we'll need to do surgery right away."

"Oh, my God," Margo cried out. "Is that necessary? How could that be, he wasn't even on the side where we were hit." Jefferson continued to hold her hand.

"The impact threw Evan into Ian, and without any-where to go, Ian suffered the most from the weight of Evan and Margo," Dr. Anderson stated. "Right now, I need your permission to proceed. Dr. Betts and his team are anxious to get Mrs. Myles to the operating room."

"Yes," Margo and Jefferson replied in unison. "Please save my babies," Margo cried.

"Just tell me where I need to sign," Jefferson said, taking the documents from Dr. Anderson. "I'll handle the paperwork for all of them."

"Good, but before we proceed, we noted that after taking Ian's blood sample, his blood type is A with an RH negative factor. I need your blood types so I'll know which parent to go to in the event you may need to donate blood."

A cold chill enveloped the room. Jefferson stood still and looked over at Margo, whose eyes were now shut. Dr. Anderson swiveled her head to the side, arched her eyebrows, and looked at both Jefferson and Margo, then up at Dr. Betts. "Is there a problem?"

"I don't believe either of us is blood type A…in fact, I know that Margo and I are both O positive. None of our other children has ever presented an RH negative factor."

"This complicates the issue," Dr. Anderson said. "Your little boy may be dependent upon replacement blood, and his twin is too small to even be considered as a donor. We need to make a decision right away."

Jefferson glanced at Margo again, dropped the papers on the bed, and walked out. A few minutes later he walked back in.

"Is there something you aren't telling me, Mr. Myles?" Dr. Anderson asked. "Ian's life is on the line."

"I'll sign the papers, but Mrs. Myles needs to make another phone call."

## Thirty-Three

I vy lay on the bed exhausted and emotionally spent, but she was happy. Not only had her husband satisfied her in ways unimaginable, her conscience was free and clear—her pregnancy no longer a secret. Malik seemed genuinely happy about the prospect of finally becoming a father and now they could move on with their lives and flourish with thoughts of nothing but good times ahead. For sure, Ivy expected that Malik would win the senate seat for Cumberland County.

Malik strolled into the room and sat on the bed next to where Ivy lay, bringing his arm down beside her. "You're beautiful, Ivy." He leaned down and kissed her lips tenderly, and she kissed him back in the same manner. They savored the moment and then Malik pulled up, raised her silk nightgown, and caressed her stomach gingerly. "Life…our baby." He smiled, then reached down and kissed her tummy that only gave a slight hint that a new life was growing inside.

"Our love child that we'll cherish and watch grow into adulthood."

"Not so fast, girl. I want to play ball with my son or

daughter, take them to their first kindergarten class, watch them become a teenager, have a girlfriend or boyfriend, watch them go to their first dance..."

"Now, hold up, Malik. You're getting serious on me."

"Of course, I am." He rubbed Ivy's stomach again. "There's a human life growing inside of your belly—one that we created. And yes, I've been doing a lot of thinking since you told me. I'm excited and thrilled about bringing our child into the world, and I love that you're going to be our baby's mother. I want to do everything right. He or she is going to have a good upbringing, have a good education to include higher education if they so choose, and I want us to be the best parents we can be."

Ivy smiled and sat up. "Thank you, Malik. It means so much to hear you say that. This baby will have two special parents who will love him with all they've got." A tear escaped and rolled down Ivy's face. "I'm glad you're my baby's father. Our child is so blessed."

Malik held Ivy, then kissed her passionately. She prayed for this moment, this day. She was happy.

She felt Malik retreat and reach in his pocket. He grabbed his cell phone and answered it. "Perry, what's up?"

"Where are you? Sterling Garrison has moved ahead of you by five points in the polls, man. You need to get down to campaign headquarters and put the spark of life back into this campaign. We need you down here to get us back on track. It would be a disgrace to lose this race to that fool."

"You're right, Perry. I'll be down there later on. Right now, I'm trying to spend some quality time with my wife." Malik smiled at Ivy.

"You can spend time with your wife later. The campaign will be over if you don't get your head out of the clouds or wherever you got it, if you get what I mean."

Malik snickered. "Okay, Perry. I got your drift. We're going to win this thing. Sterling may have a few points on me, but it isn't checkmate yet."

"All right, Malik, but I'm warning you, brother. You need to get serious."

"Okay, gotta go. I've got another call." Before Perry could say goodbye, Malik switched over, looked at the caller ID, and allowed a puzzled look to cross his face.

"What is it?" Ivy asked, her face now voicing the same concern.

"Hold on," he said to Ivy. "Hello?"

"Malik?"

"Yes."

"This is Margo."

"I know. How may I help you?"

"What is your blood type?"

"What do you mean, what is my blood type?"

Ivy sat up and listened.

"What is your blood type?" Margo screamed.

"A."

"We need you to come to Wake Med in Raleigh right away. The babies and I were in an accident today, and one of the twins needs surgery and may need blood. His blood type is A with an RH negative factor. Neither Jefferson nor I are A-positive. You need to come right away."

Malik looked at his phone. "I'm on my way." Malik hit the END button and stared at the phone and then at Ivy, who was staring at him.

"What is it?" Ivy asked, afraid of the answer.

"That was your mother. She and the twins were in an accident."

"Oh my God," Ivy said, jumping to her feet and covering her mouth with her hands. "Nothing...nothing bad has happened to them...I mean they're all right, right?"

"No, there's going to be a surgery."

"I'm going with you."

"Are you sure you want to do this, Ivy?"

"Why would you ask me a stupid question like that, Malik? You're talking about my mother and brothers. Yes, I'm going with you. Let me jump into something real fast. I'll be ready to go in ten minutes."

"Okay," Malik said in a hushed voice. He sat on the side of the bed, lost in his thoughts.

## Thirty-Four

The drive to Raleigh was met in silence. Eyes shut, Ivy pressed her head firmly against the headrest, while Malik navigated the interstate, going a little above the speed limit but not too fast that it wasn't safe. He knew that Ivy was saying a prayer for her mother and baby brothers, no doubt feeling some guilt for being selfish for not contacting her mother to let her know that she was all right, back in town, and getting married.

Malik reached over and rubbed Ivy's arm for reassurance—reassuring her that things would be all right. While she didn't open her eyes, Ivy squeezed Malik's hand, and he could hear her praying out loud.

Repressing a sigh, Malik concentrated on the road, knowing that the worst was yet to come. They were twenty minutes from Raleigh, and he never got a chance to tell Ivy why Margo really called. How was he going to explain to his wife that her mother's children might be his own? In fact, there was a very good chance that the baby boy lying in the hospital and possibly in need of a blood transfusion was his because neither Margo nor Jefferson carried an A-positive blood type with an RH negative factor, but he did. But there were two babies—twins. God help him.

As they neared the exit to turn off for Wake Med, the nerves in Malik's body were strained. He seemed to be unable to catch his breath, unable to separate himself from what seemed like more of a dream than that of reality. Malik pulled into the hospital parking lot and found a place to park, glancing periodically over at Ivy. He could see that she was as tense as he was, bracing herself for what was yet to come.

"You all right, baby?" Malik asked, rubbing her arm.

"Yeah, baby." Ivy sighed. Her eyes began to water. "I hate myself because now that my mother may be in critical condition, I show up, but when my mother needed me…when all that she cared about was my welfare, I abandoned her. I don't blame my sister for the way she acted when she saw us at the restaurant. Winter, I believe, is so much more mature than I am, although I'm the oldest. She has that *get up and go and just because I'm a woman don't think I can't handle it* attitude that I wish I had. I miss her a lot. We better go and see about them."

Malik opened Ivy's door and they proceeded to the hospital emergency room. They clutched each other's hand, put on a brave face, and walked in together. Ivy spotted Winter first. She dropped Malik's hand and ran and hugged her sister who had been pacing the floor. Winter was surprised but eagerly hugged Ivy back.

Winston and J.R. got up from their seats when they saw their sister and brother-in-law. They hugged, and Malik could see that Ivy was happy that she'd been reunited with her family.

"Where's Margo?" Malik asked.

"My dad is with her," Winston said, his arms crossed over his chest, exerting himself as the family spokesperson. "They're not allowing any of us to go back just yet. Dad has been out once and told us that they're taking Mom to surgery as well as Ian. They still have Evan back there under observation. A car hit them while they were crossing the street."

Malik sighed. "My God." He sighed again. "Margo called me and said that I needed to come right away."

"Why would she ask you to come? I'm her daughter," Ivy said with a huff.

"Well, I aim to find out, and I'll let you all know," Malik said in his defense and walked away from the group toward the nurses' station.

Ivy, Winter, Winston, and J.R. stood and stared in puzzlement. "I know he's not getting in to see our mother when her children are sitting outside waiting," Winston said.

"Pop isn't going to let him get within five feet of Mom," J.R. interjected.

"Okay, you guys," Ivy began. "Although I love you all to death, Malik is my husband. I know I don't deserve my mother's love right now, but I love that woman with every fiber of my being and all I want is for her to be well. I only hope that she can forgive me for how I've treated her."

Winter held Ivy in an embrace. "Mom loves you, Ivy. You're her favorite."

"You're lying, Winter. Mom loves your behind better than me because you're just like her."

"Well, that may be true." Winter laughed. "But you look like her. Anyway, she loves all of us the same; she told me so. She'll be glad that the prodigal daughter has come home. And…I want to say while I'm thinking about it, that I'm sorry for how I showed out at The Mint. I was hurt because my mother hurt, but it wasn't my place nor was it becoming of me to act like a jackass out in public."

"It's okay, sis. We're cool now, okay."

Winter kissed Ivy, and they hugged again.

"I've got a surprise," Ivy said.

"What?" Winter asked, looking into Ivy's eyes for clues. "Don't keep us in suspense."

"Hey," J.R. said, cutting Ivy and Winter's conversation short. "They took Malik to the back. What's that all about?"

The four of them—Winter, Ivy, J.R. and Winston— looked from one to the other. Winter wrinkled up her nose like she might have an idea as to what it meant.

"I guess we'll soon find out," Winston said.

Instead of waiting on Jefferson and his sons to get her website operational, Toni went back to her condo, sat down at her desktop computer, and began typing on her blog. Several hours had passed with no word from Jefferson. He had left her high and dry the moment Margo had come calling.

Toni had a huge email distribution list that crisscrossed the state of North Carolina as well as the entire United States, and the recipients were going to get their fill tonight. She'd been gathering information on the candidates who were running for state office, and she was surprised to learn that Malik Mason out of Fayetteville, North Carolina, was running for a senate seat but had also recently married Jefferson and Margo's daughter, Ivy. That story had been told, but who knew what might come of it, and she began her blog.

Thirty-Five

**T**ension in the emergency room tightened when nurse Cassandra approached with Malik in tow. Jefferson glared, but this was not the time to display his animosity toward his archenemy. Jefferson's hatred for Malik had mounted upon learning that he had slept with Margo, but it went through the roof when he learned that behind his back Malik had married his daughter.

Now he'd been served with another slap to the face. It appeared that his enemy was not only the husband of his daughter, Ivy, but he was also the father of his soon-to-be ex-wife's babies. Genetics didn't lie, and right then and there he wanted to kill somebody. But he reserved his hostility for one of civility, although it was difficult to keep up the façade for long. For a brief moment he thought about Toni who he left in his office...who ached to be with him and he with her. But he quickly concentrated on the present.

Malik presented himself but didn't look at Jefferson. Jefferson watched as Malik seemed shaken seeing Margo laying on the gurney. Dr. Anderson looked to Jefferson for an explanation.

"He's the babies' father," Jefferson said with a sneer.

"Oh, I see," was Dr. Anderson's reply.

"We've just got clearance for the OR," Dr. Betts said, getting off of his cell phone. "We're out. Jefferson, you are going to hang around?"

"I'll be here."

Malik listened as Dr. Anderson spoke about what baby Ian was going through, and before long, an orderly came and whisked Malik away to obtain his blood.

"I'm sorry if that was awkward," Dr. Anderson said, looking at Jefferson, "but saving the baby's life is what we're interested in."

"Understood," Jefferson said flatly. "Here are all the signed papers."

Before Dr. Anderson turned to leave, another orderly came into the room. "Something's strange about the other twin's blood test. He tested O positive...not A with an RH negative factor."

Dr. Anderson looked up at Jefferson. "Congratulations are in order. We're taking Ian to the operating room."

"May I see, Evan?" Jefferson asked, a sudden flush of excitement coming over him.

"Yes, follow me. I'll do a last check on him while they take Ian up to the OR. We may be able to release him today."

Jefferson grinned from ear to ear. Somehow he felt vindicated. He followed Dr. Anderson to where Evan was being cared for by a nurse. Dr. Anderson checked him thoroughly, noting that he'd been cleaned up and the small lacerations had been tended to.

"He was very lucky," Dr. Anderson said. "Now, I've got to take care of Ian. I hope you're still here when we're finished."

"I'll be here," Jefferson said a second time, his thoughts totally on Evan. He reached down and kissed him on the cheek. Evan smiled back. "My son," Jefferson said. "My son."

"Damn," Perry Rush said out loud, running his eyes over the text in the blog that BlackAmericaWeb.com puts out daily. "Who in the hell is this Toni Gillette?" He re-read the excerpt that appeared in the blog. *State senate campaigns are well underway in North Carolina. Black candidates seem to be cashing in on the Barack Obama coattail as an astounding record number have put their names in the hat. In particular, the race in Fayetteville, North Carolina, in a black supported district, is heating up as Sterling Garrison, a former basketball star standout for the University of North Carolina at Chapel Hill who turned pro for the Los Angeles Lakers over a decade ago, just moved ahead in the polls over favorite, Malik Mason. Mr. Mason is heavily supported by Alpha Phi Alpha Fraternity.*

*It's interesting to note that Malik Mason recently married the daughter of Jefferson Myles, a once celebrated business-man in Fayetteville, and Margo Myles, a prominent real estate broker in the same city. Sources say that candidate Mason's wife is twenty-two years his junior.*

*In Raleigh, North Carolina, Dr. Shelton Wright, well-known psychologist, is well ahead....*

"I've got to find out who this woman is," Perry said out loud. "If Malik Mason thinks he's going to win this campaign without a fight, he's got another thing to think about. He needs to focus on what's important." Perry hit the FORWARD button, checked URGENT and sent the email to Malik. "Maybe he'll pay attention to this since he seems to be ignoring me."

## Thirty-Six

Happiness and delight were painted on Jefferson's face and spilled over to his body language as he emerged from the inner sanctum of the ER with a bandaged Evan. His older children stood when they saw him and rushed toward the pair to get an update.

Jefferson stopped his advance when he saw Ivy among the group but put on a smile when she wrapped her arms around his neck.

"Hey, Daddy, I'm so sorry. I love you."

Jefferson gave Evan to Winter and hugged Ivy. He pushed back to get a good look and kissed her on the cheek. Moisture formed in his eyes as Jefferson scanned her face. He hugged her again. "I love you, too, baby. Welcome home."

"Okay, okay, okay," Winter started, trying to break up the love fest between her dad and sister.

"Don't hate, Winter," Ivy said. "I haven't seen Dad in a long time, and I'm so happy."

"What's up with Mom?" Winston asked. "Is she in surgery or what? And is Ian going to be all right?"

"One question at a time," Jefferson said, taking Evan

back from Winter. "Your mom is in surgery. She has a broken hip and busted leg. She's going to need help, which may mean we'll have to get a live-in nurse. She won't be able to do anything for awhile, let alone care for two little ones."

"What about Ian?" Winter asked, anxious to hear about the other twin.

"He suffered more trauma than Evan, and the doctors will have to perform minor surgery on him since they believe he's had some internal bleeding."

"My God," Winter said, holding her face as if she couldn't fathom her father's words.

As if she noticed Malik's absence for the first time since celebrating her triumphant return to her family, Ivy scrunched up her face as if trying to reason things out. "Daddy, where is Malik? You didn't beat him up back there, did you?"

A painful look crossed Jefferson's face. He repositioned Evan in his arms then looked thoughtfully at Ivy. As if on cue and before Jefferson was able to offer an explanation, Malik resurfaced from behind the walls that were intended for patients and medical staff only.

A look of concern and bewilderment enveloped Malik's face. He stared at the group, who in his mind were there to lynch him, until he turned and zeroed in on Ivy. His silence heightened the questionable looks that everyone gave him, and Malik knew there was little chance that he'd be able to avoid the inevitable.

"What's wrong, Malik?" Ivy asked, all eyes trained on him. "What were you doing back there and what did Momma want with you?" Ivy looked from Malik to Jefferson who eventually turned his head.

As if an answer had finally materialized, Malik answered with confidence. "They needed to draw my blood."

"Daddy was back there. Why didn't they draw his blood?"

"Uhm hmmm," Winter murmured, turning away from Malik to give her brother Winston the eye.

"Ian has a rare blood type, and Margo somehow must have remembered me talking about my blood type in a conversation I had had with her some time ago."

"I'm not getting it. Why call you?"

"Why don't you tell the truth?" Jefferson said, his mood suddenly not so cordial. "Your wife deserves an explanation."

"Uhm hmmm," Winter muttered again under her breath but loud enough for Ivy to hear.

Ivy turned and looked at her sister, then back to her father, before looking at Malik head on. "Tell me what?"

"Why don't we go outside? This is a personal matter that I need to discuss with you in private."

"I don't understand why you can't say it in front of my family since it appears they seem to already know what you're going to say. Right, Daddy?"

"Oh, your husband knows we know."

Malik was seething and drew in a breath. He looked

at Ivy with disgust. "Ask your daddy since he knows every-thing." Defiant and angry, Malik turned on his heel and marched out of the emergency room.

"Malik, wait," Ivy said as she ran after her husband. Jefferson, Winter, Winston and J.R. watched in silence.

"So what is the deal?" Winston asked Jefferson who held onto Evan like his life depended upon it.

Jefferson dropped his head, then looked back at his three children who looked as if they would pick him apart if he held out on them any longer.

"Okay, Dad," Winter cajoled. "We aren't your little babies anymore. We are grown-ups, adults…"

"I get it, Winter," Jefferson said with a frown on his face. "The truth is Evan is my biological child and Ian is Malik's biological child. Go figure."

"Shit!" J.R. said. "No disrespect, Pops, but how in the hell did that happen?"

"Uhm hmmm," came Winter's unrelenting chant.

"I'm the wrong person to be asking that question to, son. I have a gut feeling that Ivy's family reunion isn't going to have a happy ending. Winter, maybe you should go outside and check on your sister."

"Dad, I just got my sister back. I'm not meddling in that mess." Winter exhaled. "I'm going to the machine and get a Coke. Anybody else want one?"

"I need something stronger than that," Jefferson said.

"Ditto," Winston chimed in.

"How in the hell did this happen?" J.R. repeated again.

## Thirty-Seven

T oni Gillette pulled herself up from in front of her computer and headed for the kitchen to fix a salad. She was hungry, but more than that she seemed agitated because she wasn't getting the kind of fix or better said, satisfaction from what she was doing. More than she had let on, Jefferson Myles had pricked something in her…something that made her feel needy, vulnerable, and made her realize that her heart wanted more. Jefferson was more than a good catch and a good lay, he was a man with intelligence—a true businessman with goals and a plan to back it up.

She looked at her watch. Several hours had passed since she left Jefferson's office and she'd posted her political blog. Toni thought for sure Jefferson would have called by now. Maybe Margo's accident was more serious than she first thought, and she didn't blame him for being the man he was because Toni hoped that one day Jefferson would be as attentive to her.

Pushing the thoughts to the back of her mind, Toni went to the refrigerator and pulled out some romaine lettuce, tomatoes, red onion, cucumber and some chicken breasts she'd grilled the day before. She heated the chicken in the microwave and placed it on top of the salad greens and sprinkled bits of the onion and grated cheddar cheese on top. Next, she poured a tiny bit of vinaigrette on top of her salad and proceeded to the table.

Before she was able to sit her food down, her BlackBerry began to hum on the counter. Toni quickly sat her food down, picked up the phone, looked at the caller ID and smiled.

"Hi, Toni."

"Hey, Jefferson. I'm glad to hear your voice. How's everything?"

"I wanted to apologize for how I had to run out on you this afternoon."

"It's okay. I understand."

"While Margo and I may be going through a divorce, she's still a part of my life...we share children together."

"No need to apologize," Toni said, not sure where Jefferson was headed. "I'm just glad you called.

Jefferson coughed as if he had to get something out of his throat. "Anyway, ahh, ahh, Margo is in surgery, and the kids and I are hanging tough. The twins...well, Evan is okay; he suffered a few lacerations on his head and hands, but he made out better than the other. Funny thing is..." There was quiet.

"Jefferson, what's wrong? What happened to the other twin? Are you okay?"

"No, I'm not okay."

"What is it, Jefferson?" Toni asked, giving Jefferson her full attention and ready to hear a bit of news.

"Are you sitting down?"

"No, but I can find a seat. Hold on; this sounds serious." Toni sat in one of her kitchen chairs and laid her elbows on the table. Her eyes were bucked in anticipation. She had no idea what Jefferson was going to drop on her, but she was glad that he chose her to share his obvious concerns with.

"The twins...the twins," he repeated, "the twins that Margo birthed are not identical twins."

Toni arched her eyebrows and made a face. What was the big deal? Twins either are or aren't. But it was what Toni heard next that almost made her drop her Black-Berry.

"That's not the big deal," Jefferson continued, prolonging his mysterious reveal to Toni. "I have little Evan in my arms, and I found out today that he's my child."

Toni frowned. *Whoop-de-do-do-do*, she thought to herself. It didn't take a rocket scientist to figure that out.

"And Evan's twin, I also found out is not mine."

"What are you talking about, Jefferson? You're not making much sense."

"I didn't make much sense to me either at first. But it's all crystal clear to me now."

"What is? I don't mean to rush you, but this is agony, the way you've got me wondering and guessing at the suspense of it all."

"I'll just say it."

"That would help."

"Toni, you're not letting me tell it in my own way."

"Tell me what, Jefferson?" Toni's patience was running thin.

"Malik Mason, my former best friend and my daughter's husband, is Ian's father."

"Shut the hell up."

"Now you get it?"

"Oh my goodness. I see why you had a hard time conveying this. But exactly how did you find out?"

"Ian has a rare blood type, and without going through all of the things that transpired after hearing about it from the doctor, Margo knew whose blood type Ian was carrying. And Ian needs surgery and Margo had to call Malik because his blood may possibly be needed in the event they have to do a blood transfusion."

"This is too much."

"Tell me about it. Look, I've got to go. My daughter, Ivy, is on her way back into the hospital and she doesn't look happy." Almost as an afterthought, Jefferson asked, "Would it be all right if I stop by tonight?"

"My door is always open to you. Call me and let me know when you're on the way."

"Will do; gotta go."

Toni hit the END button on her BlackBerry and began to smile. "Oh my God," she said out loud. She put her hand to her mouth to keep from grinning. Toni picked up her fork and nibbled on the lettuce leaves. *This is a headliner for sure*, she thought to herself. *Watch out, Malik Mason. My cousin, Sterling, is getting ready to whoop your ass. And not only that, this will not only shape up the Fayetteville senatorial race, but it's going to put me on the map as well. I've got to be the one to break the news first, but I must be careful how I go about it since the man I want for myself is the source, and the last thing I want to do is run him away.*

Jefferson may have taken his time getting his news out, but it was news worth waiting for. And later, she would bestow the most fabulous reward to the man of her dreams; she was going to love Jefferson up something fierce for dropping the biggest piece of sensational journalism in her lap. She was going to make him feel so good—from the crown of his head to the soles of his feet—that Jefferson would spill everything and beg for more of her at the same time.

Truth be told, Toni wanted Jefferson, the man. She wanted his mind, soul, and body. She wanted to feel his arms caress her in a deep embrace. She wanted to feel his tongue exploring her mouth and whatever else he found on his expedition. She loved the way he smelled, the way he felt when he was all into her. She wanted him for more than the story that was going to rocket her to stardom. She wanted him to love her, as she was falling for him.

One day, she would be Mrs. Toni Gillette-Myles, and satisfy him in the way Margo never could. Well, she didn't

## Thirty-Eight

I t had been more than a few minutes since Malik
had stormed out of the emergency room with Ivy
close at his heels. However, no other member of
the Myles' clan ventured outside to see what was going
on, although Jefferson occasionally looked back at the
door. They hugged their seats as if it were going to be a
long vigil until they saw nurse Cassandra heading their
way. As if on cue, they all stood at once—Jefferson with
Evan, J.R., and Winston, and Winter.

"Hi, Mr. Myles." Cassandra directed her attention
toward Jefferson. "You all may want to go to the surgical
clinic and wait for Mrs. Myles to come out of surgery.
At the end of surgery, the doctor will speak with you up
there."

"Thank you, Cassandra," Jefferson said, shifting Evan
to his other arm. "Let me get my other daughter, and we'll
go on up."

"All right. I'll give your children directions to the surgical ward waiting room."

"Let me take Evan, Dad," Winter said. "That way you
can rush out there and hurry back."

"That makes sense. Take care of him." Jefferson winked at Winter.

Jefferson moved through the lobby while Cassandra rattled off the directions to the surgical clinic. Once outside, Jefferson didn't see hide or hair of Ivy or Malik. It was late afternoon, and the sun was still shining bright in the summer sky, but with all that light, Jefferson was unable to locate them.

In panic mode, Jefferson began to pace, looking high and low. He ventured out into the parking lot, looking left and right as he traveled through the maze of cars. Nothing. And then he heard what sounded like a muffled woman's voice. Then a man's voice—tit for tat. The conversation was obviously heated and Jefferson walked in the direction of the voices and stopped in front of a black BMW 750i with its passenger door standing open.

Jefferson tapped on the windshield. And the voices stopped and Ivy peeked through the window. Tears were in her eyes and a severe frown on her face.

"What are you doing here, Daddy?"

"Worried about you?"

"There's nothing here for you to worry about," Malik barked from his side of the vehicle.

"I beg to differ. My daughter is in there, and I don't give a damn if she is your wife."

"It's okay, Daddy. I'm all right."

"So you know about Ian?"

"I told you to mind your damn business, Jefferson. You

have no jurisdiction here. This is my wife, and don't you forget it."

"And remember what I told you before. If you hurt my daughter, I will find you and beat you into oblivion. My word is bond, dog. Ivy, we're going up to the surgical ward to wait for your mother to come out of surgery. Just wanted to let you know."

"Why is this happening to me, Daddy?" Ivy jumped out of the car and ran into Jefferson's arms. He hugged his daughter and hung on for dear life. Ivy was his heart; she was the most like him. He stroked her hair and lifted her chin.

"It's going to be all right, baby." Jefferson kissed her on the forehead. "We'll get through this."

Malik was out of the car and approached them. "I'll take care of my wife."

"Just remember what I said." And Jefferson walked off.


"Maybe we should go on back to Fayetteville," Malik said, as he turned and watched Jefferson head toward the hospital. "I've had enough of your family today."

"My family didn't get you into this mess. You did it all by yourself. You wanted my mother so bad, you pursued her until you got what you wanted. But don't think I'm going to raise your bastard child."

"You mean your brother."

"Whatever, Malik. I'm sick of you. Every time it seems

like we make a giant leap forward, we take twenty steps backward."

"Look, Ivy. It doesn't have to be that way. We have our own child that you're carrying. Margo probably won't let me get near Ian."

Ivy gazed into Malik's face, taking his comment for sarcasm. "And what if she does allow you to be in Ian's life?"

"Then I'm going to be the best father to Ian as well as our baby. We had that one time together...and I believed that we were going to be together. Your mother was adamant about leaving your father because she thought he was seeing Angelica, but by the next day, she'd changed her mind. I didn't even know she had conceived...that she would allow herself to be unprotected."

"Humph. Were you wearing protection? You see, it's not only the woman's responsibility, it's also the man's."

"I guess I don't learn from my mistakes because I didn't wear protection with you."

*Slap.* "You can go back to Fayetteville. I'm going to stay and wait for my mother to wake up. I've got a laundry list of questions to ask her."

Malik reached out and grabbed Ivy's arm. "You don't want to do that."

"Take your hands off of me, Malik. You heard what my daddy said, and he wouldn't hesitate to come after you if I told him you were manhandling me."

"You do that, Ivy. His blood will be on your hands.

Now go on and be with your family, but you need to take this time to think about us and what you're doing. You are going to be a senator's wife soon, and we need to deal with this issue of Ian in a private way. You are my concern, Ivy, and I don't love you less because I found out that I have another son."

"A son who also happens to be my mother's child."

"I can't do anything about that now, Ivy. I will treat you as the woman you are. I hope you'll stand by my side."

Ivy was touched by Malik's sentiment, but she wasn't sure that she could trust him to not get deeply involved in Ian's life and the life of her mother, especially since her mother and father's divorce was close to being final.

"I'll think about it, Malik. Right now, I'm going to join my family—get reacquainted. I'll spend the night with Winter. Don't worry about me getting home."

"Don't do this, Ivy. I love you."

"How am I supposed to feel, Malik? Earlier today you found out that you were going to have a child...with me, and less than six hours later, you learn that you have a child with your mother-in-law. It hurts, Malik. It hurts badly. I can't help it. I feel betrayed, and I feel like my life is getting ready to spiral out of control. I want to believe you; I really do. Let me get through this day. I'll be home tomorrow."

Malik sighed. He gently pulled Ivy to him. "Okay, baby. I understand. We're going to make it. We'll show your family what we're made of. May I have a kiss?"

Ivy looked into Malik's eyes. She wanted to believe him. "Yes." She kissed him but didn't linger.

"I'll walk you to the entrance of the ER. I'm going to get a hotel room in the city. That way I'll be close if you need me...if Ian should need me. You can reach me by cell."

"Okay, baby," Ivy said. Malik put his arm around his wife's waist and escorted her to the door of the emergency room.

# Thirty-Nine

**M**alik watched as Ivy rejoined her family and then moved out of view. He heaved a momentary sigh of relief, and then rubbed his forehead. His head was pounding and made it difficult for him to think. In his wildest nightmares, Malik didn't know where this one had materialized.

It started when he went in pursuit of Margo when Jefferson was still an occupant of Raleigh Central Prison. If only Margo had left Jefferson then, Malik might have convinced her to be with him. They were together almost every day after his wife died. Margo needed him like he needed her. They were friends lifting each other up—Margo as she waited on Jefferson to come home and him recovering from the aftermath of his wife's fatal car accident.

Thinking back, he should've moved in early—made his feelings known. It should've been a risk he was willing to take, but he was a coward because he was afraid he'd lose Margo altogether. Instead he settled. He settled to just be near her...to hear her laughter, enjoy her chatter, and enjoy her company. And when he did make his move it was too late because the husband Margo had waited on for so long got an early release from prison.

In his heart, Malik knew that Margo felt something for him. She was clingy and into his every word. It would be in the way she would touch him, although she exercised her boundaries, but yet in a playful manner excite him. He teased. She'd tease back. But he wanted more and wasn't sure how to approach her, especially since she saw him as a brother friend and her husband's best friend.

But little did Margo know that Jefferson was dust to him. He had long ago torn up his friendship card. Malik recalled the numerous times that he cautioned Jefferson about his infidelity...how he was treating Margo, and in the end when Jefferson needed Margo, she was there and willing to wait for him. Twenty years he got, but he got out in five.

Malik reached his car and hit the remote to unlock it. He eased into the car and pounded the steering wheel. What in the hell was he going to do? It wasn't going to be easy to deny his son by the woman he once loved—in truth still loved. But he was married to that woman's daughter who was also carrying his baby. And now he was caught up in a four-ring-circus—he, Jefferson, Margo, and Ivy. He turned the key in the ignition and started the car.

He needed a drink and he needed a friend. "Call Perry," Malik announced out loud. The Bluetooth system obeyed his command, and within moments Malik was talking to a familiar voice who would offer calm in the midst of his predicament.

"Perry," Malik said before Perry was able to utter a word.

"Where are you, Malik? I hope you're in Fayetteville and have read the email I sent you."

"What email? I've been at the hospital."

"Something happen to Ivy?"

"No it wasn't Ivy but close enough. Her mother was in an accident this afternoon. She and her twin boys were hit by a car."

"Damn, I'm sorry to hear that, Malik. Are they okay?"

"Margo is in surgery at this moment and one of the twin boys also may need surgery. The other twin fared much better. But that's not the half of it Perry."

"What do you mean?"

"You better brace yourself for this one, man. I'm a daddy."

"Ivy had your baby and you're just now telling me about it? That's going to hurt your campaign."

"Perry, I'm not talking about Ivy. I'm talking about my mother-in-law. One of the twins has my DNA."

"What in the hell are you talking about, Malik?"

"I just told you. I'm the father of one of Margo's twins."

"The father of one...one twin? You aren't making any sense."

"It is complicated, man. But you heard right. I'm the father of one, and Margo's husband is the father of the other."

There was deathly silence at the other end of the receiver. The call wasn't going as well as Malik had hoped. What did he think? He dropped a bombshell on Perry and he needed to give him a few minutes to recover.

"Have you told this to anyone?" Perry finally asked.

"Not a soul. I'm sure Margo isn't anxious to announce it to the world either."

"Malik, if you're serious about this race, you need to get it together. Remember the woman I told you about who is writing a campaign blog? Well, last night, she posted her blog and said that Sterling was ahead of you. I'm afraid that if she gets a hold of this juicy tidbit, you can kiss your short and sweet campaign run for the senate goodbye."

"Don't worry, Perry. I've got this. I'm not going to let nothing get in the way of nabbing that senate seat. Sterling has to get up early in the morning to pull the rabbit out of the hat on me. I like a little competition, but it's time to leave his washed-up-used-to-be-in-the-NBA playing self in the dust. We'll figure this out. We've got to sniff Ms. Gillette or whatever her name is out into the open."

"We will, frat?"

"That's what I'm paying you for, Perry."

"You must not be paying me enough. My advice is for you to do some hard thinking about how you're going to handle your end of things because if the brothers get a whiff of this stink, they're gonna drop their endorsement of you like an overcooked potato. And you need to worry about what your ex-frat friend, Jefferson, might do."

"I don't see him as a problem. The dutiful father is not going to do anything that will hurt his precious daughter and soon-to-be ex-wife."

"Man, you are so nonchalant. I hope you know what you're talking about because I'm not going to sit around and get mixed up in any scandal."

"Don't be scared, Perry. What you should be afraid of is what your wife, Shirley, might do if she suddenly finds out that you're still hitting on that pool girl. Didn't think I knew, did you?"

"Don't threaten me, Malik."

Forty

S everal hours passed. There was an awkward silence in the waiting room where the Myles' clan had gathered. It was so quiet one could probably hear a pin drop. They sat like crash-car dummies—stiff and robotic waiting for someone to push their buttons or give them a nudge.

The group sat at attention, even perked up a little as the tall, sandy-red haired doctor dressed in light-blue medical scrubs approached them. Jefferson stood, gave Evan to Winter, and shook the doctor's hand. "Dr. Betts, this is my family."

"Hello," everyone said.

"Mr. Myles, Mrs. Myles is in recovery," Dr. Betts began. "She's going to be just fine." A collective sigh came from the group. "Of course, she'll be unable to do much on her own for the next few weeks, in which case I believe that she would be best served by being admitted to a rehabilitation facility for two to three weeks so that she'll be able to get the best care."

Jefferson nodded.

"Unfortunately, that will leave you all to take care of the babies because Mrs. Myles won't be able to do so."

"That won't be a problem," Winter spoke up. "I can take a leave of absence from work. What about Ian?"

"I haven't spoken with Dr. Anderson; however, someone needs to go to the pediatric wing to see what's going on there. Mr. Myles, why don't you follow me to the receptionist desk, and I'll have the reception nurse call over there for you."

"Sure," Jefferson said, looking back at Evan who sat on Winter's lap.

Jefferson leaned over the receptionist's desk and waited while she called the pediatric surgical ward. His feet were crossed as he stood, and he bounced one continuously against the floor, his agitation very apparent.

It wasn't that Jefferson suddenly had a disdain for Ian. After all he was only a defenseless baby. But it boiled Jefferson's brain to the point of no return because it was Malik's blood that coursed through Ian's veins, and where in the hell was he anyway? But Ian had a twin brother named Evan and neither asked to be born into a mixed-up, twisted DNA pool that defined their parentage. And no matter what Jefferson thought, Ian and Evan were a pair.

The receptionist nurse informed Jefferson that Dr. Alexander would be waiting for him on the surgical ward, at which time she would explain Ian's procedure. The receptionist gave Jefferson directions to the ward, and he turned around and rejoined his family.

When Jefferson stood in front of his family, he let out

a little sigh. "Ian is out of surgery, and I'm going over there to get an update from Dr. Alexander. I'll be back when I can. I'm sure you want to be here when your mother wakes up."

Everyone nodded. Jefferson glanced at Ivy, but she avoided him. All of sudden Ivy stood up and threw her hand out. "Daddy, I'll go with you to see about Ian." She looked around at her brothers and sisters who had puzzled looks on their faces, then turned back to Jefferson. "Let's go."

"You sure, Ivy?"

"Yes, Daddy. I'm doing this for me."

Jefferson put his arm around Ivy's shoulder and she relaxed her head on his. And then began to walk away.

"We'll be back," Jefferson admonished again, tuning around to look at his remaining children again. He turned back around, and he and Ivy were gone.

"What are you thinking, Ivy?"

"Daddy, I don't know and yet I do, but I don't want to talk about it."

"If you should want to talk about it, I'm here."

"Daddy, uhh...uhh, I'm really sorry for the way I've been toward the family. I was so frustrated with you and Momma's mess, and then after she waited all that time for you and then she just ups and walk out, it pissed me off. I can't explain it because for a long time, I was pissed at how you treated Momma before you went to prison. But when Momma was so adamant about keeping the family together and you were released early, I had it my head that our family was going to be all right again. But it didn't happen that way."

"There's something I need to tell you that you may not be aware of. The boys know; I'm not sure if Winter does. Linda gave birth to a son. Your mother and I ran into them at Cold Stone Creamery in Fayetteville. There was no denying that little boy was mine because he was the splitting image of J.R. except he was much fairer. Well, needless to say, witnessing Linda and her boy put your mother over the edge, and our marriage bottomed out. The next thing I knew, your mother had served me with divorce papers. So don't go blaming your mother."

"But, Daddy, how is it that Momma could sleep with another man and it not be on her conscience? She's no better than you. And now she's been exposed because not only did she have twins, her babies have different daddies."

"You're talking about your mother, Ivy. She's been a good woman for as long as I've been with her. It looks bad, but she's not the only one to blame. I hate your husband."

"*Hate* is a strong word, Daddy. Especially since you and Malik used to be best friends."

"I know, Ivy, but Malik crossed the boundary of our friendship. He was the one who preached to me about my infidelity and how I was disrespecting your mother, for him to turn around and do the same thing."

"Daddy, do you think Malik loves me?"

"That's not a fair question for me, Ivy. Since he married you, I would hope that he does. All he needs is one time for you to come and tell me he's treating you badly before I seek him out and beat his lousy ass."

"It's not going to come to that, Daddy."

"I hope not, baby girl. But I do have a question for you."

"What?"

"Do you love Malik?"

There was a long pause. Ivy stopped in front of the elevator and turned to look at her dad. "I do, Daddy. I really love Malik. Now, I've got something to tell you."

A frown crossed Jefferson's face. "What is it, baby?"

Ivy smiled. "You're going to be a grandfather; I'm pregnant."

"A grandfather? I wasn't expecting that."

"I'm going to have a baby—Malik's baby. That's why finding out that one of my baby brothers is also my husband's child hurt me so much. I want to hate Ian, but I realize it's not his fault. He didn't ask for this. But I want to be the bigger person, Daddy. If I have to take care of Ian, I want to do it. At least that's what I'm saying now."

"Your mother isn't going to let that happen, but do your part while she's recuperating."

"Daddy, you have so much wisdom. I've missed you."

"Missed you too, baby girl." Jefferson reached down and kissed Ivy on the forehead.

They both stopped as Jefferson's BlackBerry began to sing. Jefferson pulled the phone from its cradle on his waist and viewed the number. He held a finger up to Ivy, asking for a minute, then answered the phone.

"Hello," he said.

"Are you still coming? I've been waiting for you."

"I'm still at the hospital. Getting ready to talk to the doctor about one of the twins. I'm not sure I'll be able to make it."

"Look, Jefferson, I know that your family needs you..."

"I'll be there later on, but I've got to see about my family right now." Jefferson didn't wait for any goodbyes; he hung up the phone.

"Who was that?" Ivy asked playfully. "Don't tell me you've got a girlfriend already."

"No girlfriend. It's a client that I'm on a deadline with, but I'll make sure I'll finish their work this evening."

"It's okay if you don't want to tell me. I know motor mouth Winter will give me the lowdown."

"I promise you, there's nothing to run down. Now, let's get in this elevator and see Ian."

"Okay, Daddy. Love you."

"Love you, back."

Forty-One

**D**isgusted, Toni threw her BlackBerry on the bed. After Jefferson's earlier call, she'd been anticipating their rendezvous, but his attitude a moment ago was almost foul. Maybe she was wrong about him, but she knew that he had enjoyed her company on last evening as much as she enjoyed his. But she hated to be set aside like an appetizer that had gotten cold, regardless of the reason.

She crossed the room to her office and stared at her computer. She thought about the tidbit of information Jefferson had volunteered about Malik being the father of one of Margo's twins. That piece of news would eat up the airwaves when it hit, but Toni had to think rationally. There was no way she could let loose this cannonball because her only source at the moment was Jefferson, and she had no plans at the moment of abandoning her conquest to capture this man as her trophy.

She went back to her bedroom and picked up her BlackBerry and thought about calling Jefferson again. Then her rational self took over and she gently laid the phone back down. There was no reason to seem desperate.

She knew where Jefferson was and why he was there. She needed his heart and mind clear when he came to see her, and if that meant waiting another day, so be it. She reminded herself that Jefferson was a caring man, and right now his family needed him. She'd wait.

Dr. Anderson was waiting for Jefferson and Ivy with a warm smile when they reached the pediatric ward. She extended her hand when the two approached.

"Hello, Mr. Myles," Dr. Anderson began, "and this must be your..."

"My daughter, Ivy," Jefferson said. "How's Ian?"

"Ian is going to be just fine. He suffered lacerations and abrasions as you know, and he also endured a small puncture wound, no doubt from the metal on the stroller on impact. There wasn't any internal damage as we first thought. We've cleaned and bandaged his wounds. He can be released tomorrow, but we want to keep him overnight for observation. Will you be picking him up?" Dr. Anderson asked Jefferson.

"My sister, Winter, and I will," Ivy replied.

Jefferson looked at Ivy in amazement, but remained quiet. "May we see Ian now?" Jefferson asked.

"Yes, follow me. He's resting. He's been fed and may sleep for the balance of the evening if you'd like to go home and get some rest after you see him."

Jefferson and Ivy followed in silence until they reached

an area similar to the baby room in the maternity ward. There were three other small infants—two in an incubator and the other in a crib with wires and tubes attached to several parts of its tiny body. Dr. Anderson stopped in front of a small acrylic bassinet marked Myles. Ivy stood over Ian and stared. Dr. Anderson backed away. And then as if she knew that Jefferson and Ivy needed time to themselves she spoke up. "I'm going to leave you now, but should you have any questions, please have the nurses get hold of me. Your little man is going to be fine." And Dr. Anderson was gone.

"He's so small...so fragile. He didn't deserve what happened to him." Ivy took her baby finger and brushed the side of Ian's face. "He's handsome."

"He is," Jefferson replied. "He looks a little like J.R. when he was born."

"Really, Daddy?" Ivy asked. Jefferson nodded and Ivy reached over into the bassinet and placed a kissed on Ian's forehead. "If I have to take care of my brother, I will."

Jefferson smiled and squeezed Ivy. "You've grown up, baby girl. You've grown up."

"I'm ready for something good to happen in my life. I'm having a baby, and he may have someone to play with. I'm down with it, Daddy."

"I'm glad. Now let's go see your mother."

## Forty-Two

Winter, Winston, and J.R. were no longer in the waiting room when Jefferson and Ivy returned. They looked around as if they had lost something, but the suspecting nurse called them over with her hand.

"Are you with the group who were here to see Margo Myles?" the nurse asked.

"Yes," Jefferson said. "Did they leave?"

"Mrs. Myles has been placed in a private room and you can join them there." The nurse gave Jefferson the room number, and off he and Ivy went.

Upon their approach to Margo's room, they could hear Winter's big mouth. Yep, they were at the right room all right, but Ivy wasn't sure she was ready to see her mother.

Making amends with her father hadn't been as hard as Ivy had anticipated, but the reunion with her mother wouldn't be easy. It wasn't just that she'd stayed away and refused to contact her mother, it was the knowing that her baby brother, Ian, was the product of her mother and new husband, and that made seeing her a more difficult pill to swallow.

What kind of conversation would she expect to have

with her mother? A hey, mom, I'm home conversation? Why did you have to screw up my life by having a baby with the man I married? Was she supposed to tiptoe on eggshells and not say a word? She had to make a decision fast because her daddy had pushed open the door to her mother's room and Margo was wide awake and staring at her.

It was as if the air had suddenly been sucked from the room. The crew, who only moments before had been lively and animated, were now zombies, watching the prodigal sister as she entered their mother's room. Ivy held on to Jefferson, as if that would give her comfort but more like a crutch as she inched her way forward. And Margo's eyes stared, not believing her eyes as Ivy continued to approach.

Margo seemed groggy to Ivy, but she forced herself to move ahead. As she got closer, Ivy noticed a slight smile form on Margo's face. She stood by Margo's bedside and slowly reached over and patted her hand. "Hello, Momma. How are you feeling?"

"Could be better," Margo managed to say in a soft whisper. "Happy to see you."

"Happy to see you, too." Ivy glanced away and looked in the direction of her siblings who watched with curious eyes. She turned back to her mother. "Daddy and I went to see Ian. He's going to be fine."

Margo searched Ivy's face before speaking. "That's good news. The poor little thing suffered a little bit." Then

Margo's eyes traveled to Jefferson. "Thanks for coming, Jefferson. I knew I could count on you."

"I'm always here for you, Margo. You know that. You're going to be all right; the girls and I are going to take care of the twins."

"I'd like that," Margo replied. "Come sit next to me, Ivy." Margo patted the bed lightly with her hand.

Ivy could feel the whole room watching her like she was some kind of spectacle. She wished she could be swallowed up by a giant whale, but if it wasn't now, it would be another time. She needed to face her mother.

"I need to talk to Ivy in private," Margo said to the others.

"No," Ivy said almost too hastily. While she might have been a spectacle, her siblings' presence gave her a sense of security from whatever Margo was about to say. True, she had her own questions to ask of her mother, but this was neither the time nor the place to entertain them. She would wait for the opportune moment to sit down with her mother one-on-one and unburden her heart. She sat on the bed next to her mother. "Yes, Momma?"

"There are so many things I'd like to say to you, but above all, I want you to know that I love you. You were the one person that kept me sane when I sometimes wasn't thinking straight. I know that you have questions about..." Margo looked up at Jefferson, who looked away, then walked out of the room. "Questions about me and Malik...and Ian. I wish this wasn't my reality, but it is. I want you to know that I made a terrible mistake, and now I have Ian, but I also have Evan who is a product of your father and me. You getting married to Malik was a shock to my system, but it's something I have to deal with. I want you to know and hear it from me that we all make mistakes and I'm sorry for anything I might have done to make you withdraw from me."

"Stop, Momma. It's not you; you know how selfish I can be. I hated to see our family fall apart and I blamed you more than Daddy for not trying to keep it together. I love you and always will. I have to deal with me."

"Umm hmm," Winter said from the peanut gallery.

"You don't have to explain," Margo said, intertwining her fingers with Ivy's. "When I'm up and able, we'll have brunch—just you and me—and we'll sit down and have one of our mother-daughter, heart-to-heart pow-wows."

"I'd like that, Momma. You get some rest now. Winter and I are going to take care of the boys." Ivy got up and leaned over the bed and kissed her mother on the forehead. "We'll talk later." Ivy mouthed the words *I love you*. And Margo did the same.

"Mom, Evan is getting restless," Winter said. "We're going to your house and take care of him. Where is his car seat?"

"My car is still in the garage downtown. Maybe Winston or J.R. can pick it up for me tomorrow. Maybe the hospital can provide you with one for tonight. If not, you'll have to take extra precautions with my baby in the car."

"Okay, we'll check with the hospital," Winter said. "We're going to go. Love you."

Margo's eyes fluttered. "Love you both. I'm tired."

"J.R. and I are going to stay with you, Mom," Winston interjected. "We're going to park in these chairs."

"You can go home if you like."

"Naw, we've got this watch," J.R. said. "Now take your beauty nap."

Margo had pricked a nerve when she tried to talk to Ivy about her relationship with Malik. Maybe it was Jefferson's pride that was at stake. He paced up and down the hall, trying to quiet the animosity that had risen up in him. Malik's child was ill, but where in the hell was he? In his own selfish way, Jefferson was glad that he wasn't still at the hospital. Malik's presence would've only provoked his bitterness toward him that much more.

He pulled out his BlackBerry and placed a call to Toni. Jefferson wasn't in the mood to be romanced, and he didn't want to leave Margo's side. He'd been through a lot with that woman, and this was only another family crisis that the Myles' would get through. Unhappily, he heard the excitement in Toni's voice when she answered the phone.

"I'm not going to be able to make it tonight. We've got one twin in the pediatric ward, Margo on the major

## Forty-Three

The longer Malik sat in the room, the more irritated he became. Knowing that he and Margo shared a son put a new perspective on things. He couldn't get Margo off the brain, and his desire to be with her increased two-fold. Unfortunately, there was a dilemma with his desire to be with her—he was married to Margo's daughter, who was also carrying his child.

He paced back and forth, trying to come up with a solution for the complicated mess he found himself in, but there was no immediate remedy. Then he heard Perry's voice echoing in his ear, admonishing him to get his head back into the campaign or call it a day. While in his hotel room, he called his campaign headquarters, and they confirmed the news that Perry had given him about Sterling's slight lead over him.

Maybe it would be best to put the Margo thing on the back burner. Maybe if he could talk to her alone, he'd feel better about things. He'd call Ivy later and get an assessment of what was going on. Right now, he needed to get the hell out of the prison of a room and get a drink.

Malik picked up his room key and stuffed it in his wallet. He jammed the wallet in his pants pocket and headed downstairs to the bar. As he approached, he could hear light jazz coming from the bar area. There were more people in residence than he had anticipated.

Finding a seat at the bar, Malik ordered a Bloody Mary. Then he looked back over his left shoulder as the scent of Pleasures Delight invaded his nostrils and shuddered when the lovely lady traced his neck with her finger that boasted a large, diamond-encrusted ring.

"Hey, baby, is this seat vacant?" the honey-colored lady, who looked to be in her late-thirties, sporting a black, full-body weave that hung just below her shoulders, asked.

Malik gave her a full-body scan, noticing that she was about five feet, eight inches in her heels, wearing a tight-fitting, black knit dress that framed her breasts right above the nipples. She had a pleasing smile and lovely teeth that were accentuated by a plum-colored lipstick on her full Nubian lips and reminded him a little of Toni Braxton about the eyes. He smiled. "Yes, the seat is vacant. Sit down. What are you drinking?"

"Long Island Iced Tea."

"Bartender, a Long Island Iced Tea for the lady," Malik said, giving the lady a half-smile.

"So, where's your wife?" the lady inquired. There was a blank look on Malik's face. "Your wedding ring is a dead giveaway."

"My wife is at the hospital with her mother. She was in a terrible car accident today."

"I'm sorry to hear that. I hope she gets better soon."

"So do I. And what is your name?"

"Anissa." She grinned, took her drink the bartender extended to her, and took a sip. "This is good."

Malik looked around. "So, Anissa, what brings you here to-night...alone?"

"Some friends of mine and I went to see a play downtown. We stopped at the hotel for dinner afterwards, and I thought before going home I'd stop in here to see what was happening. I love jazz, and it was speaking to me when I walked up. Do you like jazz?"

"Love it."

"So, may I ask why are you here and not with your wife?"

"You may ask, but it's no big deal. My wife is staying with her mother at the hospital and I got a hotel to be close. Simple as that."

"You're cute, but I am sure you hear that all the time."

"No, not really. I don't hang out and don't subject myself to the leers of women who might find me attractive."

"Oh, excuse me. So, I guess tonight was different. You seem to be wearing the blues."

"Truthfully, Anissa, I've definitely got the blues."

"Why don't you tell me about it? By the way, you never told me your name."

"Malik."

"Does Malik have a last name?"

"Does Anissa have a last name?"

"Okay, you want to play games. Forget the last name. Why do you have the blues, Malik?"

"I found out something today that's got my world turned upside down."

Anissa took a sip of her drink. "I'm not going anywhere right away. I've got time, if you want to talk."

Malik took a look at Anissa and felt that she was safe. He bent his head down and exhaled. "Bartender, another Bloody Mary, please." Malik looked at Anissa, who seemed to be studying him. "I've been in love for a long time with a woman I couldn't have—she was married. But the moment she became free I didn't pounce on her like I should have. I was there for her because her loss seemed great to her at the time, and I was there as the dutiful friend to encourage and be there for her for whatever it was she needed. I think she had some feelings for me, but things happened and she wasn't suddenly free anymore, but we finally had that moment that seemed magical. We made love to each other. But it was over as soon as it began."

"That's so sad. So did you ever find true love?"

The bartender slid Malik his Bloody Mary and he took a sip. "I loved only her, but when our lives drifted apart, I did fall in love again. But it wasn't the same as before. The new love of my life filled a void, but it still wasn't the same. Nevertheless, I married my new love and now we're going to be parents."

"Oh, I get it. You're going to be a father and you aren't comfortable yet in your new role. Depending on how many months your wife is, you've got plenty of time to get adjusted to the idea of being a father because when the baby gets here, that's when the real pressure begins."

"No, that news isn't earth-shattering. In fact, I welcomed the news with open arms."

"So what's got you in a tizzy?"

"You need your drink refilled. Bartender, another Long Island Iced Tea for the lady."

"Coming up," the bartender said.

"Thank you, Malik. Now finish your story. You've got me all curious."

"I learned today that I have a son."

"Whoa. I missed something; that came out of left field."

"Damn right it did. My mother-in-law..." Malik seemed to drift off in thought.

"You mean your wife's mother...who had the accident and is in the hospital?"

"You were listening."

"You tell a good story."

"Yes, the woman in the hospital. Her twin babies were also in the accident and one had a rare blood type."

"That's not so awful, is it?"

"The doctors thought he might need blood, but neither my mother-in-law nor father-in-law have that blood type."

"So are you trying to tell me that you have this same rare blood type and you are the baby's father?"

"You are so discerning, Anissa."

Anissa put up her hand. "Recap. You got down with your wife's mother and sired a son, and now your wife is having a child for you as well. Jesus. This is a bestseller, and if I were writing it I'd call it, *My Wife and Mother-in-Law—My Babies' Mommas.*" Anissa giggled and took a sip of her drink.

Malik grunted. "It isn't a funny place to be."

"I guess not. So what is your father-in-law saying?"

"If you can find any humor in this, my father-in-law used to be my best friend. We're frat brothers."

"Let me take a guess. You're a "Q.""

"How could you tell?"

"I'm discerning, remember, and you have Q written all over you. In fact, I know a lot of Q's."

Upon hearing that, Malik became silent, collecting his thoughts and running over in his mind what he had shared. Who was this Anissa? Who did she know? She seemed harmless. Damn, he'd talked too much. He could cut his losses and go back to the room, ending what seemed at first to be an opportunity to unload a burden with a stranger.

"Did I say something wrong?"Anissa asked.

"No," Malik said matter-of-factly. "Just thinking."

"Well, Malik, I wish you well with your situation. Hopefully, you can sort it all out. It's time for me to go home and get ready for Friday. I've got a lot of work to do in the office tomorrow. It was a pleasure meeting you, and thank you for the drinks and your company." Anissa reached in her purse and pulled out a business card. "If you should need a shoulder to lean on again, give me a call." She got up from her stool and patted Malik on the shoulder.

Malik looked at the card and put it in his shirt pocket. "Thanks for listening, Anissa. If I should need a friend, I'll be sure to call you." And Anissa evaporated into thin air.

Malik was grateful he hadn't given Anissa his last name. He couldn't afford to have any slip-ups on his way to winning a state senate seat. He was going to take Perry's advice and step up his game. Malik finished off his Bloody Mary and prepared to leave.

"Malik Mason?" the gentleman asked, approaching from behind.

"Yes, and you are..." Malik squinted.

"Dr. Shelton Wright, the people's candidate for state senator out of Raleigh."

Malik perked up and shook Dr. Wright's hand. "Hello, Dr. Wright. I didn't recognize you, with it being so dark and all. What brings you here?"

"Had a meeting with some of my constituents in the hotel—trying to feel the pulse of the people I hope to serve one day. How's your race going down there in Fayetteville?"

"It's going good. Campaigning is hard work, but I want this and hopefully we'll be officemates soon."

"Well, it was good to see you, Mr. Mason. I've got to

tell you, though, stay off of the sauce and away from women other than your wife. You never know who might be lurking about, ready to get some tidbit on you so they can put your business in the street. If you plan to win, you have to keep a squeaky-clean image. Well, I've got to run home to the wife and love up on her awhile."

Malik looked at Dr. Wright thoughtfully and sober enough to understand his meaning. "Thank you, Dr. Wright, for the words of wisdom." Malik watched as Dr. Wright took his leave and then looked at his watch. He needed to call Ivy, but it could wait until the morning.

## Forty-Four

Ivy watched as Winter pulled out her key and opened the door leading from the garage into the foyer that led into the kitchen in Margo's townhouse. It was close to midnight, and everything was dark and still. Ivy navigated her way in and followed behind Winter as she flicked on lights in several rooms. Evan was fast asleep, and Winter was eternally grateful that the hospital staff had offered milk and Pampers for Evan.

"Mom's house is nice," Winter said, taking the stairs to the second floor to put Evan in his crib. "She deserves it after helping everyone else to acquire prime real estate."

Ivy was taken aback but wouldn't say out loud how much she loved the place. It felt warm and cozy, and she could feel her mother's presence running through it. "Do you think Momma is lonely?"

"Because Daddy isn't here? You know their divorce is going to be final in a few weeks." Ivy put on Evan's sleeper and laid him in the bed. "Let's go into Mom's room and talk."

"My God," Ivy exclaimed as they entered Margo's bedroom. "This room is massive. Fireplace and how big is that flat-screen? I know she's not enjoying this all by herself."

Winter sat on the bed and Ivy followed. "Feels like old times, big sister."

"Yeah," Ivy said.

"Truth, Ivy? Mom is putting up a big front. Yeah, she thought she wanted to be alone; she's been through a lot. But, girl, when I dragged Daddy over here so he could see the boys, you should've seen the chemistry between him and Mom bounce in the room. She still loves him, but her pride won't make her change her mind. It's as if she had to get her point across, and she did so by making a bold statement in filing for divorce."

"How does Dad feel?"

"That man loves that woman. He told Winston and J.R. several times that he loved Mom."

"Maybe, she'll look at things differently after this accident."

"Girl, our mother is stubborn...just like you."

"Don't go there, Winter. Anyway, who was that fine brother that was following behind you at the restaurant when I saw you last?"

"You mean Phillip?"

"If that's his name, he's the guy I'm talking about. He looked as if he had the hots for you, girl."

"Believe it or not, I'd just met him. He's studying to be a doctor, and his father is running for a senate seat in Raleigh, just like Malik. I went on a date with him the other night, and I think we could have a future. It's too early to tell, though. I'll let you in on a little secret; he can kiss. Oh my God. I almost lost it when he touched my lips. He set me on fire."

"What about the rest of your body? Did he make it tingle? Did you let him touch…"

"Okay, enough." Winter patted the bed and lay on her side. "Let's talk about you."

"There's nothing to talk about."

"Sistergirl, I must look like some kind of dummy. You've got a lot to share with me."

"What are you talking about, Winter?"

"That big rock on your finger, girl. My big sister went and got married and now I'll never be a maid of honor in my sister's wedding. Remember when I said that I'd get married first?"

"I proved you wrong."

"You did, Ivy. Why Malik?"

Ivy sighed. She didn't want to go there with Winter, but the discussion was inevitable. "He was there. No ulterior motives."

"Come on. You had to have feelings for him. I'm not stupid, I keep telling you. But Malik is so much older than you and he used to be Daddy's best friend."

"I know." Ivy dropped her head. "Malik loved Momma, in fact, I believe he still does."

"So why did you marry him, Ivy? Was this your way of getting back at Mom?"

"Don't judge me, Winter." Ivy jumped off the bed and began to huff.

Winter got up and went to Ivy. "Sis, I'm sorry. I'm not trying to start anything. I was just asking. I guess I was trying to understand the rhyme or reason. You and I were always able to talk and when you cut me off, cut the whole family off, I couldn't figure out why."

"Look, Winter, I'm going to be honest with you. I'm scared."

"Scared of what, sis?" Winter took Ivy's hand and led her back to the bed. They sat on the edge.

"That Malik will either try and get custody of Ian or pressure Momma in some kind of way to let him into her world."

"Listen up, Ivy. Mom doesn't want anything to do with Malik. To tell you the truth, she can't stand him. That's why it hurt her so much when she found out that you and Malik got married. Not because she wanted him, but because she realizes that Malik had it bad for her and she doesn't want to see her eldest daughter hurt."

"Oh, I want to believe that, and even if it were true, I don't trust Malik. Why hasn't he called? He has just as much at stake in this matter as the rest of us do. I did fall in love with him, Winter. I truly did, but I'm not sure I did the right thing by marrying him."

Winter hugged Ivy. "You can talk to me anytime you need, sis. I'm sure Malik loves you or he wouldn't have married you."

"I've had some time to think about it, and sometimes I think he married me so that it would look good on his resume...so that he can say Senator and Mrs. Malik Mason."

There was a loud, cackling sound. Winter couldn't stop laughing. "You should've heard yourself—Senator and Mrs. Malik Mason."

It was Ivy's turn to laugh. "Did I really sound like that?"

"Yes, you did. Anyway, don't worry about Malik. I think he's going to make my sister proud. And anyway, if he steps to Mom, you heard what Daddy said. He was going to whoop his ass into the ground."

Ivy laughed. "Sis, I do have something to tell you."

Concern was written on Winter's face. "What's wrong, Ivy?"

Ivy smiled. "You're going to be an auntie."

"What?" Winter screamed. "I'm going to be an auntie?" Winter jumped up from the bed and screamed. "I'm going to be an auntie. My sister is pregnant." Winter pulled Ivy up from the bed, hugged and kissed her on the cheek. "Sis, I'm so happy for you. I'm going to be a good auntie, and this child, girl or boy, is going to have the best of everything."

"Thanks, Winter." Ivy held on tight. "Thanks, little sister."

Winter pulled back. "We've got to tell Mom and Dad. Oh my God. We've got to tell Winston and J.R."

"Slow down, Winter. That's why no one wants to tell

you anything. You don't know how to absorb a little information and massage it for awhile. Anyway, I already told Daddy, and he's cool with it. I'm looking forward to bringing this life into the world."

"Girl, you've turned a somewhat bad day into a good one. Give me another hug." Winter hugged Ivy. "I love you, Ivy."

"I love you, too."

Forty-Five

The room was close to being silent except for Malik's snoring that could have awakened everyone in the hotel. His sleep was sound, probably a product of the two or three Bloody Marys he had gulped down the previous evening. His labored breathing seemed to intensify as the morning wore on.

A loud knock on the door caused Malik to stir. He wasn't quite sure where he was and he fell back asleep.

*Knock, knock, knock.* "Housekeeping. Can I come in?"

With the loud knocking, Malik's body jolted upright. "Damn, what time is it?" Malik said, wiping saliva from his mouth while taking a deep breath.

"Housekeeping. May I come in?"

"Go away!" Malik shouted.

Malik laid his head back on the pillow and fell easily asleep until the alarm on his watch began to chime. He reached over and turned off the alarm, and after another minute of lying prone, he finally sat upright. Pulling his legs over the side of the bed, Malik wiped his eyes before looking at the clock that stood on the table next to the bed. "Oh my God, I can't believe it's ten-thirty,"

Malik said out loud. "I've got to get to the hospital to see Margo...to see the baby."

Malik sprang into action. He got up and went into the bathroom to relieve himself, then jumped into the shower. The steam revived him...almost made him feel like a new man. He scrubbed his body as if he was getting rid of the stench of a thousand men but smiled and when the task was done, he exited the shower a new man.

He admired his naked body in the mirror that lay on the wall between the armoire and the desk with all the hotel information sitting on it. He patted himself on the chest and nodded his approval. His body was still in good shape and he wondered absently if Margo would approve.

Malik toweled his body dry. "I've got to see Margo; I've got to talk to her. I have to let her know that I'm here for her and our son." Malik exhaled. "What am I going to do?" He punched his hand with his fist. "I want both of them."

Malik quickly dressed and put his wallet in his pants pocket. He picked up his cell and called Reggie, updating him on the situation with his mother-in-law and that he hoped to return to Fayetteville by nightfall. Next he called Perry, the one call Malik dreaded but had to make anyway. Fortunately, Perry didn't answer and Malik left a voicemail.

"Perry, this is Malik. Still in Raleigh at the hospital. Will see you this evening." That done, Malik checked out of the hotel and headed for the hospital.

Malik was surprised that he hadn't heard from Ivy, but he was fine with it. He wasn't ready to deal with her and the issue of Ian—the baby that had him joined to Ivy's mother. He hoped she wasn't at the hospital and that he could have some one-on-one time with Margo.

As Malik stepped out into the sunshine, his head turned in the direction of a group of women who were chatting rather loudly. At that moment, Malik froze, scanning the group in quick fashion, suddenly remembering the lady at the bar—Anissa. The last thing he wanted was to run into her again. He couldn't be sure what she looked like because the light in the bar was dim, although he was sitting next to her. However, the light on this bright, Saturday morning made it difficult to discern one lady from the other. He counted six women, but they hadn't glanced once in his direction. And then he remembered Anissa saying that she had only stopped by for a drink.

Feeling safe to do so, Malik walked briskly to his car, got in, and drove away without looking back. The streets seemed crowded—almost like a weekday—with people taking care of business, out for a jog in the park, getting groceries at the supermarket, or on some family outing. Before he knew it, Malik pulled into the hospital parking lot, parked his car and headed inside.

He was on a mission and Margo was his target. He walked up to two ladies who sat behind a desk marked INFORMATION DESK. One of the ladies gave Malik the location of Margo's room and he proceeded to the elevator to make his ascent to the floor she was on. Malik constantly turned his head left and right as if he was on the lookout for someone. Pleased, he proceeded to his destination more relaxed than when he came in.

Malik stood outside of Margo's door but was unable to move forward. He prayed a silent pray that she would be alone so that he'd be able to tell her how he felt and what he could offer. He scratched his head, counted to three, and went inside the room.

There was a sigh of relief as the room was void of visitors. Margo was partially hidden behind the make-shift wall made of muslin that was used to divide the room. He could tell that one leg was in some type of cast, but the rest of her was covered up by a thin, white bedspread. But it was Margo's stare once he was upon her that scared him...that caught him off-guard.

"You timed it just right, didn't you?" Margo asked.

"I'm not sure what you're talking about," Malik replied.

"You saw Jefferson, Winston, and J.R. walk out of here. They haven't even been gone a minute. What were you doing? Hiding behind a wall or in the bathroom?"

Malik smiled. God heard his prayer. "No, I didn't see them at all," he mused.

"So, why are you here? I hear you left the hospital before Ian was even out of harm's way. Did you know that Jefferson stayed and watched vigil over him last night?"

"Margo, I didn't come to argue with you. In fact, quite the contrary, and I'm glad we are able to be alone. Finding out that one of the twins belonged to me blew my mind, and I wasn't able to deal with it at the moment. You have to understand where I'm coming from."

"I'll give you that."

"I'm here today to let you know that I'm here for you and Ian. Whatever you and the baby need, I'm prepared to man up to the plate."

Margo continued to stare. "What about Ivy? How does she feel about you obligating yourself to Ian and me? Have you even spoken to her about it?"

"She'll understand. I have always taken my responsibilities seriously, and this is no different. I still can't believe this has happened. I truly wished that I had found this out before I married Ivy."

Margo stared at him, her eyes twitching back and forth. "You need to take back what you said. You are married to my daughter and I won't allow you to disregard her as if she's one of your conquests. She is your priority. Furthermore, I can take care of Ian. In fact, I want you to sign over your parental rights to me."

"Damn you, Margo. Why do you hate me so much? Why do this to me? Ian is the thread that holds us together. I haven't stopped loving you. And I haven't forgotten the afternoon you came to see me when you thought Jefferson was with Angelica and begged me…I mean, you pleaded with me to make love to you. You gave of yourself so freely, and I fell deeper in love with you at that moment. And now to find out that you bore our love child—a gift from God."

Margo held her hand up. "Shut up, Malik. Don't do this.

I don't love you and what you have for me is nothing more than pure lust. It's in your eyes—the way you always look at me, stalk me..."

"That's a lie, Margo. I felt nothing but love for you then as I do now. Why do you think I was always around after Jefferson went to prison and after Toni was killed in the car accident? I was afraid to come out and say it, but I was madly in love with you. In fact, I was in love with you long before then. I wasn't coming around for my health; I couldn't stay away. I wanted to be there for you in any way I could. I enjoyed our talks, our dinner outings, the way your hair smelled, and the way you smelled. I was too afraid to come out and tell you how I felt because I thought you'd run away. So I settled for being near you as often as I could."

"That was then, Malik, and this is now. You have chosen my daughter to be your wife, and it's she you are now beholden to. And I hope and pray that you're not playing with her emotions and affection for you. I will personally rip your heart out if you hurt my child."

"Margo, please don't do this. I want to be in my child's life; I want to be in your life. We can make it work, and I can still be a husband to Ivy."

"Malik, you need to leave now. You make me ill. If I never see your face again, that would make me happy. I do want something from you, however. Sign the waiver of your parental rights."

"What if something should happen to Ian that he needs my blood?"

"We'll cross that hurdle when it happens."

"You're being a bitch, Margo. What have I ever done to you but love you?" Moisture formed in Malik's eyes. "Don't dismiss me like I'm your disobedient child. I love you. I want to be with you. If not now, later; I'll wait. I'll do whatever you want me to do."

"I want you to get the hell out of my room."

"You heard my mother," Winter said, her voice booming. "Get the hell out, you bastard. How could you come up in here and say those things to my mother when you have a wife who's carrying your child?"

Malik looked up and saw Ivy. He had no idea as to how much she heard, but he could tell she'd been crying. He pushed past Winter but Ivy was out of the door.

"Wait, Ivy," Malik called out and the door closed behind him.

Winter pulled back the curtain and went to her mother. Tears were streaming from Margo's face. Margo looked up at Winter and tried to raise her hands. Winter held her mother's hands and kissed her forehead.

"Not one time, Winter, did Malik mention that Ivy was pregnant. I hope he rots in hell."

"He'll get his. Now I've got to find Ivy before Malik does. I'll be back."

## Forty-Six

There would be no more waiting on Jefferson Myles to show his face at her place. Toni had been there, done that for many of her adult years, and as of today, she was going to put her foot down. Maybe she thought she needed a man, but her days of chasing tail were coming to a close. True, she wanted that good-looking hunk of a man who was still in his prime and could still break hearts if he wanted to, but how much was she to sacrifice to have him as her own?

Toni had her taste of the younger men, who only seemed interested and desperate to see what she could add to their dossier. A cougar she wasn't, and if anyone was to be kept, it wasn't going to be her doing the keeping. Her life was not defined by any man; in fact, she didn't want a man that bad that she'd be handing out jewels and money to keep them interested.

It was a beautiful Saturday afternoon. The sun was high in the sky. A quick run to Saks at the Triangle Town Center Mall would assuage her spirits. Last week she glimpsed a nice Louis Vuitton bag that would go nicely with a pair of shoes she'd been dying to wear.

Toni swished her hair as she stared in the mirror for

the last time before making her exit. Her hot pink multi-colored spandex top made a blazing statement as it settled at the edge of the pockets on her white Wrangler jeans. She was hot.

Picking up her purse and BlackBerry, Toni prepared to leave. She put on her large, black Chanel sunglasses, looked around, set the alarm and closed the door behind her. Before she could take another step, her phone chirped...rather it sang one of her favorite love songs that she'd recently assigned to Jefferson. She paused, then answered, not sure she was doing the right thing given his seemingly lack of interest. "Hello," she said in a rather distracted voice.

"Hey, sorry about yesterday. What are you up to?"

"In fact, I'm on my way to Saks to treat myself. I got a little stir crazy sitting in the house, especially since it's a beautiful day, and..."

"Would you like some company?"

"Aren't you at the hospital?"

"Need to get away. Thought seeing you would lighten my mood."

Toni smiled. "Well, I don't have to go to Saks right now."

"No, why don't I meet you there? I'd like to tag along on your shopping expedition and see your taste in clothes. But I want to take you back to your place and make love to you. Now that the boys are out of the woods, I can't think of anything else but being with you. I want to hold you, feel you, and taste you. The other night only fueled the passion that is wracking my body right now."

"Well, maybe we should forget about shopping."

"You think?"

"Jefferson, what about Margo? Um, isn't she going to need you?"

"Winter and Winston are there. J.R. went into the office for a little while."

"What about your other daughter and her husband?"

"Malik, that's his name. He's been hanging around the hospital this morning. I can't stand the sight of him. I stayed with the twin that shares his blood type all night, and now after the crisis is over, he had the nerve to show up like he's the big D."

"So this is why you want to come by. To let off some steam."

"Toni, that was unfair."

"The truth is the truth."

"Toni, I really want to be with you. Margo and I will never be again. Our divorce will be final in a few weeks, and she's made it very clear that she wants to be alone—that is without me."

Relief shadowed Toni's face like a total eclipse. She couldn't contain her smile. To think she was ready to throw in the towel so early. "Okay, meet me at Saks. I'll be there in about fifteen or twenty minutes, and then I'm going to take you home and make you forget what day it is. You won't even remember that you were at the hospital caring for Margo before finding out that your daughter's husband is the father of one of Margo's twins."

"Ouch," Jefferson said. "But I do like what you're saying. It sounds like a place I want to be and in full submission to you. I'll be there as fast as I can get there, and keep stoking that fire that's got you saying just what I need to hear."

"Oh, baby, it's already a forest fire, and not even Smokey the Bear can put this out."

"I'm on my way."

Malik emptied the paper cup that had been filled earlier with Coke. He sat alone in the hospital cafeteria, going over in his head all that had transpired today. It hurt him that Ivy was a witness to his proclamation of love for her mother, while he yet loved her. But he couldn't help himself because this was how he truly felt.

He wanted to slap Ivy's sister, Winter. She had gotten all up in his face, threatening him if he hurt Ivy. Hell, he loved Ivy, but not the way he loved Margo. Winter had one more time to step to him because he wouldn't be responsible for his actions the next time.

Looking up, Malik saw Jefferson enter the cafeteria. He wasn't sure if Jefferson was stalking him because this was the third time he had seen Jefferson in a matter of an hour, but it appeared something else was on his mind. Jefferson walked past without blinking an eye and, within seconds, he left the way he had come. It was hard to fathom that they had once been best friends.

Malik got up and threw the cup away. Before he left

for Fayetteville, he wanted another opportunity to speak with Margo. He had to convince her that he meant no harm, especially as it concerned Ivy, but he was serious about how he felt about her. How he was going to manage loving two people at the same time had yet to be worked out in his head. He had no choice because his heart told him so—that he belonged to Margo and Ivy.

## Forty-Seven

I t was like a rumble in the jungle. They tore at each other like carnivores—kissing, licking, sucking, and tearing each other to shreds as if the world was coming to an end and this would be their last tryst on earth. Their bodies were entangled as one flesh and they continued to devour each other until there was nothing left to eat. Spent, they lay motionless, falling under their own spell.

With arms outstretched and eyes closed, Jefferson lay next to Toni satisfied, although his thoughts had now turned to Margo. Only hours earlier, he'd been surrounded by his boys, making sure that Margo was being treated well as she lay covered in Plaster of Paris. Jefferson thought he saw a twinkle in her eye—one of the moments that their eyes locked on to each other, bringing back a flood of memories they shared as husband and wife.

Toni shifted her body and nestled up against Jefferson, interrupting his thoughts temporarily. Something other than sex had attracted Jefferson to Toni, but he couldn't quite put his finger on it. In the past few days, it caused him to question his true motive toward Margo. But even at that moment, lying so close to Toni, feeling the tender curves of her buttocks on his groin, Margo's name was imprinted in bold letters on his mind.

He kissed the back of Toni's head, and she ran her hand over the length of his thigh, feeling for his manhood that had sent her into a villainous frenzy. Aroused, Jefferson cradled her breast in one hand and kissed her on the back of the head once more, then squeezed her breast intermittently to stimulate Toni's passion that rose in her like a beast. Not even a minute had passed before the sucking sounds of the beginning of their ravenous foreplay could be heard, almost as if each were auditioning for a part in a play. And then the curtain opened, and the well-rehearsed drama unfolded— Jefferson and Toni playing their roles, perfecting them from the time before. And the ending was spectacular— Jefferson roaring like a lion as the taunt muscles in his body pushed outward after which his body shook as if a thousand volts of lightning had hit him. And Toni followed with the passion of a mother lion protecting her cubs, her roar almost as loud as Jefferson's. Then her legs fell from around Jefferson's waist and her wet body soaked up the sweat that fell from his dripping body as she lay limp from exhaustion. And then he moved from over her and fell on the bed face up and drifted off to sleep.

The room was stark quiet except for the heavy breathing of the two lovers who lay asleep upon the coolness of the satin sheets. The closed blinds hid the afternoon sun, which soothed the lover's souls and allowed for uninterrupted peace.

Without warning, a loud noise rocked Jefferson and Toni from their slumber. They jumped at the sound of Beyoncé's voice serenading them over Toni's BlackBerry. Toni reached for her phone to quiet the noise that threatened the tranquility of the moment, but when she saw the caller's name, she decided to take it, scooting from the bed in her birthday suit. Jefferson watched groggily as Toni sashayed across the room until she disappeared from view.

Closing the door to the spare bedroom behind her, Toni resumed her conversation. "What is it, Anissa? I'm right in the middle of romancing the man of my dreams."

"Didn't mean to interrupt your lovemaking session, although you didn't have to answer the phone, you know. But I've got something hot for you."

"It better be good. I left my hot hunk of a man, who for the last hour has been snuggled up against my body."

"Ooh, too much information. Maybe I should call you later."

"No, let me hear what you've got so I can go back to my man in peace."

"Okay then. I was out with some of my girlfriends last night, and afterwards I stopped in the lounge at my favorite hotel for a nightcap and to hear the band. This guy was sitting at the bar sipping on his drink by his lonesome, and I went over and sat down. Like a perfect gentleman, he offered to buy me a drink and we began to talk."

"Okay, now that you've gotten the preliminaries out of the way, I trust this conversation is leading to something more meaningful."

"Hold your horses, Toni; I'm getting there. Anyway, I wasn't as interested in what he was saying initially, but once he began to pour out his soul and spill the reason he was sitting alone, he had my undivided attention. I asked him his name, and when he told me Malik, I was none the wiser. But when I got home and turned on the TV, there he was in living color."

"Well, who is he and what did he say?"

"Ready for this? I was hobnobbing with Malik Mason."

"The Malik Mason out of Fayetteville who is running for a North Carolina senate seat?"

"The one and only, girlfriend. But that's not the half of it. He found out that he's the father of his wife's mother's baby. Can you believe that? But it gets even better. His mother-in-law has twin boys, but he's the father of only one of them."

"Damn! And who's the father of the other one?"

"The mother-in-law's soon-to-be ex-husband."

"Shut-up. I owe you for this tidbit. This is gossip at its best." Toni smiled to herself. Now she had her story as given to her by someone other than Jefferson. She needed to move on it; otherwise, old news wouldn't pack the kind of punch she intended. Cousin Sterling would owe her big after she let this story leak into the political sewer. "Let's meet for an early dinner, and you can finish giving me the sorted details."

"Let me see if I can fit you into my schedule." After a slight pause, she said, "I believe it's doable. What time?"

"Anissa, you're crazy and I'm not mad at you for the interruption. Let's say five-ish at Macaroni Grill. Now, I've got to go. I'll have my recorder with me."

. "See you then."

Finished with her call, Toni left the room and headed back to her bedroom. She jumped when she saw Jefferson's fully clothed silhouette blocking the sun from the living room window. At that moment, she felt like Eve in the Garden of Eden—naked before God and Jefferson, her mind rapidly assessing the situation, wondering if Jefferson had overheard any of her conversation with Anissa. One thing was apparent, though; their romantic interlude had been abruptly terminated—kaput for the day. Anissa's timing might have been off, but Toni saw her interrupted time with Jefferson only as a momentary setback. He'd be back, but in the meantime, she was going to sell this story to the highest bidder. Hell, she no longer needed a website.

## Forty-Eight

**M**alik cased the hospital like a secret service agent, making sure that he didn't overlook any nook or cranny. He crisscrossed the hospital from one wing to the other, but there was no sign of Ivy. He peeped into the small snack bar, but without any luck.

As he exited the snack bar, Malik ran into Winter who rolled her eyes and scowled at him. "If something happens to my sister, you're gonna wish you were dead."

"Save your rhetoric for someone else, Winter. You need to watch your mouth and learn how to talk to your elders. I'm sure your mother taught you better. And so that you know, you don't scare me in the least."

Winter waved her finger in Malik's face and did a snake shake with her head. "So long as you heard me."

"Whatever, little girl." And Malik walked off.

Ivy walked blindly through the hospital corridors until she found a public telephone booth and walked in. She willed her tears to subside, but she was unable to shut off the steady stream that flowed from her eyes. Tears marked her path but she was determined to get as far away from the hospital as she could.

She fumbled through the Yellow Pages until she came to the page marked Taxis. Reaching in her purse, she pulled out her cell phone and dialed the numbers that were written in bold black print in the advertisement for Cardinal Cab. Painfully, she gave the dispatcher her whereabouts and turned to exit the phone booth.

Her eyes became as big as saucers as she saw Malik walk past. She ducked and turned her head to avoid detection. After what seemed like an eternity, Ivy took a chance and peeped out of the booth and was glad Malik was nowhere in sight. As fast as her body would allow, she bolted from the telephone booth and ran outside. She was in luck as the cab pulled up to the curb about the same time she arrived. Hurriedly, she got in and shut the door.

"Please take me to Fayetteville. My address is…"

"Ma'am, I don't go that far."

"I'll make it worth your while. How about a fifty-dollar tip on top of the fare?"

"I don't think anyone would miss me. Give me the address and we're on our way."

Ivy's tears were gone, but she had an awful pain in the pit of her stomach. The hurtful things Malik said about wanting to be with her mother were still audible in her ears. Her husband loved her mother, Margo, more than he loved her, and she blamed her mother for some of it.

If Margo hadn't slept with Malik, regardless of what her father may have done in the past, the pain Ivy felt deep down inside wouldn't be.

Ivy sniffed and closed her eyes, hoping to wipe out the memory of Malik pleading with her mother to give them a chance at love. Malik hadn't even given any thought that she, his wife, was carrying their baby. The bastard was going to pay. There was no way in hell that she was going to stay married to that heartless son-of-a-bitch or have his baby.

When Ivy looked up, the cab driver was staring at her in his rearview mirror. She diverted her gaze, but when she looked up again, he was still staring at her. It frightened her a little, but so far he hadn't veered off the interstate. And then she froze at the sound of his voice.

"Miss, are you okay? You seem troubled."

Ivy stared at the face in the mirror. "It's none of your concern. I need you to drive as fast as you can without breaking the speed limit."

The cabby looked straight ahead and proceeded on in silence. But somewhere between silence and Ivy's last words, she lost it. She began to cry uncontrollably and without ceasing. Before long, the car slowed to a crawl and then abruptly stopped.

The cabby leaned his arm on the back of his seat and turned toward Ivy. "Miss, what is it? I can't drive wi' you screaming like that. Do I need to take you bac' the hospital?"

"No, no, don't do that," Ivy shouted. "I don't want to go back there. They've taken away my dignity."

"Who, Miss? Who's taken away your dignity?" There was silence. "Talk to me so I can help you."

"My sorry ass husband, that's who. He and my mother have stripped me of my dignity."

"Is there anyone I can call? You don't need to be by yourself."

Ivy's face was stained with her tears. Her chest heaved in and out as her inner turmoil got the best of her. "I don't need anybody. I've had it up to here with people, especially the liars and cheaters. Every time I put my trust in someone, they disappoint me. People disappoint you when you think you can count on them the most. No more."

"May I ask what happened?"

Ivy sat up straight and wiped her face with the back of her hand. "Do you really want to know? Do you really want to know?" she screamed.

"If it will help."

"I'm going to tell you. I recently married what I thought was the man of my dreams." Ivy picked up her left hand and fumbled with her rings. "He put this nice big rock ⟨o⟩y finger, and I believed we were going to have a ⟨⟩ life together. I was hiding a secret when we got ⟨⟩ I was pregnant with our child, but when I finally ⟨⟩ he seemed happy that he was going to be a

"Yesterday, all hell broke loose. My mother and her twin baby boys were hit by a car while crossing the street."

"I'm so sorry…"

"Don't interrupt. I haven't even gotten to the good part of the story. Anyway, they were rushed to the hospital. My mother and one of the twins were pretty banged up. Come to find out that one of the twins sustained an injury that might require a blood transfusion. And because of that, my parents found out that the baby had a rare blood type that neither of them has. But guess who did? You guessed right if you said my husband. Can you believe that crap? My husband has the baby's blood type and carries the baby's genes. Do you want to know why? You don't have to respond because the answer is obvious. My husband slept with my mother."

"Whoa," said the cabby. "Now I understand why you're so upset. Don't worry; they'll pay for what they've done to you."

Ivy pounded the back of the driver's seat. She wasn't about to tell the cabby that her mother and husband conceived those twins long before she'd been with Malik. In fact, her fascination of Malik started a long time ago, however, when she suddenly ran into him in Atlanta, she pursued him for the hell of it. Little did she know that they would end up as man and wife. "They sure as hell will," Ivy said, continuing her rant for her lone audience. "They're going to pay. I don't care if I never see them again. If I was driving this damn taxi and saw my husband on the side of the road, I'd run over his ass and wouldn't even look in my rearview mirror to see if he was dead or alive. I'd keep on driving."

"You can't mean that."

"The hell I do." Ivy took a breath. "I think I feel better now. Please take me home."

The cabby started up the car and pulled back onto the interstate. He looked into his rearview mirror. Ivy had a severe frown on her face. "Are you sure you're going to be all right?"

"Oh, yeah, I'm fine. Don't you worry about me. Your job is to get me safely to my destination. It's the other folks that have used and abused me for the last time that need to worry."

Forty-Nine

**T**oni quickly showered and dressed. She couldn't wait to meet Anissa for dinner to get the four-one-one on Malik Mason. The itch was so great to get the scoop that she hadn't heard the phone ring.

Picking up her BlackBerry, Toni smiled. The call was from Jefferson. He missed her already, she surmised. She'd talk with him later. Her focus was somewhere else, and this wasn't the time to deviate from her train of thought. Not only was she helping her cousin, Sterling, to win a senate seat, she was about to get paid.

Ever since Anissa dropped that juicy tidbit in her lap, her mind had been racing. In order to realize the full benefit of this salacious bit of gossip, she was going to have to take it to a higher source, one that would be willing to pay top dollar for a good, juicy story that had all of the characteristics that reporters and editors called headline news—a story that was about to turn a political race upside down, cause a sensational scandal, and sell lots and lots of papers.

Toni took one last look in the mirror. She ran her tongue across her front teeth, sighed, put a dab more of her favorite MAC lipstick on, then exhaled. *You look fabulous*, she thought to herself.

Grabbing her hobo bag, Toni sashayed out the door. She trotted to her red BMW coupe that sat parked in an underground garage, got in, and high-tailed it to the restaurant. Toni was excited and her adrenaline flowed like oil in an Alaskan pipeline. She felt giddy and anxious, as she salivated at the thought of the feast of gossip she expected to hear from Anissa. For sure, she'd have to break off a few dollars for Anissa when she got paid. The one thing Toni wasn't sure of was how Jefferson would react to the whirlwind she was about to create that concerned his family, but it wasn't her immediate concern. Getting paid for what America wanted to hear— the unflattering backside to a candidate's good traits so they'd have something to talk about at the water cooler the next day—was all Toni cared about.

Toni found Anissa already nursing a Long Island Iced Tea when she arrived. They greeted each other with air kisses, then settled into their seats. Toni couldn't hide her smile.

"Girl, you look radiant," Toni said to Anissa, who was dressed in a pair of navy-blue crepe slacks, a white military style blouse with navy-blue trim around the collar and around the base of the three-inch cuffs, with round gold buttons that ran down the front of the shirt and also down the length of the cuffs. On her feet, she wore four-inch navy designer peep-toe pumps.

"You look fabulous, too," Anissa exclaimed. "That new man of yours must be polishing all of your bells and whistles."

"And then some," Toni confirmed.

"Well, you are blushing and I need some of that to rub off on me."

"What about the guy you see off and on?"

"You mean Perry Rush? Toni, he's a married man with no plans of leaving his wife. I see him now and again when I require an escort or need the fire between my legs extinguished." Toni laughed at Anissa's banter. "But that's all he is to me, and frankly, I like the arrangement because it's safe," Anissa continued. "When the night is over, he goes back to his wife and I go back to my carefree life."

"As beautiful a person that you are, you don't need to settle for less. There are some good, single brothers out there that would love to take you home to momma and put a ring on it, as Beyoncé would say."

"So is your man getting ready to put a ring on your hand?"

"Ouch. I'll say this, Anissa. I'm working on it. I understand his divorce is getting ready to be final any day. I'm working on it. Now let's talk about Mr. Malik Mason, the baby maker and heart breaker. Give me the full scoop... the uncut version."

Anissa gave the rundown, as little as it was, while Toni's voice recorder picked up every word. "Oh," Anissa said, shaking her finger in Toni's direction, "I forgot to tell you that Malik Mason's wife is pregnant. He's got a crappy-looking family tree to showcase in front of his supporters—a son by his mother-in-law and child by his wife. I can't wait to see how that's going to look in ink."

"Believe you me, all of black America is going to hang their heads in shame, while the white folks will say, *there must be something in the water in North Carolina because that state is full of scandal.*"

"Edwards will probably welcome the diversion since the attention has been on him for so long. Scandalous."

"Dinner was great, but I've got to run and write this story. Thanks for sharing with me."

"While I'm not one to go and drop a dime on someone, there was no way I could keep this to myself. Be good, Toni. I'll hit you up later in the week."

"Sounds good. Love you, girl."

"Love you back. And I hope I get to meet the new man in your life, soon."

"You will."

Toni sashayed out of the restaurant and jumped into her car. She felt like someone who'd won an Oscar—a golden statue in the hand that she'd melt into liquid gold as soon as she returned home. Oh yeah, the Associated Press, CNN, MSNBC, BET, *Ebony* magazine, *Jet* would all vie for the four-one-one. True it was a local affair, but by the time she put the finishing touches on this story it would not only draw the attention of the citizens in the great state of North Carolina but it'll be publicized nationally. Given the political climate and all of the misdeeds of the past, whether senate hopeful Malik Mason realizes it or not, he's going down in the archives entitled Political Hall of Shame. Shelton may be on his way to winning the seat in Fayetteville, North Carolina, but she, Ms. Toni Gillette, will be recognized for her journalistic capabilities.

Fifty

"Has anyone seen Ivy?" Winter asked, as she walked into her mother's hospital room with Evan on her hip. She watched as her brothers hunched up their shoulders followed by blank stares. "I've called her cell at least a dozen times and she hasn't answered." It seemed no one was in any real panic at her announcement.

"I'm sure she was upset when she left here," Margo offered, not knowing what else to say. "Set Evan on the bed with me."

"Of course, she was, Mom," Winter said, depositing Evan next to Margo. Margo kissed him. "To hear her husband professing his love for her mother would make anybody sick."

"J.R. and I will go look for Ivy, Winter," Winston said. "She may be in the snack bar or outside on the hospital grounds."

"Maybe Malik caught up with her," J.R. offered. "He may have taken her home."

"Without saying a word to us? That would be just like him," Winter said. "However, I hope Ivy isn't with him.

She needs to be around positive people right now. All they're going to do is argue. Ivy's got her plate full after what she learned yesterday. God, I hate Malik. He's changed so much."

"Some friendships weren't made to last," Winston said. He looked over at his mother who was watching the trio without uttering a word. Winston looked away. "Come on, J.R., let's go look for Ivy."

"All right. Winter, call me when Elaine arrives." J.R. smiled.

"I like her, J.R." Winter said. "She'd be a nice addition to the family."

"Not so fast," J.R. said. "We've talked about marriage, but we're going to take it slow."

"Oh my goodness," were Margo's first words in the last fifteen minutes. "My son is in love."

J.R. grinned from ear to ear and before long, the room erupted in laughter. This was the first bright spot since Margo was hospitalized.

"I'm happy that you're happy, J.R." Margo said.

"Thanks, Momma. That means a lot to me."

"Okay, scoot and find Ivy," Margo said, trying to wave her hand. "And Miss Winter, I need for you to check on Ian. When will your daddy be back?"

Winter blinked her eye at Margo. "Worried about Daddy? He had to run home. Said he'd be an hour or two and then he'd be back."

"Okay." Margo turned from Winter and hugged and

kissed Evan. "I love my babies, and I'm so proud of the way your daddy stepped up to the plate."

"Mom, I've got to ask you this. It may be none of my business, but I've got to ask anyway."

Margo stared at Winter without saying a word. Her face was void of expression, possibly anticipating Winter's next words. She held Evan tight and braced for the question.

"What are you going to do about Malik being Ian's father? You know Ivy is very hurt."

"You're right; it's none of your business."

"Ivy is going to always be reminded that her little brother is also her husband's child."

Margo found the remote on the bed and raised the head of her bed as far as she could stand it. She held Evan tight and glared at Winter. "Let me tell you something. I'm not proud of having made that one mistake of sleeping with Malik...and heaven forbid that I'd have a child because of it."

"You know where babies...."

"Don't let me have to get up from this bed and knock you into next week, Winter. I'm still your mother and you need to be careful what you say to me. Now I'm going to talk, and all I want you to do is listen. No one knew that Ivy and Malik were having a relationship, but for your information, it was long after I'd been with Malik. I'm not sure why Ivy chose to be with him. I've always felt that Ivy liked older men because once she had a secret crush on Angelica's husband, Hamilton. Whatever the reason, I'm not responsible for the complex situation Ivy is in, at least not directly.

"I love my daughter, and if she hadn't shunned me for so long and was forthcoming about her relationship with Malik, I might have been able to save her from this awkward place we've found ourselves. I know she's upset and hurting, but sometimes, we bring on our own calamity, although I'm sure Ivy never had any reason to see the train wreck that was about to enter her life.

"I hope the boys find her so we can talk. I need to talk with her right away before this situation is blown even more out of proportion. I want Ivy to understand that I love her and in no way would I ever try and hurt her. Malik is the one Ivy needs to worry about. I'm not sure his intentions were pure when he married Ivy."

"He's in love with you, Mom."

"Winter, I don't love him. Not then and not now. Oh, I'll admit he was great company when your father was in jail, but that's all it was...a platonic relationship. In the five years your father was incarcerated, Malik never once touched me."

"Thanks, Mom. I needed to hear that. Why don't you get some rest? I'll take Evan. He probably needs to be fed and his diaper changed. I'll see if Winston and J.R. have located Ivy."

"What time did you say your daddy was going to return?"

Winter smiled. "Asking about Daddy again, huh? He'll be here shortly."

"Thank you for taking care of Evan. I appreciate you."

"You're welcome, Mom. I'll go over and check on Ian and let you know what's going on if Dr. Anderson doesn't beat me to it.

"Okay, baby girl. Love you."

Margo kissed Evan on the cheek. Winter picked him up from her mother's bed and left the room.

# Fifty-One

After stopping home for fresh clothing and checking in at the office, Jefferson headed back to the hospital. He wanted Margo to know that he was there for her if she needed him.

Driving along the busy Raleigh streets, his mind drifted to his liaison with Toni and what it all meant. Jefferson wasn't sure how she fit into the equation, but in the back of his mind he still had reservations—something wasn't sitting quite right. He recalled Toni's sudden phone call that she had to take—in another room no doubt, and the blank look on her face when she came from behind the closed door and found him dressed. It was a look you see on children's faces when they've been caught stealing cookies from Momma's cookie jar.

Jefferson drove on and parked his thoughts temporarily. He was nearing the hospital, and all of his attention needed to be centered on the twins and Margo. Just as he was about to turn into the hospital parking lot, a car—a black BMW—whizzed by. Jefferson did a double take and realized it was Malik. He wished he had another opportunity to talk to Ivy. It felt good that he and his daughter were able to communicate.

Scrambling out of his car, Jefferson hurried through the hospital lobby and up the elevator to Margo's room. Just before he proceeded inside, he took a deep breath. Not even an hour had passed since he'd been with Toni, getting a quickie to calm his nerves. Toni was mysterious and he was fighting some internal feeling that wanted but at the same time warned him to not pursue a relationship with this woman. And now that he was at the hospital door to his soon-to-be ex-wife's room, his heart was doing a flip-flop.

Margo was surrounded by her family and she felt comforted. Dr. Anderson had even allowed Jefferson to bring baby Ian to her room as his prognosis was good and would probably be released in the next day or so. Margo smiled as idle chit chat passed from one to the other, sometimes drowning out the voices on the television that was anchored to the front wall that no one was watching. She smiled to herself as she watched the playfulness between J.R. and Elaine, happy that J.R. had settled down and was thinking about the rest of his life.

With the help of Winter, Margo cuddled her baby boys. She kissed and hugged them as if there were no tomorrow. She looked up and saw Jefferson staring at her, his gaze piercing her heart. With a wave of her hand, she invited him to sit on the edge of the bed with them, and when he came and sat down her heart skipped a beat.

He was still handsome with the same rugged good looks that stole her heart all those years ago. He seemed to get better with age—like a fine wine. While he may have picked up a tad bit of weight, he still had the body frame of a twenty-year-old. Smidgens of gray now streaked his hair but gave him a distinguished persona that she knew women loved.

Jefferson picked Evan up from the bed and placed him on his lap and kissed the top of his head. This made Margo melt. They'd endured a lot of things together, neither of them blameless for what their lives had become, but at that moment, Margo realized that rather than be apart she wanted her husband.

"Winter, how long has it been since you've tried to get in touch with Ivy?" Margo asked.

"It's been more than a half-hour; I'll try again." Winter pulled out her cell phone and dialed Ivy's number. She waited while everyone looked on. Glancing around the room until her eyes connected with her mother's, Winter shook her head sideways. She hit the OFF button, squeezed her lips together, and didn't say a word.

"I saw Malik barrel out of the parking lot as I was pulling in," Jefferson said. "I didn't see Ivy in the car, although I could be wrong. I barely got a glimpse of Malik, but the car seemed empty otherwise. Did you see her this morning?"

Margo was quiet and looked over at Winter.

"What's going on?" Jefferson asked, puzzled. "Did something happen that I'm not aware of?"

"Ivy heard Malik tell Mom how much he loved her and wanted to do right by her and Ian," Winter explained.

Jefferson jumped up from the bed with Evan in his arms. "What?"

"Pops, Winston and I searched the hospital for Ivy after Winter called and told us what happened, but we haven't been able to find her. And that was over two hours ago," J.R. added.

"I can't believe that sorry-ass bastard had the nerve to come to this room," Jefferson retorted. "How in the hell could he come up in here talking about loving another woman when his wife, my daughter, is carrying his child? I can't even comprehend what she sees in that fool."

"Calm down, Jefferson," Margo said.

Jefferson turned and stared at Margo. He opened his mouth, but whatever he was about to say didn't pass from his tongue to his lips. Margo waited, anticipated what was on his mind that he couldn't formulate into words, although she had a very good idea. It was best Jefferson didn't utter them because the good feeling she had for him would have vanished in an instant.

Jefferson took a deep breath. "I'm going to Fayetteville."

"And what are you going to do?" Margo asked with concern in her voice.

"I'm going to make sure our daughter is all right. If she was here earlier, tell me how did she just vanish into thin air? Surely, she would have told someone that she was leaving. And if she's not with Malik, where in the hell is she?"

"Dad," Winston cut in, "maybe she was in the car with Malik and you didn't see her."

"Well, I'm troubled by the fact that no one has been able to talk to her since she left the room. Winston, you want to ride?"

"I'm going, too," J.R. cut in.

"You take care of Elaine."

"Elaine is coming with us," J.R. said in final. "I want to make sure my sister is okay. And Malik better come correct because if anything happens to Ivy, I'm going to eat him alive."

"That settles it. Winter, take care of your mother and the boys." Jefferson kissed Evan on the top of his head and crossed the room where Ian was still sitting with Margo and kissed him also. He gave Evan to Winter and turned to look at Margo. He leaned over and kissed her on the forehead. "We'll call you after we get to Fayetteville and let you know what's going on."

Margo sighed. "Okay. Please don't go and make matters worse for Ivy."

"All we want to know is that she's all right," Jefferson said. "If she's fine, I'm fine. We'll turn around and come right back to Raleigh."

"Don't worry, Momma," J.R. said. "We're only concerned about Ivy's well-being. Elaine will keep me straight."

"I'll keep them all straight, Mrs. Myles."

"Thanks, Elaine. I feel better that you're going to be there to supervise my men. They can get crazy sometimes."

"No problem."

"We'll let her think she's supervising," J.R. said.

"Let's go," Jefferson said. And the room was suddenly quiet.

"What's going through your head, Mom?" Winter suddenly asked.

Margo gazed at the nameless faces on the TV screen. "I hope Ivy is all right…that she hasn't allowed what Malik said this morning to get to her. After all, she's going to be a senator's wife and a new mother down the road, and she'll need all of her strength."

"Mom, let's be real. You know that what Malik said hurt Ivy. She loves him, and now you have threatened her chance at a happy marriage."

"Oh, don't blame me for what her marriage has become. Ivy wasn't clueless about what had gone on between Malik and me."

"I don't mean you had anything directly to do with it, but because Ivy is married to Malik it changes everything, and I'm sure she sees you as a threat."

"I'm no threat to her or anyone else. My pulse doesn't jump for Malik. I have no desire for him in any way, shape, or form."

"What about Daddy? I saw the way you were checking him out…pimping him with your eyes."

"Winter, you need to take your brothers, change their diapers and feed them. If you don't mind, I need to rest." Margo kissed her babies. "Momma loves you. Mind your sister."

"Mom, I can't take Ian with me."

A hushed silence came over the room at the sound of the door opening. Margo waved her hand. "Here is the nurse to take Ian back to the pediatric ward. Now let me rest."

Winter placed Ian in the nurse's arms, picked up Evan and his diaper bag, and left the room. Tears slid down Margo's face. She prayed that Ivy was all right, wherever she was.

Fifty-Two

The political climate in North Carolina was at fever pitch. Staunch democrats battled staunch republicans for incumbent and vacant seats in the upcoming primary. The NC senatorial races in districts throughout the state were getting nasty, pitting foe against foe, helped along by unhealthy negative campaign ads on television, political blogs, Facebook and Twitter. Not a day went by that a candidate didn't try to assassinate their opponent's character, beliefs, and credibility. Even Dr. Shelton Wright's integrity was put on the hot seat more times than he cared, but the God in him kept him from going off and responding in the way the devil would've been pleased. He had his eye on the prize, and winning the senate seat in his district was within reach.

Dr. Wright smiled when he saw his son approach his office at campaign headquarters in the late of the afternoon. Phillip was going to be a fine doctor one day and Dr. Wright looked forward to him joining his practice.

"Taking a break from the studies, son?" Dr. Wright asked.

"Yes. Just completed some exams and had to get away

from hematology and carotid arteries for awhile. I came by to see how the senior Dr. Wright was doing on his campaign."

"Things are going well. I couldn't do it if I didn't have two very fine staff doctors at the clinic to back me up. I need to get a new ad out, but I haven't been able to get any of the Myleses on the telephone. Haven't you gone out with the daughter…what's her name…?"

"Her name is Winter, Dad. And she's a very nice woman. She doesn't know it yet, but she's going to be my wife one day."

"Hold up, young man. You've got studies that demand all of your attention, which means that you have no time for distractions. You don't need anything to take you off course from what you're trying to achieve."

"Spoken like a true parent…"

"Yes, a parent that has invested lots and lots of money toward your success as a future doctor. And don't you forget it. Lord knows you wouldn't want to disappoint your mother."

"Dad, I want to be a doctor, so there's no way Winter will be a distraction. But what I was about to say before you went on your tirade about me keeping my focus, Winter's mother was in a bad car accident yesterday. Her father and brothers have been at the hospital."

"I'm sorry to hear it. I thought the Myleses were divorced."

"Their divorce isn't final yet, but from what Winter

tells me, her father didn't want the divorce and she believes that her mother has had second thoughts about it. It may have something to do with her new babies. Twins."

"Babies? How old is Winter's mother? I'm sure she isn't a spring chicken, but if she looks anything like Winter, she's probably worn it well." Dr. Wright laughed at his own joke.

"I haven't met her yet, but I was planning to go to the hospital to meet up with Winter and meet her mother. I'll let you know whether or not she looks like she's too old to have newborns. But on the serious side, Dad, I'm digging this girl."

"But, Phillip…"

Phillip threw up his hand. "You have nothing to worry about, Dad."

"All right, all right, all right. Give my regards to Winter's mother and to Jefferson. Tell him I'd like to speak with him in the next day or so to discuss a new television ad campaign."

"I will. Since you seem to be doing all right, I guess I'll mosey on over to the hospital." Phillip held up two fingers and made the peace sign, flicked it in his father's direction, then left the premises. Dr. Wright smiled.

Toni Gillette sailed across the keyboard on her laptop, her French-tipped acrylic nails tapping the keys at the rate of sixty-words-per-minute, as she recreated the story given to her by Anissa. Sensational storytelling was one of her greater attributes and she colored Malik's encounter with Anissa with words and phrases such as "candidly admitted" and "shocked to find out." And everyone, while they weren't aware of it yet, was going to be shocked when they found out that one of North Carolina's senatorial candidates, Mr. Malik Mason, had fathered a son by his wife's mother—one of a pair, whose twin brother's DNA doesn't match Malik's, which takes family relations to a whole different level. And if one thought that bit of news was a bombshell, wait until they learn that Malik Mason's newlywed wife is carrying a package of her own in the oven.

Two typewritten, double-spaced pages that would probably be reduced to one stared back at Toni on the monitor. Toni was pleased with herself. She already had several buyers for her story with several more in negotiations. With her high-level media contacts, she was able to navigate her way to the publications that would pay her for what she was about to deliver. It was true that Malik wasn't as big a player as John Edwards when he ran for President, but with her cousin Sterling's name attached to the story with implications that this would be a better story, Toni maneuvered herself on to several payrolls. She was given less than twenty-four hours to deliver the goods because everyone wanted to be first to break the story.

Satisfied with the content of the article, she saved it again and prepared to deliver it to the various publications. She had to admit to herself that she was doing this more for herself than she was for Sterling, but it would be a proud moment in their family for Sterling to go from the basketball court to a state senate seat. Others had done so, and it was Sterling's turn.

Toni gave her story one last going over and then hit the send key. Yesterday's news was only a rumble in the jungle; tomorrow it was going to be a full-fledged war.

Fifty-Three

**M**alik was mad as hell. He'd been all over the hospital looking for Ivy, who seemed to have vanished into thin air. He was concerned about her well being, especially since she had walked in on his conversation with Margo and heard him exclaim his love for her.

Malik had no intention of hurting Ivy, but then he received her phone call in which she calmly told him that she was going to ruin him...pay him back for the heartache he'd caused her. If he wanted to talk, she'd meet him at home because she was already on her way.

Driving in a fog, Malik hadn't noticed that the traffic on Interstate 95 was suddenly at a standstill. He slammed on the brakes and hit the steering wheel hard for being so careless in not concentrating on the road. He dialed Ivy's cell number, but there wasn't an answer. Then he tried his home number, but no answer there either.

Irritated, Malik tried the number for campaign headquarters and was about to hang up when he heard Milo's friendly voice.

"Mr. Mason, we've been worried about you since we haven't seen you in a couple of days."

"My mother-in-law was in a car accident, and we had to go see about her. Is Perry there?"

"Yes, Mr. Rush is here. I'll get him. I hope your mother-in-law is all right."

"She's going to pull through just fine. Thanks for asking."

Malik waited patiently for Perry to get on the line. His mind was going in and out, wondering how he was going to handle the new developments in his life. The situation was what it was, but now he had to refocus on his campaign. He hadn't ventured into political waters and drummed up support to not win. Everything Perry said to him earlier came running back. Malik knew that if he was to be a serious contender in this race something was going to have to give.

"Malik, I was wondering when I'd hear from you."

"I'm on my way back to Fayetteville. There's been some kind of accident on the interstate so I'm stuck in traffic."

"Well, stop by headquarters before you do anything else."

Malik thought about Ivy's threat, but she could wait until he stopped by headquarters and his computer store. He needed to handle his more pressing business first. After all, what was Ivy going to do? "I'll be there as soon as I can maneuver around this traffic. Give me about thirty or forty-five minutes."

"Okay, dawg."

"How's everything going? Is Sterling still ahead?"

"Contributions are coming in, things have mellowed out, and Sterling is still in the lead…only by a slim margin. He won't keep it for long."

"No, he won't. I'm back and refocused. We're going to do this, Perry."

"That's what I'm talking about. If you feel confident, then I feel confident."

"I am, Perry. And I'm going to leave all this other BS behind. Got me distracted for a moment, but I'm back on track. We're going to kick Sterling's butt to high heavens. Have you been able to get anything on his wife?"

"I'm still digging. Hopefully, we won't have to go there. It appears that the article Ms. Toni Gillette wrote didn't hurt you too bad. I don't get her angle, but it didn't carry the kind of punch she was looking for, I guess. She's a tabloid wannabe, but the only way she can do so is by smearing your good name."

"Well, you need to get information on her so that if we have to put her in check, we'll have the ammunition to do so."

"Gotcha, Malik. You're sounding like your old self again. Glad to know that our work isn't in vain. By the way, the number of people requesting yard signs has doubled since last week."

"That's a good sign, Perry. Keep up the good work. I'll see you as soon as I can."

"All right, dawg."

Talking with Perry gave him the relief he needed.

Some of the stress and tension that had formed in the base of Malik's neck and along his shoulders seemed to dissolve. It was a great relief to know that his current family situation hadn't completely spilled over into his campaign. He was on sure footing again. He called his store and was happy to know that sales were steady and that Reggie was on top of things.

## Fifty-Four

Jefferson barreled down Interstate 40 with only a few miles left before he could exit onto Interstate 95 that would take him to Fayetteville. With Winston in the front passenger seat and J.R. and Elaine in the back, the conversation was light with each person, except Elaine, giving their assessment of all that had transpired since Margo's accident.

"I hope Ivy doesn't allow this thing with Momma and Malik to destroy her self-confidence," J.R. said. "She and I were always close, and the one thing I can say about my sister is that she's not always that smart when it comes to dealing with the male species."

"So what happened?" Winston wanted to know. "Why Malik of all people? He has had more women than I've got fingers and toes. Every Christmas we wondered who he'd bring to Christmas dinner at our house. Remember that, Dad?"

"Nothing but the truth. He was my frat and we always wondered when he'd settle down. When I heard he had gotten married, it threw me for a loop."

"Yeah, he married Toni…I can't remember her last

name," Winston interjected. "She was real nice and sweet. I know Malik went crazy when she died."

"Speaking of Toni, Pops, did you ever get up with Ms. Gillette…show her that you could still mack?"

"Elaine, I don't know what your boyfriend is talking about," Jefferson said, as he grinned. "She's one of our clients, which reminds me we have a retainer and haven't done any work on her project yet."

"We'll get on it first thing in the morning, Pops. Winston and I are going to the office tomorrow. But you didn't answer my question."

"J.R., I've always prided myself on keeping my professional, business life separate from my personal one. The two combined are like fuses waiting for a spark to ignite and most times to the detriment. I'll agree that Ms. Gillette is an attractive woman and deserves a backward glance, but I'm not ready to get involved with anyone at the moment."

"That's because he still has a Jones for mother dearest." Winston coughed. "I would love to see him and Mom back together again. What about you, J.R.?"

"If that's what Pops want. However, if he and Mom are unhappy and feel they should be free to go and explore other options, who am I to meddle?"

All was quiet on J.R.'s last note. And out of nowhere, Elaine spoke up.

"What about us, J.R?" Elaine asked.

"Oooooh, she got you on that one," Winston said.

"I'm serious, J.R. What about us? Do you see yourself with me in a committed relationship? I love you, but I won't give up five years of my life waiting on you to decide."

"My, my, my," Jefferson said, snickering under his breath. "I'm with Elaine. Don't string her along forever. If you intend to build a life together, don't wait until her hair turns gray."

"Pops, you aren't helping at all. I didn't ask for your two cents."

"Your mother and I stayed together for twenty-five years, although there were some rough spots…"

"A tidal wave," Winston reminded him.

"Whatever. But I knew that Margo was going to be my wife the moment I laid eyes on her. I pursued her until she couldn't run anymore. We were both in good places at the time we got married—both successful in our careers, even though we were a young couple at the time. We knew we wanted to start a family, and the rest is history."

"That's a nice story, Mr. Myles," Elaine said. "I'm sure that J.R. feels the same way I do and that sooner or later it will happen."

"What?" Winston asked, turning around in his seat to find J.R. and Elaine making goo-goo eyes at each other.

"Marriage," Elaine managed to say as she placed a kiss on J.R.'s lips.

"All right, no making out in your daddy's car," Jefferson said. Everyone erupted in laughter.

All of a sudden Jefferson put on the brakes. "Damn, what's going on? Interstate 95 is backed up. I've got to get off of here if we're going to get to Fayetteville in a reasonable amount of time."

"Dad, let's get off in Dunn," Winston said. "I know the back way into Fayetteville. Anyway, where are we going to look for Ivy?"

"We're going to start with their residence. She moved in with Malik, and if he hasn't moved, I know exactly where he lives. Give me some directions, Winston."

"Okay, Dad. Get off at the next exit."

Winston, J.R., and Elaine rode in silence as Jefferson navigated the back roads into Fayetteville. Jefferson's mind wandered from Margo to Malik, Malik to Ivy, and then back to Margo. A myriad of emotions ran through his brain, unsure of where he fit in any of the equations he'd conjured up in his head. At the moment, though, Ivy's welfare became paramount in his thoughts, given how she'd suddenly disappeared from sight.

"Home of the 82nd Airborne," Jefferson called out. "This is the last place I was stationed before I got out of the service, Elaine. Yes, Margo and I plus four hyperactive, hormone-enraged teenagers had left the safety of the United States Army and settled into civilian life."

"Hormone-enraged, Dad?" Winston asked. "You've got to be kidding me."

"Well, you weren't all that bad. They were good kids, Elaine. Don't get me wrong. They were just into everything. Girl problems…boy problems, especially Winter."

Elaine laughed from the back seat: "Mr. Myles, you're so funny. Now I know where J.R. gets his humor."

There was a collective sigh from Jefferson and sons as he slowed the car, pulled to the curb and stopped in front of an upscale condominium community. The city of Fayetteville boasted a lot of hidden secrets—its beauty sometimes lying behind veils of tall trees and shrubs and in the depths of enclaves with their winding roads that twisted and turned, not lending itself to the casual visitor or long-time resident who shopped and banked in their immediate local area.

Hands still gripping the steering wheel, Jefferson finally glanced up at the condo where Malik now lived with his daughter, so he assumed. Vivid memories of good times came to mind when the two best buddies would get together, shoot the breeze, or chill out in front of the television to watch an NFL or NBA game with a cold one in their hands. Jefferson grunted and let out another sigh.

"We're not going to just sit, are we?" Winston asked, twisting his neck to look at the now stoic group. "I mean… we drove all the way down here to see if Ivy was here… didn't we?"

"I don't see Ivy's or Malik's car," J.R. offered.

"You're right, Winston," Jefferson said finally. "We came to see if Ivy made it home. I had a moment; that's all."

"Why don't you let J.R. and I go and check, Dad? I know this is awkward for you, being that you and Malik are estranged."

"I came here for my daughter, Ivy," Jefferson shouted. "I don't give a damn about Malik. Let's go. Elaine, it might be wise for you to stay in the car."

"No, problem, Mr. Myles," Elaine said, squeezing J.R.'s hand. "I'll be all right."

Jefferson, J.R. and Winston exited the car and strolled up to Malik's condo. They surveyed their surroundings as if they were casing out the place like thieves who planned to rob the place at another time.

Jefferson rang the doorbell, while J.R. and Winston bounced from one foot to the other in anticipation. After ringing the doorbell two more times, Jefferson put his ear to the door but was unable to hear anything. "Call Ivy's cell," Jefferson said.

J.R. was quick on the draw with Ivy's number already on speed dial in his phone. He looked up at his father, then at Winston, shaking his head from left to right to let them know that there wasn't a response. While J.R. redialed Ivy's number, Jefferson placed a call to Winter.

"Hey, Dad, did you find Ivy?"

"We're at the house now, but no one seems to be at home. I'm still worried because she isn't answering her cell phone either. I guess you haven't heard from her."

"No. Ivy is acting out. When she gets like this, it means she wants to be left alone. We have to hope and pray that she's all right."

"I want to believe that. I wouldn't have made such a rash decision to come down here if she hadn't just walked out without telling anyone where she was going. I don't understand her thinking, although I'm aware what's at the root of her disappearance. But that's been hours ago now, and there's no sign of Ivy or Malik anywhere."

"She'll show up. But like you, I'd like to know where that crazy sister of mine is."

"How's your mother?"

"She was fine when I left the hospital. I'm at Mom's place with…Phillip Wright."

"What's he doing there?"

"He was on his way to the hospital to see Mom when Evan and I were leaving. We are seeing each other."

"And when were you going to tell me? After the wedding?"

"Dad, you are tripping. I'm not Ivy. And you'd be the first person I'd tell if I was to make that kind of decision because I'm going to make you spend every dime on my big day."

"Now who's tripping?" Both Jefferson and Winter laughed.

"Phillip said his father, Dr. Wright, would like for you to call him at your convenience."

"I'll do that. And you and I are going to have a father-daughter talk when I see you. All right, I'm going to let you go. Call us if you hear anything from Ivy."

"Okay, Dad."

Jefferson clicked the END button on his cell.

"Who's getting married?" J.R. inquired after Jefferson was finished.

"No one. Winter is entertaining a new boyfriend."

"Yeah, she and Phillip Wright are getting a little cozy," Winston put in. "He's the one who has his hands full because Winter, although she's my sister and birth mate, is a piece of work."

The guys laughed.

"So what do you propose we do now?" Winston asked. "We didn't come all this way not to get any answers."

"Clearly, Ivy doesn't want to be found," Jefferson said. "Winter hasn't heard from her either. Let's hang around for at least thirty minutes to see if anyone shows up."

Fifty-Five

It was business as usual when Malik pushed through the doors of his campaign headquarters. The few volunteers who had come in were busy talking to constituents about their needed support by way of their vote and money. Malik nodded to a couple of the ladies who looked up with phones glued to their ears as he walked past, but his main mission was to talk with his campaign manager, Perry.

Perry looked up when Malik entered his office. A smile jumped on his face, delighted to see his good friend.

"What's the good word, Perry?"

"Man, there's some bitter stuff going on out there. Negative campaign ads are heating up the airwaves pitting this one against that one."

"What about Sterling? Have you seen anything from his group?"

"No, dawg. This is going to be a cakewalk for you. Checked the polls this morning, and you're getting your edge back—up a few points, and every point counts."

"Well, Perry, I'm in it to win it. Good job. Keep your eyes and ears open. Where are all the volunteers?"

"Don't worry about that, dawg. They'll be here later this afternoon. Some took a lunch break. You aren't paying me to slumber. By the way, we've received almost ten thousand dollars in the past three days. That comes from aggressive campaign marketing and doing it the Obama way. People don't mind letting go of five or ten dollars they might have spent on lunch this week when they know that their seed money is going to help elect the candidate for the people."

Malik sighed and allowed a broad smile to cross his face. "My man, Perry. I have all the faith and confidence in the world that you will do the job. I'm going to stop by my store and then head home to check on Ivy."

"Oh, how is her mother? And the other thing?"

"The other thing meaning my bastard child?"

"Ooooh, that was...was...I don't know what to say except...nasty."

"Well, Margo is going to be fine. She broke her hip and will be bedridden for a while. As for the baby, Margo prefers that I have nothing to do with him unless he gets ill. I suspect since I'm the only one with the baby's blood type, she'll come begging for my assistance. And with that said, I'm going to concentrate on winning this election. So for now, my dear friend, that's a taboo subject that I've put on the back burner."

Perry let out another smile. "Great to have you back, dawg. Now go on and take care of your business and I'll see you in a little while."

"Carry on, Perry. I'm out. I'll see you around six this evening."

"Okay."

As much as Malik tried to push Margo and Ian from his mind, he was unable to. The one thing he always wished for was an heir, a carbon copy of himself that he could boast and brag about as he moved through the various stages of his life. How could Margo, in good conscience, invite him to give blood to the son he sired but in another breath say that she didn't want him involved in their son's life. There was no way he was going to allow that to happen. For now, he'd let it ride…let Margo think he was honoring her request. Once the election was over and had his senate seat, he would make his move.

Malik stopped at the store and found all to be good; so he took his leave and headed home, whistling a tune he conjured up. Perry had certainly been a contributor to his mood change. He promised within himself that he'd make it up to Ivy; as extreme as his actions had been lately, he did care for her. Plus, Ivy was carrying his legitimate heir.

## Fifty-Six

K anye West was rocking his hit "Stronger" on the radio when Malik jumped into his BMW and switched on the ignition. Feeling the moment, Malik bobbed his head to the beat, even taking the liberty to rock his shoulders up and down like he was on the dance floor. His confidence had returned with a vengeance after his brief visit to campaign head-quarters and his computer sales center. Everything seemed to be in order, and with the one to two percent-age points ahead of his political rival, Sterling Garrison, Malik was back in the game and well on his way. He knew for sure, he'd have to the leave the drama with Margo and the baby in the closet for now because he wasn't going to let anything or anyone steal his thunder.

Driving toward home, Malik activated his Bluetooth and dialed Ivy's cell phone with his voice command. It rang and rang before finally going to voicemail. Malik clicked the Bluetooth off without leaving a message and let Kanye take the lead. "Stronger," Malik sang along with Kanye, his shoulders still moving to the beat. "I'm stronger."

As Malik slowed his car and pulled up into the driveway of his condo, he noticed he had company—unwanted company. There were four heads sitting at attention in the black Mercedes parked in front of his home, and immediately he was aware that his wife's side of the family had come to pay a visit.

Malik got out of his car and looked back at the group that stared back at him. At first, he was going to just go into the house, but on second thought, he strolled over to the passenger side of the Mercedes as the window slowly eased down.

"Hey, what's up?" Malik said, looking into Winston's face.

"We're looking for my sister," Winston replied. "Have you seen her?"

"I've been looking for her myself. She hasn't responded to any of my phone calls. I figured she was still in Raleigh with you all, after I went in search of her at the hospital and came up empty handed."

"Well, no one has seen or heard from her," Jefferson said, speaking for the first time. "I find that kind of odd. I would have at least thought she'd be in contact with her husband."

"I feel the same as you do. Check my cell phone. You'll find that I have been concerned as well. If you all want to come inside, you're welcome to do so. We can try calling her again."

"We'll do that," Jefferson said.

Without another second wasted, Jefferson, Winston,

J.R., and Elaine got out of the car and followed Malik. The confidence Malik felt only moments ago had suddenly evaporated into thin air. It wasn't just that his ex-buddy and sons were in pursuit of their daughter and sister, they looked like a motley crew who would spill blood if they didn't get what they had come for. Malik put the key in the door, unlocked it, and pushed it in.

Malik called out Ivy's name upon entering, but all was silent. The Myles clan stood in a cluster in the living room as Malik moved throughout the house—first the kitchen and then into the bedroom. And then he screamed.

The group rushed toward Malik's scream. "Ivy, my God, what have you done?" Before Malik could utter another word, everyone had piled into the room. Ivy's limp body was sprawled on the floor.

"Dammit," Jefferson said, "call nine-one-one. Does she have a pulse?"

"I don't know," Malik said through tears.

"Grab her arm and feel for a pulse. God knows how long she's been like this."

"She's taken an overdose of pills," Winston said, picking up the empty container of Percocet from off the comforter that covered the bed.

"Has someone got nine-one-one on the phone yet?" Jefferson screamed, stooping down to examine his unconscious daughter himself. "She has a very faint pulse."

"They're on the way," Elaine said, handing J.R. his

cell phone where he was now on the floor next to Ivy holding her hand.

"Come on, sis, don't leave me," J.R. said, rocking on his knees. "Hang in there, Ivy."

"She needs some air," Malik said, as he stood up, his face flooded with tears. "I don't believe this."

Jefferson stood up as well. "I told you that if you hurt my daughter, I was going to bury your ass."

"This is not the time or place, Jefferson. Ivy has overdosed, and that should be your first concern."

"Oh, she is my first concern, all right. But you're the reason she's in this condition."

"Always blowing hot steam and don't know what in the hell you're talking about."

*Blam*, went Jefferson's fist as he punched Malik in the stomach. Malik stumbled back, almost losing his footing as he hit the end of the chaise longue that sat in a corner of the bedroom.

"Dad, stop," Winston called out, wedging himself between Jefferson and Malik. "This is not the time or the place."

Still holding his stomach, Malik backed away. "You're going to pay for that, jailbird. Let's see how big you are when I press charges against your ass."

"If my little girl doesn't make it, you'll have every reason to press charges. You better hope and pray that nothing happens to Ivy."

"That goes for me, too," J.R. said through clenched

teeth, still rubbing Ivy's hands with eyes full of tears. "I'll kill you myself," he shouted to Malik.

"Enough of that kind of talk, guys," Elaine said, throwing her hands in the air. "We need to pray that Ivy makes it. All this talk of killing one another is not the way. God is not pleased and isn't going to even hear our prayers if you all keep talking like that."

"I hear a siren now," Winston said, moving from the bedroom to the living room. "I'll go and get the door."

Malik stood and looked down at Ivy, tears streaming from his eyes. He couldn't believe that after all the good reports he received today regarding his campaign being back on track, Ivy would take this moment to retaliate. No matter how hard Malik tried to shake it, he was connected to the Myles family in some crazy kind of way, and it seemed that their purpose was to make him pay for something…for what, he wasn't sure.

The paramedics rushed into the room at Winston's direction and took Ivy's vitals. The two paramedics looked at each other and immediately put Ivy on the stretcher. "We need to hurry," one of the paramedics began, "if she's going to make it." Winston gave them the bottle of Percocet, which they believed to be the culprit.

"She's pregnant," Malik said to them as an afterthought. "Please don't let anything happen to the baby." And they followed the paramedics outside, and then they were gone.

Jefferson grabbed the front of Malik's shirt and pulled

him within an inch of his face. Malik slapped Jefferson's hand away, and pulled his shirt down.

"I'm giving you fair warning," Jefferson began. "If anything should happen to my daughter, I will beat you to a pulp and serve your carcass to the vultures."

"As soon as I know Ivy is out of the woods, I'm going to the police and have your sorry ass arrested," Malik retorted. "Put your hands on me again, and I won't wait."

"Dad," Winston called, "Forget him. We've got to go to the hospital to see about Ivy."

"Be glad I have urgent business elsewhere." Jefferson spit on the ground and turned and walked away.

Malik watched as Jefferson and family got into their car and drove away before turning to get into his own. "You're going to pay, Jefferson," Malik said out loud. "No one disrespects me and thinks there's no consequence."

## Fifty-Seven

Toni Gillette dialed Jefferson's number, but her call went straight to voicemail. It was now nine in the evening, and for sure he wasn't still at the hospital worrying about the woman who was soon to be his ex-wife. She thought about the morning they had—steamy, juicy, and full of unadulterated sex. Toni blushed at the thought.

Her objective met for the day, Toni thought about her life as it was now. It was empty. Yes, the new career that she was remodeling for herself was off to a great start. To stay on track, she had to nail down some loose ends and stay on task according to the business plan she had created. Once the website was finished and her online political magazine was up and running, she'd be able to move full steam ahead. Having those juicy tidbits about Malik Mason had already done more than she had anticipated, giving her the jumpstart she needed.

A glass of wine would mellow her out. Toni went to the fridge and pulled out a chilled bottle of wine that was less than half full. She poured the remnants into a wineglass and took a sip.

Lonely was the word that best described how she felt. Fifteen years had passed since the one man she truly loved was killed in a boating accident off the coast of Florida. He was Cuban and went by the name Carlos. They'd been together for five glorious years. Toni called him her canary because he could make her sing high notes when they made love. Carlos was Toni's heart and soul—a breath of fresh air. He was a great dancer, exciting her with his sultry moves whether he was doing a Latin tango, a salsa, the cha cha cha, or a slow-moving rumba, especially when he wore a white linen shirt and slacks that lay against his olive-brown skin. And as a Latin lover, he was all that—nimble and passionate. He was the best!

Toni took another sip and closed her eyes to the memory. And then Jefferson came into view, although she wasn't certain why she'd become asphyxiated with him. But then she remembered how Margo talked about her good man who had fallen from grace—now tainted and labeled a bad boy. The picture Margo painted had Toni wanting to meet him, and when the opportunity presented itself, she made her move. He wasn't her Latin lover, but he was darn near close. But it was his warmth, grace, and the way he approached intimacy that made him almost Carlos' equal.

She'd make an appointment with him to see how the website was progressing. He'd have to give her time then, especially since she had already given him an advance for the project. Toni grabbed her BlackBerry and sent a text. It was business but she would settle for an intimate evening with him in a heartbeat. She hoped he would respond soon.

The anxious group sat huddled together in the emergency room waiting area. Elaine held J.R. as he rocked back and forth, trying to calm his nerves. Winston jumped up from his seat and went outside. He dialed Winter's number once more, hoping to reach her in order to let her know what was going on. Jefferson and Malik were on opposite ends of the waiting room, Jefferson getting up from his seat every three minutes or so to pace the waiting room floor, while Malik didn't move, say a word, or bother to look in the others' direction.

Seconds, minutes flew by without any word. Forty-five minutes later, a nurse appeared from behind the main door of the emergency room and stopped in front of Malik. Jefferson stood and began to walk to where Malik stood talking to the nurse. However, before Jefferson got there, the nurse whisked Malik away. Just before they disappeared through the doorway that led to where Ivy was being treated, Jefferson called out.

"Excuse me. I'm Ivy Mason's father. Is she all right?"

The nurse cocked her head and frowned at Jefferson. "She will be." And then they were gone.

Jefferson was defeated and uttered a string of curses.

He sighed, then walked over to where Winston, J.R., and Elaine were now standing, each of them waiting to find out what was going on with Ivy.

"What did the nurse say?" Winston asked excitedly when Jefferson was in front of them.

"The nurse said that Ivy will be all right. It pissed me off that the nurse dismissed me like I was nobody. I'm Ivy's father and I have a right to know what's going on with my daughter."

"Malik might have said something to her," J.R. added. "I wouldn't put it past him."

"He can't keep me away from my daughter," Jefferson retorted. "It's Malik's fault that she's here in the first place."

"It's going to work out, Pops," J.R. interjected. "I'm sure that when this ordeal is over, she'll want to be as far away from Malik as possible. I wished she had come and stayed with me when she returned to North Carolina."

"Don't beat yourself up over it," Winston stated. "No one had any idea what Ivy was up to and that it would come to this. You couldn't have prevented it if you tried."

"Listen to your baby brother," Elaine said, squeezing J.R.'s hand. "Ivy is going to be all right."

"I guess there's nothing we can do but wait," Jefferson said. And they sat down and waited.

# Fifty-Eight

Malik followed the nurse and was taken to a private room. His stomach was in knots and tiny beads of sweat dotted his forehead. He wasn't sure how Ivy was going to look, so he braced himself for the worst, although the nurse had already said she was going to make it.

They entered the room, and an ER doctor and nurse were checking Ivy's vitals. Ivy's eyelids were closed and she lay still in the bed. Fear gripped Malik, his stomach muscles tightening even more. He exhaled and waited to hear the doctor's prognosis.

"Mr. Mason, I'm Dr. Sexton. Your wife is a very lucky woman. If she had arrived in our ER even ten minutes later, I don't think there would have been a happy ending. Having said all of that, I can't say that all of my news is good. We've pumped the pills from her body; however, the fetus that was growing inside of her did not survive."

"No!" Malik said out loud in desperation. "No, please don't tell me we lost the baby. Please say it's not so."

"Mr. Mason, as I said, you're fortunate to have your wife with us. She's young, and you can have more children."

Malik went and stood next to Ivy. Tears welled up in his eyes, and he cried unashamed. "Ivy, I'm sorry, baby. Whatever you were thinking when you took those pills, if I'm the cause, I'm sorry."

"Mr. Mason, we're going to keep Mrs. Mason over-night for observation," Dr. Sexton began. "I'll need you to go to the administrative office so we can admit her. The nurse will give you papers to do so. You can stay with her the night if you like. We'll have to report the overdose to the police."

Malik straightened up. "Do you have to…ah…report this to the police? My wife is rather private, and for whatever reason she took the pills, I'm sure she wouldn't want this to go to press."

"Do you know why she would try and take her own life, sir?" Dr. Sexton inquired, searching Malik for a clue.

Malik looked at Dr. Sexton with a puzzled look on his face. "No," Malik said defiantly.

"All right then, as soon as you've taken care of the paperwork, we'll move Mrs. Mason to a private room. I'll see you in a bit."

Malik let Dr. Sexton's words roll around in his mind. *Do you know why she would try and take her own life?* Yes, he had a good idea but he wasn't going to sing like a canary when his political career was on the line. Political career? Oh my God. He needed to get out of there fast and call Perry. Malik took the paperwork from the nurse and left the room.

He avoided Jefferson and his sons by exiting the ER through a set of doors that led into the hospital's interior. Out of earshot, he immediately pulled his cell phone from its holder on his waist and called Perry.

Malik plunged forward, not waiting for Perry to extend his customary greeting. "Perry, don't panic."

"Malik, what's up? Sounds like you're the one in panic mode."

"You won't believe this. Ivy took an overdose of pills. I found her in time, though."

"Damn, Malik! Is she all right? Where are you?"

"I'm at Cape Fear Hospital."

"The hospital?"

"We had to call the ambulance because Ivy wasn't responding when we found her."

"Who's we?"

"Her father and brothers. They were worried about her and drove to Fayetteville to see about her. I can't believe this is happening."

"You and me both. This couldn't have come at a worse time. Your numbers are going up and all I can see is our hard work going down the drain. Maybe we can keep this quiet."

"That's just it, dawg. The doctor said he had to report it because it was an attempted suicide."

"Damn. Malik, your middle name must be sabotage. You need to take a moment to think about whether or not you want to continue this campaign. This little event with Ivy is not going to be good headline news material. We're in a sinking ship."

"I'm not giving up, Perry. Now if you want to jump ship, be my guest. I'll get someone else to run it. I thought you were in it for the long haul—for better or worse. Hopefully the news about Ivy will blow over as quickly as it happened."

"Why did she try to kill herself, Malik? The press is going to want an answer to that question. I'm not a quitter, dawg, but I know what it looks like when the chips are down."

"We're going to pull this off, Perry. Just hang in there. I can make this right."

"You better because this is the last straw, friendship be damned."

"Okay, frat. I'll make it up to you…don't cop out on me now." And the phone conversation ended abruptly.

## Fifty-Nine

Two-and-a-half hours passed without a word from Malik or the doctors. Jefferson tried unsuccessfully to gain access or get an update on Ivy's condition. When the group looked up, Winter and Phillip rushed toward them with Evan in Winter's arms. Winter looked as if she'd make a great mother.

"What's up with Ivy?" Winter asked out of breath. Elaine got up and took Evan from Winter's arms, while everyone else got up to give Winter a hug and Phillip a fist bump.

"We believe Malik has prohibited the hospital staff from telling us anything," Jefferson said. "If it weren't for your brothers, I would've stormed the place by now but I'm smart enough to realize that it's not the way to get answers. So here we are waiting to see if Malik is going to do the right thing. He's only seconds away from an ass whooping anyway."

"That selfish son-of-a-bitch isn't going to get away with this," Winter rushed to say. "Malik knows good and well that Ivy is in this hospital because of what he said. If it didn't mean that I'd be locked up behind bars, I'd beat his brains in myself. I don't understand how he could destroy our family like this when he was once someone we looked up to and held in high esteem. Makes me sick."

"Believe me," Jefferson said, "Malik is not going to get away with this. He may think he's off the hook, but I guarantee he's going to have a heavy price to pay." As an afterthought, Jefferson said, "I remember when I loved him like he was my own brother."

"Hold that thought, Dad," Winston said. "Malik must have heard you because he's walking this way."

"He looks strange," Winter added.

Jefferson stood with his arms folded across his chest. There was no warmth in Malik's face as he moved toward the hostile-looking group. Malik stopped and stood in front of Jefferson.

"Ivy is going to be all right."

There was a collective sigh from the group. "Can we go and see her now?" Jefferson asked.

"She's being admitted for observation and I've just completed the paperwork. I'll let you know as soon as they've placed her in a room." Malik sighed. He looked from Jefferson to the rest of the Myles clan. "Ivy lost the baby."

"Oh my God," Winter cried out. "She wanted that baby so badly. God, why did this have to happen?"

Malik was quiet with downcast eyes. He finally looked up. "I'll be back." And he was gone as quickly as he had come.

"What's happening with this family?" Winter pushed. "First Momma, now Ivy. Who's next?"

Phillip put his arm around Winter. "It's going to be all right, Winter."

"Yes, it's going to be all right, sis," Winston chimed in. "The Myleses are a family and we stick together. Right, Dad?"

"You got that right, son."

"Ivy must be out of it knowing that she's lost her baby," Winter blabbered on. "I need to see my sister now."

"We all want to see her, Winter," J.R. put in. "We haven't been here all night for the fun of it."

"It's all right, J.R.," Winston said, being overprotective of his twin. "Winter always gets emotional."

"Hell, I'm emotional, too. Ivy and I are very close..."

"So close that she didn't tell you she was marrying Malik?" Winter remarked.

"Okay, guys," Jefferson jumped in. "This is not the time. Anyway, I see Malik coming down the hall. Don't let him see us disjointed."

Lips shut, everyone watched as Malik approached. Malik handed Jefferson a piece of paper. "This is the floor and the room Ivy is in. I'll stay here so that you all can go up and see her. She's only been awake for a half-hour and...and she," Malik sighed, "doesn't know about the baby."

Everyone looked in Jefferson's direction as the spokesperson for the group. Jefferson was seething, but he decided to keep his emotions in check. "Thanks for the information." Jefferson looked around at his family and nodded for them to follow.

"I'm sorry," Malik said.

Jefferson turned around as did the other family members. There was no love lost and the only thing Jefferson could do was stare. When he couldn't look at Malik any longer, he turned and headed for the elevator with the rest of the family tagging behind.

"Can you believe that sorry SOB had the nerve to say he was sorry?" J.R. said to the group. "God knows that I'm trying very hard to act as an adult should, but something in me wanted to slap his face and stomp him into the ground." J.R. looked at Elaine. "I guess going to church has done some good because pastor's preaching reached the sane part of my head in time."

Everyone laughed.

"Believe it or not," Jefferson began, "I felt the same way. I wanted to make good on my threat to Malik. The urge to beat him into oblivion was so at my fingertips, I could taste his blood. However, something inside made me back down. I feel sorry for Malik. He's been searching for something his whole life that he's yet to find. Oh, he was always the good friend with the positive outlook on life, and he was for awhile. Now the real person has shown up. Even made me take notice of my own life and what I've done to my family. I love you all; I love your mother. I've been praying that this family can become whole."

"Oh, Daddy," Winter said, reaching up to give him a big hug. "You are my hero at this moment. You've said the first positive thing tonight. Now, I'm ready to go see my sister and help her any way we can."

"I'm there for your mother if she wants my help," Jefferson said.

"Uhm hmmm," Winston hummed. "Yeah, right, Dad."

"Pops, I'm proud to be your son," J.R. added. "I believe the Myles family is on its way to recovery."

"Yes, we are," Jefferson said. "Yes, we are."

*DING!*

"This is our floor," Winter said as everyone exited the elevator. "Is Evan all right, Elaine? He's so quiet."

"I guess he's trying to figure out what you all are talking about. He's being a good little boy."

"Ian gets out of the hospital tomorrow," Winter said. "I don't know how I'm going to do it and work, but I'll work it. Dad, I may need your help."

"I said I'm here to help, and I mean that. This is Ivy's room and our focus is on her. Let's leave all the other stuff outside the door." Everyone nodded yes. "All right, let's go in."

Sixty

The room was quiet when the Myles family walked in with Jefferson leading the pack. Ivy seemed so fragile, so lifeless, lying on the metal hospital bed with the rails pulled up on either side. It was almost an eerie sight, viewing her that way. Then her head turned ever so slight in the direction of the convoy that had descended upon her.

"Ivy, baby, how are you feeling?" Jefferson asked as he reached down and held her hand and kissed her forehead.

"Hey, Daddy, it could be better," Ivy whispered. "Why is every-one acting as if they've come to a funeral?"

J.R., Winston, Winter, and Elaine looked from one to the other without saying a word. Then Winter moved in next to Jefferson.

"Sis, we've been so worried about you. Between you and Mom, I don't what we're going to do. But I do know for sure that this family is going to take good care of you."

"That's right," both J.R. and Winston echoed.

"Ivy, this is your big bro, J.R. I'm not going to let anyone hurt you ever again."

Ivy tried to laugh. "I'm sorry, guys. I keep making one foolish mistake after the other. I let what Malik said to

Momma drive me over the edge. My good senses checked out for a moment, but I'm back in control. Knowing that you all have my back, I'm going to make it. I've got to get well so I can take care of this baby growing inside of me."

Silence invaded the room. No one dared to be the bearer of bad news. It was Malik's responsibility as Ivy's husband to tell her that she was no longer carrying a baby, and it appeared to be the consensus of the group by virtue of their silence.

"You all all right?" Ivy asked. "You guys are acting weird."

"We're only happy that you'll be all right," Jefferson said.

"I want to go home with you, Winter, whenever I'm discharged."

"My home is your home, sis. I'll be here to whisk you away."

"I haven't told Malik. In fact, I don't want to have anything to do with him. I can't stand to look at him right now and feel good about myself."

"Baby girl, we've got you covered," Jefferson said. "Don't you worry about a thing. You won't have to put up with Malik ever again if you don't want to. Your sister, brothers, and I will help you with whatever you need."

"Thanks, Daddy. I'm ready to go home now."

"Ivy," Winter began.

Jefferson cut Winter off, fearing that she was about to tell Ivy about the baby.

"What is it, Winter?" Ivy asked with concern in her eyes. She asked Jefferson to raise her bed.

"Nothing. I was wondering what time you were going to be discharged so I can schedule myself accordingly. Ian is being discharged from the hospital tomorrow, and I was going to pick him up."

"I'll stay overnight," Jefferson said, "and the rest of you can catch a ride with Winter and Phillip."

"Phillip? Who's Phillip?" Ivy inquired.

Winter motioned for Phillip to come stand next to her. "This handsome guy is Mr. Phillip Wright." Winter made eyes so that Ivy could only see her. "He's the guy I was telling you about."

Ivy smiled. "Oh, that guy...the special person in your life?"

"Yes, this is him."

"Nice to meet you, Ivy, although it's under these circumstances."

"Nice to meet you, too, Phillip. I'll be as good as new tomorrow, and then I'll come search for you to find out what your intentions are with my little sister."

"Come on, Ivy." Winter giggled.

"That's fine," Phillip said. "Winter is a very sweet young lady and we are taking the time to get to know each other."

"Good for you. Wish I had been smarter."

"Ivy, Phillip is studying to be a doctor."

"Well, we need one in the family, if you know what I mean," Ivy said. "Every time you look around, one of us is in the hospital."

"You're putting the cart before the horse, Ivy," Winston said. "Nobody said they were engaged and getting married. We are working on the media portion of Phillip's father's campaign. Dr. Shelton Wright, Phillip's dad, is running for a state senate seat like Malik is doing but in a district out of Raleigh."

Ivy was quiet and seemed to retreat. No one said anything until Ivy finally spoke. "Oh, okay. Look, I'm tired. Are you going to stay with me, Daddy?"

"Yeah, baby, I'll be here."

"Well, I guess we'll be going," Winter said. "Don't worry about a thing, sis. Dad will let me know when you all are on your way to Raleigh."

"Who's going to Raleigh?" Malik asked as he let the door close behind him. Everyone turned around and gasped.

"Ivy is going to stay with Winter while she recovers," Jefferson said to Malik.

"Like hell she is. Ivy is my wife, and I'm going to take care of her. That's what's wrong with you people; you always try to take over and end up making a mess of things. Ivy is my responsibility and if you don't like it, you can kiss my black ass."

"Tomorrow, I'm going home with my daddy," Ivy said. "Malik, you have no say so over me. You should have thought about the consequences when you were telling my mother how much you wanted her...how much you were in love with her and would take care of her and

Ian. I don't want any man that doesn't want me. My baby and I will be fine all by ourselves."

"You lost the baby."

Ivy stared at Malik. Then she saw Winter's hand go to her mouth and the expressions of hate jump on her brothers' faces. "Why do you have to be so cruel, Malik? What have I done to you?"

"Why don't you ask your family? They know about the baby."

"You're lying, Malik," Ivy said in a calm voice.

"Malik, you are so mean," Winter jumped in. "As her husband, we felt it was your place to tell Ivy, especially since that was the impression you gave us. Oh, we wanted to tell her, but we were being considerate of you."

"You are a joke, Winter. You were being considerate of me. Yet, on the other hand, all of you were ready to kidnap Ivy and take her to Raleigh. Where was the consideration?"

The room was silent again as everyone turned in Ivy's direction. Tears were barreling down her face. Winter and J.R. were at her side, but she couldn't stop crying.

"It's time for everyone to go," Jefferson finally spoke up.

"And that means you, too," Malik said, trying to suppress the anger in his voice. "I want to be alone with my wife."

"No, Malik, you get out. I want Daddy to stay right where he is. I'm not going home with you. You and I are done; no strings attached. Good riddance."

"Ivy, come on."

"You heard her," Jefferson said. "Now get your black ass out of here before my sons and I throw you out of the window."

"You haven't heard the last of me, Jefferson. I'm going to send your ass back to prison."

"Do it."

Malik stormed out of the room without saying good-bye to Ivy.

"Malik is dangerous," Jefferson said. "I'm not going to move from Ivy's side until she's safe in Raleigh. Why don't you all go on home? Poor Evan is tired." Jefferson went to Evan and kissed him on the forehead.

"I'm going to stay with you, Dad," Winston said. "I've got to protect you from Malik."

Everybody laughed. "And just what are you going to do, Winston?"

"I'm going to have your back, Dad."

"You're going to be hiding behind Dad saying...don't hit my daddy, don't hit my daddy," J.R. said. The room erupted in hearty laughter.

"Thank you for being here for me," Ivy said. "Family is all I need."

"You got it, sis," Winter said as she kissed Ivy on the forehead. "We'll see you tomorrow. Got to check on Mom and get Evan home. Love you."

"Love you, back."

"Elaine and I have got your back, too," J.R. said to Ivy.

"You're like my twin. We used to fight each other growing up, but you are my heart, Ivy. I'm not going to let nothing happen to you."

"Oh, J.R., that was so sweet. I love you, too, big brother. Elaine, he might make a fine husband, should you all get to that point."

"Got you, sister-in-law."

"It's time to get up out of here," Phillip said. "Too much of that commitment talk in the room."

"Remember what I said, Phillip," Ivy said, shaking her finger in his direction, "we're going to have our talk."

"Okay, sis, we're out," Winter said, threading her arm through Phillip's, who was now carrying Evan. "And don't be afraid of the big bad wolf. I'll see you tomorrow."

"Okay." Ivy waved to everybody. After the group departed, Ivy turned to Jefferson. "Daddy, please don't leave the room. I'm afraid."

"You don't have to be, baby. Daddy is here. Winston will be back up after he sees everybody off. I'm not going anywhere. I do have to make a phone call."

## Sixty-One

Malik got in his BMW and tore out of the hospital parking garage. He was pissed off and he needed to let off some steam. He couldn't believe the week he had had—going from finding out that his mother-in-law had borne a child with his DNA and that his wife tried to commit suicide and then losing the baby they would've shared together. He needed Perry to meet him.

"Perry, this is Malik. Can you get away?"

"Everything all right with Ivy?"

"No! I mean, she's going to be fine, but she's going to try and leave me. Her insane family has finally convinced her to leave me."

"What are you talking about, man? You're not making any sense whatsoever."

"Listen to me, Perry. Ivy said she wasn't coming home with me. And she lost the baby."

"Oh, Jesus." Perry sighed. "I don't know, Malik. Your credibility is going down the drain."

"Look, meet me in the bar at Carrabba's so we can hash this thing out logically. I'm on my way there now."

"I'm on my way, but I don't know what we're going to be able to do to salvage your campaign."

"You need to come up with something. This thing with Ivy is only temporary. I won't need her for any appearances anytime soon."

"Whatever you say, dawg, but I'm getting a little tired of cleaning up your messes. Look, I'll be right there. I've got another call coming in that I need to take."

"All right, but don't take too long." Malik disconnected the call and for the next few minutes rode in silence. "Damn you, Ivy," Malik said out loud. "You are my wife and a wife is to stand by her husband. I'll be damned if you're going to Raleigh tomorrow."

Toni Gillette was having a fabulous morning. The ink was already dry on a couple of contracts that netted her a nice little fee for her story about Malik that would break sometime today. Stuffing a dry piece of toast in her mouth, she smiled at the thought of how easy it was to land a payday. Her communication skills and talent had enabled her to break into several lucrative media settings, although she hadn't been able to realize anything more permanent from it. However, the real and immediate goal was to land a primetime spot on national television.

She looked up periodically at the small, flat-screen television set that was mounted underneath the kitchen cabinets. The newscasters were chatting about human-interest stories, which was refreshing from all the other gloom and doom that seemed to be the only news worthy of reporting these days.

Toni lifted her glass and took a sip of juice, washing down the remnants of the toast. As she prepared to nibble on a piece of bacon, her BlackBerry chimed. It was Anissa, and Toni let the call go straight to voicemail because she didn't feel like listening to off-the-wall gossip this morning. The only gossip she wanted to hear was how a certain Malik Mason who was running for a state senate seat out of Fayetteville, North Carolina had sired a child with his mother-in-law. She smiled at the thought—*ka-ching*.

Dabbing her face with a napkin, Toni picked up her dishes and put them in the kitchen sink. The morning news hadn't been forthcoming so far, and they were about at the top of the hour. She shuffled her two feet to the kitchen table and picked up the television remote. Before she was able to hit the OFF button, the newscaster made a startling announcement about a story they were going to air in the next half-hour—Ivy Mason, wife of Malik Mason...suicide attempt. How did she miss this one?

There was no time to waste. Toni put down the remote and reached for her BlackBerry and dialed Anissa.

"Did you get my message?" Anissa asked before Toni had an opportunity to say anything.

"What message?"

"I just called and left you a message. I thought you were responding to it."

Toni waved her hand under her chin in an attempt to cool off. She was having a full-blown menopausal attack. Stress was a killer, but this wasn't the kind of thing she wanted to stress over. The likelihood of this story coming out at this time was going to lessen the impact of her story. It was like watching a balloon fizzle before all of the air was in it. No pop!

"I saw that you called but I haven't listened to your message."

"Girl, Perry called me last night…"

"Hold it a sec," Toni said, interrupting Anissa's train of thought. "There's something about Malik's wife on the news."

"That's what I called to tell you."

"Hush."

"We've just learned that the wife of N.C. Senate candidate hopeful, Malik Mason, out of Fayetteville, North Carolina, was hospitalized on yesterday. Yesterday afternoon, Ivy Mason was found by her husband, father and siblings in her home on the floor, unconscious from an overdose of Percocet. We have not been able to find out how many pills Mrs. Mason consumed or ascertain why Mrs. Mason may have attempted suicide, but we do know that Mrs. Mason is doing well under the watchful eye of her doctor.

"We've also learned that Mrs. Mason was pregnant; how-

*ever, we understand the unborn fetus did not survive. Mr.*
*Malik Mason did not respond to any of our phone calls. I'm*
*Charlotte Wilson, reporting to you live for WTVD Channel*
*11 News."*

Toni smiled. While she felt bad for Ivy, the bit about
the baby was the best segue for her story. "Anissa?" Toni
called out when she put the phone back to her ear. The
line was dead.

## Sixty-Two

"**D**amn," Malik said when he hung up the phone after talking to Perry. It was seven-thirty, and the news about Ivy's attempted suicide had already hit the air-waves. So much for damage control because no amount of convincing would repair the harm this bit of news had rendered. Perry said he was ready to throw in the towel, but Malik believed he would prevail and begged Perry to stay on a little longer.

Years prior, Jefferson Myles was the buddy he counted on. They were inseparable—joined at the hip, brothers for life. No matter what, they had each other's back. And then Jefferson went to prison for embezzlement and Malik had a roving eye. The woman Malik was to protect while his buddy Jefferson was incarcerated became the object of his hidden affection—Jefferson's wife, Margo.

It wasn't obvious to the casual observer that Malik had a thing for Margo. Malik used every opportunity to visit her, whether it was to help with something that needed repair at the house or running some type of errand. He was there at Margo's beck and call so that he could be near her.

Malik cleared his head of the clutter—memories that wouldn't die. He got up, showered, shaved, and dressed and made up his mind that he was going to bring his wife home. He didn't care what Jefferson had to say on the matter; Ivy was his wife and she was coming home with him.

Traffic was brisk as Malik headed toward the hospital. Commuters were on their way to work and at this time of day weren't tolerant of drivers who squeezed in front of them to turn left before the light turned red.

Malik was now at the hospital and parked his car in the parking garage. After turning off the motor, he sat a moment to gather his thoughts. He hoped there wouldn't be any confrontation, and coming to pick up his wife would be a mere formality. He dreaded having to deal with Jefferson at all, but he was a candidate for state senator, and he knew how to conduct himself.

He exited the car, entered the hospital, and rode the elevator to Ivy's floor. Malik was alone in the elevator, so he bowed his head in silent prayer that all would go well. Exiting the elevator he proceeded to Ivy's room but was soon bum-rushed by news reporters.

"Hell," Malik said under his breath as media news cameras and reporters descended upon him.

"Mr. Mason, can you tell me what prompted your wife to take an overdose of pills?" a reporter asked.

"No comment," Malik said. At least he knew enough to say that without an attorney present.

"Mr. Mason, is it true that your wife was pregnant and may have killed the fetus by taking the pills?" another reporter asked.

Malik stared into the face of the obnoxious reporter. "Get the hell out of my face. You people don't have any sensitivity skills. What kind of damn question is that to ask?"

"I'm sure it will be one that the police will be asking if they haven't already."

Malik pushed the camera and cameraman against the wall. "You all are the problem with America—sticking your noses into people's private affairs. I bet if you turn the camera on your own lives you won't like what you see."

"Mr. Mason, are you a proper fit…proper representative for the people in the state of North Carolina?" another reporter asked.

"Yes, my campaign has always been founded on principals of service to the constituents I represent. I will do all that's in my power to fight for the rights of everyone in Cumberland County—be they Democrat or Republican, and…"

"Sir, did you sire a baby by your mother-in-law?" The question came out of left field; Malik didn't see it coming.

"You've got it twisted. My wife was the one pregnant."

"I have information that you found out that one of the twins your mother-in-law recently gave birth to has your DNA," said the smooth, sultry reporter who was now in front of Malik. She was African-American and in her mid-to-late-thirties, and she was rocking a nice figure, although she was dressed appropriately. Her long, healthy mane was thick with a lot of body, and Malik felt sure that if he ran his hands underneath the top layer, he'd find a head full of tracks. Malik took a second look and then it was back to business.

"I didn't get your name," Malik began trying to resist danger, "but my private life is none of your concern."

"So I take it that you not answering the question means yes."

"Miss…"

She looked down her nose at Malik. "That's Ms. Douglass."

"I'm not denying or confirming it."

"So it's true."

"Answer the question," another reporter shot out.

Malik sealed his lips and pushed through the crowd that had gathered. "F y'all."

"Did he say what I think he said?" Malik heard a reporter ask.

Malik pushed through the door to Ivy's room. He stopped short when he saw Jefferson and Winston standing off to the side as they waited for Ivy to gather her things. Ivy looked up and then away as she continued to collect her things in preparation for departure.

"Ivy is going home with me," Malik said bluntly. "I understand you are her father, but I'm her husband. I'm the responsible party who will be checking her out of this hospital and paying the bill."

Irritated, Jefferson moved closer to Malik. He threw his hands up in the air. "Malik, I come in peace. I don't want any drama today. Ivy is still ill, and I think it would be prudent if she went home with us so that her family will be able to give her the attention she needs."

Brushing his mouth with his hands, Malik sighed. "I don't know how to make this any plainer than I already have, Jefferson. As her husband, I will take care of my wife."

"Ivy tried to take her life, and you're the reason why. So you need to move out of the way and allow me to take my daughter home."

"Over my dead body."

"If that's the only way, I guess that's how it's going to be. Ivy, are you ready?"

As soon as Jefferson turned his back, Malik pushed him in the back. Jefferson slid forward, regained his footing, and turned around and rushed for Malik. Before Jefferson could make contact, Winston caught him around the waist and pulled him back. "Don't do it, Dad. He might have you arrested, and we don't want that."

"I'll go with him, Daddy," Ivy said as she stared Malik down.

Malik shook his head as if he was shaking off dust. "That's more like it."

"Ivy, you don't have to go with him."

"It's okay, Daddy. I'll call you if I need you."

"You won't need him," Malik remarked snidely. "He's not dependable when he needs to be."

No one said a word but looked up when they heard the knock on the door. Before anyone could respond, two plainclothes detectives, one female and one male, entered the room.

"Excuse me," Malik said, stopping the detectives almost at the door. "You must have the wrong room."

"No, we have the right room," the blonde female said. She pulled out a badge and flashed it in front of Malik. "I'm Detective Sabrina Martin and this is Detective Jim Levine," he flashed his badge, "with the Cumberland County Sheriff's Department."

"Again, you must have the wrong room."

"Your name?" Detective Martin asked, preparing to write the answer down.

"I'm Malik Mason, husband of the patient."

"You're also running for state senator, I hear."

Malik's demeanor changed slightly. He still had to present himself as an upstanding citizen for his constituency regardless of how Jefferson was irritating the hell out of him. He spoke in a much calmer voice. "Yes, I am, Detective. Before you arrived, I was in a heated family discussion, which explains my tone of voice. So please forgive me for being a little abrasive when you first arrived. How may I help you?"

All eyes were on the detective. "It has come to our

attention that in Mrs. Mason's attempt to commit suicide, she may have killed her unborn child. We need to get some information from Mrs. Mason…"

"I object," Malik said.

"She would not intentionally harm her unborn child," Jefferson added.

"And who are you?" Detective Martin asked.

"I'm Mrs. Mason's father and I'm here to take her home."

"I'm confused," Sabrina began, "You're taking Mrs. Mason home. What about her husband, Mr. Mason?"

"Detective Martin," Malik began, "there is nothing to read into this. While I'm out campaigning, Ivy's family will be caring for her. We were working out the logistics."

"All right. I still need to speak with Mrs. Mason."

"I will stay with her while you ask your questions," Malik said.

"Of course. I wouldn't have it any other way."

"Winston and I will wait outside," Jefferson said, nodding at Malik. "We'll be ready to take Ivy home when the detectives are finished."

Malik watched Jefferson and Winston exit the room without a word. So they won round one. Ivy sat down on the bed and waited for the interrogation.

Detective Martin approached and stood in front of Ivy while Detective Levine looked on. "Mrs. Mason, I know that this is a touchy subject for you right now, but I need to ask these questions."

Ivy sat expressionless and waited for the question.

"Mrs. Mason, were you deliberately trying to get rid of your baby?"

Ivy looked into Detective Martin's eyes. "Not at all. In fact, I was overjoyed at the possibility of becoming a mother. And if you're going to ask me if I was trying to kill myself, the answer is still no. I was distraught at the time that I took the pills, but it was never my intention to kill myself."

Detective Levine watched Ivy, analyzing her facial expressions and tone of voice. She dropped her head and glanced at a note that was written down on a piece of paper. "So if it wasn't your intention to kill yourself, what prompted you to take the pills in the first place, even if it wasn't a lethal dose you were trying to take?"

Malik was fidgety. His eyes darted back and forth, almost as if he was trying to give Ivy some kind of signal. But Ivy didn't look in his direction. She mulled over the question and then opened her mouth to answer. She sighed. "A family matter…a family matter had upset me, and I only took the pills to get rid of the migraine headache I was having," she lied.

"Does this family matter have anything to do with your husband…?"

Ivy turned her eyes sharply at Malik. "What about my husband?"

"Never mind. We will be in touch. Thank you for your assistance."

Ivy sat without saying a word. She took a chance and looked up at Malik. Her eyes burned a hole in his soul.

"Are you ready to go home?"

"I heard it with my own ears. You told those detectives that I would be going home with Daddy and that's exactly what I'm going to do."

Malik grabbed Ivy's arm, thought better of it, and let her go. "Don't do this, Ivy. My campaign is in full swing, and I need you by my side."

"That's all you care about…that damn campaign that you're not even going to win. You're pathetic; I don't know why I stooped so low. It doesn't matter anyway; I'm done. And my momma, she doesn't want you either."

"Ivy, please."

"Forget it, Malik." Ivy picked up her few belongings and left Malik in the room.

Ivy wasn't ready for the host of reporters and photographers that lined the hallways. She spotted Jefferson and waited until he saw her. Immediately he went to Ivy with Winston following. They brushed the reporters aside and grabbed the elevator that had just deposited another reporter on the floor.

Safe in the elevator, Ivy hugged her dad and he hugged her back. As soon they hit the lobby, Jefferson whisked Ivy away to safety.

## Sixty-Three

Winter was all smiles when she opened the door to her mother's townhouse and saw her sister, Ivy, on the front porch along with her dad and brother, Winston, staring back at her. Spontaneously, Winter reached out and hooked her arms around Ivy's neck. Ivy did the same, holding the embrace longer than she had planned.

"Are you going to let us in?" Jefferson finally asked.

"Sorry, Daddy," Ivy said.

The trio followed Winter into the house. Ivy seemed calm as she settled into a chair in the den.

"How is Evan?" Jefferson asked.

"He's fine and sleeping at the moment. He must be worn out from yesterday."

"What time do you pick up Ian?"

"In another hour."

Ivy looked from her sisters and brothers to her dad. "Thank you all for being there for me. You don't know how much it has meant to know that my family has my back."

Jefferson sat down next to Ivy and put his arm around

his daughter. "You never have to worry about family… and that includes your mother."

"That goes for me, too, sis," Winston interjected. "We're all we've got! Together the Myleses stand; divided we fall."

All was quiet after Winston's philosophy lesson. Winter wondered if everyone was thinking the same way. It would be great to see her mother and father back together, but it didn't appear that it was going to happen.

"While I have you all here, I need to share this with you," Jefferson stated. Ivy's eyebrows arched while concern was written on her face. "Your mother will be coming home day after tomorrow. She has refused to go to rehab, preferring to be surrounded by her family. There will be in-home visits by a nurse a couple of times a day." There was relief on Ivy's face. Winter stood, trying to make heads or tails out of what her father was trying to say. "It's going to be difficult for Winter to handle Margo and the twins by herself."

"Don't worry, Daddy," Ivy said. "I'm feeling much better and I'll be here to help Winter."

"Your mother will be down for awhile, and she'll need constant help because she won't be able to do anything."

"We've got this, Dad," Winter said, holding her hands up in surrender.

"J.R. and I are going to do our part," Winston put in. "Whatever running around you need us to do, we've got you."

"Hear me out. I've called someone besides the nurse

to assist your mother. This way, the pressure won't be totally on Winter. Ivy, you need to take it easy. You're in a vulnerable state and we need to take care of you, too. Your recovery time won't be nearly the same as your mother's, but I need you to relax for a little bit."

"I agree with Dad on that, Ivy. So who is this mystery person?"

"Angelica."

"For real, Dad?" Winter asked with a frown on her face. "Have you asked Mom?"

"Your mother and Angelica have mended their friendship."

"Where is she going to stay?" Winston asked, his arms wrapped around his waist.

"Not with me," Jefferson said, matching nasty looks with Winston.

"Momma has four bedrooms," Ivy said. "I can go home if it's going to be a problem."

"You're not going home, Ivy," Winter interjected. "Mom's master bedroom is downstairs and that's where she's going to be since she won't be using any stairs anytime soon. You and I will sleep in the large room that Mom uses so she can be close to the twins and Angelica can use the room that serves as Mom's office. It has a day bed in it. Look, I just got my sister back, and I'm going to take care of you."

"I guess it's all worked out, Daddy," Ivy said. "Angelica will be good for Momma."

"I still say Mom won't like the idea of Angelica being here, but you're her husband. You should know."

"Enough, Winter."

"Well, if you and Mom get back together, you could be here to help out, too." Now she had finally said what was on her mind. "What are you all looking at?" Winter asked her sister and brother.

"Winter, Dad and Mom are getting a divorce," Winston said. "Face it. It is what it is, and you knew it was coming to this."

Ivy got up out of her seat and held her sister. "I would like to see Momma and Daddy back together again too, but they are grown people and they've made their decision."

"It's just that this family has been through so much. I want it the way it was."

"Nothing stays the same, Winter," Jefferson interjected. "I love your mother, and if it were up to me, we wouldn't be getting a divorce."

"Well, Daddy," Ivy cut in, "if you feel that way, I'm with Winter. You need to tell your wife that you still love her and claim what's yours."

"Listen to my sisters," Winston added, jumping into the fray. "Give Dad a break, although, I think he led you all into that one. What about it, Dad? Are you going to tell Momma that you're still in love with her or do you have reason not to rush into this burning bush?"

Jefferson threw his hands in the air. "Okay, enough. I love your mother, but she doesn't want to be with me.

No, Winston, there is no one else that has captured my heart, even though I've done a little window-shopping." Everyone laughed accept Winter. Jefferson went to her and gave her a hug and afterwards lifted her chin. "If your mother would take me back this very moment, I'd be with her."

"I know you love her," Winter said.

"Okay, we've had our reunion. Winter, you need to get to the hospital to pick Ian up and Winston and I need to run to the office. We've got some unfinished business. I'll be picking Angelica up from the airport tomorrow around one-thirty. Winston and J.R. should have your mother home by then. This is a surprise."

"I don't know if that's the best thing, Daddy," Winter said, "but it's on you."

"Welcome home, Ivy," Jefferson said. "We're out."

Ivy gave Jefferson a warm smile. "I love you, Daddy."

Not to be outdone, Winter echoed, "I do too."

Jefferson blew them both a hearty kiss, and then the men were gone.

"Time for you to get some rest," Winter said to Ivy.

"Don't go treating me like an invalid, little sis. Why don't you sit next to me so we can have one of our old-fashioned sister talks? Anything you want to know, I'll tell you, and we'll talk until Evan wakes up."

"Okay. First question. Do you really love Malik?"

Sixty-Four

Malik was seething. He was losing control of the persona that had gotten him close to the pinnacle of society that he was trying to claim as his. He had come a long way. His grandparents were sharecroppers in Alabama and was able by the grace of God to raise his father and his four siblings to be outstanding citizens. They all went to college, which is where Malik's dad met his mom, and Malik's dad, aunts and uncles, as well as his mom all became educators. Malik's parents wed right out of college, had him, and as soon as Malik finished high school, there was no if, ands, or buts as to what he was going to do with the next phase of his life. It was a short summer and before Malik could catch a breath, he was off to college in North Carolina at North Carolina A&T.

A&T changed his life. Malik knew immediately that he wasn't going to return to Alabama. College life agreed with him, and it was there he met Jefferson Myles. They became fast friends and joined the fraternity together. They both joined ROTC, but while Jefferson made a life of the military, Malik did a short stint and got out, vying to make more money with his computer programming skills outside of the military.

With his head pounding, Malik drove around town and decided to go back to campaign headquarters. Talking with Perry would perhaps calm the stress in his body. Before he was able to move another inch, the Bluetooth in his car signaled a call. Peeking at his phone, Malik was happy that it was Perry calling.

"Hey, Perry, I'm on my way back to headquarters."

"No, let me meet you somewhere. Have you taken your wife home yet?"

"She's in Raleigh."

"What happened, dawg? I thought you were picking her up from the hospital today?"

"The press and the damn police."

"Okay, Malik. Tell me what's going on."

"I'll tell you when I see you. Meet me at IHOP on Raeford Road."

"I've got some news too, and you're not going to like it. I've been trying to tell you to keep your personal life under wraps because if the press gets a whiff of your drama, they're going to pick you apart like a school of piranha and scatter your bones across the airwaves."

"I've done nothing wrong, Perry. I'm a victim of circumstance, and that doesn't minimize the person I am. I'm still qualified to be a state senator."

"Not after the public finishes ripping your ass apart. The piranhas aren't going to leave much for them to suck on either, but whatever is left on the bone, they're going to have a field day."

"What is this news and whose side are you on, Perry? I'm not sure you're the person I need to be speaking to right now. I've not conceded my spot in this election and for sure Sterling Garrison isn't going to get it—at least not over my dead body."

"Be careful what you ask for. I'm on my way. I got a call from my friend, Anissa, and..."

"Repeat the name?"

"Anissa."

"Your friend?"

"My friend that I was in the swimming pool with... and I'm not talking about my wife..."

"I met a woman the other night, and her name was Anissa."

"Bingo."

"I'll see you in fifteen minutes."

Toni Gillette paced the floor waiting for the evening news. She'd received confirmation that her story was already circulating on the online publications that she sold her story to, which meant the local media would possibly be feeding off of it any minute. It was amazing how the viral network could balloon so quickly from the small seed she planted, and it was even more amazing how that seed, when watered, could make or break someone's career in a twinkling of an eye. It wouldn't take but a second for Toni to confirm that her story was in circulation, but she wanted to hear it with her own ears as the newscaster blasted the daily gloom and doom report live across her television screen.

ABC Television now aired news at four o'clock in the afternoon, and Toni clasped her hands over her face when a press photo of Malik Mason flashed on the screen. It gave her a rush when they said Malik's name, as she anticipated the rest of the story.

The newscaster began with the news of Ivy Myles' suicide attempt and the loss of her baby. There was speculation that the discovery that Malik was the father of one of his wife's mother's twins had started the sudden windstorm, and when Ivy overheard her husband professing his love for her mother, it was the event that sent her over the edge. The bizarre part of the story was that Margo Myles, Ivy's mother, had given birth to twins, and that her soon-to-be ex-husband, Jefferson Myles, was the father of one and Malik Mason, her son-in-law, was the father of the other. If anything could dismantle public trust, this story definitely would take first place.

Toni smiled broadly, proud of her prowess in getting paid for a story the world was going to hear anyway. She could almost bet that Malik's story would land on the national news. She hadn't counted on the extra bit about his wife's suicide attempt but was elated because it only helped to confirm everything she'd already stated in her piece. Toni's only thought now was that Jefferson couldn't find out that she leaked this story. However, if he did, she hadn't made any pretenses about who she was and what she did. She was a journalist whose goal was to make a name for herself, unfortunately at another's expense. However, this victory was sweet because it meant that her cousin, Sterling Garrison, would undoubtedly win the state senate seat for his district out in Fayetteville, North Carolina. Toni was pleased.

Sixty-Five

Malik hit the roof when Perry dropped the bomb—that his business was all over the Internet and wherever the grapevine travelled. People were tweeting about it, serving up commentary on blogs and radio talk shows—the great black hope was tainted before his name could be printed on the election ballot. Malik's phone was blowing up, but he refused to answer, leaving the dirty work to Perry.

Suddenly the atmosphere in IHOP wasn't conducive to Malik's attitude. He was in a foul mood, and he wanted to make someone pay for the mistakes he made. For a brief moment he thought about Ivy and her threat about making him pay for his sins, and it appeared she had won, at least this battle.

"You're going to have to give some kind of comment," Perry said, after fielding a call.

"I'm not available for any calls. You handle it, Perry. I'm going home. I have a headache."

"You didn't ask me who leaked it to the press."

"What's there to ask? There were so many reporters at the hospital this morning, they could've gotten the story from any one of Ivy's family members. I'm sure it was Jefferson; he's had it in for me ever since he found out I made love to his wife."

"And that you're the father of one of her twins."

Malik let go of a smile. "Yeah, I did that, but I love her, Perry. I really do love Margo."

"So why in the hell did you marry her daughter?"

"Good question, Perry. I believe Ivy has always had a schoolgirl crush on me. When I ran into her that day in Atlanta, looking so much like her mother, I flipped. Truth is, Ivy came on to me, and I rather enjoyed the cat and mouse play. And when I kissed her that first time and felt her pulse as she opened up to me, I had to have her. Why not? If I couldn't have the real thing, there was nothing wrong with having a good replica. Ivy and I could've made it, though, if the baby thing hadn't materialized."

"Well, dawg, you've done it now...made a big ole mess. Neither Margo nor Ivy want your ass. Shoot, you aren't even going to make political history because it's over."

"Go on and kick me further into the ground. It seems like you've been itching to do that all along. Anyway, if not Jefferson, who do you think leaked the story to the media?"

"Hold on a moment; it's Anissa again." Perry listened intently, uttering the words "what" and "you've got to be kidding" over and over. His eyes roamed around in his head and occasionally he would look over at Malik. Then he hung up.

"What did she say?" Malik asked, bracing for the news.

"Remember that woman I told you about who was starting a political news magazine to air candidates' dirty laundry?"

Malik sat up straight in his seat. "Yeah, I remember."

"Her name is Toni Gillette, and guess what I just found out?"

"My mind is blank."

"Her cousin is Sterling Garrison."

"So that's what this is all about. He couldn't play ball at Carolina, so he figured he would play hardball with me. Well, he's got a fight on his hands, and if I'm going down, guess who else is going down?"

"I'm afraid to ask. Look, Malik, don't go and do something stupid. You may still have a monkey's chance to correct this thing. We've got to keep the door open. Anyway, you have a company to operate, and if you want to continue to pay your mortgage as opposed to living in a sleeping bag underneath the bridge downtown, you need to steer away from trouble. Payback is a dog."

"So what are you going to do, Perry?"

"Who said I was going to do anything?"

## Sixty-Six

Sleep had been the best answer to the stress and pain Ivy was feeling about losing her baby and the man she called her husband. All of Winter's grilling had taxed her to the max, and she was happy for the reprieve when sleep decided to creep upon her.

She scratched her head as she lay awake in her mother's bed, wandering what Malik was doing and what her mother would think if she knew she was lying in her bed. Stretching her neck, Ivy sat up on her forearms and took the liberty to roam around the room with her eyes. There were individual pictures of Winter, Winston, J.R., and herself across the length of the dresser. There was a picture of the entire Myles family that they'd taken at the studio when Ivy was eighteen. There was also a recent photograph of the twins and tucked at the back on the dresser was a framed picture in oil of her mother and father that they'd taken years ago. In her heart of hearts, Ivy believed that her mother still loved her father, regardless of her actions.

Ivy jumped, startled by Winter staring at her in the doorway. "Are you spying on me?"

"No, sis. I came to check on you, but you were so peaceful and I didn't want to disturb the quiet. What were you thinking about?"

"Do you really want to know?"

"Come on, Ivy. I care about you, sis. I know you're hurting and I'm here for you."

Ivy smiled. "Thanks, sis. That's the kindest thing you've said to me in a long time."

"That's not true. Well, I know I've been a little rough on you."

"I was thinking about my baby. I killed my baby, Winter. What if they cart me off to jail and lock me up for murder? Do you think they'll do that?"

"You were under duress and not thinking straight. It was certainly not intentional."

"How are the twins?"

"Ivy, I know all of this is hard, especially with Malik being Ian's father."

"Please don't mention Malik's name around me. I'll have to deal with him at some time, but I'd rather be free of him for the moment."

"No problem."

"Look, why don't I help you get the house ready for Momma's homecoming and Angelica's arrival? This I've got to see."

"Why don't you just rest? I'll do it. The twins are asleep, and I've already started washing the linens."

"Don't treat me like an invalid, Winter. I had a setback,

but I'm not going to dwell on it, and I'm sure as hell not going to waddle in self-pity. Sometime this week, I want you to help me get things in order so I can have my fake marriage annulled."

"Are you sure you want to do that, sis?"

"I can't believe you of all people are asking me that stupid question. I know you hate Malik's guts. Wow, I said his name. Yuck. Saying it leaves a bad taste in my mouth."

"I'll help you take care of it. J.R.'s girlfriend, Elaine, is taking some time off to help me with the babies and Mom."

"She's seems to like J.R. a lot."

"Sis, they are in love. Can you believe that? And they go to church together. J.R. has changed for the better. He and Dad get along so well together."

"That's great. You know what, Winter?"

"What, sis?"

"Wouldn't it be nice if our family was back together again?"

Winter walked over and sat on the edge of the bed. She took a good look at her sister. "I've been praying for Mom and Dad to get back together for a long time. They are both so stubborn, but they love each other. Dad might be seeing someone he just met, according to Winston, but if Mom would say the word, Daddy would come running like lightning had struck him. You should've seen how they looked at each when I brought him over here to meet the twins. They were eyeing each other like they were seeing each other for the first time. And I'll tell you this, Ivy; there was lust in those eyes."

The sisters laughed together. Winter fell back on the bed next to Ivy. "Remember how we used to get up in Mom and Dad's bed and lay there until they'd kick us out?"

"I was thinking the same thing," Ivy admitted. "I want our family to be whole."

Winter's cell phone interrupted their good thoughts. She glanced down at the caller ID. "It's Dad," Winter said, before pressing the TALK button. "Dad, what's up?"

"How's Ivy doing?" Jefferson asked.

Winter gave Ivy a wink. "She's progressing. She had a good nap and we've been yapping our lips about old times...when we were all a family."

"That's nice, but I need you to listen. Whatever you do, don't turn on the television. Ivy's suicide attempt is headline news along with the bit about your mother giving birth to twins who have different fathers."

"How..."

"Just listen. I don't want Ivy to be exposed to all of this nonsense right now. She'll have to address it sooner or later, but not now. How you handle our phone call once you get off the phone is up to you, but right now we've got to protect Ivy from the elements."

"Okay, Dad," Winter finally said. "What time are you bringing Mom home?"

"Around noon. Winston is going to the airport to pick up Angelica instead of me. Her flight arrives early afternoon. Okay, I've got to run. I have an important errand I need to make."

"Okay. Love you, Dad. Oh, Ivy is throwing you a kiss."

"Tell her I caught it, and I love her, too. If I'm not too late running my errand, I may stop by later on. I'm out."

"Bye bye." Winter ended the call and looked away from Ivy.

"What was that call all about?" Ivy asked.

"What do you mean?"

"Honey, I know when you are talking in code."

"Daddy was being overprotective of you. He told me to be on the watch in the event Malik tries to show up here."

"Daddy worries too much. Malik is too self-absorbed to even give chase to my whereabouts. He claims that his BMW drinks gas like a cat drinks milk, so he's not going to waste any gas to come up here."

"He came up here looking for Mom after we saw you at the restaurant, but I sent his ass packing. Mom was at the hospital with Evan. He had an ear infection. Mom was so pissed off when I told her he'd stopped by. I even threatened to tell you."

"Why didn't you?"

"We weren't on speaking terms then."

"But my baby would still be here, if I had known that back then."

"Even though we weren't speaking, Ivy, I was still your little sister in protect mode. I somehow knew that Malik's sins would find him out, but I had no earthly idea it would play out as it did. I hope you won't hold it against me."

Ivy sighed. "Not this time."

Sixty-Seven

J efferson was fuming. He couldn't believe that his family was being dragged through the media slaughterhouse again. He had finally faded from the limelight after all the backlash with his ties to organized crime and subsequent prison time, so much so he was able to launch a successful business. And now after he'd been so careful to do things right and on the up and up, the media was having another field day at his expense and that of his family.

He understood how the news media was able to report on Ivy's attempted suicide. As soon as they landed at Cape Fear Hospital and they realized that Ivy was the wife of Malik who was running for a state senate seat, the media came running from near and far, camping out at Ivy's hospital door in order to be the first to air the story on the local news. But how in the hell did they find out about Margo and the twins and that the babies had two different fathers? This puzzled Jefferson.

Sitting back in his chair, Jefferson turned on the small, portable flat-screen television he kept in his office. All the local stations were airing their story, and he listened intently until it suddenly dawned on him. He took his fist and banged it on his desk.

He grabbed his keys from off his desk, put on his black leather jacket, and peeped in on Winston and J.R. "Look, fellows, I've got to make an important run. I hope to be back in an hour or so. If not, I'll see you both tomorrow. I'm picking your mother up around noon."

"Pops, don't forget you need to touch base with Dr. Wright," J.R. said.

"I know. Maybe you should call him, J.R. I hope all of this negative media blitz won't hurt our relationship."

"It shouldn't," Winston piped in. "Mom and Ivy are the main topics of discussion, although you are part of that love triangle they keep talking about."

"Whatever. If you need me, call me on my cell. If you don't get me right away, leave a message."

"This wouldn't have anything to do with the lovely Ms. Gillette, would it?" Winston asked, faking a laugh. "I know what a man looks like when he's in heat."

"You're wrong...way off base, Winston," Jefferson lied. "Tomorrow, you need to get in touch with her to finalize the design of that website she's placed a down payment on."

"Don't try to throw me off the trail, Dad. Even J.R. is over here laughing because game recognizes game."

"Whatever it is you think you recognize, it has nothing to do with Toni Gillette. I'll see y'all tomorrow." Jefferson walked out of their office, turned around, and stuck his head back in. "You got it right. I changed my mind; I'm leaving for the day." Jefferson turned around to walk away but not before he heard J.R. and Winston howling with laughter. But Jefferson wasn't amused.

Jefferson jumped in his Mercedes and barreled down the street. Gripping the steering wheel tight in both hands, he went over and over in his mind the last conversation he had with Toni. Then the bell rang in his head; the moment was crystal clear in his mind. He'd been a damn fool to go jacking off at the mouth about his family's business to a woman who was a...who was a gossip columnist.

"Damn, double damn," Jefferson shouted out loud, hitting the steering wheel with his hand. He shouted to the Bluetooth to get Toni's number. He had an important call to make.

"Jefferson."

Toni's voice was cold and seemed to tremble a bit. *Self-control*, Jefferson kept thinking as he dismissed Toni's obvious annoyance. *Do not let her hear in your voice how pissed you are.* "Hey, Toni, what are you up to? Do you feel like some company?"

"No...ah, I'm not really up to it. Actually, I was on my way out to meet a friend, but if you can come by now, I can spare a few minutes."

"I wasn't looking for a quickie. I want to spend some

quality time with you. In fact, I want to mix a little business with pleasure since the boys and I are delinquent in getting your project underway."

"Jefferson, this is not a good time. If the website can be put up sometime this week, that would be great. There's no urgent need."

"Is that because you've already written your story and sold it to the media? I trusted you, Toni. I even had the nerve to feel something for you. I shared things with you because I was hurt and needed someone to talk to. But you betrayed my trust the moment I turned my head."

"You knew that I was a journalist. I didn't bite my tongue or sugar coat what my intent was for the website. You should've been a smarter businessman. You're the one who told me you couldn't mix business with pleasure."

"So it's like that. You betray me with a kiss."

"If it'll make you feel any better, I enjoyed being with you. In fact, I'd hope that we'd be able to make this a long-term relationship after the dust settled."

"Well, that's not going to happen."

"Have it your way, Jefferson. Right now, I'm busy and not interested in entertaining your thoughts about me."

"You will listen; I'll be there in thirty minutes." Jefferson ended the call and relaxed his lips into a scowl. "You don't mess with my family, sister," Jefferson said out loud. "We'll see how much you have to say when I break those hateful hands of yours."

Jefferson parked in front of Toni's condo in thirty minutes flat. He turned off the ignition and sat a moment, trying to control the anger that was eating him up inside so he could have a civilized conversation. He exhaled and got out of the car.

He rang the doorbell, but there was no answer. Jefferson was seething. He waited a moment and then began to bang on the door. "Open the door, Toni. I know you're in there. You knew I was coming. You opened your big, fat mouth about Margo, and you can't face the music. I'm going to sue your ass."

Jefferson kicked the door and prepared to leave. He turned his head slightly at the sound of the late model, candy-apple red Lexus as it drove up in Toni's driveway. He stood and waited for the occupant to get out of the car. "Anissa, is that you?" he asked when the beautiful woman stepped from the car. She was dressed in a caramel-colored, lightweight wool blazer, brown slacks, and a print blouse that matched the colors of both the jacket and slacks.

"Jefferson? What are you doing here?"

He watched Anissa size him up. "I'm here on business."

"Don't tell me you're Toni's secret lover that she's been keeping under cover. No pun intended."

"We're just business partners. I stopped by to bring her up-to-date on what we've done so far with her website."

"House calls? Uhm hmm, I'm not that stupid, Jefferson. How's your wife?"

"She was in an accident, but she's doing better now. I'll be picking her up from the hospital tomorrow."

"I heard you were getting a divorce."

"She's still the mother of my children."

"You mean your grown children." Anissa had to laugh at that one.

"Well, she gave birth to twins not too long ago; I'm the father of one of them," Jefferson said with a smug look on his face.

"Oh, no. Please don't tell me Malik Mason is the father of the other one."

"How in the hell did you know that?"

"I ran into him at a bar in a hotel he was staying in and he told me that he had found out that very day he was the father of one of his mother-in-law's babies. I didn't even know he was talking about Margo—in fact, with all the Q parties I've been to, I've never met Malik Mason before that night."

"You still sleeping around with Perry?"

"That ain't none of your business."

"Although I haven't hung out with the frats very much since I've gotten out of prison, you know how the streets talk. If I didn't know you before you became a Q-girl, I might have had a different opinion of you."

"Well, I'm not interested in your opinion, Mr. Jefferson Myles. And thank you for not giving it. Toni and I are going out to celebrate her big payday."

"Did she win the lottery?"

"You could say so. If you heard the news today, my girl was partly to blame for those news stories about Malik Mason. He can kiss his political career goodbye. And he's not the only one."

Jefferson watched Anissa telling on Toni in her animated way. There was no smile on his face. "Tied up in that story about Malik was information I had accidently shared with her. Who is the other person?"

"Oops, I guess we both have to be careful what we feed to a blabbermouth because I'm the one who told her about Malik. So this is the reason you're over here... to give Toni a piece of your mind."

"I spoke to her thirty minutes ago and told her I was coming by to talk about the news story further. She also said that she was going to meet a friend; I guess that's you. So why isn't she opening the door?"

"Maybe because she's afraid of you?"

"I gave her no reason to be."

"Well, I know where her spare key is hidden; I'll get it."

Anissa felt along the underside of the welcome mat and produced the key that was hidden in a secret compartment. After knocking again and with no response, Anissa secured the key but tried the doorknob before she turned the key.

"It's unlocked," she said to Jefferson.

"Maybe she's in the bathroom and didn't hear the doorbell. Let me go in first as a precaution."

Jefferson entered the condo with Anissa at his heels. Before Anissa could call out Toni's name, she screamed. Anissa almost fell on top of Jefferson when he stopped abruptly and dropped to his knees.

Blood was everywhere. It appeared that Toni had been hit in the face by one of her porcelain vases, the broken pieces scattered next to her body that was sprawled out in the foyer. Toni was dressed in a black Christian Dior pantsuit that was now splattered with blood.

"Toni, can you hear me?" Anissa said as she knelt down beside Jefferson. She grabbed Toni's wrist. "I feel a pulse. Call the police."

Jefferson pulled out his BlackBerry, dialed nine-one-one, and gave the dispatch the information. "Hurry," he admonished. "She's got a pulse."

Jefferson paced the floor, relieved that he hadn't gotten to Toni's any sooner. Maybe the perpetrator was already in the house when he called. All he could think about was that if he had arrived fifteen or twenty minutes earlier, he might have walked into something terrible and even been part of the crime scene. Jefferson was mad and angry at Toni, but she didn't deserve this. He was going to start going to church on the regular because God had spared him from being a statistic. It wasn't fate; it was a miracle.

"A..nis..sa."

"Toni," Anissa screamed. "You're going to be all right. Jefferson called the paramedics and they're on their way. Who did this to you? Tell me."

Toni's eyes were swollen and half shut as she tried to look at Anissa. "I don't know," she whispered.

"Well, we're here now; you're not alone."

Jefferson didn't say a word. He hated how he felt but was glad that Toni wasn't dead. When she was better, he was going to return her retainer. He breathed in and out, again grateful that he hadn't arrived at Toni's house a minute earlier.

The paramedics were there in record time, followed by the police. Toni was unable to give them a description of the attacker, so for now, whoever it was had gotten away. For a moment, Jefferson thought about Margo and what his daughters had said about wanting the family to be together. Maybe he'd talk to Margo about their request tomorrow. "Anissa, I'm going to give you my cell number so you can update me on Toni's progress." And then he left Anissa to attend to Toni's needs.

## Sixty-Eight

M argo was dressed by the time Jefferson arrived to pick her up from the hospital. He halted before he reached the bed, and drank in her beauty. She wasn't the young woman he first met when he was in the Army, but like fine wine, she had grown even better with age.

He went to her and kissed her on the forehead.

"What was that for?" Margo asked, giving him a once over on the sly.

"You're beautiful, Margo. I don't know how we got off the beaten path to be where we are now, but before the day is over, I'm going to lay at the mercy of your court and convince you that we were meant to be...forever."

"Don't do this, Jefferson. We've managed to become good friends, and I'd like it to stay that way. Let's not complicate the issue. How's Ivy?"

"She's coming around. You'll get to see her soon; she's staying at your house."

Margo smiled and it was infectious. "Jefferson, are you saying that my daughter is at my house...that she's not mad at me?"

"For sure, she's at the house. Whether she's mad at you or not is something you have to find out for yourself. We haven't had a father-daughter conversation in a few days, so I don't know what her true feelings are about things, except for one."

"What is that?"

"She wants to see her family back together again. Now, if you're ready, I'll take you home."

"I'm ready."

Everyone was there to greet Margo when Jefferson brought her into the house. Unable to walk, Jefferson lifted her up and carried her inside. She had a temporary wheelchair to enable her to get around, but Margo was pleased to see Winter, Ivy, J.R., and Elaine standing around with great big smiles on their faces, especially Ivy.

"Look at my children. This is a happy moment for me...come to help Momma out. Where is Winston?"

"He'll be here in a little while," Winter offered. "Mom, you don't have to worry about Ian and Evan, we've got it."

Margo smiled. "How are you doing, Ivy?"

"I'm doing okay, Momma. Malik keeps calling but I refuse to speak to him. I'm glad to be with my family." Ivy went to her mother and kissed her on the cheek. "I'm glad you're home."

Margo grabbed Ivy's arm. "I love you, Ivy. I've prayed for this moment."

"Momma, I wish I had confided in you. Maybe I wouldn't have messed up so bad."

"Baby, we all make mistakes; look at me. But if we learn from our mistakes, then it wasn't all for naught. I hope it won't be difficult for you...with Ian and all."

"Okay, okay," Jefferson said, cutting off the melodrama that was playing out in the living room. "Your mother needs to rest, and everyone is going to take turns assisting her."

"Thanks for being here for me, Jefferson. It means a lot."

"Well, we want you to have a speedy recovery. And I've got a surprise for you later on."

Margo arched her eyebrows and looked at Jefferson quizzically. "Aren't you going to give me a heads up?"

"No, because then it wouldn't be a surprise. Okay, I'm going to lift you to your bed. The girls will take it from there."

"Thanks, babe."

"You're welcome. I'll go check on the twins while the girls attend to your needs."


The house was quiet when, out of nowhere, the harsh sound of the doorbell pierced the quiet of the afternoon. Even Margo, who had fallen into a deep, restful sleep, woke up with a jerk at the sound of the doorbell. On cue, the Myles family, except Margo, moved from their hiding places and spilled into the hallway as if the bell was a signal for them to gather. Jefferson went to the door like he was the head of the household and opened the door.

On the porch stood Angelica all statuesque and dressed in a sharp, dark chocolate Chanel pantsuit, chocolate-colored boots with four-inch heels, and a chocolate Dooney & Bourke handbag. A large, sterling silver motif with a brown star-sapphire stone planted in the middle and suspended from a sterling-silver chain, hung around her neck. Her light-brown hair streaked with golden highlights fell around her honey-colored face and just two inches below her shoulders. It made her hazel eyes come alive. She wore her age well.

"You look fabulous, Angelica," Winter said, scooting around Jefferson to get a better look at the diva who graced her mother's doorway.

"Thank you, Winter," Angelica said, giving her a kiss on the cheek.

"Excuse our manners, Angelica," Jefferson managed to say. "Come on in. I trust Winston took care of you in grand style."

"That and more. My God, look at Ivy, J.R., and Winter. They are all grown up and gorgeous."

They all took turns giving Angelica a hug and kisses. "And who is this beautiful young lady?"

"Angelica, this is my girlfriend, Elaine," J.R. said. "In fact, I plan to make her mine forever one of these days."

Everyone gasped. Ivy and Winter fanned their bodies with their hands, trying to digest the news."

"Congratulations, J.R.," Angelica continued. "She's very pretty."

"Thank you," Elaine said.

"Why don't we get Angelica settled," Jefferson said, trying to move the conversation away from everyone else.

"Now where is the mother of this beautiful family?" Angelica asked as she took the liberty to look around her. "This place is fabulous. I know Margo had to lay out a bundle to decorate it. It's drop dead gorgeous."

"I don't know how much she paid," Jefferson said, "but let me take you to her. She has no idea that we asked you to come, so don't feel slighted if she appears to be in a state of shock."

"I see. Well, lead me to her."

Winston took Angelica's bags and took it to the room she would be staying in upstairs. The others followed Jefferson as he led Angelica to Margo's room.

Margo's pillow was tucked neatly behind her head and a burnt-orange and wine-colored comforter pulled up to below her breasts when Jefferson and entourage waltzed into her room. There was no expression on Margo's face, only a look that was faraway and frozen in time. And then with sudden recognition, her eyes zeroed in on Angelica. Margo cocked her head to the side and out of nowhere a slow grin traveled across her face. And then the other silent faces become wide-eyed when Margo suddenly broke out into laughter.

"Angelica? What are you doing here?"

"Girl, you scared me. For a moment, I thought your illness was worse than what Jefferson told me."

"Jefferson told you about my accident?" Margo looked from Angelica to Jefferson.

"Yeah, baby. Angelica will be here to assist you while you are recovering," Jefferson said, pleased that everything was progressing along so far.

"The girls are here to help me. Angelica, I don't want to inconvenience you or anyone else. I'm sure Jefferson meant well, but…"

"But Margo, I'm here for you. I'll be here as long as you need me."

Tears sprang out of nowhere and rolled down Margo's face. She drew her lips together and tried to suppress an all out onslaught of tears. "Angelica, this is the nicest thing you could do for me. I welcome your help." Margo let out a long sigh. "Okay, why are the rest of you standing around staring at me like I lost my best friend?"

"We're happy you found your best friend, is all," Winter said. "Thank you for proving me wrong, Dad."

"Angelica will be good for your mom. In fact, I bet they have a lot of catching up to do."

"That we do," Angelica said. Angelica moved to the bed, sat on the edge, and rubbed Margo's arms. "I'm going to take good care of you." Turning her head, Angelica looked at the smiling family members. "I want to see the babies!"

"We're glad you're here for Momma," Ivy finally said. "This feels like old times. Now, if only my mother and father would stop all of their foolishness and call off this silly divorce, things will really be back to normal. I've said what I needed to say, and I'll be glad to take you to the babies, Angelica."

No one moved or said a word, but stared at Ivy, Margo and Jefferson. Angelica peeled herself from the bed, shook her head, and pushed back the laugh that was biting at the bit to be released. "Since this is family business, I'll excuse myself."

"There's nothing left for me to say," Ivy said. "It's now up to Momma and Daddy. I'm ready when you are, Angelica." Ivy spun around, blew kisses to Margo and Jefferson, and laughed as she escorted Angelica out of the room and up the stairs.

"Why are you looking at me like that, Jefferson?" Margo asked, her eyes piercing his.

"Uhhm, uhhm, just surprised at the turn of events, that's all. We've come together as a family to see about you, and now our daughter has tried to make it into something else."

"Well, regardless of what Ivy said, don't go and get your hopes up, Jefferson," Margo said. "I've got these two babies I've got to raise."

"One of which happens to be mine that I have every intention of taking care of," Jefferson said matter-of-factly. "Right now, I need some air." Jefferson pinched his lips together, took a last look at Margo, and left the room. And then the front door opened and closed.

Sixty-Nine

Hurt and humiliation made Jefferson kick the wrought-iron banister that was attached to the steps as he walked toward his car. He loved that woman, and deep down inside of her hardened core, Margo loved him, too. There was nothing that could make him understand why she was so adamant about bringing final closure to their marriage.

Before Jefferson could get to his car, his BlackBerry began to vibrate. He jerked it from its holder, hoping it was Margo wanting to call a truce. But when he looked down, it was a number he didn't recognize, but he answered anyway.

"Hello."

"Jefferson, this is Anissa."

"Anissa," Jefferson said with hesitation in his voice. "How's Toni?"

"Dead, Jefferson."

"Dead? What in the hell are you talking about?"

"She died five minutes ago and you were the first person I could think of to call."

"Damn, what happened, Anissa? She was conscious when she was transported to the hospital."

Anissa broke down and began to cry. "One moment she was doing all right, and then I'm not sure what happened. The doctors said something about a ruptured blood vessel…brain aneurysm, I believe."

Jefferson huffed. "God almighty; I don't believe this has happened. Look, I'm at my wife's house now, and honestly, I don't want to get involved. You're going to have to call her family."

"I'm sure the police will question us again."

"I have nothing to hide. We both found her at the same time. I'll deal with the police when it happens. I'm sorry, Anissa; I don't mean to sound cold and callous, but I've got…"

"I understand, Jefferson. You've got your wife and daughter to see about. I'll handle it as best I can. Can I call you if I need to?"

"Yes, by all means. Thanks for understanding, Anissa. I'll talk with you later."

Jefferson ended the call and stood perplexed on the sidewalk. Who in the world had it in for Toni, other than Malik, that would do this awful thing? Malik, now that was a thought. Jefferson shook his head, wondering how in the world he'd gotten wrapped up in a mess like this.

Before he was able to calm his nerves, his cell phone began to vibrate again. This time he recognized the caller. It was Dr. Wright, and as much as he wanted to ignore the call, it was in his best interest to answer it. He hit the TALK button.

"Jefferson, this is Dr. Wright. I've been trying to catch up with you. How's your wife?"

"Dr. Wright, I've been meaning to call you, but with both my wife and daughter ending up in the hospital, I've had a lot to deal with. I brought Margo home from the hospital today and my daughter on yesterday. They are both on the mend. I told Winston only thirty minutes ago that I would be getting up with you. How's the campaign going and what can I do for you?"

"Well, that's what I wanted to talk with you about. The campaign is going well, but with you and your family receiving so much publicity, it would be appropriate for me to separate myself from your company. I don't want to be tainted with having been associated with you. I'm sorry to be so blunt."

It was quiet for more than a few seconds. Jefferson needed a moment to digest what he heard.

"Jefferson?"

"Dr. Wright, I can assure you that you have nothing to worry about. You're already reaping the benefits of our work and we've invested a lot of time and energy into making your visuals a class act."

"That I won't deny, however things are going so well, and I'd hate for my good name to be dragged in the mud because of my association with you. There's a woman out there...a Toni Gillette, who's having a field day with the political candidates, and I hear she's doing a muck-up job on Malik Mason in Fayetteville."

"Sir, I don't see why you have anything to worry about. Your reputation precedes you, and from all I hear, your seat on the NC Senate is a wrap."

"We can't be over confident."

"Is there something you aren't telling me, Dr. Wright?"

"Oh, no, Jefferson; I don't have any secrets."

Jefferson sensed tension in Dr. Wright's voice. What was this phone call really about? Something wasn't adding up. "Ah, Dr. Wright, I heard moments ago that Toni Gillette was dead."

"Dead? My God, what happened to her?"

"I'm not sure. I received a call that Ms. Gillette had expired. She is one of my clients."

"You live by the sword; you die by the sword. Messing with people's careers by writing terrible things about them is horrible."

"I agree, although Malik, if that's who you're referring to, is by no means a saint. If Ms. Gillette didn't write that piece on him, someone else would have eventually. He only has himself to blame."

"I guess you're right, but I still say that it didn't give Ms. Gillette the right to destroy him in the press the way she did."

"I wasn't aware that you and Malik Mason were that familiar."

"We aren't, but I hate how women take it upon themselves to castrate a man for no reason of their own and think they can prosper from it."

Jefferson gave Dr. Wright's last statement some thought. It made a lot of sense, but it didn't make sense to him. What did Malik's welfare have to do with Dr. Wright? Jefferson decided to dismiss it for the moment. "Well, are we still business partners?"

"Yeah…yeah, yeah." Dr. Wright hesitated. "If one of your sons could stop by tomorrow, I need to talk to him about a new promotional announcement I'd like prepared."

"I'll make it happen." Jefferson ended the call, but he was more perplexed than ever.

Seventy

Angelica removed her traveling clothes and put on a pair of denim jeans and a black, form-fitting T-shirt with the word DIVA embossed on it in large gold letters. She hung up her pantsuit and placed her boots and handbag in the clothes closet. Before leaving the room, she glanced in the mirror and made sure that she was acceptable. Happy with what she saw, she proceeded downstairs to Margo's room.

Margo smiled when Angelica entered the room. She patted the bed and Angelica sat.

"I'm here for whatever you need and for however long you need me," Angelica said. "When Jefferson asked if I could come, I jumped at the chance, Margo. Besides me being a help to you, it would give me the opportunity to tell you how much you've meant to me as a friend over the years, even when I knew you didn't like me. I like what I've become, and I'm so happy."

"You look happy, Angelica. Are you and Ari still going to tie the knot?"

"Oh yeah, baby. I love that man. He's so kind and gentle, and he's taught me a lot about life. I didn't think there was anything to learn for an old goat like me." Margo laughed. "But Ari, with his tenderness and concern, showed me what true love is, Margo. I'm confident, self-reliant, and I've started my own business."

"You've started your own business, Angelica? Doing what, may I ask?"

Angelica smiled. "You know how much I love jewelry."

"Yes, I do."

"I went to school at Ari's encouraging, and I studied metal art. I found a new passion, Margo, and I've designed some very beautiful pieces like the one around my neck. Ari knows a lot of people in the art world and introduced me to some people who love my work and offered me a contract to produce them for special clientele. And, of course, I make pieces for everybody's taste and pocketbook. Being in New York has its advantages; these rich people don't mind spending their money for unique pieces."

Margo smiled. "I'm so happy for you, girl. I'm glad that you're doing something you enjoy." Margo paused then continued. "I've missed you."

"I've missed you, too. I often talk about you to Ari. He has made the difference in my life, Margo. He truly loves me. Now what can I do for you? I'm at your disposal."

"I don't want a thing right now. I'm enjoying our conversation, and I want to hear all that you've been doing since you went back to New York."

"Okay, but before I do, I want to know how Margo is

doing. Your baby boys are absolutely gorgeous. You know, Margo, Jefferson loves you so much. He doesn't want the divorce. Have you talked to him…"

"Will you raise me up and put a couple of pillows behind me?" Margo asked, cutting Angelica off.

"Sure." Angelica stood up and placed several pillows up against the bed's headboard and lifted Margo up to a sitting position. "How does that feel?"

"Much better. Now I can see you eye to eye while we're having this conversation."

"If you rather I change the subject, I will. Remember, I'm here to make things better for you—not uncomfortable."

"It's all right." Margo turned her head and gazed out of the window. She seemed far away and then as suddenly as she turned her head, she was now looking straight at Angelica. "Truth be told, I've never stopped loving my husband, Angelica. Jefferson has been the love of my life as long as I can remember. Seeing him almost every day has been difficult for me because I know, too, that I don't want this divorce."

Angelica's face lit up like a Christmas tree. "What are you saying, Margo?"

"That…that I don't want the divorce."

"So when are you going to tell him? He needs to know right away before he gives up all together. I knew there were sparks flying around me. I have an idea."

"Angelica, let me handle this. I have to tell him soon

because our divorce will become final a week and a half from now."

"Yes, tell him. What I was thinking, though…was that we could make it a double wedding—Ari and I will say our vows and you and Jefferson will renew yours. It sounds perfect."

"Angelica, it sounds wonderful and all, but you and Ari deserve to celebrate your special day without Jefferson and me upstaging the two of you."

Angelica laughed. "Upstaging Ari and me? Girl, it's on. We are going to set the date for…"

"Why don't we have it here?" Ivy said, bursting into her mother's room unannounced. "I know Daddy won't mind."

"Ivy Myles, you were snooping. Nothing seems to be private around here."

Angelica laughed. "Girl, it's no big deal. Anyway, Ivy's idea is great. We can have the ceremony next weekend."

"This is going much too fast," Margo countered. "I haven't had an opportunity to convey any of this to Jefferson. After how I've dismissed him, he may have had a change of heart."

"Don't try and talk yourself out of it, Margo," Angelica reasoned. "We're going to make it happen. You owe it to yourself to be happy."

"I don't feel comfortable about any of this without talking to Jefferson first. How can I make plans when the other party doesn't know what's going on? Angelica, you and Ari will have to get a marriage license. That may take a long time."

"Angelica's right, Momma," Ivy said. "You're trying to talk yourself out of what you know you want. I do agree, though, you need to talk with Daddy first." She walked to her mother's bedside and placed a kiss on Margo's lips. "I love you, Momma."

"What's going on in here?" Winter asked with Evan in the crook of her arm. "I know you aren't having a hen party without me."

"Baby, you aren't the star of this show; I am," Margo said, giving Winter a wink. Ivy laughed and Angelica joined in. "Bring Evan to me so I can give him a kiss."

Winter took Evan to her mother and sat him on the bed next to her. "Whatever. So what did I miss?" Winter said flippantly.

"Momma and Daddy are going to renew their vows." Ivy grinned. "Yep, it came straight from the horse's mouth."

"Hold it, Ivy. I said I wanted to talk with your daddy first."

Winter looked perplexed. Her mouth hung open. "Does Daddy know?" Winter asked, ignoring what Margo said. "Daddy is still outside brooding."

"Well, Winter," Angelica spoke up, "your mother wants to renew her vows, so now would be a good time to call him inside so he and your mother can talk. Ari and I are going to get married—on the same day."

"Next weekend," Ivy interjected.

"I can't believe you heifers left me out of the planning," Winter stammered. "Look, I may want to join you."

"What do you mean, Winter?" Angelica asked.

"I've got a special man, too." A smile radiated on Winter's face like a balloon being blown up. "His name is Phillip and he's studying to be a medical doctor. Maybe I should call him and see if he wants to make this a threesome."

"No, Winter," Margo said, somewhat exhausted. "While I never said that I was going to partake of this renewing of the vows, if it should happen, I'd like to do it with my best friend." Margo rubbed Angelica's arms and gave her a huge smile.

Angelica patted Margo's arms. "I'm glad to be able to help my best friend. Now I've got to call Ari and tell him the plan."

"Who's going to tell Daddy?" Winter asked, her eyes fixed on Margo.

"Call him and tell him to come up to the room and that I need to speak with him."

Both Ivy and Winter grinned.

"Oh my God, there's going to be a wedding," Winter said.

"No, two weddings if everything goes the way we want it to," Ivy corrected. "Sis, we've got to do some fast planning to pull this off by next weekend."

"No problem, sis. I have a good friend who is a wedding

planner. She's awesome. We've got to get invitations to send out right away. I'm sure everybody from Mom's old church in Fayetteville as well as her clients will want to come."

"We can't invite everybody, Winter. Remember, Angelica has friends also."

"Like who?" Winter wanted to know.

"Has anyone called your daddy yet?"

Both girls turned around and looked at Margo who seemed the happiest she'd been in a long time."

## Seventy-One

Jefferson's breathing was labored. What started out as a fairly good day suddenly morphed into one that had headed downhill at a speed of fifty miles-per-hour. Margo's straight-up-and-in-his-face denial of her love for him was the first devastating blow. She hadn't even masked how she felt—a resounding no, although stated in a round-about-way was worse than any bee sting he'd ever received. And then there was the call from Anissa about Toni. He still couldn't fathom that she was dead. One moment they were exchanging insults on the phone, and the next moment, she was lying in a hospital bed with a white sheet pulled up over her head. But the call that perplexed him the most was the call from Dr. Shelton Wright. There was something unsettling about his call that Jefferson couldn't quite put his finger on.

Jefferson moved into the street and unlocked the driver's side door of his car. Just as he was prepared to put one foot inside, his BlackBerry vibrated again.

"Damn, who in the hell is it this time?" He jerked his BlackBerry out of its holster and looked at the caller ID.

It was Ivy. He didn't answer the call but ran back to Margo's townhouse. Before he could ring the bell, the front door opened and Ivy stood off to the side. "What's wrong? Is something wrong with your mother?"

Ivy slapped her side, then broke into laughter. Winter, who had been standing on the landing with Evan, looked at her dad below and howled with laughter. "Daddy, you should see your face," Winter said.

"Okay, I must have interpreted something wrong by the looks on your face. Maybe I should have answered the phone call."

"Come in, Daddy," Ivy said. "Momma wants to see you."

A puzzled look replaced the anxious one Jefferson had on his face. "Okay, what are you girls up to?"

"Momma asked us to call you. You'll have to go and see what she wants."

Jefferson shook his head and dismissed his daughters, although he kept looking from one to the other. Still unable to ascertain what the sudden crisis was all about, he moved forward and knocked on Margo's door, although it was open.

"Come in," Margo said.

When Jefferson stepped into Margo's room, Angelica was sitting in a side chair with Ian in her arms. Angelica swiftly jumped from her seat, and she and Ian walked out.

"Close the door," Margo said to Jefferson.

Surprise registered on Jefferson's face but he did as he was told. He moved to the foot of the bed and relaxed his shoulders. "Is everything okay?" he asked with a puzzled look on his face.

"Everything is…is okay. Sit next to me on the bed."

There was some reluctance to go and sit on the bed next to Margo. It was more out of fear because Jefferson had no idea what Margo was about to say. Although it was a mere second stroll from the end of the bed to where Margo patted her hand on the bed, it seemed that it took forever for Jefferson to move. Once seated, he looked at her, his eyes roving back and forth like an accomplished pianist's hands running up and down the scales of a Wurlitzer. Jefferson wished he could read Margo's mind so that he could brace his heart from the sting her words might render. He continued to look, and then she smiled.

Margo sighed while sifting through her thoughts and choosing the right words to say. She pursed her lips together and then released them to allow Jefferson an opportunity to relax from the anguish that was written on his face.

"Baby, I know this past year has been a rather difficult one for the both of us. You weren't happy with my decision to end our marriage, but so much had happened with us, so much so that our marriage had deteriorated right before I eyes. And I couldn't take it anymore."

"Margo, you don't have to explain anything to me. You've repeatedly told me how you feel. There's no need to dredge over the details again. I respect your decision to obtain a divorce, however, I will always be there to support you and the twins if you need me."

There was a moment of silence. Margo took another breath. She looked up at Jefferson and smiled. "I'm not trying to dredge up anything. Needless to say, I've done a lot of thinking about my life...our life together...this family and all we've been through."

With arched eyebrows, Jefferson seemed more puzzled than when he first entered the room. "So...what is it you're trying to say, Margo? Please help me to understand because now I'm more confused than ever."

"Jefferson, I need for you to get your best black suit cleaned, a tux if you have one, and wear it to the house next Saturday morning. I can't continue my life without you." Jefferson looked as if he saw a ghost. "The past few weeks have been a testament to why I married you those many years ago," Margo continued. "Through all that this family has been through, you've been there for me and the twins, now Ivy. Your love and support has meant more than you know, and I can't find any reason as to why we should be apart. Our children want this; I want this. They could see better than I that their parents shouldn't be getting a divorce. I want us to be whole, Jefferson. I love you."

Tears fell from Jefferson's face. "Margo, I don't know what to say."

"Just say that you want the same thing I do." Margo smiled.

"Yes, of course that's what I want. Are you sure about this, Margo? I don't want to get my hopes up for you to turn around and say you had another change of heart."

"Shhh," Margo mouthed as she drew her fingers to his lips. She looked at Jefferson thoughtfully, then dropped her head, brought it back up, and opened her mouth to speak. "We are going to renew our vows next Saturday in a double ceremony; Angelica and Ari will say their vows as well. We are going to do it here, probably in the clubhouse. The girls and Angelica will take care of all the planning." Margo smiled.

Jefferson couldn't stop staring. "Does this mean..."

"Yes, it means that I want you in my life forever...that we were meant to be together and not apart...that...that I love you, Jefferson. Always."

"Oh, Margo, I love you, too. I've waited for this moment for almost a year."

"Well, shut up and kiss me."

Jefferson didn't waste another moment or another word. He reached over and held Margo's face in his hands and embraced her with his eyes. Then slowly, he moved closer and softly placed a kiss on her lips, then reinforced the first one, until his head was moving in a slow, circular rhythm with their lips still attached. Careful not to sit on her leg, Jefferson got up and sat even closer and kissed Margo again. Then Jefferson felt the vibration of his phone, but he didn't bother to get the call.

Margo pulled away first. "Next Saturday."

"I love you," Jefferson said in return. Jefferson eased back and pulled out his cell phone. It was Dr. Wright again. "I'll be here with bells and whistles on my feet. Now, I've got to go and handle some business for Dr. Wright, but I'll be back later this afternoon."

"All right, baby, and thank you." Margo smiled.

Jefferson rose from the bed, elated. This moment had come at the right time. All of the mishaps from earlier in the day had all but evaporated. As he walked toward the bedroom door, Jefferson suddenly turned around and went back to Margo and kissed her again. "Don't ever leave me again." Then he opened the bedroom door only to find his nosey daughters glued to the other side of it.

"Surprise," they said in unison.

## Seventy-Two

**N**othing under the sun could dampen Jefferson's spirit. He was riding high on a cloud that he had no intention of getting off of, at least no time soon. There was nothing in Margo's body language or her salty words that prepared him for how he now felt. He sprinted from Margo's townhouse, got in his car, and drove away with a sense of purpose.

Dr. Shelton Wright was his first order of business, although his mind became fixed on something else he wanted to do. It was a long way to Charlotte, but a couple of hours by car wasn't too long of a trip to make to purchase something special for Margo for when they renewed their vows next weekend. It would be an expensive trip, but there was nothing too good for the woman he loved for more than half of his time on earth and who brought passion back into his life. So instead of going to Shelton Wright's office himself, he would send Winston. He headed toward Charlotte, more specifically to Tiffany & Co.

Jefferson cruised down Interstate 85 excited about the prospect of selecting the perfect diamond ring for Margo. He was now on the outskirts of Charlotte having just passed the sign for Concord Mills, a large shopping outlet that drew many to Charlotte. It wouldn't be long before he hit Interstate 77 that would take him close to his destination.

Smooth jazz oozed from the stereo, and Jefferson popped his fingers as he let the lyrics of the sultry number consume his soul. Only thoughts of Margo roamed around in his head. Just as he neared the exit to enter Interstate 77, the car's Bluetooth blared. It was Winston.

"Hey, son," Jefferson said upon answering. "Did you take care of Dr. Wright?"

"Dad, brace yourself because you aren't going to believe this."

"Do I need to pull off the freeway to listen to what you've got to say?"

"That might be a good idea."

"I'll call as soon as I get to where I'm going. It won't take long."

"Where are you anyway?"

"In Charlotte."

"Charlotte? For what?"

"I have to get something for your mother. I'll call you back in fifteen or twenty minutes."

Jefferson ended the call, not sure that he wanted to hear what Winston had to say. He didn't want anything or anyone to spoil his good mood. It seemed that the last couple of weeks had been scripted as a movie starring the Myles family.

His exit was upon him before he knew it; the call to

Winston would have to wait. Jefferson took the exit and headed straight for Southpark Mall, and upon his arrival headed straight for Tiffany & Co. In less than a half hour, he found the ring he wanted to give his wife. It was a Tiffany Legacy diamond ring that came with a fifteen-thousand-dollar price tag. Jefferson would have to take out a loan, but he was putting this splendid piece of jewelry on Margo's finger next weekend. After the ring was boxed and ready for him to take, he prepared himself to hear what Winston had to say because nothing could be worse than the news of Toni's death and what they had been through as a family.

Back in his car, Jefferson called Winston. "Okay, what was it you had to tell me?"

"Did you get lost? You were supposed to call me thirty minutes ago."

"Shoot before I hang up."

"Dr. Wright was arrested."

"Arrested? Are you talking about our Dr. Wright?"

"Yeah, Dad, I'm talking about Dr. Shelton Wright. They arrested him for murder."

"What in the hell are you talking about, Winston?"

"Remember Toni Gillette, the woman you've been wagging your tongue at?"

Jefferson's throat went dry at the mention of Toni's name. "What's your point? And I'm not wagging my tongue at no one but your mother."

"Well, the good Dr. Shelton Wright was arrested for her murder."

"What? Shelton Wright arrested for murder? Why would he want to kill Toni? I had no idea he knew her, although I do recall he spoke about her in the third person blogging about political candidates."

"Can you believe that Toni Gillette is dead? I don't know what's going on. Everywhere we turn, somebody or something keeps trying to break our family down—first Mom, then Ivy, and now this."

"I'm on my way back to Raleigh. There has to be a reasonable explanation for this turn of events. I refuse to believe that Dr. Wright had anything to do with Toni's death. He doesn't have an evil bone in his body. Not the man I know."

"All that means is that you can't judge a book by its cover. I believe everyone has two faces—their real self and their alter ego. I hate to say it, but Dr. Wright's campaign is over. It must be some kind of conspiracy. First Malik and now Dr. Wright. This must be the workings of the Republican party."

"Okay, Winston. It's time for you to get off of the phone and redirect your energy. This is a damn shame. Why would Shelton Wright want to kill Toni?"

"Good question, Dad. See you back in Raleigh."

"Yeah, later." Jefferson ended the call. His body shuddered all over—an appropriate reaction to such horrific news. Jefferson reached over and lifted the Tiffany bag from the passenger seat. Neither Dr. Wright, Toni, nor Malik were going to steal his joy.

## Seventy-Three

Malik walked nervously about his condo, waiting to hear from Perry. It had been more than twenty-four hours since he last heard from him, and now Malik was afraid that Perry might have taken his word as bond and done something crazy after they talked about doing something to get back at Toni Gillette.

Malik had also attempted to call Ivy more times than he could count, but she hadn't bothered answering—not even one phone call. His world was crumbling around him, and it was all because of his lust for one woman. If he hadn't been so bent on having Margo as his, there wouldn't be a baby and he'd still have his wife. Now he had nothing—no wife, no campaign, or his dignity.

He turned around at the sound of pounding on the door. Maybe it was Ivy wanting to give him another chance. Malik flew to the front door, jerked it open, and stood petrified as he looked out at an angry Sterling Garrison standing on his front porch.

Sterling pushed Malik with his powerful hand, a hand that could hold a regulation-size basketball in its palm.

Malik stumbled backward, surprised at this display of violence for which he had no earthly idea what caused it.

"Nigga, I know you had something to do with it."

"Something to do with what, Sterling? What are you talking about?"

"Don't play me, Malik. I know you had my cousin killed."

"Whoa, whoa, whoa. Back it up. What in the hell are you talking about?"

"You heard me, fool. You had my cousin, Toni Gillette, killed because she wrote that stuff about you and sold it to the press and the tabloids. You weren't going to win anyway."

"Toni Gillette is dead? And you think I did it? Not in a million years. My God, what else is going to happen?"

"Don't put on a show for me, you crooked wannabe politician."

"So you're Toni's cousin. I'll be damned. But get this straight, brother, I didn't know that Toni was dead and I sure as hell didn't have anything to do with it. Now you need to get your ass up out of my house before I call five-o on you for trespassing. Maybe I should do it anyway so you'll know what it feels like to have the bottom fall out of your political career."

"That won't be necessary; I'm going. Be warned, though, that if I find out that you had anything to do with my cousin's death, your body is going to be floating down the Cape Fear River."

"Is that a threat?"

"Interpret it however you like." Sterling left the way he came in and slammed the door behind him. Malik shook like Mount St. Helens when it spewed its lava all over Washington State.


"I'd like to make my one phone call," Dr. Shelton Wright said, as he sat at the conference room table in the interrogation room.

"What were you doing at Ms. Gillette's home yesterday afternoon? What made you so angry that you'd kill her?" the detective asked, pounding his fist on the table.

"I'm not answering any questions until I get my lawyer. I didn't hurt Ms. Gillette."

"So you admit you were at her residence yesterday."

"I didn't admit to anything. I'm not saying a word."

The detective slammed his fist on the table so hard Dr. Wright jumped. "Boy, you are going to answer my questions, and if you don't, you won't have a chance in hell to get that phone call."

Dr. Wright clammed up and refused to speak. A frustrated detective all but clobbered Dr. Wright for what he perceived to be insubordination. After thirty minutes of silence, the detective left the room and let Dr. Wright sit there for the next two hours without food or a potty break. Wearily, Dr. Wright looked up when an African-American detective walked into the room.

"Somebody was praying for you," the detective said. "Your wife is outside with your attorney. You've made bail. I'm going to send him in."

"Thank you," Dr. Wright said, sitting up straight but obviously aware that the mirror that covered one wall was a two-way mirror.

Dr. Wright's attorney entered the room and patted him on the back. "We've already posted bail and you're free to go."

"I didn't kill that woman," Dr. Wright said. "I was at her house; she's one of my patients, but I didn't kill her."

"Enough, don't say another word," the attorney warned. "Let's go."

## Seventy-Four

B etty Wright stood at the entrance of the magistrate's office in an ashen-brown, linen pantsuit with a frown on her face—by no means the look of a happy woman. Her eyes pierced her husband's frame as Shelton Wright, flanked by his attorney, walked toward her, a little worse for wear.

Dr. Wright sighed when they were in front of Betty. "Hi, honey, what an ordeal I've been through. I was treated like scum in that place; I'm a respected doctor after all."

"Save it," Betty said in a voice barely above a whisper, holding up her hand. "I hope you can explain what you were doing at that woman's house, especially since you stopped making house calls a long time ago."

"Let's wait until we're miles away from this place. The only thing you need to know is that I didn't kill anyone."

"Okay, it's time to go," the attorney said. "This isn't the place to have this conversation."

Shelton Wright returned Betty's gaze. Without another word, he turned and walked along with his attorney and Betty the few feet to the car that was parked down the street. He wasn't able to assess Betty's anger fully, but whatever information she was privy to had put her in a bad mood. How could he tell her that Toni Gillette was blackmailing him to the tune of twenty thousand dollars to keep their affair out of the tabloids?

Malik jumped when he heard the doorbell ring. This time he wasn't going to be careless and rush to the door without finding out who was on the other side. He crouched down like a hunter getting ready to attack his prey, then eased up when he approached the door and looked out of the peephole. He jumped when the doorbell rang again but breathed a sigh of relief and opened the door.

"Where in the hell have you been, Perry? The world is spinning out of control and you can't be reached."

"Relax, Malik. I've been running interference for you."

"What kind of interference? Not the kind of interference that ends in murder I hope."

"Man, what's up with you?"

"Toni Gillette is dead—murdered. I'm surprised you aren't in possession of that bit of news since you've got all of these connections. Man, Sterling Garrison showed up at my door about thirty minutes ago and accused me of the dirty deed."

"Toni Gillette...dead? Damn, dawg. So why did Sterling come to see you?"

"Remember, Sterling is Toni's cousin. And I guess he figured I was the one who did it."

"So, she set your tail up. Damn, damn, damn. But... you don't know anything about it?"

"Do I look like a murderer to you, Perry? Give me a break. I'm a sad blues tale if there ever was one. I lost my wife, my son, my unborn child all in one week. What would I gain by killing Toni?"

"Satisfaction?"

"You're not funny at all, Perry. Did you hear anything I said? My life has spiraled out of control, and killing Toni wouldn't fix a damn thing. You've been gone awhile, maybe you know something."

"Okay, Malik, what do you think I was going to do? Kill her? Look, I have no plans of going to jail for you or nobody else. I can't believe you allowed that thought to cross your mind."

"So, where have you been? You said you were going to fix things."

"I got some goods on Toni, and I didn't get it from Anissa. I heard from a very reliable source that Toni was having an affair with a good doctor in Raleigh who's also running for a senate seat."

"Please, Perry, I know you're not talking about Shelton Wright. That man is so straight-laced, I couldn't imagine him going into Victoria's Secret to get a pair of lacy underwear for his wife. She probably wears cotton panties."

"Whatever, but Dr. Wright is the kind of person who'd do his work undercover—sneaky. I'm telling you, my source is reliable."

"Even if it is, what are we going to do with the information?"

"It doesn't matter now since you said Toni is dead." Perry scratched his head. "I wanted the bitch to get payback, but killing her never crossed my mind."

Malik sighed. "It doesn't change things for me. My political career is over."

"Not quite yet, young man. That's why I rushed over. I wanted to give you this good news in person."

"Don't keep me waiting. I've been dying for some good news since all of this mess with Margo."

"Is your hand out?"

"Why?"

"Malik Mason, you're about to get a big endorsement. Dawg, your campaign is not over. The mayor is putting his chips on you. In spite of all the things that have gone on with you, the mayor, as well as a lot of people in this city, are aware of all that you've done for this community. You're an honest businessman, and you were a single man when you slept with Margo..."

"Who begged for it, by the way."

"Well, it depends on whose story you listen to; however, it was before you entered into this senate race. Also, you didn't know that she was pregnant and conceived a son by you."

"For some reason, Perry, I'm not feeling that good about your assessment."

"I guess what I'm trying to say is that we all make

mistakes and hopefully we can learn from them. The main thing is your campaign isn't dead. There are people who believe in you."

Malik sighed. "I hurt my wife, Perry. I love Ivy. I was caught up in the fact that Margo bore me a son...a child who had my genes, and I lost it."

"I get that, dawg, but now you have an opportunity to redeem yourself. If you love Ivy, you've got to pull out all the stops and make her understand you love her. You've got to go and fight for that girl and let her know that you want to be the best damn husband to her that you can be. I'm not only saying that so that you could look good as you continue your campaign, but it's a reality check about what's most important in life...about being a good person, and as you've said time and time again, be the right person for the people of Fayetteville and Cumberland County."

"Thanks, Perry, I needed that pep talk. I only hope that Ivy will believe me."

"Make her, dawg. Even I can see that you do. Also, she may be the only person who can redeem you at the polls." Malik stared at Perry. "I'm just saying, dawg. Call it as I see it."

"When I left the hospital the other day, I had hoped that when I looked in my rearview mirror I'd see Ivy running after the car, shouting for me to come back. Instead, I saw nothing...no one. Ivy won't take any of my calls, and she certainly hasn't called me. However, I'm going to be optimistic about the whole thing and pray that she'll let me back into her heart."

"Well, you need to get on bended knees now and ask God for divine intervention. You're going to need Him for this task."

"Yeah, you're right. I believe He already hears me."

"That's a good thing. I'm really feeling sorry about Toni Gillette, though. I hope they catch the person who did it to her."

"So do I."

## Seventy-Five

There was very little conversation on the ride home from the police station. Dr. Shelton Wright gazed a time or two in his wife's direction as she barreled down the highway, but it was very obvious to him that she was taking no prisoners and the last thing she wanted to do was *talk about it*.

Shelton wasn't sure what information Betty had in her possession, but if looks could kill, the information had to be lethal. While Shelton wasn't by any means a henpecked man, any attempt to talk to Betty seemed to be futile. That is until Betty suddenly unleashed the dragon that had been eating her up inside.

"Why did you do it, Shelton?" Betty snarled.

"Betty, I didn't kill that woman. My God; I'm a healer, not a killer."

With hands on the steering wheel, Betty looked straight ahead, navigating through a couple of traffic lights. At the next red light, she put her foot on the brake and turned in Shelton's direction. "Why did you have an affair with that woman? I've given you the best years of my life. I've stood beside you through thick and thin, when your practice had only a few patients, then prospered to what it is now. I've been a dutiful wife, standing proudly beside you at every major medical event when you were being honored or otherwise, and you betray me? Was she that good, Shelton? I wonder what your son, Phillip, will think of the dad he has emulated all of his life."

"What are you talking about, Betty?"

"There's no need to lie to me, Shelton." Betty began to cry. She smashed her foot on the accelerator when the light turned green. "I know about your secret trysts, pretending that you had to go to a medical conference that would tie you up for hours. Oh, I've seen the receipts for the hotels and motels you claimed as business and the receipts for the diamond bracelets and other trinkets you lavished on the bitch. Was that to keep her quiet… to keep your secret from the viewing public that held you in high regard? Well, was it?" Betty shouted when Shelton didn't respond.

"Betty, I never meant to hurt you. Ms. Gillette was one of my patients who came in with a bunch of problems. I began providing her with counsel and without even realizing it, one thing led to another. You…you weren't interested in taking our lovemaking up a notch, and I didn't mind, but…but Toni did things to me and we explored an intimacy that I hadn't experienced in our marriage."

"You dirty bastard. I gave you a loving son and when

we created him, we did it in love. You men and your sick fantasies are going to burn in hell. And to think you didn't even try any of your newfound sexual exploits with me. You know why? Because you knew that I'd recognize that you'd been cheating."

"I'm sorry, Betty."

"Sorry my ass, Shelton! Why did you go to her house? Did you go for one last fling before you became a state senator? Everyone said you were a virtual shoo-in."

"Watch out, Betty, you're going to run into that car. Let's stop talking about this before someone gets hurt."

"Hurt isn't a strong enough word. My world has been shattered. The man I loved gave his soul to a whore. Oh, I know all about it, Shelton. I followed you to her house."

Shelton bucked his eyes and pushed against the dash as he turned to look at Betty. "What are you talking about, Betty? Pull over; you're too emotional."

"I'm driving and you better listen, damn it. I heard your sorry-ass pleas, begging Miss Toni to keep your name out of her blogs because you didn't have twenty thousand dollars to give her so she'd shut up. Fool, she was using you to get paid. Why would she pay any attention to you anyway? You ain't that good in bed. To tell you the truth, you don't know a damn thing about pleasuring a woman. I've always had to take care of myself. I tolerated you because I truly loved you, and to think I was the real fool."

"You were there, Betty, in Toni's house?"

"Did I stutter, Shelton? Yes, I was in her house. You were so anxious to plead your case that you didn't even close the door all the way. I slid in the door like a phantom. You didn't even see me—a piece of cake. It couldn't have gone any better if I had had an actual plan. I jumped into the bathroom just off the foyer.

"Shelton, do you know what was so disgusting about it all? It was watching you touch her body as you pleaded for mercy. Sickening is what you were. Oh, she had a smugness and arrogance about her I didn't like. Didn't she know that you were not only going to the North Carolina senate, but you might even become governor of the great state one day?

"She toyed with your emotions. Even when she took that phone call, she was basically inviting someone else to stop and wet her whistle. You see, I'm a woman, and I know how a woman thinks and plays the game. She was ready to toss your ass out with the night's trash. And there you were groveling like a spineless, dickless fool. I couldn't take it anymore."

"Please don't tell me you were the one who killed Toni Gillette."

"Yes, I hit her with that expensive vase, but I wasn't trying to kill anybody. In fact, I heard that she was going to live."

"But you left her to die."

"Listen here, you cheating bastard," Betty screamed. "I was tired of her games, and you failed to take control.

That slut talked down to you as if you were somebody off the street begging for a few dollars. You are a well-known doctor of medicine, but she couldn't see that. Only the woman who's been with you for the last thirty years recognizes your true worth.

"You hadn't been gone but all of five minutes when she primped and pampered herself in the mirror for whomever was next in line after you. If you need to know, I felt much better when all of that screaming ceased. You were long gone by then, but you should've heard her when I surprised her bourgeoisie behind. I thought she was going to die for real."

"Why did you do it, Betty?"

"Shelton, for sure I haven't been wasting my breath for the last fifteen or twenty minutes. I've already explained it to you. That nasty woman was violating something that belonged to me and she had to suffer the consequences for her actions. You see, I don't blame you totally for what happened between you and Ms. Gillette. As powerful and prominent a man that you are, I know that your ding-dong still does the dictating when a woman comes between you and rational thinking. And Shelton, she wasn't even that pretty—nice body but not pretty."

Betty pulled into the driveway of their North Raleigh home. She let up the garage door, turned off the ignition, and sat still when Shelton didn't move.

"Betty, I'm going to call the police."

## Seventy-Six

"Hey, baby, are you ready for our big day?"

"Margo, I can't be any happier. I'm feeling a little heavy after attending Toni's wake last night."

"That was so tragic. Have they caught the person who did it?"

"No, but Dr. Wright hasn't done any campaigning since they picked him up for questioning last week. I can't believe he and Toni were having an affair. What she did to people in life, she reaped in death. It's a shame because she never got to see the headlines that were written about her. Plain-clothed policemen were sprinkled throughout the room, though. You couldn't miss them even with all the people who showed up."

"Well, let's not talk about Toni anymore. This is our day, Jefferson. I feel that God allowed us to go through our stuff to bring us to where we are now."

"I feel blessed to be renewing my vows to the only woman I've loved, besides my momma, of course. And God gave us this beautiful fall day to enjoy. Are Ari and Angelica there?"

"Yes, baby. We're all at the clubhouse waiting on you. We've got a little crowd."

"I'm down the street; I'll be there in a minute." Jefferson ended the call.

Jefferson felt good as he rode down the street. His car was detailed to the letter so that the black of his Mercedes had a perfect spit shine and the chrome on the bumpers was like a mirror—you could see yourself in it from ten blocks away. He brushed down the lapel of his black tux and smiled. His prayers had been answered.

Jefferson pulled into the parking lot of the clubhouse and was surprised to see quite a number of cars. After turning off the engine, he sat a moment and reflected on what the day meant to him. He was getting his life back although he had to pay a price, but it was worth all he'd gone through to be with the woman he loved.

He took one last look at himself in the rearview mirror, brushed the sides of his hair, and got out of the car. Walking with purpose, Jefferson opened the door to the clubhouse and was overwhelmed with what he saw. It was as if David Tutera from the popular television show *My Fair Wedding* had popped into the room and gave it some of his magic. It was a page out of a Hollywood magazine.

The room was breathtaking with ten rows of golden-backed chairs that separated the aisle that would usher forth the brides. Six five-foot flower arrangements that consisted of beautiful apricot-colored English Legend roses with pussy willows that extended beyond the flower cluster were positioned on the floor and strategically placed at the entrance of several rows along the aisle. A large chandelier hung overhead. But what made Jefferson blush was his bride who looked like a cherub with all of her children gathered around.

Although in a wheelchair, Margo was stunning in an ivory knit, square-necklined Donna Karan dress that hit her at the knees and boasted enlarged and elegant cap sleeves. Swarovski crystal teardrop earrings fell from the lobes of her ears, while silver pumps adorned her feet. Margo's happiness radiated like the sun and Jefferson couldn't stop the grin that danced about his face.

As soon as Margo spotted Jefferson, she put her hand over her mouth. Jefferson could tell she was pleased. Although she and Jefferson were only renewing their vows, Margo had Winter to push her out of the room until the service was to begin. A Greek-looking gentleman with a silver mane, who appeared to be in his late-fifties, was engaged in conversation with Winston at the front of the room. Jefferson walked over to them, and Winston introduced him to Ari, Angelica's husband-to-be. They shook hands.

Jefferson was surprised to see Pastor Dixon as he approached both him and Ari. Pastor Dixon shook Ari's hand but pulled Jefferson to him and hugged him as if he were the prodigal son.

"Welcome home, son," Pastor Dixon said. "Welcome home."

"Thank you, Pastor," Jefferson responded.

"We're going to start the services in a minute. Turn around, Jefferson. Many of your old friends from the church are here."

"It's a sight for sore eyes." Jefferson waved to a few of the guests he recognized.

"Ari, I will perform the ceremony for you and Angelica first after Margo has entered the room. Then I'll go through the ritual of renewing of the vows for you and Margo, Jefferson. I will make this a double-ring ceremony and will pray for both couples together. Follow my lead."

Both Ari and Jefferson nodded.

"You nervous, man?" Ari asked Jefferson, giving him a pat on the shoulder.

"My palms are a little sweaty if that's any indication of how I feel, but I'm ready."

"So am I. I feel lucky to have met and fallen in love with Angelica. It was a bit scary and rocky at first, but once she conquered her fears, she mellowed into this wonderful woman."

"I'm glad to hear that, Ari."

The music began to play and Winter, followed by Ivy, strolled down the aisle with beautiful bouquets of roses in their hands. They both wore Donna Karan bone-colored, cotton slash dresses with a full skirt accented by black-and-silver-beaded, four-inch peep-toe heels that made them look like scrumptious eye candy. Winston, who stood in as best man for both Ari and Jefferson, moved to the center and pulled the runner down the middle of the aisle.

Angelica, dressed in a simple, strapless Vera Wang gown that was form-fitted, glided down the aisle. She was a radiant and blushing bride as she rushed toward her man. Tears of joy streamed down her face. Then Margo was wheeled through the doors by her son, J.R. Jefferson shook his head in awe.

Pastor Dixon performed the ceremony for Ari and Angelica, then Jefferson and Margo. Just before Pastor Dixon prayed, J.R. asked Elaine to come to the front. Everyone watched with amusement, but soon there were sighs of relief and joy that replaced the rather awkward moment when J.R. handed Pastor Dixon his marriage license. Stunned, Margo and Jefferson stared at each other and smiled.

The uniting of the three couples was a reason to celebrate. After being pronounced husbands and wives, congratulations were heard all around. Each of the couples hugged one another, but the Myles family had a lot to rejoice about—Margo and Jefferson Myles; Jefferson Jr. and Elaine Myles—two marriages made in heaven.

"Let's get this party started," Angelica howled. "I's married now!" The audience roared with laughter.

After the picture-taking session, the bridal party and well-wishers moved to another room in the clubhouse for the reception. It was decorated as beautifully as the room where the wedding ceremony was held. Twelve round tables and a head table were decorated with beautiful china and floral centerpieces that made one think they were in a dream world. Everyone was happy.

"My ring is beautiful, Jefferson," Margo said, not able to take her eyes away from it. "You really shouldn't have. I know this set you back a pretty penny."

"No amount of money would've kept me from giving you this token of my affection. I love you, Margo, forever and always."

"I love you, too, Jefferson. I'm so glad we're together again."

"Where are the twins?" Jefferson asked as if he'd noticed their absence for the first time.

"I hired a nanny to help out. Although Angelica insisted that she would be with me as long as I needed her, I let her off the hook. She needs to be with that fine man of hers. She's truly happy, Jefferson. I appreciate you bringing us together. Our friendship is on the right track."

"Finally."

"What a surprise about J.R. and Elaine getting married. The girls kept it from me."

"J.R. is truly happy and is going to make Elaine a wonderful husband and vice versa. Margo, our family is on the mend."

"Yep, you're right. Now give me a kiss, Mr. Myles."

"Gladly." Jefferson placed a tender kiss on Margo's lips. "This feels so good...so right."

Angelica and Ari took over the dance floor. Everyone seemed lost in their own individual worlds. Ari and Angelica cut their cake, followed by Jefferson and Margo. Winter and Ivy had seen to it that there was a wedding cake for J.R. and Elaine also. This was going to be a day to remember for all time.

As the evening was about to wind down, an unexpected guest arrived at the festivities. Jefferson was the first to see Malik and headed in his direction, followed by Winston.

"Malik, I don't know what you're doing here or how you knew we were here, but this is not the time or the place for your antics."

Malik held up his hand. "I've come in peace, Jefferson. I'm not here to disturb…"

"Daddy, I told him he could come," Ivy spoke up when she finally reached the men.

Jefferson had a puzzled look in his eyes. "Why would you do that, Ivy? Hasn't he caused this family enough pain?"

"I guess I got caught up in all the nostalgia with helping to plan the weddings. When Malik called and said his peace, I asked him to come. Daddy, please understand. After seeing you and Momma getting your second chance, I thought long and hard. Believe it or not, I wanted it for myself."

Jefferson looked at Ivy in amazement. "I'm shocked. Why do you want to put yourself through this after all you've gone through?"

"I've done a lot of soul-searching, and if I was to tell the truth, I'm not totally innocent. I used Malik to get what I wanted, and it sort of backfired on me. After finding out that Malik was the father of one of the twins, I totally lost it. The truth of the matter is, however, I fell in love with him in the process." Ivy couldn't look in her father's face, but she was happy because a weight had been lifted off her chest.

A half-smile crossed Jefferson's face. "Is this what you want, baby?"

"Daddy, Malik and I have a lot of soul-searching to do. I want to see if we can salvage what we had before everything spiraled out of control." Ivy looked at Malik and watched the color come back into his face. "I'm going to take it slow. He wants to talk; I'm going to listen. I'm not going to return to Fayetteville right away." Malik seemed dejected.

Malik cut in. "Jefferson, I love Ivy very much. I've been so out of sorts with all that has gone on and have done some soul-searching of my own. The one thing I can say without a doubt is that I love my wife and I want her to come home. I want us to be a family, and I pray to God we can produce another grandchild. And if you can find it in your heart to give me another chance…to forgive me, I would be forever grateful."

Jefferson sighed. Malik wasn't going to be let off the hook that easily. Jefferson looked at the two of them. "If this is what my daughter wants, then who am I to stand in the way? But I want to remind you that if you in any way do anything to hurt my daughter ever again, I will find you and…"

"Daddy, come on," Ivy begged.

Jefferson sighed. "All right, I'm sorry. This is supposed to be a celebration."

Everyone turned around when they heard her voice. "What's going on?" Margo inquired with a puzzled look on her face, especially when she saw Malik standing next to Ivy.

"Yeah, what is Malik doing here?" Winter asked, jumping into the middle of the discussion. "Are you all right, Ivy?"

"Yes, sis. My husband and I are going to try and work on our marriage. Look at Momma and Daddy. Today, they are two happy people."

Margo stared at Ivy. "Are you sure you're doing the right thing?"

"Yes, Momma. I've got to do this for me, for us. I'm going to take it one day at a time. We've been through a lot, and I'm ready to move forward. Look at how you and Daddy came full circle? It's because of the love you have for each other."

"Ivy, listen to you," Winter rushed to say. "All that you've gone through and all of the hurt Malik has caused, you can't mean that you're going to go back to him. So this is why you were on the phone most of the morning."

"Winter, this was a beautiful day," Ivy began. "Momma and Daddy, J.R. and Elaine, and Ari and Angelica getting married put some things into perspective for me. I want to try and make my marriage work, and if it doesn't, I can't ever say that I didn't try. We're going to take it a day at a time. I'm going to stay at Momma's for a few more days until Malik and I can sort some things out. Be with me on this, sis." Ivy reached out and held her sister's hand. "We can still have our sister outings, and how about you being godmother to my firstborn when I get pregnant again?"

Winter moved back, wrinkled her nose, and tried to smile. Then she grabbed Ivy and hugged her sister for the longest time. "You better be good to my sister, Malik, or you won't live to see the light of day."

Malik mustered a half-smile. "I know how deep your fangs go, Winter, but you don't have anything to worry about. I'm going to take good care of my wife. Now may I have a piece of cake and whatever else you all have to eat? I'm starving."

Jefferson held Margo's hand as the crowd moved toward the buffet. "This is a miracle. God couldn't have shown me this one any better than He did today. Why don't we join Ari and Angelica? It's not fair to let them have all the fun. They're making the DJ work for his money." Margo laughed. Jefferson reached down and placed a kiss on Margo's lips.

"Okay, baby, push me to the dance floor."

Seventy-Seven

C heryl looked up from the paperwork on her desk when she saw the door to the office open out of the corner of her eye.

"Good morning, Dr. Wright. Are you all right?"

"Yes and no." Looking at the nameplate that graced Cheryl's desk, Dr. Shelton Wright looked at her thoughtfully. "Ms. Richards, is Jefferson Myles in his office today? I need to speak with him as soon as possible."

"Let me check to see if he's still in his office. Please have a seat." Cheryl dialed Jefferson's intercom.

"Yes, Cheryl?"

"Dr. Shelton Wright is in the office and would like to speak with you right away."

"I'm finishing up with a client, but I'll be happy to see him. Give me fifteen minutes."

"Okay." Cheryl clicked off the intercom and called to Dr. Wright. Dr. Wright stood and walked the few feet to Cheryl's desk, anticipation written on his face. "Mr. Myles is with another client at the moment, but he'll meet with you in approximately fifteen minutes."

Dr. Wright seemed agitated and fidgety. He placed his

hands on Cheryl's desk. "Is there any way possible I can meet with him right now? This is very important."

"Let me get you a cup of coffee, Dr. Wright. He's just about finished with his appointment; I promise you it won't take long." Dr. Wright went and sat down in one of the few chairs that were in the small waiting area.

In twenty-five years of practicing medicine, today was the first time that Dr. Wright decided not to go in to the clinic for other than business. His heart wasn't in it, although he still had a heart for people. He hadn't known a time that he'd cancelled all of his appointments because he didn't want to be there.

He looked up when Cheryl approached him with the cup of coffee. Cheryl reminded him so much of Betty when he first met her working at the student bookstore of the college they both attended. Betty's shoulder-length hair swung when she moved her head, and he was captivated at that very moment. Digressing from his memory, Shelton took a sip of the black nectar and placed the cup on the magazine table that sat next to the chair.

"Dr. Wright, Mr. Myles will see you now," Cheryl said. "Come this way."

As Shelton headed back toward Jefferson's office, a man passed him on his way out. They both turned as soon as they passed.

"Dr. Wright?" the man asked.

"Malik Mason?" Shelton inquired. "What are you doing here?"

"The Web Connection is handling my advertising campaign for my senate race. I've got it like that when your father-in-law, and hope-to-be-best-friend-again, is the owner of the company. I'm sorry about your wife's troubles. Toni hurt a lot of people, and maybe she got what she deserved. I'm just glad she's out of my life. Take care."

Shelton Wright watched as Malik exited the building. Tears erupted from nowhere and began to flow down his face. He placed his hands over his face to cover the stain they'd made and the embarrassment he felt because his sins had been found out. He'd been on track to make history for his family—a prominent Raleigh doctor elected North Carolina senator. Now, it was a dream that was fading fast. Shelton Wright couldn't move.

"Where is…" Jefferson started to say when he bounced around the corner looking for his visitor. He saw Dr. Wright leaning against the wall in a bent over state, crying his heart out. Jefferson went to him and wrapped his arms around this broken man. Jefferson knew Dr. Wright's pain; he'd been there and suffered through it. Somehow, God had given him another chance to get it right, and he hoped the same would be true for Shelton Wright.

For Jefferson, it was like looking in his rearview mirror and seeing the reflection of his past as he moved forward. There were moments when the demons of the past called out to him, tugging and pulling at his spirit in an attempt to lure him back to the dark side, but faith and family brought him through, even enough to forgive an old friend. The pain he saw in his rearview mirror was in the past. New hopes and victories became his new yellow-brick road.

Jefferson squeezed Dr. Wright's shoulders and wiped the tears from his face. "It's going to be all right after a while; just keep the faith and take care of yourself and your family."

About the Author

Suzetta Perkins is the author of several novels including *Behind the Veil, A Love So Deep, EX-Terminator: Life After Marriage, Déjà Vu, Nothing Stays the Same, Betrayed, At the End of the Day,* and *Silver Bullets.* She is a contributing author of *My Soul to His Spirit.* She is also the co-founder of the Sistahs Book Club. Suzetta resides in Fayetteville, North Carolina. Visit her at www.suzettaperkins.com, www.facebook.com/suzetta.perkins, Suzetta Perkins' Fan Page on Facebook, Twitter @authorsue, and nubianqe2@aol.com.

*Discussion Guide*

I n *My Rearview Mirror* tackles family dynamics and what happens when dysfunction within the family disrupts and tears it apart. The Myles Family—Jefferson, Margo, J.R., Ivy, Winston, and Winter—have been through some hardships as a family, but the challenges they face in this novel are greater than most as the consequences of infidelity, betrayal and political scandal eat at the fabric of their lives.

1. As this story opens up, what event is taking place that has the potential to be an explosive time bomb? What has the main character shared that alerts you that trouble may be on the horizon?

2. After twenty and some odd years of marriage and four grown children, Margo and Jefferson Myles' life together as husband and wife will soon be final. What is Margo's feeling about the finality of her divorce? Jefferson?

3. An old foe and former best friend of Jefferson's has

embarked on a new career. What is his name and what career move has he made?

4. A career move wasn't the only thing Malik was making. He was making beautiful music with a woman. Who is this woman and how does her relationship with Malik become the Achilles heel for what might possibly be the biggest scandal in North Carolina politics?

5. There is an old saying that says what happens in the dark will come to the light. What traumatic event did Margo endure, and what transpired because of it, that will certainly cause war between Margo and her daughter, Ivy?

6. Should Ivy be angry at her mother, Malik, or both?

7. If you were in Ivy's shoes, how would you have handled knowing that your brother is also your stepson?

8. Jefferson and Margo's marriage suffered a lot of turbulence in its final years. It is apparent that the love they once had for each other has not been completely extinguished, although Jefferson has been in the arms of other women and Margo has sought the comfort of Jefferson's best friend. What

is Jefferson's reaction upon realizing that Ian is not his child? Do you feel that this is reason enough for Jefferson to move forward with his life and give Margo her freedom? Why or why not?

9. How does Malik deal with the same revelation that Ian is not Jefferson's child? What does he do that could possibly cost him everything—his life, his unborn child, possibly his marriage, and a seat in the state senate?

10. What is the name of the woman and her occupation who sought to bring down Malik's house of cards? Was she successful?

11. "Political suicide" has become a common phrase in our society today. Besides Senator John Edwards, Democratic nominee for President (2008), name some political figures whose political careers were compromised because of scandal.